TWO COINS

Jeffrey Owen Thomas

Cover artwork by Albert Thayer
Cover design and author photograph by Sean Banton

For you, Emily

TWO COINS

Part One

I

I made a pact with the Professor to squander all of my allowance on the gay life of a rake and speculator, saving for my future only two coins which I swore to then hang from brightly colored strips of ribbon, like medals on my chest.

It was Good Friday, somewhere on a brown hillside south of lower Mayfair territory, when I bade farewell to Bidwell, my trusted aide, engaging from that instant upon my youthful pact, womanizing and gambling for the honor of my word and principle before the Professor.

My father, upon receipt of Bidwell's epistle on the frightful state of my affairs, managed half a dozen blows upon the undeserving conveyer, whose only good fortune included Bidwell's complete ignorance of my incarceration, escape and subsequent marriage to the daughter of a gentleman whose leave one evening from his reading chair into the rainy street would be the last description of his person Mrs. Gentleman could ever reconstruct.

We settled for our first summer in a small apartment off a courtyard ringed by windows blackened from the soot of a regiment of chimneys puffing hard against what little light and sky had managed to impress their way beyond the church spires and the gloom.

As for accommodations, I cared little for such essentials as a settee or a phonograph; concerned most about which illustration she might choose to hang between the curtain which described the nether reaches of the kitchen and the dormer where we placed two chairs before the window and a lamp of brass with a satin shade, a stage on which we passed the quiet hours reading.

She chose a scene of gypsies by a fire and a young dog with its nose pressed deep into the trouser pockets of a man in colored rags who held a frayed bow in his one hand, a violin pressed inside his chin; a lithograph I admired as much for its detailed depiction of a squirrel in a cage and guinea fowl as for its showcasing of the printmaker's skill.

A portrait of her mother stood inside a lacquered frame upon the side table where she clipped her smoldering cigarettes which wisped their trails like dragons through the shade, on to the open window, cracked just enough to carry the smoke-filled air out into the alley where the neighboring windows formed their ring.

It would interest the reader to know, that it was right there, below the window in the courtyard where I first observed my dear Bidwell, returned from Mayfair these many months later with new instructions from my father, when at the same instant from the toilet came a cry from Mary confirming my half of the responsibility for bringing yet another mouth into the world.

I had no sooner tossed the key into the courtyard toward my old friend below when rounding the gate came Mrs. Black, my irritable creditor and nemesis, no doubt burdened with the single thought of collecting on the back months and interest I had promised in a drunk some nights ago to have for her this morning.

Our humble digs, being up on the precipitous top floor of the old house, presented little enough chance for me to fail at some excuse in exchange for an empty purse; yet as the Professor did correctly theorize, assuaged my anguish with the comical image, provided by these two elder statesmen of life's myriad hardships, singularly intent upon their separate business; one tall, angular and arthritic from a lifetime of reticence and studied grace, the other short, round and prohibitively masculine; both mounting the dark staircase, step by moaning step, in the self-absorbed silence one could anticipate from two assumed strangers, totally unaware that soon enough the climb should end for both of them at my apartment door.

There came a knock.

II

Bidwell was absorbed, examining the tangle of pins and hideous bare, livered spots on the top of the old woman's head when I greeted them at the door, managing the same insincere expression of delight I hadn't time enough to reconcile from the recent news of my impending fatherhood. "Bidwell! . . and Mrs. Black. Such a surprise. Please, come in, won't you?"

"I'm here for my rent," she demanded, ignoring the invitation with accusatory indifference.

Bidwell excused himself past the short bulk of the woman and entered my apartment by respectfully stretching his limbs to employ what little free space remained within the jambs after subtracting her dull mass, as was consistent with his refined manner.

We embraced briefly, yet with just time enough for me to discover the appearance of skeletal protrusions about his arms and shoulders bearing witness to both the fellow's advancing years and the uncharacteristic fatiguing of his dress.

"Master Giov! After these many months, so wonderful to see you once more!" He spoke with his distinctive sincerity while I managed the jacket from his shoulders, as one might remove the glass balls and garland from a tree past Christmas time, only to discover once more, the • stark branches beneath.

"I'll have the rent . . . all of it. I'm not interested in lingering."

She bore a manner that would have certainly erased all light and life from our very same, full dressed tree; a tribute to her *acumen métier* yet reciprocal to any sense of her humanity.

"What is your meaning, my dear?" snapped Bidwell turning to address the escalating irritation firmly planted in the hall. Mrs. Black had a way of screwing her eyes to avoid moving that thick neck when dismissing someone, and Bidwell discovered immediately the coarse effectiveness of such technique.

"What's all that noise dear? Are you talking to someone?" My young wife's voice came from behind the bathroom door. "What's going on, Love?"

7

"I'm here for the rent money!" shouted Mrs. Black, loud enough for my wife, and all the tenants two floors down, to hear.

"It's all right dear," I replied, "I'm just taking care of things right away! I have a surprise for you. My old friend Bidwell has come to call. I want you to meet him!"

It was about this same time, to my considerable chagrin, Bidwell, a character of finite patience and infinite intuition, had let slip from the side pocket of his vest, a dark brown purse embellished by tightly drawn embroidered threads in the likeness of two figures from an ancient time of heraldic majesty, by which an avalanche of sentiment raced the downward cants of my bewildered mind like glacial shards loosed by an unusually eventful morning of consecutive shocks to my now unstable summit.

"And what figure madam, would release the young couple from any further obligation to you?" He spoke, not breaking his measured surveillance of our tiny home for even the briefest instant, withholding any glance upon the reprehensible subject of his wager.

"Bidwell, please," I began weakly.

His stiffened index rose in gesture toward me, like a battle standard from a palm of marbled bone, a basket of clenched fingers extending from the dark sleeve hole described commandingly by a well starched, gold pierced cuff; summoning me to silently reflect on the impossibility of the situation in the absence of any such intervention.

"That'll be three months, including his leaving me without notice and a tidy interest added for whatever work I got ahead of me to fix the place to let again," replied Mrs. Black, stiffly.

I watched him count out coin sufficient to settle all my trespasses with interest generous enough to keep the old lady in gin and cigarettes for half the coming year.

"Out by Friday," she coughed, descending back into the blackness of the stairwell, where she may as well have vanished.

"Pack your things Master, excuse me, *Mister* Penworth. Alas, the joy of this wondrous reunion is tempered by a gravity of such cause as I dread with requisite allowance, for I've come to bring you news that grieves me profoundly to tell."

The remaining days until Friday morning were occupied with introductions, updates and wine induced recollections, for which my dear wife bore in measured intervals, both a fascination and discreet tolerance, washed across her countenance in a fine spun intelligence reserved for my singular detection; the balance of hours spent packing for the long travel back to the continent where my father's grave and appointment waited impatiently upon my arrival to claim them.

"And what does one wear when sailing?" she asked one afternoon, rolling the linens into a last small space inside the crowded trunk.

"I've never been, you know."

"Never been what?" I breathed, lost in some tangential thought which teased me from the slender glint of the harbor, squeezed as it were between the dozen blocks of black brick buildings, belfries, chimney pots and skeletal roof antennas; like the proverbial reeds inside the clutched fingers of a drowning man.

"Sailing," she replied.

III

Despite what a more seasoned traveler might reasonably observe with petulant despair, the modestly endowed Cumberland more than compensated for her narrow beam and proportionately understated keel by virtue of a web of well-manicured, fresh strung lines, bright sail-cloth and meticulously preserved and ornamented architecture. She was a splendid thing which bobbed apparently weightless upon the waves.

Our curious passage aboard the relatively small barquentine was little more than the product of Bidwell's prior knowledge of her Captain by reputation among various members of the court and sundry anecdotes spun by the Professor between lessons to retrieve my youthful intellect from pure distraction, back onto a chalk board drowned in dull equations. There was, besides, the measured decision to act with such discretion as to keep our movements well beneath the radar of both a hungry press and certain inevitable and unscrupulous agents of opportunity for whom the value of my sudden reemergence from obscurity would provide ample occasion for political intrigue and collateral profit. We had, you see, never met the Captain face to face.

Being a gentleman of the most diligent ethics, Bidwell wasted little time managing the introduction, for the twin purposes of assuring some degree of care regarding my confidential passage, while additionally securing some commitment for an exclusive invitation to supper with the skipper, as was the custom, that he might relieve some of the tedium of sailing by entertaining us with, among other topics, embellished tales from his years spent crisscrossing the globe.

The meal itself was the culinary expression of the same lavish atmosphere of the whole; a vessel lovingly endowed by the anonymous engineers and craftsmen who first divined the Cumberland's fabulous configuration, drawn as it were, from the ethers of artistic genius and proportion, evident throughout every post, portal, pin and plank of her construction.

For the sea in all her vast bounty, as is well accounted, withholds from mankind the greater variety of his more civilized, albeit refined, indulgences, for which his tireless ingenuity over-compensates at mealtime; few things aboard a ship are managed with equal attention nor matched with an exuberance of execution.

A four course supper was therefore commissioned by the skipper, then exquisitely prepared by a gaunt, silver haired cook, whose fondness for a wild pig, sardonically christened Chops, a veritable mascot aboard ship, extended to her name and likeness scratched in ink across his arm; and who subsequently, with mixed sentiments, succumbed to his master's insistence that she be served up on a dish of his finest Chinese porcelain, surrounded in a wreath of fruits, nuts and bright red tendrils of tassel flower, fresh picked from a nearby island; a sharp, molded cheese beside, which required several swallows of decent burgundy to digest; all to be served in his cabin that evening at approximately nineteen hundred hours.

There was, I noticed, no soup.

It was in consequence of the evening's long conversation and sudden drop in barometric temper that Mary, in a losing battle with her progressing condition and the pitching cabin, eventually succumbed to an advancing vertigo, spilling the contents of her glass across her brand new blouse, miraculously sparing the exquisite blazer, a jacket of the most discerning combination of color and weave, presented to her by Bidwell last week upon the startling announcement of her recent introduction to the house of Penworth, and cordially excusing herself from our company retired to recover, through sleep, alone in the privacy of our marital quarters.

"Good night, Mrs. Penworth," bade our host.

IIII

"She appears to have accepted her situation with remarkable appreciation, Mister Giov."
Bidwell stared unblinking into the foggy blackness which stretched menacingly over the poop deck from across the taffrail, tapping a cigarette onto the etched silver case as he spoke into a steady, salted breeze.

"Yes, Bidwell," I replied, grateful for both his approving assessment of my dear wife, whose relatively recent discovery of my station and her new capacity as accessory to its profound responsibilities, its myriad misgivings, exposed the very wizened instincts necessary to enforce it; and secondly, for securing, at long last, an opportunity to speak in confidence with my trusted aide, outside the Skipper's cabin, about the dreadful situation deduced from this evening's lengthy conversation with the *ersatz* Captain, the Imposter, with whom I found ourselves to suddenly be nefariously engaged.

There was, as I recall, some matter of an anecdote related by the good Professor, of a scene some years ago, created by the Skipper at a banquet where the first course was a plate of *angels on horseback,* followed by a glimmering platter with a long necked goose. The third and fourth courses came and went before the eccentric Captain finally raised his voice, arresting all conversation, and upbraided the cook at a full squall, demanding to learn why the chowder on the *carte du jour* had not made it to the empty bowls still stacked vestigial in the breakfront's gaping maw. There was no more sincere enthusiast of the briny arts than Captain Fiske, none more passionate about the cultivation of a good stock. Fiske was known to punish and reward his entire galley crew on the single merit of a bowl of bisque.

"So then," he rejoined, startled at my brief summation, "what have they done with the *real* Captain Fiske, do you suppose?" tossing the dog-end over the rail where the relentless wind blew it smack into the transom window below, opened to the weather by our surreptitious host, perhaps attempting to relieve the dense atmosphere of pipe and cigar smoke collected over the period of the night's earlier entertainment.

"That's exactly what I'm anxious to learn Bidwell. The answer to Captain Fiske's disappearance and the identity of that charlatan in his quarters

11

could very well shed some light on our own fate as well, as I'm almost certain the two situations share a common motive. And please, not a word of this to Mary until I'm satisfied with my theory."

"A theory based on the eccentric utterances of a self-promoting polymath," he argued, describing my former mentor, epistemologist and individual tutor, for whom he had always reserved a personal disdain and intuitive mistrust, seeming at the time to blossom at a rate equivalent to my growing, youthful veneration for the Professor's breadth of knowledge and empathy for my station as a child of the court.

It was apparent that Bidwell's forthright tone betrayed some sense of gravity toward the potential exactness of my suspicion, emboldened further by the influence of half a dozen cups of burgundy, courtesy of our furtive host.

"It would do you well, my good friend," I replied, "to rest your suspicions of the Professor long enough to test his description of Captain Fiske against the evidence we have both witnessed tonight, as our predicament demands the utmost clarity and thoroughness of examination."

The sound of a protesting hinge surprised us into silence.

V

It is fascinating to note how difficult it was to reconcile the effect a pistol aimed at one's heart can make upon the atmosphere of a quarters employed only one hour ago to entertain with roasted swine, fine cigars, drink and friendly conversation.

"You should be more careful when you toss your butts, Mr. Bidwell, you could start a fire; someone could get hurt." the imposter teased. "Please, have a seat on the bench while I decide whether it is worth the effort to keep your friend here alive. I've observed your healthy appetite Bidwell, and it is most likely I shouldn't get my money back from selling you."

"I gather you are not Captain Fiske," I mocked.

"Captain Fiske is no longer anybody's concern. Sad how such a splendid career could end with so little glory. Please take Penworth back to his room and keep him safe, won't you?"

"Aye, Mister Blick," said the other.

12

The pistol never left my back as I was led through the narrow compartments below-decks toward a solitary light which, in its dimness, roughly defined the shape and placement of my portal.

"I'll be right here, outside your door all night, should you require anything," the man coughed.

"Goodnight," I said.

Mary lay under a thick pile of soft blankets fast asleep as I quietly tore through the trunk looking for anything I might use to turn the tables on the situation. There was, as I already knew looking back to the bed, examining the peaceful image of my newly expectant wife, nothing.

Heaven help us.

VI

I managed to break from my confinement amidst the chaos occasioned by the next morning's unexpected turn of events, and savor from my precarious hiding place behind two great barrels, the faintest rush of retribution, witnessing the final conjoined expression of surprise and anguish wash across the scoundrel's face; the counterfeit Skipper, forced to his knees and shot through his hat by two pirates from the crew which boarded the Cumberland on a dawn raid; armed with aging rifles and the brazen courage Mother Nature reserves solely for those forgotten souls, who from birth are schooled in the cruel consequence of indigence and mature to mete equally cruel justice on the inequities of abundance. Mary however, was not as fortunate, being swept from my protection by one miscreant while I was left to engage with and subsequently overpower a second.

Last night's weather, to the picaroon's relief, was broken by a cool current of air from the mainland some seventy-five miles east of our position; the lonesome Cumberland no safer in these waters than a tethered goat; fair and fitting booty for the hundreds of young thieves who menace the region, popular with the merchant vessels going to and from the mines and lush plantations in the south, back up, along the coast to the dense gray cities of the separate continents farther North.

Blick's fatal attempt to broker our lives in exchange for his own was perceived as little more than impertinence, perhaps contributing to the impetuous execution as our surprise guests appeared to already have established uncontested possession of the schooner and everything aboard, including Mary and Bidwell whom I have not seen alive since this morning's earlier struggle.

I was determined to save them.

VII

Half a century and many a thousand miles away in some dim lit past, a great ship pushed its rusting hulk through the shimmering waters of an exotic harbor; audibly groaning as she steered, then pulled and stretched herself ever closer to the ancient wharf where the one legged black gulls and shabby cormorants watched patiently for the arrival of the small fishing boats, sailing home from another sunrise at work, darting like dragon flies between the massive merchant vessels from far away; racing to tie off and sell their morning's haul with a spirit and confidence clearly at odds with their meager wages. A slight man in hemp trousers waited at the pier beside a wide nosed carabao, whose yoke of loose leather straps secured the animal to an old wagon borrowed from the moderately prosperous brother of his wife's mother, impatiently clutching a notarized manifest and watching for the lines and chains to secure the great boat so the business of unloading could begin.

Deep in the belly of that rusted boat, amongst the sacks of grain, machinery crates and other assorted containers of contraband, was a second-hand loom from the farthest side of the globe, for which the slight man's title secured him the right to fix onto his uncle-in-law's cart and begin the daylong journey back to a small home in the country where his wife and young daughter anxiously watched for sign of his return.

The manifest, you see, represented eleven arduous years of frugal sacrifice, the price of a Danish loom which was their best and only hope toward earning the money needed to feed themselves and pay a doctor to one day examine their only daughter who had not heard a sound nor spoken one word in the ten years since she took her first provincial breath of air.

The couple worked tirelessly on that loom, with even the young girl eventually employed to toss the shuttle back and forth as if engaged upon a game of table tennis, expertly commanding both serve and volley, laughing uncontrollably at what her worried father could only surmise was some invisible adversary; and within a very few years the small family had established a reputation for weaving high quality cloth of vibrant color and patterns, which eventually brought in more requests for work than they could write.

14

"No time for games Piko," the mother scolded one afternoon, having established the habit of talking to the deaf girl many years ago, "toss the shuttle." She raised her tired eyes up from the warp beam to find the girl fixed at the window where a tired barbet used the sill for an easy chair.

A rap came against the bright doorway opening as a young gentleman in formal western dress tapped his walking stick against the jam to announce his arrival and impending business. His bleached eyes now unaccustomed and adjusting to the darkness of the room, having walked the better part of the three mile road which joined the village to what could only be referred to as the town-proper, and swept across the shadowy forms of chairs, tables and all manner of fabric spools and bolts, eventually to the window where the young girl now lay with her head resting on her folded arms just inches from the blue and yellow bird on the sill.

"I've been informed," he began to address the wife, whose English was proficient enough to conduct an estimate but sorely inadequate to the task of anticipating the social nuances of finer Western etiquette; an observation which did not escape her guest who mercifully took it upon himself to enter the home as though it were a shop and little more.

They spoke of hemp and wool and silks and dyes and weaves for a considerable time, her eye anxiously drawn back on the frozen, un-producing loom; his to the curious young girl in the window.

"No," he shook his head finally. "These bolts are not what I'm here for. I've come a great distance upon your considerable reputation in the city and see in all these weaves nothing to suggest I'm in the home of Mai Pan. My boat leaves in two days and I'll sail home with nothing before I accept anything less than your finest endeavor."

He was direct, yet he was not altogether unkind; her comprehension of his words sufficient enough to retire all preoccupation with the loom and redouble her marketing efforts with renewed confidence in her singular talent, now directing his attention to a host of special-order weaves which under any other circumstance could not be sold.

"Ahh, yes!" he began, inspired by a growing confidence in his decision to put off equally pressing business in the city for this impetuous adventure way off in the countryside. Arrangements were being made to have three bolts from this special collection delivered to the hotel address on a card he provided, when for one final moment his gaze took him back to the window where the bird lay undisturbed beside the black haired girl.

"Bear with me a moment, will you?" he motioned to the woman, slowly turning to approach the girl.

"She not hear you. She sick. See Doctor maybe someday."

"That's unfortunate. Her skirt," he started, lost in a delicacy of thought more profoundly consuming than any sensation he would ever again have the clarity to relate, ". . . her skirt is beautiful. I will buy all of that cloth in your possession, provided you swear to never work that weave onto your loom again."

"No more," the woman replied.

The gentleman slipped from the side pocket of his vest, a dark brown purse embellished by tightly drawn embroidered threads in the likeness of two figures from an ancient time of heraldic majesty.

"Send me the completed bolt at this address. There is more than enough here to cover all expenses. A doctor will be by within the week to see about her." He motioned toward the window. "I'd appreciate a letter regarding her situation, if you wouldn't mind. Good day."

It was in her new jacket, cut from that very same cloth many decades later, that I last saw Mary as she and Bidwell were kidnapped off the Cumberland.

VIII

I stole below, no longer able to watch the pirates choose which crew might live and which to cast aside; thinking how I might yet turn the tables, to save Mary, Bidwell *and* my unborn child without additional casualties; for if one fact were squarely uncertain, would be my continued ability to remain invisible topside.

The fuel barrels blew a hole the size of a sailor's trunk, splintered clear through the portside hull just at the waterline, eliminating any chance for the swashbuckling thieves to consider flying a new flag from her mast, yet forcing me to reconsider the second and arguably weaker part of my plan, which was to simply have the scuttled ship burn slow enough to secure my own safe escape.

The decision to race at top speed away from the burning Cumberland was promoted more by an instinct to place as much distance between themselves and the thick column of jet black smoke rising from the roaring, flame engulfed craft, than any fear of catching embers on the wind; for Navy ships also patrolled these waters and the smoke of distress could be seen for a hundred miles.

It could also be noted by this time that any mention of my luck would naturally have included how poorly fortune can regard an individual, but I implore the reader to consider just how the mind of your narrator works under such conditions; a spirit yet independent of all that had just been lost to me; a disposition less preoccupied upon the unthinkable danger of my situation; but a humor reflected instead on the great fortune of finding a secure dinghy at my disposal, untouched by the flames. This was in no small part another profitable consequence of the conditioning labored upon your protagonist by many months instruction by the Professor.

I had only hunger, exposure and more pirates to consider; and failing to acknowledge how I might affect any influence on these fretful possibilities, I simply settled into my tiny boat and watched the black smoke trade its baritone for the hissing column of white steam as the Cumberland, ever smaller, ever farther away, sank to its grave at the bottom of the sea. I do not remember falling asleep.

IX

I woke in a bunk aboard the *Douagiere* some weeks later; the weather having exhausted what little fight my emaciated body had to offer the circling gulls which unintentionally revealed my longitude to an observant watch aboard the merchant vessel sailing back north with a full belly and high spirits.

The captain was delighted to learn how much progress I made over the following week; my strength and memory returning to levels adequate enough that I could summon all the details necessary to finally convince my hosts of the truth of my fantastic claims; inviting me on the fifth day into his cabin to sup along with his First Mate and Navigator, a coincidence my recent experience had sapped of all keenness and intrigue.

"So you can understand then, my sense of urgency and discretion with regards to being set ashore, that I might head back south to find where they've taken my wife and child. I maintain every ambition of rescuing

17

them and returning safely back home . . . *if they haven't already met with some supplementary misfortune.* And there is also the case of Bidwell, whose family has been in the service of the Penworth House and His Majesty for seven generations." I implored, "I owe it to many that I should attempt to return him home as well."

"The coast is teeming with ships, young man," consoled the Captain.

"We'll stay on all channels 'til we've found you safely aboard the proper south bounder. Truth is, you're a bit of a black omen on the *Douagiere* and you're starting to spook the crew," he shrugged.

"Why don't you take a look, Fin, and see that the boys are on it up in the chat room, would you? Then grab two more and bring 'em back for some *hold 'em.* You play cards, Mr. Penworth, don't you?"

Those whose habit it is of bankrupting all satisfaction from another's confidence in speculating, must take it as a routine, born of instinct, to survey each gambling house with an eye toward prioritizing its exits in a narrow order of accessibility, wagered against relative utility; a ship, being somewhat unique from a house, no matter its size, provides fewer than none. To escape, one must inevitably resign to terms with Poseidon, a character not generally associated with enthusiastic negotiation; and at present, I'm already into him for at least one life-sized dispensation.

For despite the late hour and my persistent infirmities, I read the cards that evening like a stock trader devouring the morning paper, managing in my vulnerable condition, however, to trespass against two of the cardinal rules of hustling which I learned early in my university years; never smile at your adversary and second, never lure the Captain into a mugging.

"You done damn good for yourself tonight," he said to me after the room was cleared. "The money's one thing son, the pistol," he paused, "let's just say old Billy O's gun's brought you just enough bad luck to justify winning it. For a bright lad, should've seen that one." After which he burst into a fit of laughter. "I'd check her to see that it's loaded at the very least!" he howled again.

I felt pretty tired about this point and bid the Captain goodnight.

X

A lot could be said about my decision to leave the Captain's compartment with no reference, symbolic or otherwise, to a safe journey back to my bunk; the hour was late and the weight of the empty pistol in my belt was a testament to the inevitable certainty that I should collect any number of adversaries in my attempt to rescue Mary and it would undoubtedly prove a formidable deal breaker in this cause.

The six or seven men who initially surprised me I discovered soon enough to be nothing more than a pair of my former poker mates, executing a blunt edged assault in the dark to reclaim some cash, a small crumb of their personal sense of dignity and for the handsome one, his pistol which was, I deduced, fortunately unloaded; I having neither the speed or strength to protect it from being instead used as a hammer against the thin layer of flesh stretched across my thick skull.

The loud ringing in my ears gave way to the developing sound of the Captain's roaring instruction that my two assailants cease kicking and clear back from my curled position on the deck.

"You. Mister Penworth, get up from there and come with me. There's news come from the radio. Soon as I can get you off my ship ain't soon enough." His temper had apparently caught up with him.

No one likes to lose.

"You're a holy mess son! What happened to you? Looks like you fell through an open hatch!" he laughed.

"Yes Captain. That must have been what happened," I replied, finally spitting the tooth I had been rolling around with my tongue. It made an impressive click as it struck the ground and rolled toward the handsome man's boot.

"Mr. Billy O', I believe you found Penworth's pistol; that's it there in your mit, ain't it?"

"Captain-," he protested.

"We ain't *thieves* for Christ's sake! I don't much care for this grifter any more than you boys. He'll be off my ship by daybreak, I'll see to that." He turned to me, "You got a South-bounder within six hours' time. Get yourself washed up and look right 'n let this be a notch in your belt."

He took the pistol from the handsome man and handed it back to me. "Lucky he didn't kill you for this. Now follow me to the chat room."

19

XI

You could begin to make the rising sun's reflection off the approaching craft without the aid of binoculars; I spent the remainder of the pre-dawn morning wide awake and very much *en garde* at the ship's rail, eager to get off the *Douagiere* at the earliest opportunity and, God willing, in one piece; occupying most of the time in an imaginary conversation with Bidwell, wherein I was waylaid into admitting my foolish handling of the card game despite my ultimate, noble object of securing the funds necessary to pursue the trail of my enemies. The pistol, I successfully explicated, was simple providence. I imagined Bidwell pretending to look away to conceal a smirk.

The *San Nicolas* was outfitted at tremendous expense for scientific research; her deck as fascinating to the intellect as that of the *Douagiere* was uninspiring; the organized profusion of brightly painted winches, glass enclosed gauges, precision compressors and a large pod-like device outfitted with twin propellers, a torpedo shaped sonar apparatus and a considerable number of viewing ports, lending it a disturbing fly-like intensity, diffusing any gestating eagerness I would have routinely entertained upon the outside chance an invitation to descend below inside its stainless steel belly should present itself.

"It's a great day for mollusks!" greeted the red haired gentleman whose well calloused hands directed the docking operations of my precipitated transfer off the impatient north bound merchant ship.

"Good Lord! What in bloody hell happened to you?" He leaned over the rail into my dinghy and grabbed at my upper arm through the thick wool sweater with a grip that betrayed many years practice, leaving a bruise I would nurse with relished relief for the following fortnight.

"Dark night, open hatch," I answered.

XII

Triangulated a few thousand miles north of the present coordinates of the emancipating *San Nicolas* and laterally from Mai Pan's now well regarded, graciously retired loom in the distant East, lies the tiny fiefdom of Hoffenstein, whose six hundred year old Monarchy owes much to its strategic position among the foothills of a majestic snow-capped mountain known affectionately to countless generations of Hoffench as Pater.

This noble stone, thrust upward in a prehistoric cataclysm of tectonic pageantry, out from the surrounding blanket of lake spotted foothills and dense, uncultivated woodland relegated to define the overrun stretch of landscape from which ancient Hoffenstein had come to cobble itself; whose sun torched pike thaws each year unfailingly, over filling the thirsty streams each waxing spring, dribbling down into the waking valley; *old Father*, whose pointed spruce and firs descend row upon infinite row in whispering defense against the buffeting winds far above the city, their indulging limbs a shelter for the kite and owl nests; boughs shading the brooks where the spawning penny-trout devour the blackflies; Pater the mountain, pouring its shadow wide across the marshy swath of country known as the Dortpen, defended for centuries by Hoffenstein militia against the shambolic tribes of dubious barbarians and conjuring gypsies, who with the silver-fox, black bear, the grey wolf and roan elk, have roamed the darkest pockets of these unmapped woodlands an eternity before the first stone of Hoffenstein's Palace was set onto the granite shore of the Silberfluss.

Here along the banks of the brilliant Silver River, cradled at the feet of old Pater, hides the medieval city of Touchwick, the enchanting capital of Hoffenstein, reigned over these past ten years by King Maximillian Dubious III; who, though crowned at the unpeppered age of seventeen, a consequence of the untimely death of his father, M. Dubious II, (itself an unfortunate affair involving the senior Marquis Penworth and a retinue of eleven noblemen and supplementary aides while hunting wild pigs in the Dortpen), managed the affairs of his homeland with considerable approval and was, on the whole, the direct benefactor of his people's love for their Monarchy if not entirely indulgent of the Monarch himself.

The city of Touchwick is a tight network of narrow flagstone walks and cobble streets, hemmed by blocks of three and four story homes and shops built from the timber, stones and mud-clay dragged for centuries from the outlying forest to this natural plain along the north and south banks of the river; a maze of intricate doorways shaded in stone carved porticos; meticulous vestibules and window casements stretched in panes of floated glass, adorned more often by hand-lettered signage matched in general proportion to the proprietor's sense of balance between vanity and good taste;

ornate balconies and oriels tucked under the eaves of steep sloped slate roofs embellished with copper and zinc plated tear-drop and spider-web dormers; bright colored shutters shielding double-hung windows and striped-canvas awnings in festival shades; here labor the grocers and butchers hawking fresh meats and cheeses, wine shops and savings banks; haberdashers measuring inseams for slacks, shoulders for jackets and heads for fedoras; swinging shingles announcing legal counsel for a price within and dim lit taverns to be forgotten in;

there are shoe makers, the book dealers and several television repairmen, hair salons, a multitude of barber shops and two rival clock repairmen, one north, one south, all shoulder-pressed among the dozens of other wonderfully carved, tastefully painted facades distributed in comparable proportion on opposite ends of the magnificent *Pont Dubious*, stretched in a pleasant arch over the Silberfluss; a thousand slate and copper crowned edifices rising left and right above the polite flagstone sidewalks punctuated with cafés, offering reprieve to the pedestrian from the bustle with breathtaking views of old Pater, looming like one's conscience over the city, from the spectacular *Palais Silberfluss* on the West end of town to the Holy Orthodox Cathedral of *St. Pontificate*, completed over five centuries ago on the east.

It was in this place, in the town of old Touchwick, where a middle aged cleric, a salt and pepper, spectacled man; a fellow passed over routinely by the Bishop for a collar and, in consequence, a man forgot by his congregation; by those seeking redemption inside a two minute psalm, a two verse hymn or from the strike of coins against a gold enameled collection plate; whose thin black jacket lent scant protection against the season's brisk wind; who ambled diagonally across the near empty street, half lit in gas light, the balance by dawn, to reach a welcoming bakery where the early morning hour promised golden buttermilk quick-bread to be fresh pulled and cooling from the oven.

"And the paper?" the girl at the counter inquired, observing the cleric's aberrant interest in that particular morning's news, factoring in the routine she had established for her clients over the years of devouring the stories within against the varying time it took their place on line to reach the counter and have the steaming loaf of quick bread or muffins popped into its bag, saving more often, the change for an evening's smoke, candles, or bus fare.

"Yes," he replied, not raising his nose from the page.

"The King's havin' a baby. How 'bout that?" she remarked, scanning the large type on the front page of his paper. "An heir to the throne! . . . How wonderful is that?"

"I'd wager the Queen's got quite a bit to say about it."

He closed the paper with a grin, shared by the counter girl, who realizing the slip returned his bread and change saying, "I'd sooner be a King in labor than a Marquis vanished somewhere at sea! You can bank on that, father!"

For it was also there on the cover page of the paper, down below at the very bottom in smaller type, the headline which read:

Mystery at Sea: Marquis Penworth, Truant Heir to Penworth Estate
Lost Off Africa. Suspect Pirates.

The bell rang behind the cleric who stepped back out onto the street.

XIII

"We're heading to Port Bosley to drop off some papers and recharge the tanks. We'll spend a few weeks there, most likely. Bosley's a naval base, so I'm encouraged about your chances of learning something more regarding your wife and friend," said the Skipper. There was no mention of the baby.

I passed the following week dividing my attention between tracking the uneventful journey to Port Bosley and absorbing all I could of her landscape and customs through interviews with a couple of the researchers familiar with the region; perilously aware by this stage of the hazards associated with being exposed as a Count to the court of Hoffenstein, yet all the same, longing to acknowledge my intimate relationship to a certain Professor, held in the highest regard by the team for his recently published theory regarding the effects of tidal anomalies during the tropical cyclone season on the diminishing seal and penguin populations from the barrier islands; a theory for which the *San Nicolas* had just completed a six month voyage collecting data. Everyone was rather eager to reach dry land.

XIIII

Our arrival into the harbor revealed Bosley to be considerably smaller than I had imagined during my anxious weeks at sea, with a very narrow but navigable channel, dredged through a series of long stone jetties, sounding at less than five meters, restricting therein all vessels drawing more water than the light corvettes of the Portuguese navy.

These came and went on an increasingly consistent basis since the recent renaissance in pirate activity off the Angolan coast made their service essential to the impression, if not the reality, that some degree of protection for the healthy passage of merchant ships delivering goods and resources from the exploited mines and plantations of the colonized mainland, was being aggressively pursued.

Despite its relatively quaint accommodations, the harbor's ultimate utility unleashed onto the tiny coastal village, a contemporary version of native life more beholden to the aesthetics of a military muse than the rich, timeless traditions which served their people well enough for countless generations.

I secured a room near the canteen and went directly to the base where I introduced myself to an enlisted sailor who wasted no time closing the door behind the Commander and me, who then sat to review the evidence his forces had gathered from the capture at sea of a pirate vessel whose image I immediately recognized from two sizeable photographs displayed for me across his tiny metal desk.

"So, you still haven't mentioned a word about rescuing any survivors."

"Sorry. Seems we caught the bastards outbound on a tip from Angolan security forces regarding a skirmish between their troops and these vermin whose cargo van exploited the distraction and escaped. I believe your wife and friend were part of that delivery."

"I see. But you have found something strong enough to conclude that Mary was alive at the time of the skirmish?" I asked; a developing sense that I was squandering valuable time in that office rapidly surpassed the slightest initial optimism that the military had, at the very least, a handle on the situation.

At this question, the Commander turned and met my gaze directly; pinning his shoulders back and dismissing all prior informality he replied, "We have an eyewitness account that puts your wife, Mary Penworth, in the van at the time."

I met his stare with a cold and distilled defiance.

He continued, "It is my responsibility to see you safely back home, which under normal circumstances would require you to surrender that revolver of yours. These are my orders, direct from the Admiral of the Portuguese Navy. We are two gentlemen however, and under the extraordinary circumstances, I will forgo the officious formalities and place you and that pistol on your own recognizance pending the coordination of your itinerary.

"And as I'm certain you've noticed, Bosley's a bit out of the way and suffers for want of an airport; there's the strip over by the mail office, but that hardly qualifies, so this could take some days. It's not much of a town, but I suggest you make the best of your time here while I prepare the logistics. The matter of your wife and Mr. Bidwell are now the responsibility of the Angolan police."

He read the despair in my eyes and added, "I can assure you Count Penworth, the Portuguese government, in accordance with the amicable relations between our two nations, has imposed its complete support and resources behind the effort to rescue your wife and Mr. Bidwell."

XV

It was while nursing a gin and quinine in the canteen later that evening, still ruminating over the unsettling development that my cover was compromised, when I noticed a brown leather flying jacket thrown carelessly over the back of a stool. I was further encouraged to observe the conspicuous absence of military insignia, an otherwise ubiquitous presence on the couture here in Bosley.

He was a pilot for the same mail plane referred to by the Commander, as I learned over a few warm beers and tonics, recently returned from a four day assignment into the rain forests north of the Morro de Môca; a hostile and virtually inaccessible region populated by indigenous tribes of recently converted Christian villages; up there, in the steamy tropical heat, the missionaries work diligently to frustrate the spreading influence of the corrupt traders who employ the ancient jungle as a shield from the authorities. Weighing my options within the context of my complete ignorance of the country outside the immediate region of Boswell, I was determined to sever the hold this base intended for my protection and bribe the pilot to take me up north with him on his next mission, from where I could freely continue the search for my beloved Mary and dear Bidwell.

"You'll need bullets for that pistol if you're serious about going in there," he said.

"I have given that some thought."

25

"Well, we keep a few guns and ammo back at the shack; mostly for the pilots. I'll see what I can scrounge up for you. Meanwhile, just hold tight. My next trip up to Luremo won't be for another two weeks."

I thanked him by covering his tab for the remainder of the night; confident, by virtue of his extraordinary capacity for both drink and discretion, that my private arrangements were in dependable hands; the race between the Commander's progress back at the harbor and my freedom had begun.

XVI

The first week passed with no news from the base of any headway securing transportation back north. I occupied my hours with a routine that always began at sunrise with an refreshing swim off the nearest jetty followed by a small breakfast and long walks through the brush, examining the plants and rocks as was my habit from those bygone years under the Professor's tutelage; an activity which, in its own small way, helped dispel for brief periods a persistent anxiety, tormenting me with unceasing reminders of my impotence in the face of Mary's dreadful situation and the possibility that any second could bring instructions from the Commander to pack my belongings and prepare for departure back home to Hoffenstein.

It was extremely late one evening as I lay on my cot reading an article from a publication lent to me by the same red haired biologist from the *San Nicolas* with whom I had developed over the weeks a mellowed degree of trust and respect, or what one might enthusiastically refer to as friendship; for as fate would allow, his time during the lay over at Bosley also involved a ritual morning swim off the nearest jetty, offering a fortuitous opportunity for the pair of us to engage in, among other topics, a more spirited discussion of the Professor's theory on penguins.
There came a knock on my door.

"It's late. This must be important."

"The Commander has instructed me to deliver this message."

I recognized the young sailor from my first visit to the base.

"Thank you," I replied, watching to see him disappear back into the night, before slicing the envelope.

XVII

"A Marquis?" he laughed, standing on the jetty, shaking the cold water out of his red beard, "I always suspected there was something more about you, but," he paused to look directly into the rising sun, silent for the better part of a minute while the water continued, like the voice inside a metronome, to drip off his body onto the rocks.

I dove back into the water, remaining under for as long as my lungs would allow, swimming against the strong tidal current funneling through the narrow channel emptying the harbor, unsure if I had inadvertently complicated things even further by attempting to enlist his aide in my effort to avoid being hustled onto the ship, now anchored off shore in deeper waters, waiting to bring me back toward home.

"Look, Oland," I gasped, dragging myself onto the slippery rocks, "it was impossible to tell you sooner. I could really use your help."

For the next half hour I summarized my situation, including numerous answers to the many specific questions he had with respect to the close relationship I shared with the Professor, a personality Oland claims was responsible for his initial interest in studying the ocean professionally.

Our friendship progressed that morning to a more profound intimacy, approaching brotherhood, with Oland returning to his cabin, assuring me that my secret was safe.
"You give me the sign, your *Lordship*," he chuckled, "and I'll buy you some time!"

XVIII

I walked back to my room and gathered my effects; a much humbler chore than when I first began packing for the trip home and, after settling with the clerk, made off for the mail shack to negotiate contingency arrangements with the pilot.

The mail office was set off from the general concentration of shacks composing Bosley proper, about three quarters of a mile down a dusty trail half reclaimed by stubborn shoots of elephant grass and ant mounds, the other half sculpted by adventurous jeeps carving their indelible ruts; all told, a passage knit of the most formidable and extravagant beauty the natural world has ever set upon her emptiness; everywhere in every direction, the early morning dew rose in a haze off the milkweed and slangbos, sprayed in yellow gum acacia and blue pin cushions; the pungent smell of the carrion flower luring her flies; all surveyed from a regal distance by a solitary, towering baobab tree, whose hideous branches seem to scratch against the immense African sky, lit like the day's first oven in a bread shop, by the immense, quavering disc of the new morning sun.

I approached the shack, visible finally through the last outcrop of Um Duma and wild olive trees, discovering the mail operation, an area I had conspicuously avoided during my time in Bosley, to be little more than a hut, a wind sock and a silver plane, parked within a hundred feet of the office, her engine cowl retracted to expose the motor which, by the appearance of a tool kit, oily rags and jerry can, was undergoing some involved technical procedure, sending a shock wave through my legs which responded by increasing my saunter to a trot.

A man stepped out of the office. I was now close enough to identify him as Owen and it was obvious that he found my running form an inconvenient development in his otherwise monotonous regimen, slowly ambling back to the front end of the very airplane I hoped would rescue me from the unfortunate irony of my situation back at the naval base. He wiped his forehead with the back of his hand, shook his head and turned to continue attending the motor.

"Good morning!" I exhaled, careful not to seem too anxious; he appeared to be the sort of individual who would impulsively exchange a welcome for cold dismissal at the first sign of undue complication. I was apparently not careful enough. He kept his head inside the engine compartment for another few minutes, saying not a word.

"Have you had breakfast?"

He withdrew from the motor and turned to me, "Something wrong?"

"I need to know if you can prepare to leave earlier than scheduled. Tomorrow will not be soon enough."

"Looks worse than it is; she'll fly; just regular stuff. *You* know."

My legs almost gave out with relief.

"Take me a few hours," he continued, "gotta put her back together, fill her up," he motioned to a regiment of jerry cans standing in the grass, "and then get the mail bags loaded. What's the rush?"

"How soon can she be ready to fly?" I insisted.

"Give me till mid-afternoon; won't be ready 'til then. Need me a few hours, then" he wiped the inside brim of his ball cap, "she'll take you anywhere you need to go."

"I may not have a few hours. Is there any chance . . .?" I tried.

He turned back to the motor, not saying a word.

"Right . . . this afternoon then. I'll see you mid-day. Thank you again. Oh!" I remembered, "about breakfast…"

"See you this afternoon," came the voice from inside the engine compartment.

I turned to begin the jog back to town when he called out, "Take the Jeep. Keys are in the office on a hook over by the desk. No sense wasting whatever little time you got left to untie your knot."

I was driving off when he shouted, "Three o'clock I leave!"

XIX

The *San Nicolas* made an impressive sight tied up alongside the deserted pier, her black and white hull reflected in the rippling surface of the clear green water still dropping with the outgoing tide.

"I expect to be met here by the Commander at eleven this morning," I told him, intently watching as he crawled under the hydraulic cushioning apparatus on which the submergible was restrained. Oland was attempting to feed a red cable in one direction after successfully snaking a yellow cable the opposite way.

"The *Oliveira e Carmo* leaves for the continent at two this afternoon. They should be sending a transport sometime before then."

"Grab the yellow cable and pull it away from me."

I did as he asked.

29

"That's *right*! . . .*Hard* as you can," he grunted. "So, you want I should buy you some time? How much time do you need?"

"My plane takes off at three this afternoon. She's right now under the blade of a pilot who's got her liver and kidneys on a table, promising to have the patient sewn up and fueled for take-off at three sharp."

"And his word?"

"I trust his word. He seems a competent fellow; and for that matter I've little choice, do I? I'm confident he'll keep to schedule," I answered, believing my own words for a change.

"Very well then, Duke, you're officially scheduled for an interruption in conveyance around one thirty this afternoon. That gives me less than three hours." He rose from the deck and approached me, holding his hand out as if wanting to shake farewell. "I'd better get started then."

I took his hand.

"You will be expected to visit Hoffenstein soon . . . as my guest, of course."

"I'll most likely be looking for employment," he joked.

"You'll come work for me," I laughed.

Walking back from the dock to the spot where I parked the Jeep and with no particular destination in urgent need of me, an acute chill leaked deep into my thoughts, overwhelmed by the catalog of unresolved details, compounded by the incessant reality of what dreadful consequences would befall Mary and Bidwell should the scheme fail, when out from a shaded over-hang opposite the marina came the Commander's booming voice, inquiring if I'd extend the privilege of joining him for breakfast.

He was unusually animated and spoke the entire meal about his frustration with the Angolan security force's progress into Mary's prolonged and unimaginable situation, unduly mesmerized by his own distinguishing ability to arrange for my temporary accommodations and repatriation; confident as though I were already on board the cruiser, halfway along the journey home, as I sat across the table from him, listening impatiently, eating a slice of toast with jam, a halved ugli fruit, a strip of spiced *Afrikaner* and sipping on a mug of hot, black coffee.

Unsettled as I was, the mental projection of my impending situation, should I indeed manage to be airborne at the prescribed hour, left a rather substantial void in my menu; the Commander's invitation, regardless of the nuisance, was an opportunity I could ill afford to dismiss.

I placed my napkin on the table, took a final swallow from the cup.

"So have they at least positively determined the van was headed into the Malanje region up north?"

He stopped examining his fingernails and met my gaze without subtlety.

"We," he began, "excuse me; *they* have reported specific evidence to that effect, yes. I have wired your consulate of every detail, including your recovery and scheduled departure this afternoon. I can assure you that your homecoming will be a relief to the financially depressed tabloids back home, to say the very least." He smiled.

I excused myself and stood to leave.

"The transport will be ready to shove off the dock at one o'clock. Please arrange for enough time in your schedule to accommodate the Portuguese navy, who have after all, extended considerable resources in the service of our esteemed ally, Hoffenstein. Until then."

I took his extended hand, nodded sharply and headed back to the *San Nicolas* to inform Oland of the abrupt change in plan, cautiously optimistic in his capacity to improvise.

XX

"He's below, Mr. Penworth," I was told. "Come aboard."

He was a twenty two year old deck hand named Guillaume, with whom I spoke many times during our voyage to Bosley; originally from Corsica where his two elder brothers still live in the canton of Porto Vecchio, operating the town's oldest and most prominent bakery where every Thursday one oven is still dispatched to the brothers of the Seminary of *Église St.-Jean Baptiste*, who bake the bland wafers accountable for cleansing generations of distressed Vecchian souls.

The unique dispensation traditionally afforded his family from time to time for this kindness failed, however, to extend beyond an anachronistic code of provincial Corsican, Catholic morality, unappreciative of the divine tolerance recently adopted elsewhere by a growing number of contending theologies for a greater compassion and salvation toward the difficulties presented to contemporary worship by the proliferation of illicit drug distribution and substance abuse, thereby alienating young Guillaume.

The elder brothers' advanced impatience with the spirited libertine reached critical mass at a period coincident with the young man's resolve to end the malignant melodrama and begin his new life by seeing the world, and at the tender age of seventeen, recognizing already the limited prospects for a young, moderately educated abuser in a sleepy tourist town, stepped off the wharf at Porto Vecchio for the last time.

The crew of the *San Nicolas* has since adopted him as one might accept a stray dog into one's home, to warm by the fire, away from the terrible weather outside; a kindness the young man repaid through hard work and fidelity.

"Thank you, but that won't be necessary. Will you explain that I need to speak with him? It's quite important."
"If it's anything about the delay, I can tell you that we're on it. Gonna be a riot!" he laughed.

An all-too familiar, all-too frequent chill raced through me again at the sound of those words coming from this unforeseen co-conspirator. *Was anyone still unaware of my plans?*

"Please tell him, Willy, our meeting is changed to one o-clock, will you?"

XXI

The Commander's face was a portrait in frustration and disgrace; the hour for departure had come and gone while two smaller fishing boats were continuing their efforts to drag the ninety foot *San Nicolas* away from the rock jetty where she succeeded in tangling herself in cables originally intended to winch her nose off the rocks, a consequence of a mysterious failure of the bow-thrusters in the strong channel currents now pouring in to fill the harbor. The activity had completely blocked all traffic through the narrow passage for the better part of two and a half hours. It was now closing in on three o'clock and the transport remained anchored outside the port, resting patiently for the show to end while a small single prop airplane crossed overhead, circled wide and flew off north into the empty blue African sky.

"Where is Lord Penworth now?" the Commander asked a gathering of three sailors also watching the activity from the dock. "It looks as though they have finally managed to free the *San Nicolas*."

XXII

It has been incorrectly proposed over the centuries, that a King enjoys his place above men by the will of God alone and, consequently, behaves within an aspect of habits and principles entirely superior to the reason of those outside the regal bubble, as to render unimpeachable such incongruous rituals as a blood privilege to the throne, a habit of taxation based on little more than a vacillating disposition or any misconception toward an expectation of personal discretion.

His Royal Highness, King Dubious III, now twenty seven years old and King of Hoffenstein for the past decade, stood from his seat, rolled a copy of the most recent issue of the *Touchwick Chronicle* under his arm, turned to the left, twisting his shoulder plane to approximate a twenty degree shift in alignment to his hips, reached out and pulled the toilet lever, releasing the familiar rush of water, sending his regal feces down a long series of pipes to an eventual crypt, dug beneath the lavish floral-clock garden situated three stories below the bathroom window and approximately fourteen meters from the exterior wall of the palace. It would be an understatement to suggest he was pleased by what he read.

Here it was observed and noted by the stoic Groom, that a nightgown will fill much like a parachute when fitted on the wiry frame of an eccentric potentate, given to vault in excitement on the resilient surface of a quilt laden bed; an expression of his sincerest delight upon re-reading the morning paper's confirmation of Lord Penworth's imminent return to Hoffenstein, courtesy of the Portuguese navy.

"Gee-off's coming home! Old Giggy's back!" he cried, leaping from the bed and sliding in his royal socks across the polished floor toward the door on whose opposite side the Queen lay freshly interrupted from her dreams by the familiar exuberance of her husband, bracing herself, anticipating correctly the King's imminent breach of that last defense; screaming with delight as the immense gilt door flew open to reveal her significant other in nightgown and socks make a running dive into her bed, showering her in kisses of pure and naked joy.

"Oh Max!" she continued laughing, "Whatever could make you so wonderfully happy?"

"Oh it's *true!*" he replied, "It's true. Giggy's sailing home from Africa this morning! My oldest, dearest friend; how I've missed him!"

He stacked two pillows beside the queen and propped himself on his elbows and continued,

"Nothing's been right around this God-awful palace since he went off on his damn *tour grande*; especially Lord Penworth, who's been," he stopped short, paused and began, "excuse me, who *was* a regular *bear* these past seven years with Giov out, God knows *where*; rest him."

"When does he arrive?" she asked.

A very loud knock on the front door of the queen's apartment interrupted the king, who instead of answering, shouted across the vast room to the unsolicited proprietor of the offensive knuckles outside in the hall;

"What on earth brings you to assault the queen's door, whoever the *hell* you be!?"

"My profound apologies, your Highness," came the voice from the hall, "but I bring a card from the Chancellor, His Excellency, Archbishop Grieble, who wishes to convey his humblest compunctions for presenting under such informal circumstances and waits for you downstairs in the library."

"Damn!" he dropped his face into the pillow.

"Oh Maxi," she turned to place her thin hand on his head, "what good is it to be the King when you can't even tell that despicable *vulture* to fly away? Stay here in bed with me; we shan't present ourselves a minute before the moon shines across the gardens!"

"Dear, dear Fanny, if the life of a king were only that easy. . . ."

He slid his legs over the side of the bed, sat up and turned, placing his finger on her protesting lips and labored, "I'll return after my conference with the Bishop, I swear. Nothing shall keep me."

At which point he addressed the page, "Inform his Excellency that the King will be down to greet him shortly."

34

XXIII

Half an hour had passed before His Highness entered the library; a magnificent space bathed in southern sunlight through nine towering pane glass windows, emancipated each morning at six o'clock from their thick velvet drapes, casting bright rays across the sofas, cabinets, desks and carpets of the room; long foreboding shadows visited across the scene like the tenuous chorus through some solemn Greek drama.

Here he found the Bishop turning the coals in his pipe, examining the *Touchwick Chronicle* from an easy-chair. The sound of the Page opening the hefty library door summoned the His Eminence to carefully fold his paper, place it neatly upon the side table and rise to bow his head in the general direction of the entrance; covertly securing his pipe in the cup of his opposite hand.

A scribe stood halfway up a rolling index ladder, nine feet off the floor, with a ticket in his hand searching the collection for a volume Maximillian deduced would be employed by the Chancellor to clarify his urgent reason for disturbing the King's brief domestic reverie.

"Your Highness," he coughed irritably.

"Chancellor," King Dubious replied, discreetly overlooking the Bishop's pipe. "What urgent business brings you to see me outside of chambers?"

"Yes my lord, about that" the Chancellor began, "I can assure you the information I bring will be of great interest to you. It is a serious matter, recently come about, concerning none other than the son of the late Marquis Penworth (*God rest him*) and his honor, the Portuguese Ambassador. Here comes the scribe now, delivering the text... *hurry along* boy! . . . if you would permit me."

He laid the book open on a desk and motioned for King Dubious to come over to get a good look; fixing his tiny glasses to the hook of his nose he continued, "Here, your Highness sees before you, a geographic delineation of an area of south western Africa, most specifically, the old Portuguese colony now recognized as the sovereign nation of Angola."

"Yes I'm aware," said the King rather impatiently, "it's in this morning's paper."

"If you'll permit me, your Highness," he rolled his eyes to the cherub filled clouds frescoed high above, "I believe you will learn that the paper is not quite up-to-date; something has gone terribly wrong."

XXIIII

Outside the antique wall surrounding the old city of Touchwick lay the flourishing development of peripheral city districts grown too congested over time to squeeze back once more inside the many archways cut into the otherwise impenetrable fortification;

the shops, factories and row-houses where Hoffenstein's future merchants, lawyers and burglars run from stoop to stoop chasing balls, dodging cars or trading jabs with mongers for a piece of fruit; bicycles and trucks vying for space enough to move within the narrow corridors provided centuries ago for horses and their wagons; neighborhoods untouched from dawn to dusk by the daylight struck back against the leaning walls, crooked roofs and towering steeples, peering ostensibly down onto the desperate population, always on some crooked search for absolution, always baited by the insatiable Church, yet always and inevitably abstaining from salvation in a daily gamble for a plate of food against one's only and eternal soul.

This was the vibrant scene as it must be played out by Touchwick's least prosperous citizens; those who populate the streets, shops and parks beneath the high windows of His Majesty's Palace; this rabble: they are the city of Touchwick itself, the coarse, pulsing libido of Hoffenstein's cultural loins.

It is to here that foreign conversations generalizing the whole of Hoffenstein inevitably defer, as if the outlying country beyond its gravity were nothing more than a backwoods pending subjugation; a bucolic travesty, a vacuum of sophistication, culture and intelligence, where simple minded men and women live for little reason more than want of directions to the city.

But to the folk whose lives depend more upon the weather forecast than a train schedule; to those outside the influence of the market fluctuations inside the ancient wall; the craftsman, farmers, shepherds and ranchers of the outer counties, these nether regions represent instead the entire uninfected history of Hoffenstein, frozen from the time of its purest infancy; uncorrupted by intelligence or influence from the outside world; and somewhere, way out here in this peaceful slice of sloping pastoral reverie, set nuzzled at the base of Old Pater, as it has for many, many years, a little cottage, wreathed in wild hedges, rose briar and rag weed, rests in a crook carved at the forest edge.

An old blue truck is pulled up on the shaded path near the timeworn garage around the back of the cottage, below a stand of towering hemlocks carpeting the ground with a soft bed of orange needles; a short man in a green plaid flannel and grey work trousers is slowly loading the back of the truck with noisy crates of market hens and bushels of eggs, unenthusiastically preparing for his weekly drive into the market district outside Touchwick's famous wall.

Turning the back corner of the garage to where five neat rows of hutches stood in a clearing, the sun freely bathing a patch of grass and graveled dirt, the short man in the green flannel froze instantly, intent upon a sight whose familiarity could never in a thousand years undo its sincere and fresh simplicity; then placing the two cages from under his arms carefully on the ground turned silently, rounding the garage back toward the house where another man was throwing a basin of grey dishwater out of the kitchen door.

"I'll need a shirt," said the one to the other.

"She's back to see her hens again, I gather?"

"Yes. This time she managed her shoes," he replied.

"There's a load of unfolded laundry in the living room. You'll find some tee shirts, still warm from the dryer."

The man in the green shirt climbed the back porch steps to pass the other on his way inside.

"You'll let her look at her friends a bit before you take her back?"

"I suppose."

The man in the gray pants passed into the house while the other, a salt and pepper, spectacled man, looked up to the sky, burdened by the soft wet eyes of his darling companion, whose coarse exterior could not contain his marvelous humanity; and whose fondness for the young girl always left him short on conversation.

37

"You'll be back late, I guess?" said the grey haired man in spectacles to the one in the plaid green shirt, now walking back to the rear of the garage where he will first cover the strange young girl's thin naked body before finishing his preparations for the day's business travel.

"Not if I can help it. Hope her folks ain't too cross."

"They're probably on their way over here now. I'm sure she hasn't worried them long. Besides, her mother comes regular to the church; I've gotten to know her very well over this past year and she doesn't strike me as anyone to be overly concerned about; she's got an inspired perspective on things. The Lord gives to those only what they can manage."

Turning back from the corner of the garage, the short man asked, "By the way, what'd the Bishop say this time?"

The cleric dropped his shoulders, brought back to reality from his brief holiday of sublime introspection, adopted an ironic grin and replied, "I'm still not fit for the priesthood; not quite yet my dear; seems I've offended his Eminence by choosing to live in sin with you over subscribing to his private, trademark inquisition."

The short man laughed at this news saying, "Be home for supper."

XXV

"It is a matter for the King to decide what response we should make to the Ambassador," said the Secretary, "and not the Church!"

"Very timorously stated," snapped Lord Grimstone. "Then what, may I ask, do we suppose to discuss in his absence?"

The large table was littered with papers, pitchers of iced water and crystal goblets; surrounded by thirty chairs roughly divided in equal proportions, north and south, by members either supportive of His Majesty's rather progressive outlook on the situations of the day or those who consider all legislative responsibilities divine and as such, to be conducted toward the singular object of maintaining the status quo of Ecclesiastical entitlement.

"I propose that his Lordship refrain from syllogistic exercises regarding his Majesty until such time as He may bear legitimate witness for himself," responded Lord Waxman, the King's personal Surveyor and General Council for all Royal financial litigation.

"It's been an hour!" chimed the Chancellor, Archbishop Grieble, whose uncharacteristic outburst served to mollify all commotion in the great hall, "how much longer is this legislature expected to govern with its left hand tied behind its back? I propose we draft a singular response to his most Distinguished Excellence, the Ambassador of Portugal, confirming our dismay at once; *distance* this chamber from the activities of the young, irresponsible Penworth, prepare documents of censure for the Duke and have his Royal Highness sign it and be done with the matter!"

The hall went wild.

"All nice and clean, Your Excellence, but for the matter of any legal precedent."

Silence immediately fell upon the great hall. Thirty pairs of eyes shot to the west side of the great room, toward the sound of the King, who upon entering, continued,

"Am I not at least *close* to correct, Lord Waxman?" he smiled, positioning himself in the empty chair at the head of the immense table.

"Your Highness," the Chief Surveyor bowed; reaching involuntarily with both hands to button his jacket, he continued, "I'm inclined to support your liberty to withhold judgment of Lord Penworth pending evidence to corroborate any proscribed trespass; and yet despite my relative inexperience in criminal practice, I challenge the Chancellor or any one of his *apostles* to provide any such testimony before a response is prepared for the state of Portugal!"

Thirty suits in thirty shades of somber black, deep blue and grey leaped up at this bold proclamation by the Chief Surveyor, waving sixty arms and multi-colored boutonnieres in a frenzied, vocal undertow of riotous dissonance; some with sashes, some in medals, others adorned in scrambled eggs and epaulets; the clergy, in embroidered frocks designed to subjugate, out-shone them all.

This was the entertaining view from the great chair at the very head of that immense table, where the King of Hoffenstein sat silently bemused until the moment came to calm his children and restore the chamber to some semblance of legitimacy through order.

He raised his right hand in the air; bent lightly at the wrist, his thumb and pinky extended toward opposite corners of his kingdom; he looked the Chancellor directly in the eye.

The room went quiet.

"So… what does the Chancellor have to say for my support against the activities of Lord Penworth? And be bold about it! We have an ally on our books whose nose was somewhat bent; but in the service of the evidence, wouldn't a box of Hoffenstein's most excellent chocolates salve the wound? Since when does one amputate the finger for a hang nail?"

The room resonated with the muted dialogue of thirty throats, clamped around two opposing ideologies, suppressed by centuries of protocol for the eminent domain of the Monarch; only the Chancellor looked King Dubious back; looked him directly in the eye and spoke,

"The Portuguese Navy does not run on chocolates, my liege. Perhaps his Highness fails to grasp the true gravity of the situation. Hoffenstein is in the process of closing two extremely lucrative contracts for development projects giving our landlocked nation direct access, for the very first time in our great and illustrious history, to the Atlantic coast. The Portuguese government is using the situation in Bosley to reopen questions concerning the nature and inevitable success of these contracts. Distancing this regime from the impulsive antics of this renegade Marquis, whose apostasy to our class, his own father and this chamber seems to me the only proper, nay, *moral* solution to the problem."

Shouts of support and dissent rose like the presence of a lion, sauntering slowly through a room filled with well groomed, caged monkeys.

The King then replied, "Perhaps, my good Archbishop, it might be assumed imprudent to consider marriage to a partner of such delicate skin; one must always, I believe, anticipate the terms of alimony when one slides the ring onto even the most favored finger.

"I remind you all I am a King, not some compulsive industrialist. I strongly suggest you all, every *damn* one of you, remind yourselves about *just* what makes this nation desire the King such as he is. You speak to me about contracts? What in hell is Hoffenstein going to do with a few resort hotels on the Atlantic? Are you anticipating the birth of the Hoffenstein navy? Don't be ridiculous.

"And then you would turn on one of our own to appease the Portuguese who are using the case of a desperate husband and expectant father to shake the confidence out of our deal to invest good Hoffenstein gold to develop their own soil? You then, good Archbishop, actually accuse

40

Lord Penworth, whose family has served these chambers; who've served my ancestors for centuries, with the apostasy of his class and this council on a pretext of immorality?

"No, Your Excellency, it is my duty as a King to ensure that everything achieved by this nation is done in accordance with the true spirit of our Nation's loyalty to its principles and a paternal regard for every last one of its people. Selling off Lord Penworth for some real estate on the Atlantic coast is not what I was crowned to accomplish. Unless you have developed a case beyond this premise, I'm inclined to press for a vote on the matter. What say you?"

There followed a great noise in the Chamber.

XXVI

Looking down on the wild, seemingly endless savannah, marinating in a cocktail of two parts anxiety with a splash of thrill, I conjured a distraction in order that I might refocus, regain my composure; passing the hours in the tiny plane attempting to impose some correlation between the pulsing, rhythmic forms below and Fibonacci's classic number sequence (the *Lord's thumb-print*, the Professor liked to say); and rediscover in the sun parched landscape those same equations at work that an engineer might have employed when raising a cathedral or designing an airplane.

Owen wasn't strong on conversation and the gnawing anticipation of arriving to a very strange village out in some God-forsaken jungle; to redouble my efforts and continue the search in light of a gamblers instinct toward my increasingly diminished prospects for success considering the months that had already passed; all had finally fatigued my nerves; it was everything I could do to preserve my sanity.

By using my thumb as a scale I proceeded to divide thumbs of grassland by the aggregate thumb-area of brush within the field; then by estimating the size of the zebra herds I spotted, calculate the average ratio of grassland to brush needed to sustain one individual zebra.

When I got bored of doing this I simply moved off zebras and started fresh with water buffalo, gazelles or even herons as we flew across the wide marshes and rivers; and by comparing these figures with respect to whatever scraps of information I gleaned from my studies concerning every discrepancy in the relative size, metabolism and mobility of the various species, I attempted then to determine a common number that

41

might be employed to describe a method of anticipating the herd count of the next victim in my game.

This was the equivalent of big game hunting for a nobleman of Hoffenstein; and luckily, we set down in a dusty field of what appeared to be an uninhabited region of Luremo immediately before I completely lost my mind in meditation upon my thumb.

XXVII

Owen introduced me to Kriss, the driver of a jeep, invisible under some shade trees during our landing; a fellow whose skin was even darker than the faded black paint which was all that remained of the original vehicle, now modified to include features like hand poles and foot planks for passengers not quick enough to win the animated competition for one of the more formal seating positions, which already exceeded the owner's manual recommendations by a factor of two.

There were bible caddies bolted onto the backs of both front seats; an interesting display of single shot rifles standing vertically behind the back bench and a jerry can strapped to the rear bumper guard where a spare tire was originally mounted; the driver outfitted his cock-pit with an aluminum strap, curled and riveted to the left side dash console where he kept a personal thermos of water.
I could never quite fully comprehend the smile he delivered upon our brief introduction; in its encryption, I believed, was the key to any success or failure I might achieve for the duration of my endeavor here in Angola, or perhaps the whole of Africa; the secret to knowing how to understand the intentions of every one I will need to trust, to bribe, to trick.

I dreamed many nights upon that broad grin, filled wide with yellow teeth, further obscured by a tempest of intelligence within the blackest eyes I had ever looked upon; never before have I seen their match; no pair of eyes across the most dangerous table of cards; eyes with so much to say, yet in so foreign a tongue; I can assure the reader, I never did again.

Kriss was instructed by Owen to take me to the last stop on his route, where I would be introduced to someone who had connections of immense value to my mission; a utility, I must confess, of no deliberated particulars.

I was Kriss' personal responsibility until at least that time, a commitment he undertook with apparent tenacity, as I became the sole inhabitant of the shotgun position for the entire two hour journey, an extremely rare and honored endowment judged according to the rejoinders of the nine additional regulars he accumulated along the ride.

And such was the influence of the only mail carrier in these remote regions.

It felt good, initially, to feel the rumbling ground again, resonating up from the nubby tires through my thinly padded seat, directly into my bones after three and a half hours sailing through the warm, velvety African ethers in the small, single engine Cessna; a change which proved equally tiresome after the first half hour of unpaved, stone infested travel.

It would have been an easy mistake to assume the Jeep either had no brake pedal or that it had been relocated during that eccentric period of her afore-mentioned renovation, off to an area of the vehicle physically beyond leg-reach of our stoic driver, were it not for the periodic stops along the trail at predisposed stations where one or two individuals patiently waited over long periods of time for the convenience of an automated lift to our final destination, where treasures like a package of sewing needles, boxes of stick matches and sacks of salt, flour and sugar could be procured.

The journey for these humble items represented an investment of the better part of one's entire day, so it was a sincere delight to watch as each subdued personality which greeted us at every stop invariably exploded into a child-like expression of that same sense of liberty discovered, among other rare occasions, as when passing through the ticketed gate of an amusement park.

The difficult relationship I had eventually developed with my seat was in stark contrast to the agility demonstrated by these joyous strap-hangers who displayed an almost super human agility, riding the bumps and sharp turns while standing on the foot plank, holding the hand pole, laughing and singing at the top of their lungs through the vacant bush. Things had gone on pretty much like this for another hour or so, everyone drawing from the same reservoir of excitement.

That is, until we came within half a kilometer of a dense group of Bushwillow and Jackalberry trees pouring their shade down from way

43

high above, onto the grateful thorny bush and thick flowering vines below.

Kriss suddenly found the elusive brake pedal, slowing the party to assess some ambush ahead; he quickly reached his sinewy arm behind my chair and thrust the Bible into my chest.

Breaking his silence for the first time, he turned his eyes to me and said, "You a ministah now."

Bewildered, I replied, "Whatever do you mean? What's going on?"

Looking straight ahead he said, "You a ministah or you a dead mon."

I became quite anxious.

"Eva body sing! Rock ov Ages!" he commanded.

It was only then I saw the bright reflection of the sun break through the dense leafy blind off what I could only ascertain to be the windshield of some vehicle in hiding up in the small oasis ahead.

The veins were now pronounced along the sides of Kriss' neck, a most disconcerting development, uncharacteristic of his otherwise unflappable countenance, augmenting my sudden embrace of the role so impetuously thrust upon me.

I was now, for whatever reason, Pastor Giov.

XXVIII

I am still unsure of the exact dialect, but its effect on every passenger on that Jeep was consummate terror, although Kriss alone maintained a balanced degree of subdued anger and deep concern, keeping a tight grip with both hands upon the steering wheel, head pointed straight forward as though resigned to accept the inevitable discharge from the automatic rifle, held inches from his ear, with all the dignity and protest of one consumed by an unshakable faith.

There were three men overall, traffickers I later learned, who waited for us, specifically for us, with instructions to abduct a certain *gentleman of nobility* rumored to be headed into northern Angola in search of his loved ones. Details regarding any further specifics were as yet exceedingly *un*specific, leaving these self-styled soldiers additionally vulnerable to the thespian skill-set I honed while serving out my youthful time in Preparatory School back in Hoffenstein.

I was suddenly overtaken by a pervasive sense of profound calm for which, upon reflection, I owed my life; I was now a man of the cloth, and clutching the Bible in my hands, I began to read aloud from the Proverbs: *An Evil man always seeketh quarrels: but a cruel Angel shall be sent against him,* I began,

To which our driver burst forth, admonishing me, saying, "My gud Fathah; is not a time to read your book! If you hof to read, do not read words and make them mod!"

A gentleman then lowered the butt end of his rifle onto my skull, saying something to the effect that he would appreciate it immensely were I to adopt a more humble attitude about the situation, up to and including a temporary vow of silence, *or words to that effect.*

I remember being grabbed at this moment by a firm fistful of shirt, thrown from the Jeep onto the hard, dusty ground; the whimpers of the terrified passengers filled my ears like the murmurs of an audience from the blackness of a crowded theater house, all come to this holy place, for a memorable performance.

I had only just begun.

I rolled onto my stomach, my head still ringing, pulled myself onto my hands and knees; a warm trickle running down my cheek, dripping off my jaw into the dirt; do they speak English? I wondered.

"What do you gentlemen require of these passengers?" I continued, "Can't you see we have no money? Nothing to matter anyway."

"No mistah fathah," answered the one by Kriss' side, "we aint here fah no money. Mebee we here fah yoo?!"

I looked down at the ground, temporarily distracted by the amusing sight of another tooth, lying there on Africa's great dirt stage, a smile breaking across my face at the irony of having almost thirty years of cavity-free living still unspoiled.

"Well then," I remained down on all fours and spoke, turning my head over my shoulder toward the apparent alpha-dog of this motely pack, "take me and leave these good people to go on their merry way. You've

45

managed to upset a perfect time, you realize; maybe I can use this wonderful book here to help redeem some misguided souls back at your camp."

He lowered his rifle from Kriss' head and walked around the front of the Jeep, over to where I continued to bleed.

"You a ministah man, eh?" he asked, now standing over me so close that I could no longer turn my head far enough to see his face, "den why you not hov thee cross on yaw neck?"

Apparently surprised at his own deduction, he lowered his rifle and smiled broadly.

"It is because," I began, beginning to feel some of the pain which would preoccupy me for the next two or three days, "I am just now returning from another most profound episode in this human drama we so casually call life; but which too often reminds us only of its limited autonomy."

One of the other two gunmen screwed his eyes at these words.

"The death of this young child," I continued, "though just another unnoticed, *un*-event in your barbaric land, has darkened my resolve with its exceptionally cruel circumstance; conditions which have moved me, in the absence of any substitute, to see the child buried with the only crucifix accessible, leaving my neck undressed, but my soul intoxicated. My cross will guide one child at the least, from this tropic of divine madness unto His place, assuredly beside Jesus Christ, in Heaven. God be praised."

At which time, every last passenger on the bus burst out in affirmation; "Lord hear us!" and "Praise Jesus!"

Kriss turned to me about half a kilometer from our final destination and without a word, shook his head and smiled, driving on at full speed.

XXIX

I managed some ice from the hospital tent, recently pitched by a group of philanthropic practitioners from up north attempting to out maneuver a very nasty outbreak of some serious intestinal parasite wreaking havoc in the neighboring villages. Their efforts thus far though commendable, were not entirely successful, as evidenced by the infirmary tent, set apart from the main village itself at the extreme edge of the jungle, which was not as vacant as they had anticipated, being the unfortunate new address of no fewer than five seriously ill tribesman.

"Keep the ice on your head until the cloth is completely saturated and warm. I wish we had more, but…"

"I understand; pretty hard stuff to keep around here," I interrupted.

She was less beautiful than her soft personality deserved and I found myself consumed with a desire to spend more time in the emergency tent. I was a bit less subtle than the circumstances required and she tactfully directed me to the thin screen door which seemed to swing and slam so frequently as to raise the question, *why a door at all?*

Back at my own tent, assembled specifically for my somewhat conspicuous arrival smack in the middle of nowhere, I dropped on my cot and thought about what an ass I must have appeared; hitting on the first female I'd seen in months with no recourse to follow through on the feeblest of my seemingly limitless reserve of concocted scenarios of romance in the jungle; when thoughts of Mary returned to fill the pain of long term loneliness I had managed for so long to suppress.

I fell asleep.

XXX

Vehicles came and went through the village, dispatched from a tiny mud office which apparently provided the logistics for all commercial activity coming and going from this precocious interpretation of a municipal nerve center; vehicles personalized by their sadistic owners to display impartial combinations of all compass points of the color wheel with every disregard for subtly or discretion. They were incredibly amusing to watch and starkly incongruous with the somber looking jeep directed to greet me at the landing strip a week ago. All the circumstances surrounding my somewhat enigmatic hospitality appeared to refer back to the parish, whose remarkable intervention of the conventional transportation arrangements on the afternoon of my arrival begged more questions than it provided answers for.

I decided it was time to conduct a more in-depth conversation with Father Dodd, so I left the cock fight early, content enough I had at least fed some irascible hens, and went directly for the chapel where I assumed he would be employed upon some ecumenical errands like straightening benches or polishing candlesticks. I was told by a boy in his early teens, Junior, I learned, that Father Dodd had gone over to the hospital some hours ago, that I would probably find him there still, helping the staff or praying to St. Erasmus for a timely end to this latest scourge upon the otherwise sleepy village.

I was greeted by Janis, who extended the courtesy of channeling any awkward after-taste of my initial performance into a more matured sense of amicable familiarity, acting very much the part of a sister or first cousin; I was relieved at her behavior to say the least and used the opportunity to hone my skills as the Duke of Dortpen; a rather dramatic departure from my previous persona.

It was an unmitigated success.

She informed me that the good Father was not at the hospital, but rather over at the infirmary across to the far side of the village, praying over the poor souls still clinging to life and reading a eulogy for the one unfortunate soul who checked out of the hospice sometime in the middle of last night.

She agreed to escort me to the infirmary.

The burial, in accordance with specific medical protocol, would have to be as soon as possible, so preparations were underway when we arrived, to transport her body from the cot and away from all manner of living creature and vegetation, pending her burial into the side of a small hill about one and a half kilometers from the village border.

Father Dodd was extremely busy and agreed instead to meet with me that evening at the parish to elaborate on his instructions and my role in them; until then it was apparent that my presence at the sick bay was less helpful and more of a distraction, so I begged my leave, resisting the urge to ask Janis out for a walk under the stars, and headed over to the small market stand where a few chairs were offered on the street for a weary soul to sit, drink his beer and watch the multi colored jeeps drive past; all beneath a breathtaking view of the immense, blue African sky.

XXXI

"No, I have to admit, I haven't really been here as long as it appears," he offered, watching me slowly pan about the room, admiring the tremendous collection of regional sculpture and intriguing natural artifacts discerningly mingled among the other sacred and secular representations of cultural life back home on the Northern continent; there was a portrait of an elder gentleman wearing the collar inside a lacquered frame upon the side table where his cigarette trailed its smoke out the screened window above an old fashioned vacuum tube radio.

"That's him. Father Cecil. He's the one responsible for the eclectic atmosphere of the office. I was sent here only two years ago and found myself too bewitched to adjust a lamp shade. I suppose it's a touch morbid, but I feel as though my place is simply one of a junior curator; my main purpose is to guide these villagers across the Jordan, intact; that's really what I know best, you see."

He took a long pull of his cigarette.

"Father Cecil, now he's a tough act to follow. Spent thirty years here, doing the Lord's work in Africa, mostly in Angola; the last eleven years right here. . . building the collection you see now."

I continued to survey the dozen shelves, over-filled with careful arrangements of assorted minerals, clocks and pieces of dried wood lost amongst the icons, framed paintings and ivory carvings; there was simply too much stimulation for the first time visitor to disregard; evidence of Father Cecil's interest in religious philosophies beyond even the most lenient parameters of his own Jesuit faith; articles of political intrigue and instruments of scientific purpose, showing evidence of considerable wear by someone capable enough to squeeze some drops of the fabulous nectar of divine creation from its brass rings, precision screws and polished mirrors, presently at rest, silent on the shelf collecting dust.

"Where did you get this?" I froze; stopped in the course of my fanciful examination by an article which drained the blood from my limbs.

"I'm sorry?" asked Father Dodd, "Where did I what?"

He looked up from the ashtray where he had just clipped his butt, and smiling, turned to see my back toward him, fixed to a spot in the collection that had apparently caught my eye.

"Are you all right, Mr. Penworth?" he asked making steps toward me, "What seems to be the trouble?"

He approached around my right side and saw that I held in the palm of my trembling hand, a magnificent small leather bag, suspended off of a shelf bracket from a length of the thinnest leather thong; a purse

49

embellished by tightly drawn embroidered threads in the likeness of two figures from a time of ancient heraldic majesty.

XXXII

He wasn't the kind of priest my mother introduced to me back in those misbegotten childhood days in Mayfair, out in the Dortpen. Our estate was shepherded by a Father LaValle; who took the discipline of faith in all matters Christian above everything else, with the express caveat that all matters in heaven and on earth were *in toto*, Christian. My resultant memories as a young boy of faith were somewhat sketchy, to say the least. My father, Lord Penworth, naturally thought the world of him.

Father Dodd leaned across the low coffee table with the bottle and asked, "A dram?"

I nodded my head and he poured.

"I apologize for the tactic, but you see," he continued, speaking in just above a whisper, "it was necessary to establish your true identity, things being as messy as they've become."

I lifted my eyes to his and asked, "Did they recover him?"

He placed his whiskey onto the table, looked down and said nothing. My thoughts moved immediately to Mary.

"I don't have all that much information about your wife either," he continued, listening in on my thoughts, "Save to assure you that a witness for our organization saw a woman, much like your wife's description, fairly pregnant, very much alive at the time of the engagement in which your good friend found his salvation. The purse was the lone article of evidence recovered from the camp. It is how I know you are the real Lord Penworth."

"What is with all this intrigue?" I barked. "Of *course* I'm Lord Penworth. Who the hell else would fly in here, to God knows where, to spend his time at cock fights when he could be back in an easy chair in Touchwick with his beautiful wife telling him how wonderful he is over tempranillo and snails!"

Father Dodd threw back the rest of his drink, poured another for both and spoke.

"Your activities, Lord Penworth, like everything in life, have had a proportionate, collateral effect upon certain circumstances; your newly established position in the court and recent, extraordinary activities have in this case awakened a grave, sleeping misfortune, creating tensions and alliances between a triangle of opportunists who would see in your dilemma only its potential profit at the expense of all your lives. Take this Owen gentleman, for instance, who has been known over the years to sell out to both sides. We had to be thorough, please forgive me, but the certainty that this pilot had brought someone claiming to be Lord Penworth was a gamble at best."

"But what of it? I've harmed no one. What do these people want of Mary if it's my head they need?"

Father Dodd rose from his chair and walked over to his desk where he lifted a long envelope tattooed with stamps, writing and airmail insignias; walked back to his chair, offered me the post and sat down saying, "Perhaps you should read this."

I sat quiet for a few minutes, reading in the dim light of the oil lamp, folded the paper and handed the set back to Father Dodd unsure if I understood the true gravity of my situation.

"This transmission was obtained under the most clandestine circumstances. No one but my direct superiors are even aware we have it; certainly no one from Hoffenstein's court."

"But King Dubious *must* be made aware!" I stood, pacing the small area between the couch and the coffee table.

"All in due time; if it is what God wills, it will be done. We have a mission here that your personal affairs have brought, as you say, to a head. The villages of these parts are being corrupted and destroyed by the infiltration of illicit traders, such as those who have your wife in their custody as we speak. The Angolan authorities have been onto the Portuguese government for a decade trying to make the case for additional aide; until now, the Portuguese have been tied up; no sooner repairing one banking scandal when out from under a rock crawls another; and now this *deregulation* situation has only made borrowing simpler and their future domestic problems worse off."

I sat back on the couch and curiously enough, lit a cigarette, although I'm not a smoker.

51

"Now your small nation of Hoffenstein, rather well fit financially I might point out, has miraculously come to the Portuguese with enough business to free Portugal from the immediate distress of further judgment on its credit. And here is where it gets quite dicey;

"you see Penworth, those influences from Hoffenstein; the one's prepared to profit most agreeably from this partnership, are all rather concerned by Portugal's use of your recent insubordination to leverage new terms of the deal, naturally favorable to Portugal. Seems you've embarrassed the mighty Portuguese Navy!

"Only now, your old friendship with the King has the council of Hoffenstein split, dead to rights, as to whether you are any longer even considered worth the effort of saving; that is to say, that by censuring you, the council of Hoffenstein, including most disagreeably, His eminence, Archbishop Grieble, will have out maneuvered the protests of the Portuguese authorities; their arguments to redraw the contracts will have eroded right out from beneath them. The deal, as it is, is saved."

I looked back at the letter in Father Dodd's hand.

"Then why all the fuss?" I finally said. "Censure me. I don't give a damn! Let me simply do my thing; find Mary and my child and succeed or fail by myself. Why am I even wasting my time in this rotten village; stewing in my own?"

I was justifiably angry, finally learning of the tremendous scale of the efforts working against me, wondering where to go from here.

And there was Bidwell.

"Because Lord Penworth; these are simply *some* of the details at work *against* you. To us, you represent the finest story we've ever had to bring attention to our work against the cartels which poison the jungles out here. The vast majority of people in the world admire you; you've become quite a hero in the media; these people care *nothing* for the silly Portuguese navy!

"Plus, we have connections to informants inside the jungle which are dedicated to tracking your wife and child; places and access you could never achieve; all while you and I drain this ridiculous bottle, three fingers at a time."

Being, by this hour, a bit stoned, I stood up indignantly and swore that I was to leave that evening and burn the whole forest in the search for my beloved Mary; that *Fathah Dodd-wick* was simply an amateur, playing in a man's game; for him to stand aside; that I was the *true* gamer here;

"Come on," I challenged him, "get a deck of cards; I'll show you how I'm gonna save Mary!"

He placed a blanket over me as I then passed out on the couch, slid a pillow under my head, said his prayers, and went into the next room where his cot lay.

XXXIII

It was roughly one half hour later when Gregory finished loading the old blue truck with its cages and bushels. Rolling down the gravel drive past the house he waved to the pastor, shouting a last reminder to make no exceptions for dinner time.

Stopping first to return the young girl back home, he began the drive into the Touchwick market district where his reputation for plainspoken dealing won quite a few regular peddlers over the years, which paid for itself in a developed routine for a quick day's delivery; the gratified merchants allowed then to save their best efforts at haggling for the other vendors; most notably from the Kingdom's plentiful vegetable gardens. When it came to the city's appetite for chicken, Gregory's hens were a cut above.

Having pegged the last pair of the trousers on the line, the cleric went back inside the cottage, grabbed his satchel and left the house for his daily walk into the village where the church stood beneath another tall hemlock which seemed to dominate the entire lawn with its tremendous boughs.

The struggling flower beds were but another of the preacher's failing tributes to the new aesthetics of the good house; drowned in shade from dawn to dusk; a metaphor in many ways for the cleric's own struggle to revitalize the regular congregation since the town's conscience, Father Japheth, passed on two years ago. The Bishop has, after all, allowed the situation to remain in limbo, leaving the un-collared parson to minister in Father Japheth's absence for the indefinite interim, a matter of importance far behind the Archbishop's preoccupation with the larger clerical matters of raising more capital through investment trading and international land development schemes; all in the name of preparing for future, greater works in His name.

The sight of Sharon, the young girl's mother, on her knees beside the flower beds in front of the small white chapel filled his heart with a joy matched only by the smell of fresh baked quick bread on a cold winter morning.

He walked across the sloping lawn, never losing his eye upon her, climbed the steps to the large wooden door and went inside to the chapel where he kneeled and crossed himself before making his way toward the back room where his cassock and surplice hung from a coat rack beside a folding metal chair and a table; a table at which Father Japheth once met with the ladies auxiliary each Wednesday to discuss the choice and order of the hymns for the weekly service, which they would then gather to practice the Saturday before; way back when the church had a rich congregational life.

He changed unexpectedly from his regular street outfit into a tee shirt and work trousers which he always kept around the place, buttoned his cardigan and made for the rear side door which he exited to round the side of the chapel intending to join the girl's mother in front, who was still working intently to improve the appearance of the good man's struggling flowerbeds.

They both worked from opposite ends, aerating the roots, pulling weeds and redistributing eccentric out-growths of the healthier plants to areas far less cheerful; at one point, the cleric rose to his feet, stretched and walked toward the rear of the chapel where an old barn leaned against a century of the of earth's persistent gravitational influence, ever patient and seeming more than ever determined to bring it one day crashing to the ground.

Inside he located a short spade and wheel barrow which he filled with black dirt from the mossy side of the barn and wheeled it back, over to where Sharon continued to labor, apparently consumed inside her thoughts.

Together they unloaded barrow after barrow until all the beds around the chapel were cleaned and neat again; the gray haired cleric in spectacles then, checking his watch, went toward the back of the chapel to return the tools, unable to think of something to say that could possibly complement the profound kindness of her gesture.

"Don't care about a gay preacher; all that talk," she suddenly spoke, wiping the dirt off her knees, "You're decent to my Helen."

He thanked her, thinking of all the whispers around town, all the complaints and ridicule she and Bob have endured over the years; he then invited her to bring Helen over to see the chickens any time she wanted and watched her walk down the dirt road back home where Bob was watching over the little girl.

He then rolled the wheel barrow around to the back of the church and stopped, looking at the old barn for a long, long time.

It's reasonably certain that one will never presume to know exactly where his mind traveled in that vague period in time. He wound up leaving the wheel barrow and spade outside the barn and went home to take in the laundry and start supper for Gregory.

XXXIIII

Janis got used to me loitering around the Hospital tent, encouraging me, in her own manner, to occupy my idle hours running small errands or entertaining the volunteer staff with anecdotes of my childhood as Prince of the Dortpen; a healthier alternative, I suppose, to divesting any more of my limited remaining capital away at the cock fights.

Those evenings when she had to work later than usual, I would typically wander the village alone, exploring the crowded paths between the hundreds of mud homes and small market fronts which sprouted like toadstools, randomly throughout the languid streets; mud and grass affairs with roofs of wavy tin; bodegas constructed with a striking disregard for most conventional security enhancements, providing instead, unrestricted access for the sunlight and fresh air, pouring ever freely through the conspicuous openings provided by the absence of front doors and shop windows; in their place, the bowing tables, buried beneath odd looking fruits, nuts and other produce; rice, sugar, eggs and candy; there were counterfeit handbags; woven broad brimmed hats, (the ubiquitous choice to battle the blistering sun); cassette tapes with music imported from Algeria, the Caribbean Islands and Madagascar; there were tourist shops trading postcards, poorly crafted keepsake drums, kalimbas and "authentic" African carvings of figures from the local folklore and inevitably, the dozens of tables displaying hand strung necklaces of semi-precious stones, somehow managed from the greedy snares of foreign entrepreneurs from the steel gray continents far north.

On the sidewalks were the trinket laden blankets of the less prosperous impresarios who spent the better part of their rather tedious days keeping improvised soccer games from extending into and upsetting their business by sending merchandise flying every which way but toward the goal posts.

This was a very relaxed, civilized people; quite in contrast to the puppet-like depictions employed up north by the public schoolmasters, reinforcing the diffident superiority of our culture's legacy toward the deft maintenance and practice of delinquencies for which this gentle village as yet had no name; crime, for the most part, being not yet an issue here.

The sun was getting low in the sky, and the curious mix of electric lights and oil lamps began their evening trick of separating the haves from the have-nots; where by a single glance up the road, one can distinguish at an instant which of the huts were commercial by their proud display of any variety of modern lighting choices, from incandescent to fluorescent and the rare yet always bedazzling, blinking neon, spilling their colorful stripes across the trail in uneven intervals, broken by the dark bands indicating where the other families sat inside their huts preparing meals under the mellow glow of oil lamp or candle light.

The dress code was divided even enough I suppose; half the population dressed in western tee-shirts and shorts or jeans while the other half wore the more traditional buba, whose bright colored *Kente* prints seemed to energize the smallest gesture with a power uniquely African; a manner of projecting indisputable authority in everything and anything traditional.

Over the huts about a block or two away, the unexpected sound of drums kicked up against the more prevalent tranquility of the town; the murmur of a nearby mob, invisible for a time from where I ambled, gathering enthusiasm as its numbers grew and grew; the drums calling ever louder, the tempo ever quicker.

It was reasonable to discern by this time, even from my position way around the corner, that some fresh troupe had descended into town this night, providing the extraordinary appeal required to pull these sleepy people from their huts and stoves, forming lines of thrill seekers, lured as if by some enchantment, some invisible vacuum, toward the minstrels, strangely materialized in the village square.

As it happened, I was no less vulnerable and found my place amid the swarm of traffic flowing to the music.

A fire had been set in the center of the space, where the minstrels in their ankle length skirts danced like men possessed, occasionally leaping like phantoms through the flames; landing softly again on the hard ground in bare feet; all to the pulse of four musicians pounding on their djembes.

It was quite the scene; a spectacle to thaw the coldest claim against the unity of all human-kind; this blaze of colored bubas and kangas, swaying in a tidal surge of joyous caroling, the chorus snaking through the intricate warp and weft of this embryonic heartbeat sounding from the loom of djembes; a musical expression in defense of every creature's basic right to enjoy life and be loved in return; where one night a simple market square took its bow then stood aside, there entered in its place this intrepid crucible of all the mysterious and instinctive forces of unpretentious human harmony; roiling, untamed vapors on a teasing thread of warm African night air.

I wished at that moment for a camera and a beer.

It was around this time I grew somewhat distracted, lost in a private moment of no apparent significance or sequence; at one point maybe wondering if tonight were an anniversary or something of that nature, I can't remember exactly, but I can clearly recall turning to focus at something odd across the fire, on the opposite side of the now teeming plaza; a most fascinating sight.

I've heard and read accounts of the Hyena men, given to tame and feed those feral dogs from hell; walking them on motorcycle chains in studded collars like Cerberus on a leash and there, through the dancers and the fire on the other side of the show floor, they were paraded; the minstrels in their group with four pale chimera mixed from wild boar and muscular bull terrier, spotted demons with immense smiles filled with fillet knives topped by pointed ears through which a mane of tall bristling hair stretched in its Mohawk from the crown down to the middle of it back.

These were the Hyena men and I wanted a better look.

I managed my way around the audience, now even more densely packed in a seething throng around the central spectacle; united by this time into a single throat, clapping and swaying, singing at the tops of their voices, trying it seemed, to be heard and attended in the deepest valleys of the immense surrounding jungle, where all the good and kind ancestral spirits live out their separate and mischievous eternities; the brilliant fire throwing shadows through the bright lit strips of switching faces; eyes and teeth and the beautiful, gleaming, sweated blackness of the strobe-like portraits caught in ever changing facets of pure euphoria.

The children were quite naturally adept at making the best of this priceless opportunity, running from or chasing one another through the legs of the enraptured adults; boys and girls whose young screams and taunts for once were drowned out by the pounding and the chanting of the main event.

I was very near to where I could finally examine these curious animals without compromising any acquired sense for my own safety, turning with a smile from the children toward the seated djembe players. A stick with flame charred meat as I recall, had fallen from a young boys hand, who overlooked the hungry Cerberus as he bent to pick it up; his silent screams, drowned by the deafening song, narrate my still disorganized memory of pulling old Billy 'O's pistol from my side and shooting the animal off the battered body of the child.

XXXV

Janis, I later learned, attended me back at the emergency tent, bandaging my broken arm and battered face. The sedative she administered was lovely and I was soon enough playing in a pea green field of crimson poppies with Mary and my little baby, reading quietly on a bright blue set of synchronized waves, listening to a piece of music that I often hear in dreams where I'm dancing to the djembe on a sun drenched shore.

XXXVI

"There's someone wishes to visit."

A familiar voice began to break through the haze of darkness I had pulled, like a window sash, across the screen of my tired, aching brain; the dim light of a tiny room now overpowering the pull of unconsciousness; the second hand swept past twelve upon the face of a metal clock set on the bedside table.

"He's waking up. I'll see if he's able to understand where he is."

It was Janis, my guardian angel. I began to recognize the familiarity of things; simple objects began to assume their solidity from a long holiday in some other, virtual likeness; books became real books; the bed post at

my feet was real which meant the feet under the blanket were *my* feet. If I could only lift my arm to the nightstand, I am sure as I'm the Duke of the Dortpen, that it would stop my hand from passing through it.
Everything was real again; my heart raced.

"Hello, Giov. How are you feeling today?" she asked.

Speaking was an entirely different thing. I hadn't ever given much thought to how much effort goes into producing the simplest phrase. The muscles in my neck relaxed and let my head sink back into the pillow. Questions started to take form inside my brain; a bit confused at first, but the strong sensation that there was something I needed to know continued to agitate me; beginning as a hybrid, the first half of a sensation edited to the second half of an unrelated feeling; I was drowning in frustration when there appeared a spark from the stone, a fully formed question which made me turn my lips upward, forming a weak smile.

"What the hell happened?" I breathed.

"Please, run and get the doctor. Tell him he's coming around," said Janis to the same boy I vaguely remember seeing some undetermined time ago, when I called at the Parish, looking for Father Dodd.

"You've been sleeping for quite a long time, Giov. We were all quite concerned. How are you feeling?"

There was a long pause.

"Odd," came my ginger reply.

A few days passed like this; my mind returning slowly to capacity and my sleeps interrupted by Janis to prevent any relapse.

"Good morning, Your Lordship," she woke me, ever the sardonic angel.

I looked first at the clock on the nightstand, then back to Janis, admiring the way she fit her uniform.

"Yes," I replied, "How's about a little breakfast and some answers this morning? That would be a splendid development. This room keeps shrinking and I'm suspicious that the key to my ever eloping is tied up with an understanding of how I came to be here; all this intrigue is rather stressing on the appetite, you know."

She smiled broadly, "I'm delighted to see you come around so completely, my Dear. I'll fix you up with some toast and tea, right off. Don't figure on eloping for a little while longer, however; you've had quite a nasty time and have some more repairs to consider in the next week or two."

"Oh wonderful!" I swore, "How about drawing back some shades around this morbid pit, then? I'm suffocating."

She agreed to open the window on the right side of the room, insisting that the other two windows remain covered.

"There's a man who asks when you will be well enough to receive visitors. He's quite anxious to talk with you. Are you up for it?"

"I'll see him right now if he's carrying a tray with eggs and bacon," I replied.

She left the room, now somewhat brighter for the open sash and didn't return with breakfast for another hour.

"Here we go," she said as she propped me up with some extra pillows. "So sorry about the time, but another patient died last night at the infirmary. It's too sad."

I began on the toast.

"I did bring you a surprise, however; a gentleman wishes to thank you. You've been keeping him waiting for weeks. Are you game?"

"Like I said, if he's got a lunch tray. I suppose I could clear my schedule and work him in."

"He's in the other room. I'll leave you two to talk."

XXXVII

There was a soft knock at the door. I instructed my mystery guest to enter.

I must admit I was quite taken aback to see step out from behind the door a jet black man with strong sinewy arms and the blackest, most completely intelligent eyes I had ever had the privilege to look upon once before.

"Kriss?" I managed.

He looked at me, all broken up as I was, incapable of speaking for the better part of half a minute; he never was much of a talker, I thought, but served quite brilliantly as the closest thing I had come upon so far as a mirror and as such his response helped to relieve my desire to see myself in one for some time longer.

"Mister Minister," he smiled.

The following hour was most enlightening and clarified Janis' reluctance to address the particulars of my unfortunate, though rather remarkable situation.

It seems that on the evening of the entertainment in the square, I had produced the same pistol Lady Fortune laid across the steel card table aboard the *Douagiere* so many months ago; pulled the trigger, killing a rather large hyena aggressing on a young boy; the son, as it would be revealed, of Kriss' youngest sister; a boy whose life I saved; an uncle whose lifelong gratitude I earned.

My keen reflexes in all matters hyena however, were the ironic cause of my immediate apprehension by the surrounding mob, who knowing nothing of the scene into which I discharged my weapon, proceeded to mete out a most thorough and efficient form of provincial justice on their own; regrettably far along before the true explanation could be elaborated; only then turning from my extensive schooling to the task of chasing the Minstrels and their dogs outside the village limits with every threat should they consider ever coming back again.

The boy, besides a row of stitching which will no doubt earn him awe among observers in his older years, survived the ordeal much less worse for wear than did I, having spent the past three weeks on a cognitive hiatus, testing fate, medicine and apparently the prayers of my guardian angel, who took my health on as her personal responsibility, leaving my side only to care for others at the infirmary or retiring to her dormitory each evening to sleep and begin the next day much as the one before.

The commotion of that terrible evening, most unfortunately, had the additional consequence of drawing attention to the village where I enjoyed, until then, a certain degree of anonymity from the dreaded agents of the causes Father Dodd had weeks ago laid bare. The room to which I was moved, Kriss also informed me, was one which none but a very select group would have guessed shielded me in convalescence; hence Janis' unwillingness to open the remaining two windows.

Another fine mess I've made of things I thought to myself before falling back into a late morning nap.

XXXVIII

Six white horses, fresh groomed and hitched to pull a bright red landau trimmed in gold, sat patient in the steady rain, waiting with a few hundred hardy revelers, hid beneath a canopy of black umbrellas outside the great Cathedral of Saint Pontificate where the proud and thankful King and Queen were expected to descend the wide staircase to begin a celebration of the christening of the newborn heiress to the Dubious throne; crossing back through the city where the Great Ballroom of *Palais Silberfluss* waited for the afternoon's merriments in all its festooned splendor.

Beyond the imposing edifice and surrounding city, the trees of Hoffenstein were one by one, exchanging the verdant trappings of summer for the annual spectacle of autumn's much anticipated, infinitely more vibrant collection; the peal of University bells soothing the vast, empty spaces across the great lawns and pastures dividing the nether villages, forests and farms, calling the young and promising custodians of Hoffenstein's academia and tradition back from months of idle holiday to rejoin their specified positions among the books, beakers and blackboards; the hay stacks were piling and the air was faint with the smell of burning leaves.

The rain tapped against the drowsy casements of the vestry, where Archbishop Grieble stood motionless, arms out-stretched; aides busying themselves positioning his chasuble and smoothing his hard won pallium for the impending ceremony; the soft voices of the choir floated weightless as ash, reaching into every remote crevice of the cavernous cathedral, predisposing the hypothetical observer to consider the pensive Bishop incapable of meditation upon any subject other than the birth and resurrection of the Savior; an assumption whose legitimacy would ultimately serve to disenchant.

The high pitch of the commencing organ sounded, as *With Christ we share a mystic grave* solemnly filled the nave where the throngs began to arrive; touching the font, abiding the ushers, genuflecting and ultimately taking their prized, ticketed seats among the hundreds of identical pews cut through by four main carpeted aisles, washed in the colored light from twenty four stained glass windows of the clerestory high above.

The fiefdom of Hoffenstein was, on this marvelous occasion, continuing down a path long marinated in tradition, an unbroken chain of remarkably fertile monarchs who established the Dubious lineage and its reliable, if not always revered stewardship, punctuated periodically by extravagant reminders such as this, that even the mighty Palace itself was, no more or less, likewise obliged to the good Lord above, who incontestably resides omnipotent within the hallowed walls of the imposing Cathedral; the roommate, so to speak, of his most Holy Eminence, the humble Archbishop Grieble.

A Page in thin, black framed glasses, white horse-hair head piece, a cobalt double-breasted waistcoat piped in braided gold and white knee-high silks, entered the adjacent ante chamber where the King waited impatiently for the ceremony to begin, anxious to return at the earliest opportunity back to the royal palace wherein home court provided him every distinct and time honored advantage usurped by the predicated infallibility of all matters of heaven and earth, here in the most-pious cathedral on the east side of the eccentric city.

In his gloved hand, the middle aged page balanced a small, highly polished silver tray upon which lay a tented card, effectively intended to convey an urgent dispatch to His Royal Highness; an exercise whose elaborate enterprise aroused sufficient suspicion above all competing notice; all erstwhile matters of the day out-leveraged by the impending celebration; the Christening as much a matter of State as that private milestone of fatherhood which transcends all caste distinctions.

"A telephone call for me in the office?" asked the King upon examining the brief message.

"Quite correct," replied the page.

"Where can I find this telephone, then?"

"If His Highness would do me the supreme honor," replied the Page who led King Dubious down a short hallway to the office door, lightly cracked in anticipation of the King's subsequent arrival; then dismissed himself, leaving Maximilian Dubious III to his privacy.

XXXIX

There was less than an hour of sun left for the small plane to find the dirt landing strip, scratched into the hard ground of a small natural clearing surrounded by thick vegetation, about eight miles outside the official municipal boundaries, directly west of downtown Luremo.

Kriss sat half asleep behind the wheel of the faded black jeep, eyes covered from the brightness by a tilted grass hat while napping in the hot, late afternoon shade. He knew from experience that although the plane was always late, the plane always eventually came.

In his half sleep, his mind wandered like a bee in a vast field of bright colored flowers, sampling small traces of disconnected memories before flying weightlessly to pollinate another; the ambush and the bible; the minstrels and the pistol; his sister's face when he explained to her the truth about his nephew and the hyena; the large black fish he caught from a small boat on a river a few weeks ago; one ear always trained on the sky for the sound of the mail plane.

A slight breeze passed over the wide hat brim, resonating through the woven straw to tug the sweat band on his head; twenty more minutes passed when finally, softer than the buzzing flies upon the armadillo carcass fifty feet away, the first lonely traces of the purring Cessna could be discerned, phasing in and out of audibility, gaining volume with each passing minute.

It would be another four or five minutes before he could make out the tiny spot against the immense blue backdrop; another fifteen before the dust cleared and the propellers finally stopped spinning.

It was too late to consider refueling to begin the return trip back to Bosley, so Kriss tossed the mail bag into the back of the jeep, preparing to take Owen into Luremo where he could find himself some dinner, cold beer and a room for the night. Neither were enthusiastic talkers, so the relatively short ride into Luremo was, for the greater measure, bereft conversation.

"How's my friend, that Lord Penworth fellow?" asked Owen, breaking the silence.

Kriss continued driving, looking at the road in front of him.

"You must see a bit of him in your travels, yes?" he continued.

Kriss reached into his shirt pocket, produced a cigarette and struck a match. Owen simply smiled at his blunt generosity.

"Don't know. He gone almost right away; finding some woman in the jungle," he replied.

Owen gave a short laugh. "That's odd. Heard something about him getting pretty beat up only a month or so ago."

Owen also lit a cigarette, the last from his own pack and continued, "I can make it well worth your while; you just tell me how to find him."

Kriss pulled up to a small motel across the street from an open beer shack.

"Con't help you mon, your story maybe not so good. Mister Ministah left right on. I keep looking if you want."

Owen stepped out of the jeep, grabbed a small bag and headed to grab himself the first of the night's many pints of ice cold beer. Turning back to the jeep, he smirked, looked Kriss in the eyes and said,

"Have it your way, old boy. I'll pay well for any information you want to give me. See you again, soon."

Kriss drove off, looking straight at the road in front of him.

XL

Bishop Grieble slid the tiny door back across the aperture from which he discretely surveyed the great nave through the vestry wall, growing increasingly suspicious that the phone message delivered to King Dubious might explain why the royal pews remained empty, fully fifteen minutes after the last guest took his seat and the great cathedral gates were closed, a signal that the service should typically begin.
The resourceful organist had already improvised for the delay by complementing the choir's recital of *Within the Church's sacred fold* and was now into the third stanza of *Once in royal David's city*, singing,

> *"Christian children all must be*
> *Mild, obedient, good as he. . . "*

and still no sign of the royal child's parents or the Prince, Maximillian's younger brother Eugene, who until the birth of the princess, stood next in line to the throne and spent many an idle hour lost in pleasant distraction upon the implications; accepting with begrudging consolation an emblematic chair upon his brother's council, a position the enterprising Prince employed to the fullest advantage; engineering considerable personal affluence by means of his singular influence in the brokerage of myriad hand selected interests; matters of international investment wherein Hoffenstein's eventual losses were simply the collateral consequence of Prince Eugene's up-front earnings.

Being selected, therefore, "default godfather" to the young Princess Gloria, was perceived as a double edged tribute, not gone unnoticed; both a confirmation of his inevitable, growing distance from the throne and yet testament before all Hoffenstein of his proximity to its inner sanctum; this was indeed a most epochal event for the Prince and his socialite wife, the ever fashionable Lady Belladonna.

Maximillian Dubious III finally exited the office into a crowded hallway where his agitated Queen stood among the entourage, holding the tiny princess in her arms.

"Well then. Sorry to have kept you all; shall we begin?" asked the radiant Monarch.

The Archbishop was a study in unrefined curiosity and mingled suspicion; a volatile mix which seized the reigns of his countenance in the absence of any subtlety; turning his head to hide the fact, he then motioned for the entourage to assemble for the grand entrance.

"Who could that have been? Don't you think it rather impolite to have kept the congregation waiting for so long," whispered the admonishing Queen, hastily passing young Gloria off to her Nanny.

"Waiting is entirely in the fashion, my dear," he smiled. "So much depends on what one waits for, don't you agree?"

The procession began its winding journey to the altar, where the crème of Hoffenstein's cultural elite sat impatiently, watching for the ceremony to begin.

XLI

I managed my rounds with the aid of a cane provided by Kriss some weeks ago to replace the horrid aluminum model supplied by the infirmary upon my release from the clandestine bed, provided by Father Dodd, for my anonymous recuperation. It was the interpretation of a snake, hand carved into the stubborn meat of an ancient Jackalberry tree, wrapped from head to spotted tail along the staff; a tribute I imperfectly perceived to reference the mighty Asclepius, a call to my rapid and thorough recovery, but served instead, by Kriss' sober account, to represent a snake climbing along a sturdy branch, a prosthesis to assist my rehabilitation and nothing Greek whatsoever. I grew quite dependent on old wooden Caduceus and soon racked up the kilometers hobbling here and there on my journey toward complete recovery.

It was late morning and I had just left the chemist where a curious bottle of blue pills had been prepared for me in accordance with instructions from Dr. Spencer R. Hoernfeske, MD, my attending, when I recognized the young boy from the chapel ambling down the road about half the distance from the next corner, some twenty five meters away. He carried in his hand a long switch with which he swatted at imaginary targets in rhythm to his lazy stride; a curious reflection in contrasts, he and I, I mused, brightened now by his sudden appearance.

"Mistah Ministah," he grinned "you getting on so good now 'days. You not gonna need that ol' stick no more. Mebbe you give that old cane to me?" He laughed as I promised to consider the generous offer; anxious to fulfill, in record time, every prognosis of my complete recovery and grateful independence of the vestigial, serpentine accoutrement; I bare no sentimental bond for any gift, no matter how considerate, which held so many punitive associations.

"Have you seen Father Dodd?" I asked, looking for both fresh conversation and a place to sit my tired bones for a spell.

"He's ot the 'mergency 'ospitol, last I see, Ministah," he replied, eyeing my cane with his fingers, "talkin to Miz Janis about the new baby."

"Baby eh? *Will the wonders of the amorous science never cease in its industrious campaign?* I mused. "I'm not one to pitch a fuss over babies, I'm afraid; *filthy little things, really.* Maybe I'll look in on the hens over at the gymnasium instead."

"No Ministah," the boy cut in, "I sent from the 'ospital tent jes now an fine you. Faddah Dodd ask for you. Come back wit me and talk wif him."

I followed the boy back to the infirmary, unable to keep pace with his enthusiastic fantasies of inheriting such a storied work of supreme

67

craftsmanship: "dee fable Cane of dee Marquis Penwort, Lort of dee Dor'pen" he rambled; a prospect which fueled his youthful stride to trace, in allegro hops, my linear andante-plodding, with a spiraling track not without its analogous reference to the very Greek associations of the carving in question, I smiled.

I finally arrived to within ten feet of the large tent with the big red cross, when Junior came running back out to inform me that the two had returned to the parish, taking the baby with them.

I was fairly exhausted and my leg was beginning to ache again; looking up to the sky, I grabbed the handkerchief from my pant pocket and wiped the sweat from my brow; popping a few more little blue pills I then looked disdainfully over at Junior, all *smiling* and filled with piss and vinegar, saying,

"Well then, lead on Good Sir!"

XLII

Junior made an excuse as we approached the parish house, eyeing my staff once more, and quick as that, was out of sight.

A bench was placed for the weary traveler outside, under the charitable overhang and I sat down in its shade, not at all anxious to watch as the two of them fussed over a baby while I pretended to share in the domesticity of it all.

It was another very hot morning and I enjoyed that bench for at least twenty minutes, watching the birds walk cautiously between the busy people, pecking diligently at the littered road, completely unaware of any difference that might possibly exist between the cosmic search and seizure of a table scrap and the rush against the cruel and unrelenting clock upon the workshop wall.

Here, from this humble bench outside the parish, all the cogs and springs and gears and things that constitute this messy little world, a ball of dust inside this perplexing universe, the whole of all this madness seems to spin in perfect cycles of its own configuration; the writhing jungle of warped gravities and cantankerous gasses we are all convinced at having been created for little more than us to understand; that with our textbooks and bibles we slave to navigate a ship whose tiller is, in the end, controlled by other hands on other wheels; our job ultimately revealed as not to fix nor wind or steer the day, but simply wash it's pretty little lettered face, dust a gear, oil a bushing, nothing more.

Perhaps this is the secret to it all, I realized, sitting on that bench; this God we work so industriously, so tirelessly, to create and then recalibrate is little more than the table scrap which has answered the prayers of my feathered friend; the clock on the wall is nothing more than a clock on a wall.

The door opened suddenly, it was Janis.

"How long have you been sitting out there? Come inside and have a cold glass of water. You must be dehydrated!"

I smiled, abruptly retired from my meditations and stood up, leaning hard on my walking stick.

I could hear the baby from the porch and walked into the front room where my eyes labored to adjust to the dimness. I could hear Father Dodd enter the room from the back of the house and it was obvious by the sound that he was cradling the child in his arms.

"She's such a miracle," he whispered. "Care to hold her?"

I was initially surprised to see in his arms, a tiny white baby, assuming since my first exchange with Junior that the child would naturally be black.

I was not one brought up to accommodate such a challenge and began quite respectfully to decline when it was apparent that my failure to receive the baby from the priest would result in a tumble from which serious harm might result. I held the child as one might caress a badger or wet cat; both of them laughing at me.

I must admit that I was beginning to get a bit bothered by the attention drawn to my discomfort when I turned my eyes finally adjusted to the dimness of the room, and I saw lying neatly over the arm of a corner chair, the jacket.

I sat upon the couch and clutched the child in my arms, crying so loud that the old cat on the window sill lifted its tail to stretch, and then retired into the back room.

"The child was found swaddling in that marvelous jacket. Her mother, your wife Mary, I regret to say died in captivity. We've arranged for your transportation home, Lord Penworth, through communication with none less than King Dubious himself. Your mission here in Africa is finished."

End of Part One

Part Two

I

Few events compare with a predawn snow; the immense transformation of the earth, achieved in a perfect vacuum of sound, spread like butter cream across the farthest points of scenery; where only yesterday the countless features of a summer landscape teased the restless artist's eye within us each;

particulates we trim and paste onto the balance sheet of practical experience; the pond we gave a name, the trees, the flitting leaves, the seed globe of the dandelion, the reflection of an old bay horse bent to wet his tongue; all used to harmonize the subtle yet essential differences that constitute the whole; baptized from the soup of chaos into some primordial catalogue of purpose; each atom christened with a new and useful name.

A tribute from the most eccentric atelier in this far corner of the Milky Way; in sentimental flakes of noiseless ice, dropped in our sleep upon these silly ledger-books; out there draped across the valleys and the hillsides; in whose expression each and every computation then is magically erased; there are no leaves, there is no grass, the roads are gone; the country overrun in seamless snow.

The terrace becomes the lawn becomes the moor; becomes the white washed forest edge far off, becomes a wrinkle in the great bleach blanket folded at the base of old Pater, himself pressed like the spire of St. Pontificate, ever higher from the sleeping, icy countryside against the frosted daybreak sky above.

Far out, across the meadow near the wooded edge, furlongs from the windows of the great house, *Burlwood*, throwing sallow pink and palest blue reflections back toward the inescapable retreat of night, the tiny figure of a restless man traced footsteps through this virgin spectacle; thin wisps of breath seen curling from his silhouette like frosted garland on the crisp winter air.

It had been ten full years since Lord Penworth had come home from Angola.

Little had changed of Mayfair since he left it all those many years ago; the great stone house stood as it ever had, alone on its scrap of hill, visible from clearings in the Dortpen miles off; Lord Penworth, his father, had died of course, but there were no new roads, no new houses, no old houses gone; the trees were fatter, the hedge rows taller and the stables somewhat smaller than they seemed to him as a boy.

How tall did young Charlotte now imagine her stables stood?

Arriving from the harbor in a tiny woven bassinet, the infant daughter of a much transformed man began her first of many seasons in the country, where her ancient relations defended for as many centuries all of this remote Dortpen territory from the savages and lawless gypsies yet abiding in the great surrounding forests for the honor and protection of the Crown; the great house stood as nothing less than one small token of some old King's gratitude.

II

The new King, not so very young himself these days, Maximillian Dubious III, took great delight in memories of that fateful day, ten years ago, when inside the immense chapel of St. Pontificate, before the marble Baptismal font, he loosed upon the Queen, the congregation, the Bishop and the Prince, his scandalous direction that the chrism touched upon the infant's head did not ally her soul in Christ with Uncle Eugene at the watch, but rather through his trusted aide and bosom friend, Lord Penworth whose imminent return from Africa was told to him by telephone not twenty minutes prior.

The Queen, about to have a marvelous faint, took one last glance onto the large assembly in the nave and changed her little mind, thinking much the better she should maintain a regal disposition; but not before young Gloria returned her lunch upon the Bishops vestment, wherein Lady Belladonna, jumping clear, then knocked the chrismatory flying towards the Prince, whose sudden shock was further elaborated by the stain of chrism oil now spilled across his medal covered breast.

It was a matter of many months before the delighted Sovereign could get his wife to join him in the fun and even to this day not entirely. His brother and His Eminence conversely, never shared the joke.

The Duke of Dortpen, however, squared Dubious' unsolicited tribute against this malevolent spider's web with a deft civility; for neither Eugene nor the Bishop were successful in turning even a reasonable minority of the popular sentiment against him, despite their considerable means; resurrecting the customary company of skeletons out from shallow graves, *Lord knows there were many*, then smearing these across the covers of the *Chronicle* and many other sundry periodicals; each new and shocking episode, to their chagrin, served conversely to intensify forbearance toward any further campaigns of the sort against the good Duke.

He was just what the resolute nation required, and timely come; a hero arrived from adventure far off to relieve the current system from its protracted malaise; come to resurrect the great debate; a self-made statesman reassuring Hoffenstein that Parliament was still composed somewhat of flesh and bone; an unpredicted benefit for a much indebted King.

For many years, Maximillian had ineffectually observed his adversaries in the council leverage their extensive corporate alliances with revenues that stimulated the Country's imagination without a proportionate influence upon its treasury. Certain, well positioned people in the government were indeed prospering, but the marginally apprised citizens of Hoffenstein instead habitually blamed King Dubious alone for the consequential tax burdens and lack of meaningful employment; the Duke simply reintroduced a polarizing element into the great halls of society, dormant for as many years before his celebrated return and scandalous abuse at the hands of his well-heeled adversaries.

And so it was, for these inimitable skills, the grateful Monarch arranged for his boyhood comrade, Lord Penworth, and his lovely daughter Charlotte Marie, to be well provided for, which meant a townhouse near the Palace for his frequent business visits into Touchwick, where it was arranged that Charlotte was to provide amicable distraction for the young Princess Gloria, who grew to be a spoiled little thing and made as much fuss about having to amuse herself by teasing Charlotte as she did about how enormous and lonely the Palace could be without her.

Charlotte however, seemed to enjoy the time they spent together, fascinated by the same opulence and diversity which simply agitated the bored princess; returning many nights to supper with her father asking why her young friend was so tormented by access to the very things most children claim, from want, would solve their bleak existences.

"That, my dear, is what we grown-ups call irony; and so as your lovely mother would say, *take care before you make a wish, that it might come.*"

Charlotte smiled, kissed her father and retired to her book in the small reading room where Giov placed two chairs before a window and a lamp of brass with a satin shade where she would curl herself and dream into the pages of her story, pausing every now and again to part the curtain with a hand and look across the garden to the palace where she wondered if the lighted windows of her best friend's room suggested she might be curled into a chair and looking back.

III

Deacon Frederick had finished extinguishing the candles, bowed his head and knelt before the altar preparing to rise and wipe the cup when a sharp pain stabbed him in the lower back. He rested his elbow on the edge of the altar cloth and slowly lifted himself, trying to correct the alignment of his spine; slowly, finally upright, the aging man took on a wistful air. Sure he was getting on; still preaching every Sunday; still without a collar, acolyte or a steady congregation; and still together with Gregory in love; but it was the pair of them, sitting there in the way back pew, fifteen minutes after the others had gone which gave him cause to brood. Helen was older now, perhaps eighteen, and looked very much the pretty young lady, sitting patiently with her mother in the farthest pew. The gray haired cleric fixed his glasses and continued to straighten his stance, then dropped his eyes to the altar, suddenly praying to himself as he had over many years for the redemption of this sweetest evidence of God's purity here on Earth.

Such perfection locked inside this tragic, shattered form; that Helen might yet receive the Blessing; that deep inside somewhere, the directness of her unself-conscious being, the innocence of her understanding might somehow earn her some clemency, some extra mercy from the rigid edict of his faith; that she could be closer to the *Christ* than everyone yet never know his name seemed more than a just bit unfair; it was *so damn cruel*!

He abruptly flushed, astounded by the depth of his own apostasy, staring across the chapel with the chalice slinking in his quivering hands.

Helen turned to Sharon and opened her voice, a bird song to the rafters. Her mother responded, pressing her cheek against Helen's soft curls, *"There baby, hush darling"*; smiling with the tired, tarnished expression of a lonesome brass bell rung atop a buoy many years into a heartless squall; always anchored, somehow always lost; a rosary like seaweed woven through her abstract fingers.

The chapel door swung open; Gregory was as quick to close the biting chill outside and stomped the snow from his boots. He had come this morning as he often did, to save Frederick from a long cold walk back to the cottage. Oddly enough, he was not a religious type, raised by a pair of tolerant agnostics; he had never set foot inside a chapel before his very first invitation to a wedding, a lifetime ago when he was an elder statesman of the teen years.

Gregory was however, by any standard, a good man.

Unwrapping his muffler, he stepped through the vestibule doors and entered the chapel where he noticed the two women on his right; Sharon turned to the sound and met his eyes while Helen continued her intense examination of the bright sunlight pouring through the colored glass above the altar. He nodded and leaned over to squeeze Helen's cold hand. She did not drop her gaze from the stained window, but returned his gesture and sang a pair of notes.

"Come on Dear; it's time we're going back," Sharon said; "Nice to see you Gregory."

"It's pretty cold; I'll take you home and come back for him."

"Oh no," she immediately replied, "I've got to knock some of the devil out of her, you know. Mebee the cold'll help. Thank you anyway; things been fairly crazy since Bob's gone. She's a handful you know."

"Yes, I can only imagine. Going into Touchwick tomorrow; would it be a problem?"

"She'll come if you're invitin' again."

"We always have a wonderful day. She's such a good one. Still fond of those hens, she is."

"Oh Mr. Gregory," she looked down to conceal her eyes, "you're such a dear friend. God bless you."

"My pleasure, Ms. Sharon. I'll pick 'er up around eight an' have her back before sundown. Now bundle up, it's freezin' outside."

He leaned over to kiss the top of Helen's crown; a brief smile broke across her vacant stare, which, as soon as the birdcall, was gone.

Deacon Frederick looked up from his hands on the altar, noticing the candle by the font still burning. Gregory might very well be ruined by a book, he thought.

He held the cup into the colored light from the window, watched it shine for a minute and placed it back down on the altar where it would stand, draped under a soft white cloth until next Sunday morning.

IIII

Felis stood in the warm predawn darkness with his bundle, waiting for the bus to take him forty miles away from his aunt's little room in Lubalo to the Catoca Diamond mine where his uncle arranged a job for him by stitching some connections to a few favors. The young man would stay about two weeks at the mine before catching another ride back to his aunt's with a paycheck and a pile of filthy clothes from his fortnight digging, eating and sleeping next to a few hundred unfamiliar men, most of whom fell to drinking and gambling from loneliness and wretched living; Felis would often play the scars across his face and body in a faux-offense against the inexorable pressure from the older miners trying to lure the innocents into friendships engineered to separate the young men from their wages.

Every morning, hours before the sun would rise, Felis joined the long lines of miners, waiting to enter the cages where he would be lowered through the earth's crust to the maze of squealing mineral containers rolling on their polished tracks, disappearing into dim lighted tunnels from where echoes of machinery and unintelligible hollers, laughter and fragments of song would all reverberate into a single cacophony of sensation back inside the great timpani of the common chamber.

He would work ten hours, loading containers, drilling rock or repairing the machines before taking the long cable ride up to the surface where the dim twilight of dusk softened the transition back to a sweltering African evening. Here he took his place onto another set of longer, slower moving lines where he would strip from his filthy clothes and wait for a security officer to search his naked body for any illicit vestige from his subterranean holiday; the tiniest pebble which might in fact belong to the Firm.

From the search room the line moved to the showers where Felis stood with twenty other men under a spray of cold water before putting on his surface clothes and meandering over to the mess tent where began another evening of assuring the belligerent gamblers and topers that he would prefer to sit in his tent, alone on his cot, reading the Bible until he remembered nothing but the loud horn of revelry at three-thirty the following morning when he would don his filthy dress to begin the cycle once again.

This tactic wore into the same familiar ruts as many other tales of virtuous men in dreadful situations; a story altogether unchanged since the very first shaman, around his transcendental fire, told of someone's desperate struggle between the good and evil natures battling inside his soul. Three months since he was first issued a helmet, the dozen self-appointed leaders of the various coteries of con-men and gamers fell to half the number still intrigued by the disfigured young Christian; that number to four, then three, until there was unchallenged, one single adversary with a cankerous grudge against Felis' perceived insolence; a spirit which bore down upon his temper like the proverbial itch that required a severe scratch.

The war began in earnest one evening after another day in the caves, when a circle of five men laughed as Felis wiped the plate of food from his face and chest where it had landed after Raul deliberately walked into the distracted young man.

"You should watch where you're going," exploded Raul sarcastically. "You almost messed my pretty face," his five friends laughing on cue.

Felis looked up from his shirt and stared directly into the man's troublesome eyes.

The crowd surrounding Felis grew somewhat thicker, ramping to a mean spirited howling, some men chiding Felis to strike back at the scoundrel; teach dirty old Raul to not be so proud; he was after all, unpopular to many of the younger miners for being a loud mouth; many of them having been themselves subject to the same harassment as young Felis.

Felis bent over to pick his plate and tray up off the dirt, trembling inside with a mixture of rage and fear, the dissonance of excitement dissolved into one single key-note of adrenalin; his center of gravity now swimming in a rush of fresh, hot blood racing through his ears.

"You one *ugly* mother fucka, you know that?!" Raul continued, "Would ya'll get a good look at this clumsy boy's face; what happen to you son? You walk into some big ol' chainsaw or somthin?"

Raul was on a roll; most of the older men walking away by now, familiar with Raul's tired routine and anxious to get on drinking and throwing the ivory; the younger men losing their nerve to come to Felis' defense, leaving the remainder simply amused by the sadistic break in the camp's more familiar monotony.

"Raul," a tired voice came from the lingering circle of spectators, "Just leave the boy and come lose your money with us. We got whiskey an' mebee a girl come to camp wid us tonight. "Ee's jus a stupid boy who don' know any better, dats all."

Felis turned to find his way through the circle; he was out numbered and very afraid.

"Where the fuck you going, my friend?" shouted Raul, turning back now from the older miner and grabbing a handful of the young man's shirt. Felis turned instinctively, rounding Raul across the ear with his fist, hoping only to break from the ring. Raul went down and instantly, Felis disappeared beneath the pile of five men whose fists and elbows worked like hammers into a breach of diamond studded stone.

V

"Would you prefer some ham or bacon with your breakfast this morning, sir?" asked the butler.

I had just stripped from my hat and coat and was warming my wet feet by the fire; meditating on how dependable the revitalizing effects of the morning sun rays against the crystalline ice and snow were upon a man's soul despite the repetition over numerous decades of its enigmatic consistency and variation. "It's a blessing!" I declared

"I beg your pardon, sir?" remarked the butler, "Are you referring to the ham or the bacon?"

"The *ice*, Hobbes! . . . and I'll wait to have breakfast with Charlotte when she wakes. Perhaps you'll join me for some strong coffee in here for a while?"

"That would be very nice, sir. I'll prepare some espresso and quick bread right away. You just sit right there and warm yourself; I'll be a moment."

I settled back into the recliner, pulled over to the fire by Hobbes earlier in anticipation that I should want a moment to me, before the house would inevitably shake from its nap and fill the halls and parlors with the precious reverberations of life, youth and fresh, limitless adventure.

There were still moments like this, though fewer it seemed, when the sounds of silence weighed profoundly, like a brooding spirit upon the precious fixtures, chairs and treasures of the comfortable room; pouring like a clear velvet lotion, sometimes out from the deep, dark folds of the heavy drapes; other times imparting from the eyes of the ancient Penworth gallery of frozen portrait stares recorded of my progenitors by some artist's mystical brush; while on still other occasions I could swear it leaches from the space in time between the tick and tock of the somber mantle clock above the fire; a perfect silence broken only by the gentle crackle of the flaming logs inside the pit; here I would find myself lost in an audit of the many years of loss and gain, the joy and heartbreak that did culminate in my resting where I do, dumped into an easy chair, toes against the blaze.

How did I, who worked so deliberately to shed the fleece of privilege; who made the pact so many years ago to speculate, run with unsavory company; to squander my allowance; to marry outside the formal blessings and produce thereby my lovely child; how have *I* ultimately arrived to nothing more or less than which befell and formed the trappings of my father, and his father, and his father's father's father?

Is life indeed a script which read to the end picks up only on the title page again, as it would appear?

I poked the logs with the iron, watching the sparks rise into the flu upon the tufts of blazing air, imagining as they exited the chimney, sailing high, high over the snowy house and fields where down below my single set of boot prints cut into the virgin snow like notes upon a page of the sweetest music;

I heard a low hum rise from deep within my throat; an old folk song from Hoffenstein's magic past; a tune my mother, *bless her poor departed soul*, would sing while doing cross stitch before an open window...

> *The Dortpen birds fly round and round*
> *The sunlight on their busy tails*
> *Their beaks are fill'd with scraps they've found*
> *To line the nest where the hatchling wails*

That is my triumph, I should conclude! My Charlotte upstairs asleep, my symphony; the difference all my travels and travails have made upon the script of Penworth privilege, now upstairs pouring dreams of innocence into her soft, soft pillow; the flame inside the soul of this one restless man, desperate to crack the mould, resolved to stare for centuries hereafter, out from his singular painted likeness, back onto this chamber from the silent gallery with my singular, riotous noise; that this comfortable space shall never set its vacuous silence onto any future Penworth from this moment on.

"Coffee and quick bread, my Lord." The door swung closed behind Hobbes as he placed the tray upon the coffee table and sat himself down.

"I expect to spend the remainder of the morning after breakfast in the study catching up on some mail and other business, Hobbes. Perhaps you might take Charlotte to the hill sometime today while I'm working, would you? You know how much she loves her sled."

"It would be a sincere pleasure, My Lord. Perhaps she might even allow an old gentleman a chance on the contraption," he laughed.

"You're very good to me Hobbes. Thank you; if you only had the chance to meet my dear friend Bidwell. You two would have gotten along famously, I'm convinced."

VI

Hours had passed; mind-numbing hours spent tearing into envelopes, making separate piles of folded papers in orders of descending priority, switching sometime along the way from coffee to cabernet, then to soda, to ale and back to coffee; the room, no more a refuge for me than it was for generations of my predecessors, grumbling over the same tedious necessity of mollifying one creditor at a time; fencing with one political adversary at a time, while lending support to another pair of desperate political allies. I had, *rather eccentrically I suppose*, every telephone within ring's reach torn from the walls and outlets of the study, that I might forego the added pleasant distraction of such further annoyance. Concentration was always hard won for me.

This however did not curtail my occasional stroll over to the window, looking down at the great south lawn, sloped perfectly for the curious pairing of sled pilots, making the most of a bright early afternoon snow day. I managed a smile and returned to the final bundle of carefully tied envelopes, after whose completed inspection I had every intention of abandoning my dungeon to don a pair of boots and cap, then join in the icy revelry I so anticipated as apt compensation for my morning's penance.

Let it be here confirmed, the adage wherein it is proposed that prodigious wonders spring more often from the humblest circumstances, as by reaching for the final and smallest parcel of bound envelopes I was delighted to find, on the top of the pile, a hand addressed envelope with air-mail markings and a series of four colorful stamps depicting tropical birds and traditional figures in bright native costumes, with the words *Republica Portuguesa, ANGOLA*; there was no return address on the envelope.

I took a spirited pull at the cord, anxious to unfasten the knot, but succeeded only in releasing the individual letters to burst haphazard across the desk blotter when a second envelope from the batch caught my eye, momentarily addling my attention from the first. This envelope was pale blue and bore most of the markings of the *Palais Silberfluss,* up to, however, the hand scribed address, making it appear that whatever was set inside the envelope was most undoubtedly unofficial and not parliamentary business.

Oh dear; has it been so long? Hobbes had come to the study door with a fresh tray of liquid refreshments, having ample time to change from his wet clothes and warm his bones by the fire.

"Oh, thank you Hobbes. I seem to have lost all trace of time."

He placed the tray down on the low table and poured two glasses of *Eau de Vie*, wrapping his long fingers around the snifter; holding the edge up to his considerable nose, he then closed his eyes, ever so softly and poured the precious cognac over his tongue like a fraternity lad swallowing his first goldfish of the contest. I decided to join him by the couch before I lost him completely to his addictions.

He handed me a snifter which I received gratefully. "I'm very sorry I missed your excitement out there," I began, "Charlotte must be disappointed."

He placed the glass down and smiled, "No Sir, she has a most precocious understanding of your unique position and an imagination which leaves her little time to dwell upon the more lugubrious sensibilities. I rather think she enjoys her time in the play room fashioning these marvelous tributes you proudly display about the place. No child ever adored her father so, I must say."

81

He finally placed his glass on the table. I leaned over to refill it when he continued, "a remarkably happy child." He thanked me, wrapped his fingers around the snifter and repeated his ritual.

"Nor a daughter so loved," I replied under my breath, crossing my leg and looking out the windows far across the room.

"Forgive my impertinence, but is something troubling you, Sir?"

I smiled wearily. Is it the truth, that one man is forever obliged to forgive another's impertinence simply because he predicated his impertinence with an apology? Whatever the matter, I felt somewhat relieved by the question; like a wound that's been seen by nurse, who by helping it heal, makes it hurt.

I laughed briefly and said, "I'm not at all sure Hobbes."

The old butler placed his cup on the table and leaned forward, choosing this very moment to raise the ante on my faith in him, emboldened, no doubt, by his recent, youthful jaunt in the snow.

"Might it help to discuss your situation, perhaps? For affairs confined to the margins of our mutual affiliation, I can assure you that my ears are your instruments and my soul, your safe box. For all other matters, however critical, I implore you to seek that singular council which might answer to the unrequited voice inside you. As those folkies in America have said, *friendship is a diamond,* Mister Giov, *but trouble is a diamond mine.*'"

Our eyes fixed for a time, then parted when he dropped his gaze to find the bottle. It seems that there was much more to old Hobbes than I ever suspected; astuteness I haven't encountered since I met the man who twice saved my life in a jungle, somewhere in the mountains of northern Angola.

I decided then to protect my personal papers in a very secure place.

VII

Janis poured two glasses of fresh squeezed lemonade over ice and carried them back into the study where the two men sat, silently staring at the cluttered shelves in the dim office. Outside the parish, Kriss had taken the added precaution of parking the black jeep around back to add some measure of confidence that he would not be connected to Father Dodd or the church.

She handed one glass to the priest who appeared lost in his very trebled concentration; she decided to put the glass down on the small table beside him, moving across the space to offer the second glass to Kriss, sitting hard against the left arm of the old couch, waiting impatiently for some word from Father Dodd. He declined the lemonade.

"Janis, have you heard back from Lord Penworth?" he asked, finally breaking the quiet.

"Not yet, Father. I only sent the letter last week. Giov must be extremely busy up there these days, hobbling around the fine courts in Touchwick," she said with apparent sarcasm.

"And where exactly is your nephew now? No, wait. I'm not at all sure I care to know," asked Father Dodd, correcting himself. "This is very serious, but you know that already, don't you."

Kriss looked up from the floor and over to the priest, unable to speak he simply nodded.

"Well, if no one else is going to have some, I'll drink it myself," she declared, tossing back a large swallow; the ice made its inimitable chime as the fan hummed, ineffectually by the window. It was a hot summer here in Angola.

"Kriss, the one thing you've simply *got* to understand is that we have more experience with the cartels than with the law. I can't . . . the *Church* simply can't hide someone indefinitely; I need to hear from our old friend up north before I know how to begin. Your nephew's up against it all right, but making a bad move right now will only make matters more serious for the both of us. You do understand, don't you?"

Kriss looked at Father Dodd, saying in a very deliberate tone, "My nephew is a innocent boy; he dead widout the Church; widout Mistah Ministah."

Janis turned sharply to the thin beam of light stabbing through the curtain panels, tracing her finger in circles atop the sweating glass of lemonade.

VIII

It was another bright morning in the Dortpen; the sun having had a few days to reshape the valley, exposing piecemeal, small features of the landscape as the snow began its arduous retreat; the roads, most notably plowed, returned to the utility of neighboring farm trucks and other, more audacious motorists; the occasional snowmobiles crisscrossing the shimmering fields.

Looking down from the parlor window I could see Hobbes shoveling the path between the house and the garage, preparing for my rather abrupt departure for Touchwick where Charlotte and I anticipate spending the next several days or so.

My decision to leave this morning came as somewhat of a surprise to Hobbes, as I wasn't expected to meet with the Prince until Wednesday, two days from now; acting upon my suspicion that, time being of the essence, I could best insure the probability of success by posting my reply to Janis from a more discreet location.

An announcement was dispatched by Hobbes yesterday afternoon for the townhouse staff prepare for our arrival, peeling covers from couches and chairs, lighting ovens and polishing windows; and with the Princess and her mother returned from their holiday in Greece, trading the Touchwick frost for the warm sands of the Zouroudi shoreline, I was further consoled by the synchronization for Charlotte's entertainment.

"Why didn't you ever marry someone else, Papa?" asked Charlotte, nose pressed against the passenger side window, "I wonder if I might have had a brother or sister; someone to play with."

I must admit, I was thoroughly unprepared for this and instinctively placed my right hand back upon the steering wheel and touched the brake, slowing the car a bit.

"Why do you ask that, Lotti? I should hope you're not an unhappy girl."

She smiled at this, "No. Not unhappy; I have you all to myself, don't I? It's just the things that Gloria says sometimes; makes me wonder about what it might be like. Do I sound silly?"

Oh, the trials of single parenthood! I braced myself for the answer to my next question.

"Of course not, Lotti . . . and what sort of things does she say?"

That's it; I went too far. I was now caught up in the snare of pre-teenage intrigue and there was no backdoor. The image of a card game at sea sprung to mind.

"I don't know Papa; sometimes when I think about it, I'm not sure I know whether I'm indeed angry with her at all, and if I am, I'm not sure why I even should be. Gloria is the closest person I'll ever have to a real sister, yet I'm not certain about the reason she says these things."

"What *things?*" I continued, digging myself in deeper and deeper.

"Well, she told me once that her uncle Eugene suggested there was something improper with my mother; that I might not be a true Penworth. She said that if I had a mother and a brother or a sister, that maybe I would be more like, I don't know, part of *regular* society. What does this mean, Papa?"

I asked for it I suppose, and I got it square for sure. I tried to keep the pause as brief as possible, knowing full well the intelligent young lady beside me would wager the seriousness of her mystery by the length of time it took for my explanation to progress; I must first however assume control of my temper.

"Well that's all a matter of ridiculous nonsense," I began, thoroughly aware of its feebleness; stalling to subdue my rage. "Prince Eugene knows full well that your beautiful mother was the crowning achievement of the Penworth family, until *you* were born. That your mother could not be around to watch you grow to be so kind and pretty is no reason to begin telling hurtful slanders."

Careful Giov, careful . . . not very wise to speak ill of the King's brother or Lotti's best friend.

"I'm certain she misunderstood something she overheard. Just remember, I shouldn't be Lord Penworth, Duke of the Dortpen if there was any question about your mother or my lovely daughter, now would I?"

"No you wouldn't Papa," she replied, smiling bravely.

We rounded the stone wall separating the Mayfair vineyards from the neighboring dairy farm, the last edifice before passing through the small village of Söfenzin where it would appear the snow was nothing more inhibitive than a mild rain. The shops were open and the sidewalks busy enough. We were about to cross through Monument Park where the twelve foot likeness of Lord Harry Penworth II stood atop his immense granite base, peering down for one hundred and thirty five years over the same people who seldom look back, when Charlotte remarked, "Look Papa, look at the hens in their cages."

I looked over to the right window and there crossing the intersection, headed north was a very old blue pickup truck, loaded to the last square centimeter with cages of chickens.

"That's some load. Have you ever seen so many hens?" I asked her.

"No, Papa; I've never even seen a chicken . . . close up I mean."

"Well then!" I replied, "Time that you see your first hen, then," and I accelerated, turning north to catch the chickens while Charlotte laughed hysterically. The truck was about a quarter mile ahead of me, traveling fairly slow; I was gaining on him.

I flagged him at the next stop, just outside the village limits. He looked very perplexed, which was perfectly understandable. I motioned for him to roll his window down.

"Something wrong, sir?"

"No," I laughed, Charlotte sitting with the bemused mix of embarrassed mischief washed across her pale white face. "I simply wanted to impose upon you for a brief spell; my daughter Charlotte here would love very much to admire your hens. She's never seen one up close and personal, you see."

I noticed the gentleman had a passenger with him who refused to look over to us. It was a young lady who simply sat next to him in his heated cab without a jacket. I thought it odd, but soon enough gave it no mind at all.

The man laughed and welcomed Charlotte to inspect the cages at her leisure, provided we respected his desire to make Touchwick before the midday traffic complicated travel.

"Sorry I can't really get out to show you young lady," he directed to Lotti, "but my friend in here simply wouldn't permit it. I trust your father here will do well enough."

"Thank you sir," replied Charlotte, trying discreetly to see the face of the mysterious woman in the passenger seat.

"This is really quite kind of you. My name's Penworth, Giov Penworth, that is."

"I know very well who you are, sir. Face's always in the papers, it seems; my pleasure to meet you. Name's Gregory; this here's Helen; she's very special, you know."

"Yes, I can see that. Good day to you, lovely Helen." Charlotte was dumbstruck at how remarkably real these chickens looked; how very similar they were to the pictures of hen's in her books back home.

"Come on love, let's leave these two get on to Touchwick."

I shook the old man's hand and thanked him again; it was not five minutes before I lost sight of him in my rearview mirror.

IX

I had just left the post office with no indication of being tailed, deciding to then swing back to the townhouse and see if Charlotte would enjoy spending some time at Silberfluss Park where we could feed the swans and pick up a movie or a show afterwards; we had only been in Touchwick a day and I was anxious to spend some free time with her before the actual grind of business commenced midday tomorrow.

She was delighted by the idea but had already made an appointment to meet with Princess Gloria who proposed that the two of them remain at the townhouse refining their cribbage; a suggestion neither Charlotte nor I were enthusiastic about.

"Why don't you invite her to come to the park with us? I'm sure she would enjoy herself."

"That's a wonderful idea Papa!" She squealed. "Thank you so much."

It was eventually decided that we should forgo the cinema and return to the townhouse after we visit the swans at the park; a compromise more illuminating of the young princess' predilection for her own authority than any true disclosure of her interest in either the game of cards or, for that matter, Charlotte.

I've watched the years transform these two young friends along two very different paths, as if their closeness was a test by which only one of them could survive intact; and so it has become my fate to defend this heart in only one of many ways; for a gardener will not use a bell jar to safeguard the flower that he loves, but trains it in a garden, to languish in its bloom and fragrance for a season. I need to dissuade Charlotte from the noxious humors forming in her young friends mind, but at what cost to her innocence, and absent this? Oh, Mary! What would a mother do?

The park was a magnificent study in winter, with the afternoon sun making shadows of the trees and street lamps, stretched across the many footprints tracked into the lawns and paths defined by tidy hedges where the starling nests lie cradled in the icy cold. The band shell far across the sward stood vacant as a tomb, whose solemn mouth gaped in mournful supplication of its springtime praises; the sounds and memories of waltzes and symphonies, dramas and comedies, oppressed by melted blocks of snow; a stage become a humble floor again.

The two girls spent some time feeding and teasing the swans, each, naturally to their own vocation, whereupon tiring of the river bank, advanced ahead of me to the shuttered carousel where Gloria shook the locked gate to test its mettle. Charlotte laughed at her and ran to peek inside, past the parapets where the painted horses stood in such darkness, like Henry's charge at Agincourt, yet suspended, like everything else in winter, in the deepest dream; Gloria tossed her snowball and missed which caused Charlotte to return volley.

The sun drew low, the shadows formed in ever wider, steadily connecting patterns, the street lamps began to glow and behind them, through the capillary crests of naked oak, birch and hickory, loomed the *Pont Dubois*, in its slender, graceful arch, a string of delicate piercing lights, like needles through the cold evening twilight; South Touchwick shimmering softly at its opposite end across the river.

I suggested once more that we have supper and take in a picture.

X

"It's the Prince, Your Holiness. He wishes to see you on some urgent matter," said Miss Crumbe.

The Bishop placed his knife and fork onto the plate and turned slowly toward the door where the diminutive housekeeper maintained her respectful distance. She'd seen to the Bishop's rectory for seventeen long and faithful years, acquiring an intuition about many of His Eminence's particularities, including his fondness for an undisturbed dinner and was so prepared to accept her due penance as bearer of the news.

To her relief, Bishop Grieble simply dragged the napkin across his lips and thanked her, asking her to bring the Prince to the study where he would join him in his fashion. Miss Crumbe prepared to collect the dinner dishes to carry on her way out when the Bishop interrupted;

cautioning her to avoid keeping the Prince in the parlor for a moment longer than was necessary.

"Right you are, sir," and off she ran.

When the Bishop finally entered the study, the air was already thick with cigar smoke, for which he had no particular fondness. He crossed the room and shook hands with his guest and sat down across the table into a chair designed more for presentation than comfort.

"Well Eugene, what have you heard?"

The Prince took a long pull from his *Jean Jarreau* and replied, "For starters," smoke poured through his teeth and lips in a manner most upsetting to the Bishop's digestion, "they're expecting another eleven and a half percent from the last numbers to cover, what *they* contrive, to be the specific economic damage this project will present to many of the coastal municipalities. That brings us roughly another billion further away from settling what a year ago was a very nice, clean arrangement."

There was no disguising the disgust stamped into the Bishop's face as he struggled with the news.

"We've simply got to convince the council to pass a spending proposal to match the crisis," the Bishop replied. "The Portuguese are out-maneuvering us Eugene. This is your area of expertise. Handle it."

The Prince stood from his chair and walked casually over to the Bishop's desk and raised a framed portrait of His Eminence standing next to the Pope; smiling, he imperceptibly shook his head and placed the frame back down.

"My brother is very capable of selecting advisors who can read contracts, Elmer. Our problem is not so much a Portuguese problem as it is a domestic one. Azevedo will move to draw blood only when he smells it. He is as quick to withdraw when we withhold it. Everything from the Portuguese end of the project moves like smoke in a wind. Control the breeze, control the Portuguese."

He moved back to his chair and sat down; leaning across the table, he lowered his voice and continued,

"My *brother* is another problem altogether. It's quite obvious to him, that our ability to profit from the new terminal will be outpaced by the interest on its investment for the first ten years or more, thirty five more on the principle, then come the leases, taxes and the tariffs. He's got that damn Penworth in his ear reading the figures and interpreting the costs against their immediate strains on the national infrastructure. He's filled the King's head with talk of schools, railways and healthcare; Maximillian has expressed a developing dissatisfaction with the whole terminal project; I'll handle the Portuguese, but you, Archbishop, *you* handle the people. Maximillian will listen to them, he always has."

Eugene looked at his watch, adding, "I'm also busy reviewing our losses from selling the whole mess back to Azevedo."

"Wait a minute here! We have interests pressing us from the south, mind you," protested Grieble. "Clients and suppliers are relying on access to these terminals. How can you stand there and tell me that Penworth will be the unraveling of everything when so much depends on silencing him?"

Prince Eugene rolled the cigar in his lips and walked over a set of burl wood cabinet doors which he opened to reveal a small collection of crystal glasses; a dozen green and brown bottles.

"I'm meeting with him tomorrow afternoon." he smiled, "Join me for a nightcap, your Eminence?"

XI

There was scarcely allowance enough in the present stipend for the Deacon's current, meager conveniences, so this morning's notification from the Bishop that additional austerity was a matter of imminent consideration proved a formidable test to Frederick's early morning cheerfulness; the sliced envelope lay on the desk beside the opener; the content missing from among the other papers scattered about.

The coat stand was bare save an ancient leather leash whose sentiments lay branded evermore on the good man's heart, allowing for neither future purpose nor its more dispassionate disposal; dangling from the dull brass hook; its license tags hung like wild winter grapes from reticent vines; a wistful ointment rubbed into his mind and soul; the empty coat stand stood, in consequence, never really empty after all; but for this knowledge, in the absence of the Deacons hat, jacket and scarf, the coat stand was ultimately and formidably bare.

The distinct smell of a chapel starved of heating oil in the dead of February, having frosted the drapes and carpets, cushions and prayer books; the vandalous chilled air condensing into its separate molecules upon the skin of the crucifix and perspiring ciborium up on the alter; only to revive in periodic spells of warmth upon the ministry of favors by each member of the congregation in their turn; one tribute toward the furnace; one benevolent, infrequent trip to the thermostat over time, had chance to make its impression on the fragrance of the space, a singular bouquet of mildew mixed with frankincense and lavender through which the deacon passed to take his leave and brood elsewhere, outdoors; a therapeutic drive into the forest so to reorganize his thoughts and plan some newest strategy to cut another round of expenditures in his quest to serve his Lord.

Gregory, he knew, would raise his fist to the Archbishop; demanding Frederick finally retire from the futile battle of a homosexual minister against the entire *College of the Scripture*, currently under the mindful scrutiny and enterprise of His Eminence, Archbishop Grieble, which has decided all matters of Christ's intention and interpretation for the faithful congregations within Hoffenstein's borders since the corner stone was set upon that sacred soil, crushed beneath the weight of the *Cathedral of St. Pontificate* over six centuries ago.

To which the stalwart Deacon would respond that only worse than his own suffering could come from such a decision to retreat; that his was not the case by which to validate the false accusations of a gay philosophy as an apathetic ministry of the Church; that he stood for something worth defending so long as one person still came to warm a pew in search for answers to their questions of faith; to which he believed in his heart that such tenacity might one day expose a great and systematic injustice inside the College and the faith, proceeding downward from the very top.

These thoughts accompanied him along the road to where he eventually reached the forest's edge; the fields and wind breaks now behind him as he drove preoccupied into the deepening shade of the tree covered road, the view to one side solid granite rising straight up, thirty feet from where the old dynamite shafts were drilled to blast, then scrape the road winding through the foothills of Old Pater; and to the right a forest so primordial, untouched, the snowy carpet of the floor would likely wince under the first footfall of man.

He had no notion, no travel plan and was already further from the village than he would have guessed; but there *was* this problem after all, and it required that he defer his attention from all other concerns to focus upon it.

The letter suggested that the decision to trim the funding for his parish was as yet pending; that he still had the time to respond, to coordinate confederates and a strategy for defense. But that was the sanctuary of fools, he reconsidered; an opportunity to simply discredit an even larger alliance, to be humiliated by the council who had already decided to make an example of his work; to showcase the inferiority of his breeding. It was up to Deacon Frederick alone, to stay his course and expose the systematic efforts at work against him whether or not the truth is acknowledged during his tenure; the only failure being his loss of faith; his resignation.

Gregory had always done fair enough with his poultry, he tabulated, devising a preliminary ledger of credits and debits to establish in his mind a foundation from which to begin; the repairs to the belfry would have to wait; he could reduce the candles to half the number; and best of all, spring was just around the corner; oh! Frederick was just gearing up when there, halfway down a large hill he noticed an old white van in apparent distress parked as far off the road as could be managed without tumbling over the steep drop and into the chasm waiting hungrily below.

He pulled alongside the van to greet a black haired gentleman standing by a young boy with eyes as dark as onyx pebbles set into his thin, expressionless face. There was no telling how long the two were stranded but to estimate by the joy with which the elder one greeted the Deacon, it could be guessed that the van had left them in the lurch some long hours ago.

"I must apologize, but I know nothing about engines," Frederick said. "You're welcome to a lift, if that would help."

They spent the next several minutes transferring sacks and boxes of supplies from the village out of the van and into the deacon's tiny, aged Volvo. It was apparent from the situation, the clothes, the complexion of the pair and the accent, that they were Romani; ancestors of the legendary gypsy tribes that lived and wandered in these woods and hills for centuries.

The old car now heavily loaded, they drove in comparative silence for much of the ride, the young boy saying nothing the entire way. Deacon Frederick did manage however to introduce himself and learn the elder one's name, Grigoras; the younger was his son, György; also, that no manner of proficiency in auto-motive mechanics on the minister's part could compensate for the bearded man's miscalculation of the supply funds, buying extra cheese and coffee when it eventually became obvious that more of the kitty should have been saved for fuel.

With about seven miles of the main road now behind them, Grigoras motioned for the Deacon to slow the car while he located a fine dirt covered path which he expected Frederick to simply follow, continuing the journey.

Frederick pulled to a complete stop, a vapor cloud of condensation hovering in the crisp winter air, engulfing the car.

"You can't possibly expect this vehicle to navigate that path, can you?" he exclaimed, getting out and inspecting the situation more closely. Grigoras burst out laughing so hard as to break the spell of melancholy that until now appeared to possess the boy.

"Path is good one; car is good one. You make it fine. Van make hundreds trip up and down all over again; over and over. Thank you, my friend, please," replied Grigoras.

The Deacon, resigned to his service, got back into the car, "How far along?"

"Kilometer, no more," Grigoras smirked.

They reached the camp with fewer troubles than Frederick anticipated; invisible within a few yards of the perimeter, being enclosed by dense brush and fabricated blinds. The path, as Grigoras claimed, was far more navigable once the car rolled beyond the formidable looking entrance off the main road, a fact which helped ease the mounting agitation of one very anxious minister, having already endured a considerably eventful morning.

The Volvo was surrounded, upon first entering the limits of the settlement, by three surly men and a circle of poorly dressed children, all as curious for their friends as for the strange event of their chauffeured arrival. Grigoras smiled meekly, aware of his foolishness and empathetic to the worry he had placed upon the others, and so engaged upon the

93

only course of defense a man of his wits could concoct, promptly shouting over his inquisitors in his own distinctive tongue, embellished tales of his own travails and heroism; this much was all that was accessible to the minister, witnessing a performance transcending any undue complication resulting from a more orthodox, literal translation.

Grigoras introduced the preacher to his neighbors, cousins and his wife; her mother and father, his two brothers, his brown shepherd Hoi, and most preciously, to his youngest sister, who at the time was on a small stool retrieving fresh milk from a very satisfied goat. The smoke from a rather large, perpetual fire, smoldering in a central pit, wafting through the site; at any given moment, one's attention might likely engage upon the faintest trace of ash, crossing the encampment on the chilled mountain air.

"You will have some dinner?" Grigoras' wife asked Frederick, who by midday was beginning to develop quite an appetite.

"Thank you, yes. I'd love to have dinner."

Grigoras smiled from ear to ear and packed the bowl of a large clay pipe, fashioned to resemble some form of gargoyle or mythic being from the underworld and continued to introduce Frederick to his people, all milling about the ring of trailers, vans, horses and livestock; characters in whom he expressed a tremendous and sincere pride; tromping through the snow and mud against which his boots provided a vastly superior defense than the unfortunate shoes barely clinging to the deacon's iced feet.

It was an odd sound to anyone unfamiliar with the old Volvo, but fortunately, a high pitched squeal in the key of G#, which was familiar enough to Frederick who regularly parked his car on the steep incline of the driveway which circled to the back of the house where Gregory had his hutches.

Rushing toward his car instinctively, Frederick witnessed as the children who were previously amused by the strange toy, ran away screaming as it startled from its nap when one young boy released the parking brake in a moment of inspired investigation; the car began to pick up momentum down the steep incline toward a massive hickory some thirty yards on.

He was fortunate enough to time the traveling car to a spot where he had access to intercept it, jumping through the open window of the passenger door in time to wrestle the wheel into a much closer, much softer target of arbor vitae and juniper shrubs which saved the boy inside the car from a much larger, perhaps fatal collision with the hickory, but allowed the open driver's side door to recoil and bite deeply into the young boy's tiny arm.

Deacon Frederick immediately stripped off his coat to reach his old black shirt which he tore into strips that he then wrapped around the wound, fashioning a tourniquet, a tie he twisted like the one's he practiced a lifetime ago in the Royal army. He was acting quicker than his thoughts could catch; the sounds of screams and hollers rushing down the hill from the camp to the scene below where Frederick was now finishing the knot which he prayed would hold the essence of the boy inside for the time it would take to race the Volvo back into the village for proper medical attention.

XII

There was never any waiting that I can recall when arriving punctually at the Prince's residence in the tony *Fleiss* district of North Touchwick, where blocks of exquisite townhouses overlook Silberfluss Park and the blissfully ignorant swans paddling the river.

I was greeted by Davis, the oldest butler to be accredited checking hats and topcoats inside any one of these ruinous estates; shadowed by the Parliament and Palace complex a short cab ride away; where decisions to engineer intricate arrangements to meet elsewhere to discuss nefarious decisions to empower partisan conspiracies, are born. Very little to nothing at all is ever progressed within the actual walls of that great edifice that isn't trumped by the effective facility of negotiations exercised over a glass of port, a Cuban or a plate of delicately trussed quail safe outside its echoing halls. The Parliament, as is well known, hears too much and dispenses all.

It is with the sincerest reluctance that I am suffering one of these arrangements at this very moment.

"His Lordship, the Duke," Davis announced, completing the considerable maze of staircases and hallways from the vestibule, up to the private office of His Highness, the Prince, closing the tall, hand carved door behind me as he exited.

I fully anticipated the cigar smoke, but was unprepared for the attendance of Lord Grimstone, who stood from his comfortable seat to extend his greeting with a nod, conspicuously excluding his hand.

"Lord Penworth. So good of you to be on time," greeted the Prince, circling his oversized desk to approach me with his outstretched palm.

"Your Highness," I responded, applying a well refined firmness to my half of the handshake.

"Please, do sit down."

I positioned myself in a chair prearranged to face the window across the desk where the Prince immediately returned, making his face that much more difficult for either Grimstone or me to see with any clarity, awash as it was in shadow from the startling backlight provided by a picturesque winter sun.

"I'm rather disappointed to find you here, unannounced, Grimstone; I should have thought to bring some fresh venison from back home. Are you to be joining the Prince and me for our meeting?"

Eugene interrupted Grimstone, whose flash expression warranted the intervention if the meeting stood the slightest chance of being both productive and brief, "Forgive me, Penworth; my apologies. I invited Grimstone rather spontaneously I suppose; I regret the undue surprise. It is however most fortunate for us to have him clear his schedule on such short notice, as his expertise on matters concerning our discussion will prove, I most sincerely believe, invaluable."

"I receive my annual supply of venison from sources much closer to the vest, I must confess; but thank you for your most generous sentiments," finished Grimstone, incapable of yielding.

I concluded that this conference would not keep me away from Charlotte too much longer.

"Grimstone has devised a mechanism by which moneys from your Education program could be reinvested into bonds that would yield higher future returns while securing current stability to Hoffenstein's massive investment in its industrial expansion; let's get to the point, Penworth; we're talking jobs here."

"You say 'invested', my Lord, when the word you want is 'diverted', no?" I snapped, "These jobs" I began when the Prince interrupted,

"Listen Penworth, Hoffenstein needs this project; it needs the jobs!"

"Forgive the impertinence" I rejoined, a technique of politeness for which I will thank Hobbes when I return to Burlwood, "but I see your vision of our nation's future riding singularly on the backs of our laborers at the expense of our academic competitiveness; future profits from a project already suffering from outrageous cost overruns? Hoffenstein's jobs paying Portuguese taxes?

"Grimstone, I may not have held you in the highest regard, but this 'mechanism', to which the Prince has signed your name, is unworthy even of you."

Grimstone shot to his feet. "My Liege, I am finished here! If you will excuse me, I have urgent matters to attend across town. I'll not stand here, subject to this rake's insolence another minute."

I smiled, knowing I'd eventually get to him, but was astonished at how quickly I succeeded; given that a man's skin thins proportionate to the level of contempt born toward his adversary, I concluded that Grimstone has quite a sizable distaste for me.

"You're going nowhere, Grimstone!" admonished the Prince. "It's agreed that this meeting is to be a brief one. I dare to suggest that this is an ill matched party after all; however, I have the two of you here to achieve some forward movement toward a considerable solution to a problem that won't just go away anytime soon. We can be either responsible for its success; and by this Penworth, I might also, in the privacy of this room, suggest your own, personal success; or by damn, the failure and slow, torturous death of a program that represents the investment of ten years of Hoffenstein planning, dreaming and spending!"

The Prince moved around to the front of his desk. Grimstone slowly and meekly returned to his seat. I sat with my elbows rested on the arms of my chair, hands clasped with my fingers tented upon which I rested my chin; looking down, I slowly shook my head.

"Penworth; I dare say I can help make you a very successful partner in this enterprise."

I did not need to look up. "I'm already comfortable, Your Highness." Thank you for the conversation. If Grimstone's report is in that folder on your desk, I might ask you for a chance to review the figures. I can only offer, as a member of the Royal council and member of parliament, to review the proposal, with all sworn and customary discretion, before I determine my position on it."

The Prince reached across his desk and retrieved the folder and handed it to me.

"I think you'll see quite a bit to like inside it," he smiled.

I stood and nodded to some indeterminate spot of air between the two, "Good day gentlemen. I'll see myself out."

It was apparent that I had surprised Davis near the front hallway, hoping to discreetly reach around his gaunt form to collect my top coat and hat in the absence of any further detainment from the hastiest emancipation out into the open street, unbound and away from this dark and suffocating house. His lifeless form propped upright in a straight-back chair before the coat-check, having fallen from attention to his *Chronicle* into slumber, as has become his way.

"Mister Penworth," he started with a snort from whatever place his reverie had abandoned him, "Good god! You're leaving so soon?"

He raised himself to his feet and seized the collar of my long jacket.

"What is the time sir, if you please?"

His paper dropped to the floor.

I laughed and tried to calm the old dear, insisting that it was only half past three and that he hadn't been off his guard a minute longer than was perfectly respectable for a distinguished butler of his tenure; I stooped to pick *The Chronicle* off the ground and folded it to read the most remarkable headline:

Hero Homo Deacon saves young Gypsy's Life

XIII

Most people would have referred to it as a dim, insufferable space; nothing less than hell; the blue glow of the sunlight through the tight weave of the vinyl tarp was too faint by which to read; the empty oil drums a clever ruse; but faithful Felis simply measured his present

98

lodgings as to those of an oft cited, highly revered figure from scripture, caught in a vaguely analogous situation.

Simply subtract the lions and replace with spiders and a host of other creatures he detected yet could not see; he would repeatedly excuse his earnest discomfort as the mere consequence of a coddled childhood and nothing more.

Over the first few days on the lamb, he cultivated a philosophy wherein the surreal component activities which led to his desperate situation revealed themselves, piece by piece, helping to recreate a reasonable model of the whole episode and his influence upon it, allowing for the eventual clarity of his mind; the capacity to strategize in the absence of worrisome distractions.

But as his disparity returned, an urgency of faith likewise rallied, conversely restoring his courage only to consume itself once more; and thus this cycle continued; immediately mapped upon a pattern of access to food and drink, withheld and offered by all the intervening opportunities a bustling village would refuse or permit to loving, loyal confederates engaged in surreptitious yet humanitarian ministries.

And so one evening, the resourceful Felis in a pitch of fevered strain, scratched a hole just small enough into the tarp to let a single ray of tomorrow's delicious sun pierce through the suffocating space inside his hiding place to splash against the open pages of his Saviors words; a tiny Bible that he snuck with him; the singular salvation of a frightened young man of Christ, in critical fear that his redemption for a crime, for which he has been mistakenly accused, but for which the circumstances once elaborated must acquit, will never come.

He shook the blanket, given him by Janis from the hospital and stretched out for the moment, laying his head upon his fist;

"Yea, though I walk through the valley of death," he read.

XIIII

What is it about life, that two men or two women can be born and raised in the same house; schooled by the same teachers, be employed by the same establishment, yet the fortunes of the one would appear most un-extraordinary while the other appears to have drawn upon himself a cloud of grave misfortune due in no part to circumstances of his own device? One man's crops should flourish while his brother's fail;

99

these are the facts observed of life which were never fully trusted to our sciences, there would not after all be such a thing as God if every step we dare were predisposed to fill an imprint in the soil of the one who took the very stride sometime earlier; the risk is dressed and drained of blood; the horse race run.

So it is known that one individual will prosper in their time who was a wretch, and that another may husband the passage of virtue through his generation, only to suffer unique episodes of grotesque adversity; the disparity itself enough to send the prophets to their writing desks.

Felis, the young boy savaged by the Cerberus all those years ago, who would take the childhood scars from an oddly vicious summer's night into his adolescence and beyond; the butt of ridicule by the young boys and scorn from the girls; who later lost his much beloved mother and went then to live with his considerate uncle who procured for him some work at the Catoca Diamond mines; who could not find his place even there.

This same Felis who was targeted for a mark; deemed insolent by fiends and was beaten, one day walked into a blazing fire that he could not quench; and turning from the screams to look for help was chased by a mob who testified they saw him recently attacked by those whose desperate voices subsequently filled the evening air; and thus a motive born; and in a fever let him abscond with his life, never learning how Raul had come to be burned inside that shack, who really set the flame upon it; the pattern of the evidence satisfied them all that it was Felis; that he deserved as much a head start from the resolute executioner; and so ended up at Uncle Kriss' door with such a tale.

The letter was received by Janis on the third Wednesday of that month; Father Dodd notified Kriss and the Jeep was fueled for the considerable drive to the coast where instructions were relayed for the young man to meet a sailor who would stow the fugitive inside the belly of a north bound ship where it was expected he should start upon a separate chapter of his life in Hoffenstein and leave the black clouds of trouble and misfortune, that had so defined him to this point, back home inside the jungles of his native Africa.

Kriss stood at the pier and watched the black and white ship disappear into the waves through a telescope of tears.

XV

100

It had been about six weeks since I first noticed the pale blue envelope from the Palace, tied among the other letters in the bundle that I unloosed across the blotter on my desk that snowy day; and for the period from that time to now I must confess to bearing some degree of vacillating delight and trepidation toward Charlotte's enthusiastic fascination with our handwritten invitation to the Royal Ball and all the varied trappings and formalities of social life among the Court.

"May I buy a new dress?" and "Who'll teach me to dance?" comingled with, "Gloria suggests that there will be a number of handsome young boys, standing against the wall like tin soldiers; the thought of it makes me laugh, Poppa!"

Oh, Mary! . . . How did the years pass so quickly?

It was therefore inevitable that I should find myself behind the wheel again, Charlotte beside me looking out at the passing countryside, seeing nothing of the pastures or the silos or the sheep, but imagining instead the beautiful gowns inside the windows of the dress shops back in Touchwick where I promised her some days ago that we would go and pay a call.

Arriving at the Townhouse to freshen up after the long drive, I left Charlotte to her lunch while I climbed the staircase to my office on the second floor, hoping to skim the mail before our *father/daughter* outing was to officially begin.

The letter I hoped to find had finally arrived mixed among the formidable stacks that my secretary had already collated into four categories bound by separate rubber bands in accordance to very specific parameters of subject matter, elaborated several years ago when I first established a proper office in Touchwick. It had always been my intention to keep all aspects of my political life both separate from my life with Charlotte and consolidated to a single house for business. Letters however, began arriving at both addresses causing me to squander a number of opportunities that may very well have handicapped the efforts to dissuade our philosophical adversaries among the council, who consequently scored some of the most unthinkable legislative victories.

I opened the envelope from Father Dodd, read it and slid it into the inside pocket of my jacket.

It was time to test Hobbes.

XVI

The limousines were lined up from the Palais Silberfluss to Gerund Boulevard, six blocks away; where the drivers simply parked and read their papers, napped or chanced a meal and glass of wine at any one of the numerous pubs and bistros in the area; it was dusk, the city lights were enchanting and the ball was expected to provide another six hours of idle time outside, while within the palace, the great clocks sheathed their pendulums; all the music, intrigue and romance swims eternal tonight.

The greetings were read; King Dubious was introduced and the first waltz begun; Charlotte, standing beside Princess Gloria was impossibly beautiful, a fact very few failed to compliment.

The Princess wore a most fabulous pink gown with lemon piping and chiffon sleeves, designed and handcrafted by the fussy and highly regarded Royal tailor, Arnaud, who hired an exact duplicate of Gloria for the three weeks it took from the initial clip to the final stitch; her hair was piled high with two extensions dangling down, framing her narrow, heavily made face, topped with an exquisite tiara once worn by her father's mother when she was debutante so many years ago. She held a fan.

Charlotte was all yellow in the dress her father proposed was most remindful of her radiant smile. Her hair was a natural cascade of deep golden ringlets and spools upon which the fussing coiffure had only the slightest influence. Her father, remaining incapable of compressing her full ten and a half year old person into the image of the baby she will ever be inside his heart, strongly resisted the use of face cosmetics of any kind, succumbing only after much arm twisting by the lovely technicians in the salon, to a modest shade of red upon her lips and simple accents for her inescapable eyes.

The two girls, standing side by side at the dance floor's edge, both equal to the elegance of the evening, were once again a study in complete contrasts.

"I'm Count Spurious of Lichtenstein," the young boy introduced himself to Princess Gloria, taking her gloved hand and pressing it to his lips, "and this is Marquis Deveral of Belgium. But you will call us Vincent and Jacob won't you?" he deferred to the young Marquis.

"It would do us a great honor should you dance the next waltz with us," said the Marquis.

Gloria swooned at the handsome young Count who kissed her hand with such brashness; he was no more than twelve, yet fulfilled Gloria's passionate daydreams of life in the teen years, so far in the future yet so accessible to an exceedingly self-confident princess. It was her part to play the disinterested trophy.

"I'm so delighted to meet your acquaintance, Vincent; Lady Charlotte and I were just leaving to freshen up; if you'd promise to wait, we'll let you dance with us."

Charlotte, very much her own age in size and confidence, stood petrified listening to Gloria and looking both boys up and down; from the shine of chandelier light off the pomade in their slicked back hair to the perfect kiss of trouser cloth against the topside of their patent leather dancing shoes; it was one thing, yes, to talk boldly about boys when play acting in the privacy of one another's company; quite another when they stand directly there, tall and handsome asking for you to accompany them to the ballroom floor.

XVII

I was rather enjoying the evening, discussing fly fishing with Count Visnik of the Ukraine; navigating with the Marquis Fontaigne, currently residing and yachting in and around Bermuda; and global economics with the notoriously wearisome Lord Reginald MacInnis from Dundee; all while keeping one paternal eye on the dynamic duo, currently sparring with a young pair of rather "*un*-tin like soldiers" at the edge of the ballroom floor.

I got to considering this *cheek*, so prevalent in today's young generation; trying to account for the definitive loss against one's spiritual ledger, one's soul, when youthful innocence, the instinct for caution availed through misgivings of consequence, is exchanged for mere confidence alone; the rationale traditionally fitted in hollow partiality toward the virtues of inexperience beside the vacancy of such self-assurance, as displayed ubiquitously on the streets of nearly every western city of our day.

For it is generally understood abstractly in conflict, that an army does well to advance no further than it can hold its ground; that a little battlefield timidity will serve the stomach well, *and don't our soldiers march on these?*

Yet neither can one intelligently defend the world from spinning on its side with an over busy fork and knife; . . . the questions we employ to drive ourselves to madness! And right there, right now, Charlotte and Gloria are speaking to a pair of handsome boys!
Where are you Mary, dear?

"Ah! Lord Waxman. How good to see you tonight," I exclaimed in relief from my thinking upon noticing his direct approach toward me with a face too practiced to detect the faintest purpose. He held two fresh flutes of *Laurent-Perrier*, smiling as he extended one to fill my empty hand.

"You're not exactly driving anywhere tonight, now are you Penworth?" he laughed.

I smiled genuinely, taking his hand and spilling a bit of the champagne over my lip. Lord Waxman was a tireless defender of nearly every platform before the council that inspires me to persevere in this whole dirty business. I can't say we're actually very close, but we're as close as circumstances allow, making his appearance a true and pleasant distraction from my preoccupation with the potential indiscretion of the two girls.

"You're here tonight with the young and very lovely Lady Charlotte I surmise."
I glanced over with a father's instinct to notice the girls walking away from the two young gentlemen, eager, no doubt, to discuss their separate observations and decide upon a unified strategy. It was not too difficult to find my old friend, Maximillian Dubois, surrounded by his guests about halfway across the immense room, paying no mind whatsoever to the affairs of our two young debutantes from Touchwick.

"Yes. Seems to be enjoying herself; only wish I could say the same for her father. How's your son?"

"David? Oh, David's doing quite well at the academy. He'll be entering the University next January; want's to study architecture," he made a comical frown and continued, "nothing I can say appears to make the smallest difference. He's full scholarship you know; can't even threaten him with the purse strings."

I laughed at this, wondering how marvelous it would be to have a son; to have a son who wanted to be an architect. Blast it all! Who needs another miserable politician in the family? One is surely more than enough.

"Oh Charles, *go on*! David's a very intelligent young man. He's got his whole life ahead of him. There'll be plenty of time for him to destroy it in politics."

At which the two of us burst forth with such laughter, infecting the neighboring conversations, noticeably eager to season their own discussions with conservative pinches of similar cheer.

"Anyhow, I've always got Fischer. He's another bright one. He's leaving for England in the fall to get a good secondary education. I might have more luck with him; but listen, Penworth, I've actually come to bring you a surprise of sorts."

"A surprise? Have you found support for the healthcare bill?" I joked.

"Not exactly. But if you follow me out of this noise, I'll explain myself."

I felt an immediate sense of panic; leaving Charlotte in the unsupervised company of Gloria was not my idea of good paternal sense.

"Leave me a chance to speak with the security agent for a moment and I'll meet you in the terrace."

"Yes, by all means. But I'll wait here for you instead. There's someone upstairs who asks for you. Please don't be long."

"As you require. I'll only be a moment," I smiled.

XVIII

After spying on the two cavaliers from across the great hall through a large arrangement of fresh flowers, the girls returned, deciding that Gloria would allow Vincent to escort her to the dance floor and that Charlotte would do likewise with Jacob. Vincent was at least ten centimeters taller than Gloria and extremely handsome, producing an enormous passion within the little girl's mind which she easily confused for maturity.

Charlotte however, was beginning to panic. She could no longer find her father in the crowd and became increasingly distressed about her waltz;

the lessons seemed to be erased from her mind. Passing a table with colored soft drinks, Charlotte retrieved a glass in each hand, *always remembering Gloria*, hoping to provide some transitory distraction for the moment they were to meet up again with their charming escorts.

There they still stood, infinitely *gallant*; Vincent immediately offered to free the glasses from Charlotte's hands and placed them on an empty table, turned, nodded sharply to Gloria and took Charlotte by the hand, spinning her onto the dance floor; the band now popping the cork to the *Champagne Gallop*.

A very flushed Gloria, stunned by the abruptness of her dashed dreams, turned slowly and bravely to Jacob, who offered his hand proudly beneath a broad smile.

XIX

Charles Waxman led me through the dark paneled hallway to the rear staircase along which anyone familiar with the King's penchant for billiards has at one time or another been ushered; as more often than not, His Majesty's humor was contradicted by more serious and unpleasant matters from which he preferred to distract himself; the back stair designed so to provide the adequate cover.

We arrived at the billiard room; Charles first knocked at the door with a soft rap; we hesitated for a moment, in the absence of any reply, then proceeded into the room.

The large table commanded the left half of the space under its fringe-hemmed cover as the lamp, suspended from its chains above, floated in darkness ; the cues all set up and silent in the rack against the wall. It was getting on in the evening and the long drapes were drawn so as to swallow into blackness the last and faintest glow of what little light the small lamps struggled to toss about the room.

It was obvious from the mound of embers in the fireplace that whoever lounged before it, back to the door, had been doing so for quite some time. The flames were low, but with no predisposition to remain longer than a polite greeting, I was not inclined to stack another limb onto the dying flames.

It had suddenly occurred to me that I still carried the long empty champagne glass which I then placed onto the table directly beside me, making the faint sound of glass upon wood which seemed to revive the shadowy old gentleman from his contemplation of the rhythmic flashes; the flitting, infinitely black shapes crenellated throughout the iridescent theater of the coals.

"Lord Penworth," he smiled, turning his head from the dim fire light into the greater darkness of the room; his face obscured in shadow, "My darling *young Rake*. How I've missed you."

XX

Charles sat directly across from my seat on the opposite side of our old friend; the minutes passed quickly.

"So I finally caught up with the *San Nicolas* at St. Helena, twelve hundred miles off the Angolan coast, where my theory of *Cyclonic Hypo-saturation* was successfully corroborated by their most extraordinary research, *such a vessel, indeed!*, supplying, *of course*, the metrics necessary to confirm my predictions regarding specific migration anomalies, when out of the clouds, your name surfaces."

Charles, with an industrious eye toward every detail, managed to secure another bottle of champagne and a third flute during my rapt reunion with the Professor; refills our glasses while I stood to place another log on top of the coals.

"It was Oland, as you might expect, who provided the most instructive information, helping me to understand and reconstruct your whereabouts, the preponderance of motivation, I confess, being primarily of a personal nature; *you can forgive me I'm certain*; checking my labors and investment into the composition and depth of your seasoned character.

"I trailed your movements, regrettably as I soon discovered, by an initial margin of time exceeding any real helpful advantage; meeting quite the cast of characters as I pulled at the thread of intrigue with mounting incredulity.

"Leave it to the heart, dear friend, and trust that my condolences, though belated, are solemn with sincerity; for yours, Lord Penworth, is the most acute set of unfortunate circumstances ever to be set upon my society of friends or family, making that which I have gleaned from my investigations all the more despicable."

The light, though poor, was enough to reveal the glimmer from a film of tears built inside the sockets on the old Professors long, weathered face;

I confess that I had never before seen him well a tear.

"It's alright," I consoled him, "I've had many years to sort through the worst of it; Charlotte has in many ways relieved the unbearable sense of loss I suppose. But thank you, Professor for your kindness."

The tenor of the conversation, having exceeded the more superficial parameters of Waxman's expectations, reminded him of a situation downstairs requiring his immediate attention; leaving with an improvised regret for which my mentor, *and his student*, expressed our heartfelt gratitude.

Secure in the knowledge we were at long last alone, the Professor turned to me, leaning forward from his chair and whispered, "We haven't much time and I'm sure you're anxious to return to that lovely young treasure of yours; but I have some advice which might prove vital to your success in a certain, shall I say, discreet enterprise recently visited upon you."

It was a premonition of mine that he would eventually get to this.

"Father Dodd has recruited you into the service of a magnanimous cause that will do you no benefit to support without an almost inhuman caution. Have you, in earnest, considered the level of risk you are taking upon yourself; upon Charlotte?"

It was disorienting to hear him speak like this;

"Are you suggesting that I turn my back on the boy? And how is it you know of my correspondence with Father Dodd?"

Perhaps I *was* a bit curt considering the protective context of his intervention; I was, however, no longer an impressionable pupil and he warranted, by my estimate, candid evidence of the resounding success of his *experience magnifique*;

Looking down into my glass, I choked, "Forgive me."

There was a sharp pop from the fire, bracketed by the silence of two men struggling to fit their separate and foreboding purposes into a unified, constructive dialogue.

"I'm under considerable strain these days," I continued, taking a swallow from the flute while watching an indistinct smile grow beneath the deeply tanned skin of his tired cheeks, "but that's certainly no excuse for me to behave poorly.

"I apologize, yet all the same, it's crucial for me to learn how you came to know about this affair; and mind you, it must remain in this room, with only the two of us. As for the adventure, I have no apology to make for anything I've done, for what I do these days is seldom without '*earnest consideration.*'

"Charlotte, since you asked, must appreciate above any other lesson in life, that she is filled with ancient, honorable blood; this much is true regardless of my fate, and as you once mentioned to a young man back in Mayfair, the price of the truth is *never* reasonable."

I poked the fire with the iron attempting to intensify the glow.

"I'm simply providing the only chance for justice to an old friend who has saved my life on more than one occasion; is this something you would even trouble to advise me against?"

The glimmer of amusement left the old man's eyes, replaced by a deep philosophy which transformed him from the tired old Cassandra, into the venerable ally I recall from much more impulsive, much stranger days so many lifetimes ago.

"I think I'd like some more champagne," he replied.

XXI

The scene from first violin on the orchestral podium was one of dissolute passion for a late summer's gambol; dutifully raking her bow in an evening of flying spicattos and ticklish pizzicatos across the fiddle's slender neck; now to *die Fliedermaus,* next to the *Rosamonda*; surveying from a panoramic vantage on the stage, the whirling, kaleidoscopic dance floor; the synchronized dalliances of the privileged coterie all same cut from multi-colored bolts of silk chiffon and satin blossoms, hinting of the bold hibiscus blooms.

Vivian watched the dancers surge like tree tops in a cyclone'd wood; stretched one moment to the farthest east, *so very, very far*; a subsequent and captivating swirl, that by next measure any compass point *but* east; *yet always steadfast rooted to the floor.*

And she wondered how her youth of passion and dour discipline, of bright sunlit days spent indoors; of tempting evenings, all dismissed, all these natural, youthful rites traded for a set of spotted pages on a slim black music stand; her life of sacrifice should culminate in sawing letters from her spruce and maple box into an atmosphere so sinister with vice. The music as it ever was, its very own medicine even now, she sighed.

The crowded floor was home just now to two of Touchwick's most youthful and identifiable performers, each girl independent in her shoes, making of the tutorials and the meter what they could; their escorts to their trial best, while Charlotte, as the song wore on, showed them all what can be done when the lessons are ignored; the heart instead an open door to such a melody as filled the plastered hall this night with the dulcet joy of life.

Vincent, to her great fortune, was marvelous for his years, looking down into the face of this unexpected angel in his arms, held weightless, flowing flawless out of one spin through the next; eyes closed as if the beaming smile on her charming face were of a simple, private meditation of an even more delightful time before he took her hand onto the floor. The dance ended with the pair inside the first half box; Charlotte's hem continued in an orbit still beneath her waist and back again to settle for an instant on the floor, girdled round her small bewitching shoes.

There was only time enough for Gloria to shoot an undetected glare to Vincent, who she full presumed should, in the antique fashion of a gentleman, come rescue her from Jacob who had scuffed her brand new shoes no fewer than a dozen times; when from the first seat of the violins up on the stage, a tone in undue haste was set into the air, and off again our two matched pairs commenced, this time from the slow English measures from before, now upon the true Viennese romp at twice the pace and twice the turns.

Yet in the manner of the pilot lit inside the oven of her father's wagering mind one evening over cards aboard the cargo ship so many years ago, young Charlotte's own passions set her feet on a fluid course to meet each measure of the song; as if to concentrate on any but the feelings of her escort's hands around her waist, the air upon her face and music, spilt like honeysuckle in her ears, would be to lose her place, becoming just a simple country girl again, who never dreamed of such fantastic things as these; whose feet would slow into a sleep.

There was a moment then, however brief, when Charlotte woke from her trance to raise her eyes up to view the Count's own soft expression looking down; a moment so beyond the letters on my feeble keyboard to describe, as it might as much relate the color yellow to a blind man in his darkened bed; for each it was the rush of a first encounter of the heart, a sensation every one of us who survives our own initiation fails along our lifetime to ever duplicate.

This brief instant lasted only for the time it took for Charlotte to immediately shut her eyes again, simmering in a flash of feelings which as yet she had no words to describe, no experience to match; when to their left a great commotion, sounding like two snow geese, collided in mid-air; the music stopped and all was still as the tight crowd of gawking dancers spread their ring around the young Princess Gloria, who in a corrupt spin went falling to the ground. Jacob stood above her with his outstretched hand to lend her aid which she cursed and rejected, holding back a wall of tears.

A very sharp laughter rose above the stunned silence of the room, coming from the seat where the first-violin played the last evening of her illustrious career.

XXII

The Professor wore the look of one who had chased too many things for too many years beneath too hot a sun; the additional logs just now joining in a reprise of flame and light within the fireplace, the details of his face became much deeper, better defined, and by these sharp etched shadows traced thereon, a pinch of melancholy settled into my own tired soul, knowing analogous scribblings divulged the many years of similar adventure on my own.

We were much older, both of us, from when at first he tended to my father's wish and stuffed my idle head with erudition from the wider world; this truth cannot be avoided; but neither were we one day older than our youngest thoughts, which in that dim and private room were plentiful; for the Professor continued on, confessing to precarious meddlings and hushed arrangements, more likely associated with the risks and daring of one's youth, much concerned with me, already undertook to aid my circumstance and spread a shield as best he could around my unsuspecting Charlotte, whom he took to regarding as his own blood.

"So it was understood by Father Dodd that young Felis, by Kriss' oath, is false accused; and further, the young man's single hope to escape the hangman was to come across the ocean, here to Hoffenstein, anon."

The old man reverse-crossed his legs so he could lean closer toward me, curiously lowering his voice to half and continued,

How could a scheme so large in scope and fraught with peril come to be? I quizzed myself, needing only strike one nerve for Father Dodd to seal the windows and confess. Your name, it grieves me much to learn, has gained you many favors, far more than I should have ever guessed from looking on your boney frame all those many years ago; but favors Giov, come at much too high a price I fear, and like the truth, are only useful after sorted from the false allure of all their initial, raw intensity.

"It's one matter Master Penworth, after all, to hide a saint among the husbands in one's barn, but quite another to do so when you have brought upon your house such notoriety, such ill-tempered scrutiny; I mean by this the vengeance of one Bishop and one Prince."

I knew the rightness of his point, the circumstances being what they were, but always acted with an understanding that a zone of insular cooperation remained intact; a space for sporting partisans to breathe and reinforce the structure of *le Systéme*, wherein contradictory attitudes are summoned to explore the compromises necessary to define the Nation as a Union.

"I believe you overestimate the liability," I replied, "we are merely lawmakers of a seeming insurmountable disparity, for sure, but it's unwarranted to think that I should ever live as though my every movement could attract the obsessive enmity of any two such devils, resources as they are in such scant supply; I've read the *Quarterly*, Professor, and though I'm discouraged for Hoffenstein, I'm yet comforted by the losses to the pair you fret so much about."

"Peril, my son, is but a surreptitious motive with an hyper-anxious hind quarter; and by that I mean both a reason *and* an opportunity. What stronger motive exists than *loss*? You say you've read the report, did you? Have you read it carefully?"

"Well to be honest, I've become quite sufficient at skimming though most of the more tedious papers that I stuff into my briefcase every week. But I'm sure that I can convince you of my lack of interest to these two, for the time being that is."

"What if I suggested that you were wrong; that the time calls for improved diligence toward defending your reputation and possible safety; that your very career was in the crosshairs of some greater plot than has breached the threshold of your instincts? What would you do then?"

The fire licked at his sharpened features like an artist's brush full loaded with a yellow-golden flame, lifting his brow and cheek up and away from the greater swallowing blackness of the room.

"What are you implying? . . come, speak plainly to me."

"The young Charlotte has been without her father for too long downstairs; perhaps we should continue our discussion at a time more appropriate to its relative complexity, shall we?"

The Professor stood from his chair and placed his arms around me in a hug, then whispered in my ear, "Someone has been listening. I can't say how long, but this room is not a safe place to continue."

The sour fragrance of villainy now tainted the Billiard room as I returned the old Professor's sentimental *adieu*. It was near impossible to resist a *lunge* into the darker corners where the spying culprit might be hid; but affairs of this sort seldom prove to factor out with poise; best I follow the Professor's lead and play on ignorance.

"And goodnight to you, dear Friend. Tomorrow evening then, for supper?"

"I'll be there. Tell me Giov, does Charlotte like chocolates?"

Even sarcasm was redundant here; the expression on my face supplied the old man with the necessary answer needed to include the *chocolatier* into his leather backed appointment book.

XXIII

It was a matter of only a few minutes before the band struck the chord to start the Ball afresh; His Highness excused himself politely from his throng to personally investigate the disturbance on the dance floor where gossip had already implied his dear Gloria could be found and was in some manner involved.

It was a scene that an understanding of youthful vanity and insecurity is required to explain; for no sooner had the King embraced the Princess as a father should then she rejected his ovations, turned to grab the nearest glass which held a swallow of a nice Pinot Noir and tossed it directly at Charlotte, staining her new yellow dress with blood-red wine.

Silas shaved the strings on his fiddle to *Eine Kliene*, his debut opportunity to sit as First Violin, and enraptured, managed well enough to hold the chair for the remainder of the evening.

XXIIII

The bakery was always the first shop in Söfenzin to startle the mice back into hiding from their nighttime escapades; the ovens lit at ten past four each morning by a gaunt, silver haired baker, whose fondness for a useless stray mouser, sardonically christened Guts, a veritable mascot around the bakery, extended to her name and likeness scratched in ink across his arm; who mixed and leavened and cut and rolled and dusted and washed his breads and pastries into a multiplicity of sizes and shapes, the consistent quality of which was legend. The bakery had been lighting its ovens each morning exactly as it did today for no fewer than two-hundred and thirty-five years.

Inspecting the pastry case, Deacon Frederick squinted at the various pies behind the surface of the glass which was positioned at such an angle as to catch the rising sun and throw it back into the shop, providing an almost reverent glow upon whoever stood in just the right spot at just the right moment. Today, as has so often been the circumstance, it fell to Frederick.

It was another glorious day break, promising by the chorus of cicadas and the dense mist above the fields, to be another hot and humid late summer's day in the Dortpen, with every chance for an afternoon thunder shower. Frederick never missed an opportunity in fourteen years to take advantage of the cool summer mornings, rising about six o'clock to walk to the chapel on a course which, though not the shortest distance, allowed for him to stop at the bakery for a morning cup and quickbread.

"Butter this morning?" asked the young lady behind the counter, unwise to any consonance behind the gray haired minister's decision to abstain from, or indulge himself upon a spread of sweetness over his breakfast with a tab of freshest cream from the Knöbel dairy farm, a bucolic settlement out past the vineyards in a corner meadow just this side of the Mayfair dam, which also brought the milk he loved so much to stir into his morning cup of fresh grinds.

"Butter?" he smiled, stolen from his meditation on the shelf of pies by the lady's humoring tone, "Why that sounds perfect! A little butter on one side please, while it's still nice and warm, would you?"

"But of course," she replied, "anything for the Town celebrity!" The Deacon blushed.

"And the paper?"

"No I'm afraid. Not this morning, thank you."

The girl popped the quick bread into a paper bag and handed it to Frederick, who held out the exact change.

"I'll take this only so's I got something for the plate on Sunday," she teased the embarrassed gray haired man; "I aint big with the church, not yet I mean, Father."

He interrupted, "Please Isa, you needn't . . ."

"No father," she continued, rattling on, "I got to tell you, more serious you gather, like a confession, you know. Well I been noticing quite a few more, you know, *gentlemen* who I been wanting to know more friendly like; an' they all been coming to your church on Sunday. Figures I would save a few coins and see you up there, you know, like a girl should do; like them nice families that been going again. Don't you see? How else a girl gonna meet someone outside a saloon, right?"

She handed the bag across the counter as he stood dumb, not knowing quite what to say but, "Thank you Isa."

"How much they put in that thing anyways, Deacon?"

There was a reticence to her voice that caught Frederick's attention; as if somewhere beneath her bristling sarcasm was a half karat of sincerity, desperate to appear none too eager.

"Each what they can; *some what they need to*," said the Minister, "Hope to see you Sunday, Isa."

The bell rang behind the cleric who stepped back out onto the street.

And so it came to be, that one good turn did trip the switches of a multitude of dormant sentiments, which in their sum provided all the hope as was required to wake the whole town from its pious slumber.

The *Touchwick Chronicle* published the true life story of a hapless country deacon who risked his life to save a wretched Gypsy boy from the jaws of death; and thus a hero from their very midst was appended to the civic code; as providence would validate, aroused more interest than the hearsay of a struggling preacher ever could.

And in the wake of considerable notice piqued by the recent attendance of Söfenzin's town leaders, one by one, to hear the *captivating* Deacon speak (Graham Bessel, for instance, the editor of the *Mayfair Courant* and chief perpetuator of the hero myth; once a tenor in the chapel choir under the more conservative baton of the late Father Japheth), there came the multitudes whose capillary motives followed suit.

The stoic blacksmith heard from Guy at the car dealership that Daniel the grocer knew from his wife that Father Japheth let it slip one evening with the ladies of the Auxiliary that Deacon Frederick chose to trade a collar, rightfully earned at Seminary school, to live against the book of Leviticus, in sin with the man Gregory who raises chickens to sell in the city.

The blacksmith from the darkness of his shop said nothing as he observed the town withdraw like frightened starlings from the chapel when old Father Japheth died; Guy mentioning one day how dead his showroom in the summer was this year, then struck by an epiphany, he took his stand with God and stopped attending mass on Sunday; for a good Christian should never, in those days, be seen in *that* church.

With car sales up again, Guy and the others who took to stopping at the quiet Smith's forge to drink their brew, were left with nothing more to say about the Deacon or the Lord, and the Blacksmith went about his business, hammering the galaxies of red stars from his furnace for the full ten years it took Guy to fill each new car with a good Christian and for each good Christian in the Dortpen to have in their drive, a new car.

But that, the stoic blacksmith smiled, was how Guy sold cars *before* the miracle. To sell a car in Söfenzin today, he overheard one sunny afternoon; or to sell a box of nails or a pound of lamb, a loaf of quick bread, a dress, a horse or anything (save the petrol for your car), you simply went to hear the hero Preacher speak, and there be seen by all as a good, church-going Christian.

No one bothered mention Gregory again.

The house was fuller these days, two Sunday masses; the collection grew, some tithes renewed; the belfry under considerable repair, the little Church beneath the towering hemlock fresh painted and the oil tank filled; Frederick breathed the waning summer's fragrance and made his

116

way to the chapel, a bag of quick bread tucked beneath his arm, where a letter sealed inside an envelope from the Archbishop's office waited for him in a small stack of unread mail.

Passing the blacksmith shop, still closed from yesterday, Frederick admired its tired old bay doors and black crusted windows, wondering where the smithy might go on Sundays; what he might do when the whole rest of the world was busy buying and selling cars at his little chapel under the hemlock.

XXV

It rained Sunday evening; a black gloved hand drew back the window shade to peek down on the wet cobbled street, making what confusion it could, refracting the dim rays from the beleaguered street lamp standing sentry at the driveway entrance to the side of Lord Penworth's townhouse, winding through a tunneled archway under the building to the back entrance where a covered drive-through served to shield its guests from the more unreasonable elements such as were in abundance this night.

The old Citroen splashed its way around the house, stopped beneath the car port and waited briefly for the great iron lamp, hung ponderously from a heavy chain, to be extinguished; an indication no doubt, for the two gentlemen inside the vehicle to prepare for a quick departure through the damp night from the car directly to the rear door of the great house, held open by none other than the solitary figure of His Lordship.

The two shadows, under cover of significant darkness, were assured additional obscurity by the great vestigial umbrella, unfolded to its full, opaque and vacuous utility, held close on; and in a sprint were disappeared into the safety of the great house.

It was a matter of five minutes past this strange event that a gentleman, dressed in a black Mackintosh, exited the house and drove the car into the farthest right bay of the garage on the west side of the small garden. Returning inside the house, he relit the great lamp which threw its beams like lemon drops to the orphaned puddles of rain below.

It was another half hour before a second, much larger car was driven out from the garage and around to the covered overhang where it sat idling just long enough to be loaded with a number of trunks and various parcels as for a holiday; the great lamp was once more extinguished and a company of three gentlemen and a young lady, obscured in a manner very much as before, took their places inside the car, secured the doors and drove, making off into the street.

The glove released the window shade again; shutting out the streetlight, leaving the dim room once again in total blackness.

XXVI

Two weeks together in the country was the Duke's best prescription to minister the overwhelming compression of events at war within the bewildered young man's mind.

Having gained his tentative freedom from the vicious verdicts for the crimes which were not his: a burning shack from which he fled, a savage, butchered dog for which he bled; having walked through such a door as few have in the past, all Africa behind a lock replaced by unfamiliar fields of harvest gold and red; had said goodbye forever to his beloved Uncle; was torn from everything from which his soul was spun, to be here, in this strange land of the Dortpen; without the blue sky or Lord Penworth, he may as well be in Luremo on his mat asleep.

The good Duke took him as a nephew to the woods where many times his own tired soul found solace in its dense, sublime simplicity; *thereon, the lily to consider*;

two men hiking through the meadows and the fen far off, crossing streams and napping in the shade beneath the soaring pines; some bass were trapped, a fire lit, the stars read down like letters in a story book; yet not a sound exchanged until the bedrolls, spread like Persian rugs across the moss, called out for each to trade recuperations in for dreams.

"Tomorrow," said the Duke.

Standing in the library on the second floor, the Professor drew from his pipe, looking out of a tall open window over the immense, undulating fields, checkered by the ancient walls and tree stands set by crofters long ago to tame the winds which whipped down from old Pater onto crops so plentiful in generations past; he focused on the forest edge which hemmed the view, a tribute to his pupil, now his friend, that there inside the vast magnificence of green were two men from two paths in search of common ground.

It is no use, he mused, to free a man from execution who is a hostage in his soul; that he is thankful for a kindness permits a proud man to live on again, much like one who's crossed a bridge, his gratitude the toll; but when, by virtue of its nature such a service has no end, then a man is life-sentenced; his eternity upon the bridge; a pocket full of gratitude, no *levy house*.

There is in this no place for pride nor can there ever be; a torment to a good man, damnation to a proud man, lest this kindness can be worked by other means; and hence the walk onto the foothills of old Pater, wherein the key to *other means* though devilishly hid, is often found.

He pulled on his pipe once more before turning from the window to greet Hobbes at the door standing stiffly with an envelope addressed to him which had just arrived with this morning's mail.

"Curious," he thought, "I've told no one that I'm here."

XXVII

"But would it interest you to know, dear brother, that chief among our difficulties finding traction with Azevedo, are the dalliances into diplomatic transgression by your dear friend *Gigi*; who, according to my own, very reliable sources, only recently contracted with some covert Jesuit organization to interfere with the apprehension of a desperate murderer?

"Moreover, I beg you to explain this proclivity to pestering the hapless Portuguese? Can't you place a bug into his ear against the Swiss or the Finns, for Christ's sake? *Anyone* can buy a lawyer in the States for that matter and be done with it all!"

The Prince stepped over to a portrait of his great, great uncle, Prince Bruce, Earl of Kip; a dour moment captured for eternity of an old man also having lived a life of public service in the shadow of his inferior elder sibling. With his back now turned toward the King, the faint glow of a precipitated victory shone out from his steel grey eyes; the pieces for so many years collected now settling into place;

"*Ah, Bruce!,*" he observed, "*My own likeness will no doubt reveal the very mettle by which, in its patent absence, this candid painter has so perfectly interred your grim description.*"

Maximillian despised his brother, true, but seldom more than now. One does not wear the crown so long however, who does not know the long way to an end; keeping Prince Eugene at arm's length has always been a necessity, if not a recreation for him. There were at his brother's disposal after all, resources which, for one deprived the scruples even of a brown-recluse, could prove themselves of immense, even fatal consequence.

119

Eugene born that rainy day so many years ago, it had been diagnosed, came into his mother's lap devoid a heart.

This was no blood His Majesty saluted; but for the teat of the House of Dubious on which the soul of Hoffenstein suckles, Eugene to him was better dead. He therefore spoke to Eugene as one should his brother, in whatever incarnation such a personal description might indulge.

"I know nothing of your sources, or the intrigues they describe, Eugene; as perhaps my excellent example should be one for you. The troubles we have with Azevedo are a trifle when you stand some convict on the scales with our two fine economies. I'll have a word with Azevedo myself and bind the stray and finer threads of these negotiations which have apparently escaped your barb. And don't you worry, little brother, I offer this with absolute discretion, for I will credit you as though this conversation never was."

The Prince pulled at the foil in his chest and turned away from Uncle Bruce to face Maximillian; stung to the core; his face now as crimson as it was soft pink and complacent a mere instant before.

He replied, "I believe my brother overwhelms me with his kindness; but I advise you Max to spend less time at billiards and much more of it on your throne. You are too wound up with this Duke to parry straight; Azevedo will eat you alive!

"I put the principle of justice for a killer on the scaffold where it rightly fits; the shadow, now flung downward overwhelms discussions of our checkbooks or our silly corporate plans. What price would you reason for a nation's pride?"

"If Lord Penworth is involved in any escapade King Dubious snapped, "my guess is that the effort was intended toward the correction of some wrong, some injustice. Bring me evidence that I may draw the curtains from this skullduggery and shed a proper light onto the case; meanwhile, get back on the phone with Azevedo; tell him I have declined any new arrangements to the deal pending a thorough, albeit very discreet survey of the charges; if Penworth is the hinge pin, then he'll have his day."

The Prince, reasonably satisfied, nodded, "Good day, your Highness."

The long walk through the palace was tediously familiar and Eugene descended the first staircase, then shuffled through the galleries and hallways, festooned with marble busts and Italian oils, tapestries from medieval Gaul and vitrines filled with priceless plates and saucers from all the essential Eastern dynasties;

Toby's and crystal from Britain and a prized egg from old Mother Russia, *just before the terrible revolution, mind you*; and who passed all these precious things with never having raised his eye up from his shoes; for though the objects offered not the vaguest mental inspiration for him, it was rather, an obsession with his brother's remarks upstairs that filled his mind; the gamble whether all was just now won or lost.

He spied the banister descending to the lobby entrance up ahead when from the music room he heard the tiny voice call out his name, "Uncle Eugene!"

He paused to grin, turning slowly to his young niece walking toward him like the very lady of the house; *"how she is grown!"* he mused.

"You've been to see my father." She approached with her hands outstretched.

"Yes, I have Gloria. You're more beautiful every time I see you," he lied, taking her tiny hands into his.

"So this young thing is sister to the Penworth girl," he schemed, *"how strong the bonds."*

"Where are you going? Won't you stay over for dinner tonight and play cards with me?"

"Not tonight, my dear. I've a meeting on the other side of town. I'll take a rain check if you please."

He kissed her cheek and started for the balustrade and stopped to turn toward the Princess adding,

"Wait, Gloria!"

She perked up, "Yes?"

"I believe I saw your beautiful young friend yesterday, Charlotte isn't it? She walked with a very handsome young man. I believe I saw them dancing together at the ball."

Gloria almost fainted. "But where did you see them?"

"At *Verdi's* Department store. Naturally I looked for her father to pay my regards, but he was nowhere to be found. I turned back, the two had gone."

"Well then," she exhaled, "It couldn't be. Charlotte's out in the Dortpen with her father since Monday. You must have made a mistake."

"All right young lady, if you say so," he smirked. "I'll be running off now. We'll play cards very soon, I promise."

Gloria watched her uncle disappear into the great hall downstairs and ran into the music room, slamming the door behind her.

XXVIII

It was obvious that they admired clocks; for every wall was hung heavy with the clicking boxes, separated only sparsely by the chance framed image of a scene wherein the artist shrewdly let the viewer know the time at which he froze the composition.

Entering the back door of the cottage, through the mud room, with its orderly row of rubber muckers and crusted leather work boots; a row of tarnished coat hooks saddled with slickers, umbrellas, scarves and cobwebs; its small, silt-glazed window to the east, embellished with the faintest speckled trace from a careless painting some ten or fifteen years ago; a rusted screwdriver asleep on the sill;

one steps up and through the half-door, moves into the kitchen; a classic account of the provincial galley, replete with a converted, side-scullery now serving as a greenhouse for Frederick's impressive assemblage of hearty house plants, whose vigorous proclivity to grow obstructs the very sunrays straining to pass on through the leaf blocked panes.

An old gas stove stands beside the deep-sink underneath a respectable array of copper pots and iron pans, dangling from a solid beam of hickory on which a row of fancy cups, mugs and wishbones also hung like fresh caught rabbits skinned for a pie.

Passing from the kitchen through a rounded doorframe, a fireplace of smooth-edged stones anchored on the far side of the cozy living room; whose mantle abides two anniversary clocks, the pair a study in how two craftsmen can incorporate a common principle into separate devices of remarkable contrast. On the left hand, a handsome machine, boxed by four flat panes of beveled glass, a four ball pendulum topped and trimmed in brass. To the right, a tall apparatus housed inside a crystal

122

globe, whose pendulum like its cousin to the west, suspends down from a torsion spring, though less like the four ball carousel, is instead a poised, precision disc of gold.

The clocks were in evidence everywhere; on every surface, from every spare inch of the wall.

Frederick had gotten quite used to living with the sound, his ears swimming in the chorus of the many voices, each escapement calling off the seconds like a hundred wooden crickets; the sound becoming nothing less enchanting than the endless rhythmic waves against the shore.

And here, among them in this room, sat Frederick in his reading chair, quiet in his thoughts.

The sound of Gregory's truck returning from the village was the signal to collect himself in preparation for his pronouncement; sure to be met by his partner with a concentrated mix of pride and bitterness; rightfully observed, yet somehow not as pleasant a task as Frederick presumed the news deserved; alas, Gregory lived close to his principles which on certain occasions presented more of the truth than was kind; and any news from that scoundrel Grieble was enough to set him off.

The sound of the back door sent a gale of dignity throughout the modest deacon's bones; perhaps Gregory will take the news in stride, he thought, the friar now a priest; the two might dance and celebrate with cold champagne; yet maybe not.

"Could never love a man with an ounce less battle in his soul," was all he said; they danced and drank the bottle dry.

XXIX

There, from far off in the great meadow's hub, two tired rovers cut a thin path through the waist high grass; the one a Lord, and one a fugitive; two new brothers now come home to settle in; two dark spots against an argyle field, patches specked in purple thistle, even-sprayed in goldenrod.

"I'm thinking of a hot bath and a shave," laughed the Duke, wondering if the great house on the hill was actually floating away, further with each footstep, as it appeared; the tiny spots of three individuals now discernible a short distance from the great house, milling about a strange dark structure, some curious new contraption which he, from that distance, could not identify, and yet affirmed was nothing present when they first set off those few, fine days before.

It wasn't too long before the span between them was no greater than his voice could cross, and shouting Hello!, Lord Penworth brought the attention he desired, as he saw his Charlotte recognize their forms and dash through the tall grass to reach her darling prodigal whom she missed terribly, with his strange new friend.

"Welcome home!" cheered Hobbes, relieving the two men of their bedrolls, which, in the Duke's case permitted him to carry young Charlotte less encumbered; for she had, in her excitement, leapt upon her father's back, tied her hands about his neck and rode him home.

"I suppose some change of clothes for the pair of you will be in order," remarked the good domestic, who smiled and suggested Charlotte come to help him pick two outfits suitable for the wondrous occasion.

Penworth turned back to the Professor, still smiling from his welcome and observed the old man tinkering with what appeared to be some variation of a windmill and a coil, tubes of different colored liquids attached to some form of compressor fashioned from haphazard odds and ends found inside the old garage behind the peach orchard; he shook his head.

"Searching for Uranium, Alistair?" he teased.

The Professor, engrossed upon the brass fitting of a blue tube leaving the compressor, simply muttered something under his breath before addressing the Duke,

"Oh yes, Penworth. I see you're back from your sabbatical. If you would please, hold that pulley from turning while I secure this fitting; seems to give me nothing but trouble . . . *vacuum* leak, you understand."

Giov nodded his head to Felis, thoroughly bemused by the situation.

"Best go inside and get you scrubbed up; seems my bath will have to wait a bit."

Charlotte had finally tired from the stories narrated by Felis and her wonderful Papa of the glorious travels shared among the tall trees, caves and thunderous rivers of old Pater; her heavy eyes barely lifting as Giov carried her to bed, leaving Felis, Hobbes and the Professor to talk amongst themselves before the fire.

When he got back to the parlor he saw that just the two of them remained, Felis having himself dozed off, was led by Hobbes back to his room, who then returned with a bottle and three glasses from the kitchen. The two of them now discussing which features of the old place sustained the greater changes, and whether for the better or the worse.

Hobbes, the Professor learned, was no stranger to the Dortpen, nor Mayfair to be more specific, having been the child of a chauffeur and a cook at an estate not more than ten miles distance, and so being schooled nearby. But this was many, many years ago; his knowledge of the region, being vastly more intricate than the Professor anticipated, seemed only to delight him all the more.

The pipes were filled and the snifters emptied.

"So, I'm going back to Touchwick on Monday," said Penworth after every caution from his two friends failed.

"The photographs suggest you're headed to a trap, son. How else would anyone even know to address that envelope to me here? Why won't you consider the facts?" admonished Alistair.

"Dear me, Sir," interjected the good Hobbes, "It seems to make perfect sense to me that the Professor is trying to help. Please listen to him, won't you?"

Penworth paced the carpet, struggling to resolve the truth of what must be, against the facts assembled as they were by his two confederates; how to make the pieces fit!?

"I ask you two, what else can be done to save a man's life from such a comedy that still respects the law? Nothing! Those photographs prove nothing! Which one of you will tell me that this man's freedom is worth less than the savage desire to enslave it; to snuff it?"

The Professor shook his head slowly at this; knowing that his work was done too well. Hobbes simply took a deep swallow of the brandy without breathing or savoring the drink; lowering his head, he concluded the discussion had exceeded his rank; his was restricted to a question of maintaining loyalty beyond any true understanding or agreement of the facts as he interpreted them.

"I work in Parliament after all; I will immediately begin a campaign to gather support for this whole ridiculous affair; I do have friends in high places as you know. And I can't hide forever in the Dortpen; by rights, I should have nothing whatsoever to hide, anyway! I'll just return to Touchwick earlier than I planned; start the process."

For the very first time, Lord Penworth had the hint of apprehension in his eyes.

"Then I come with you," said the Professor, firmly.

"And I?" asked Hobbes.

Penworth's worry broke into a smile as he was reminded that he was not alone.

"You, Hobbes, will guard the Dortpen; report of any more suspicions, strange mail, phone calls or surreptitious characters. Keep Felis busy, find him work. He's a good soul and disdains an idle schedule. He's very talented with his hands. But I beg you, keep him low. No one must suspect until I've found a way to make his case. Are we understood?"

Hobbes filled all three snifters and raised his, the Duke and the Professor both returned his toast.

"Now I'm tired gentlemen. It's off to bed. Good night."

The two then paid their respects to the Duke and stayed a few more hours before the fire, smoking and talking about tropical depressions.

XXX

The Cloister is situated upon what remains of a massive stone-mason yard, once used for a few hundred years to size, shape and sculpt the schist and limestone extracted from the nearby quarries during the construction of the great Cathedral of St. Pontificate over four centuries ago; the soil still rich with the chips and other miniscule artifacts from the endeavor.

Surrounded now by a quadrangle of covered outdoor passages, drizzled thick in English ivy and the ever lovely Venus-Maiden flower, the magnificent garden, so meticulously cultivated over the dozen generations, has made of itself an essential diversion; a secular tonic to the blunt sensibilities of the Archbishop, whose every morning regimen includes a walk amongst its noiseless paths.

His encyclopedic recollection of each and every Latin designation for the hundreds of flowering varieties was but a school boy's recall and little more, a trick or talent such as circumvents the soul; for him, yellow is a color, cobalt just another frequency, the spectrum nothing more; what place in these states for joy, reverie or sorrow?

"This, the *bellis perrennis*, the English Daisy," he stopped to pull the blossom over to his nose.

"Belis parenis," the presbyter dutifully repeated, "fascinating, your Excellency. But permit me to once again inquire as to your reasoning? It would appear to my congregation that he is wholly unfit for the collar; can you not agree?"

The Archbishop pulled at a full white rose, seeming not to hear.

"*Rosa Alba*; commonly, just Alba; notice the yellow stamens? Come, look closer."

The priest was getting quite impatient with Bishop Grieble by this point, for news of the homosexual deacon from Söfenzin receiving a collar disturbed some of his colleagues and a few of the more vocal members of his constituency. Father Crispe, it was decided, would travel on their behalf to confront the Archbishop with their objections.

"I mean, with all due respect, Your Excellency, where will it lead? What is the example? What do we tell our flocks?"

The priest had evidently managed to channel his nervous agitation into a more resolute supplication; Bishop Grieble, finally pulling his nose out from the Rosa Alba, sensed an imminent episode of convulsive pontification and attempted to calm the excitable clergyman, finally responding,

"The sky is still very far off, my son," and began to walk the path again, "and the healing ministries of our faith as potent as ever. Your fears are mine, *were* mine I dare say; but for my faith, would be so still."

The priest, now silent, waited respectfully for the Bishop to develop his remarks along some form of an idea; that being what Bishops are expected to do.

"*Hedera helix*, English Ivy;" he motioned to the vine covered pillars across the garden, "so beautiful on the stone, don't you think? So ancient, so dark, the magnificent accoutrement to our ancient and romantic sensibilities, our European heritage. It blankets our castles, churches; tombs . . . even our prized universities; an indispensable prop in our collective archetype; theme music to childhood fairytales and adult mythologies.

"Yet, my son, it is this same common and much venerated vine, virtually harmonic to the very songs of David, known to strangle the host; killing chestnut, elm, hickory, all tearing at the great stones like gravel out from the mountain's groin!"

The two paused briefly to watch a pair of swallows shoot out from the tall, dark bell tower, chase circles in the cloister and alight on a buttress high above.

"And still so marvelous on the wall, don't you think?"

Grieble drew a wide self-satisfied grin and clasped his hands behind his back, setting a pace so slow the Priest could only awkwardly abide.

"So you are in agreement then, that the Church cannot allow the gay pastor to perform the sacraments . . . lest the vine strangle the Scripture?" he stammered.

"And where, Father Crispe, does it say in the Scripture that two men shall not share one home?" asked the Bishop.

"It says nothing in Leviticus of two men, or three men, for that matter, living under one roof," answered the Priest. "But . . ." he began, "but two men in love are the same in sin under two roofs as under one, is that not so?"

"Are we counting roofs now, Father?" stalled Grieble.

"I'm just saying, Your Eminence, that our objections stem not so much by their choice to live in sin, but to *love* in sin."

"I have no documented account of either party having declared their inappropriate love for the other. Did not Jesus beseech us all to love one another?"

"These two men have been observed on more than one occasion, *kissing*! I think you know the kind of love I'm referring to Bishop."

The priest was shivering now, overwhelmed by his proximity to the border of impertinence; it needed nonetheless to be said, he thought.

"Well then, did Jesus not kiss Judas?" followed the Archbishop, "and where in the testaments does it purport that He withheld his love from anyone?"

The priest, full aware that Bishop Grieble held the collar like a dog-toy from the Minister of Söfenzin for the past ten years, took one more charge to test the line of insolence, asking,

"How now, your Eminence? I don't understand your play here at all. Do you truly mean the things you say?"

Grieble had a most disagreeable schedule that morning, including a meeting with Eugene at eleven, following the present discussion with Father Crispe, already exceeding the outer limits of his patience. Anxious to bring the matter to an end, Bishop Grieble turned to Father Crispe and said, rather curt,

"Calm your people down. I'll take care of the priest from Söfenzin," and then considering, added, "I've no intention of producing another *Vandermeyer* from the ribs of Hoffenstein; one martyr per continent is quite enough. However, I need you to do something for me, for the *Church*, of course."

Father Crispe looked anxious to the Bishop, like an acolyte given notice to perform at his very first Eucharist. He was quite familiar with Bishop Vandermeyer; his eccentric profile as the bane of the plutocrats; a lighthouse for the recent explosive sentiment of mass subjugation throughout a wide swath of the continent's struggling hoi polloi.

"Yes, your Holiness?"

"I want to know more about this Gregory fellow, the man living with the *Hero*. It would be as wrong for me to withhold this *priest* from all those good people from Söfenzin begging to tithe as it would be to allow this whole charade to continue without knowing more about the other one, do you understand?"

The Priest paid his respects and left Touchwick for the outskirts of Hoffenstein where he would begin the difficult task of reassuring his congregation; perhaps it was also time to pay a call on his inevitable colleague from Söfenzin after all.

Grieble looked at his watch and began the walk from the garden to his office high upstairs in the cathedral, where the Prince was expected to arrive exactly on time.

XXXI

The shiny red Fregaté waited impatiently at the roundabout, now congested with commuter hour traffic, attempting to make *Dumont Avenue* and cover the remaining seven blocks to the townhouse with all improbable efficacy, so its anxious passengers could finally park and stretch their legs after the long drive from Mayfair.

The Professor made spare conversation, preoccupied the entire ride with a private appraisal of every conceivable outcome for his two friends, drawn from the distressing pastiche of recent events; a trail leading back, each and every time, to the *Atlantic Entitlement Group*, where of his knowledge, though considerable, was compromised by the circumstantial quality of its sources.

Hearsay, though an effective contrivance of his analytical repertoire, was simply inadequate for establishing or sustaining an unassailable defense.

Being an accomplished gentleman of letters and mathematics, Alistair recognized the urgent need to secure a very specific set of documents from where he hoped to exhume the numbers essential to substantiating his preliminary deductions. This was the mind of an academic, a distressingly logical savant, at work; in here no puzzle, however intuitive, leaves the higher floors of the metaphysical taffy-pull for the ground floor of practical applications premature.

The operation, as it stood, was about formulating the correct questions from a small handful of answers which bore no obvious association, save the massive shipping port construction project; already an indispensable port of call for speculators and traffickers on either side of the equator.

There was this coercion by certain authorities, for instance, to expeditiously repatriate the young Marquis back from Bosley before any legitimate rescue efforts formalized, a tragic situation wherein pressure from the Portuguese embassy seemed to contradict every tactical precedent for similar hostage scenarios. Then there was the additional conspicuous context of the prominence of our two hostages to consider, namely Lady Penworth and Bidwell.

And where were the delegates from *Silberfluss?*

There was a disturbing, maleficent sense that the young Duke was left, abandoned to his rogue rescue efforts; that his eventual and limited success and return to Hoffenstein was a terrible setback to specific individuals with extra-judicial interests; that those interests correspond directly with those of the chief investors of *AEG* who appear ultimately beholden to Prime Minister Azevedo. This much he surmised by the coincident timing of the Duke's unfortunate adventures in Angola where, he suspected, the source of *AEG*'s first contractual crisis of many, originated.

And in a seemingly unrelated matter, why would the triflings of a young villager from the far south side of the globe warrant the cloak and dagger interest of parties from a small landlocked fiefdom nestled in the foothills of Mt. Pater if not for the protection from broader liabilities? Accomplices apparently with means considerable enough to suspect these interests proceed from the highest levels of power. The clearest presumption once again points toward some fantastic connection with the Atlantic Entitlement Group.

His intuition strongly urged him to secure the documents most likely nestled among the other reports half asleep in Giov's valise, specifically the most recent proposal from Prince Eugene's office, the same one Giov referred to obtusely in the billiard room last Saturday evening; that same study prepared by Lord Grimstone of which he had confessed to only having browsed.

The key to any feasible strategy, he firmly believed, required access to the cagey logarithms scrawled across some classified prospectus stuffed inside the brown valise; whose access stretched beyond our faithful Alistair's influence, considering the Duke's strict observance of an antique code of confidentiality in accord with his capacity as a gentleman of honor and Member of Court. The reports in that briefcase were official State property and matters of State, self-ruinous or not, protected by an ancient policy of intimacy among even the most parochial and polarizing members of the Council. Lord Penworth, to his grave, like his father and *his* father's father's father, remained loyal to this.

"So good to be out of the car!" Charlotte yawned, waking from her morning nap.

"Yes it is," agreed Penworth, stretching as he made his way to the trunk for some of the bags.

131

The professor could not seem to take his eyes from the Duke's briefcase.

XXXII

It is critical, for the health of the clutch, that the brooder be maintained and warm; all manner of disease and vice avail themselves to chicks at such a time; the parasite, the vixen's tooth; the chill of night, the torrid day; a wonder they should ever grow to lay.

It takes some time, but to the breeder all is kind; and of the kinds there are but two; one for her egg, one for the pot, and looking in upon his butter-colored brood, he thinks about the ghostly line which cuts across the peeping clutch like the shadow from the hangman's noose; which one of you to live and lay and which is served on Saturday?

Gregory pulled the hutch door open against the mischievous breezes, come whipping down the fleecy green wings of the mountain; his flannel arms loaded with half a dozen tin pails. It was market day and forty cages filled with forty hens were needed to be stacked into the truck by early light, when all the stars had slid below old Pater's sight; the crescent moon alone caught unawares against the growing brightness of the dawn.

He imagined Sharon in her kitchen, starting the stove to make a lunch for Helen who would ride with him to town today. He knows the care with which she lay her baby's clothes; the pretty blouse, the fresh pressed pants; her jacket with its mismatched buttons sewn up tight; fragmented thoughts; the sleepless night.

How does Sharon get along, he thinks, what small adventure has she planned? Does one so many years surrendered ever chance to feel the breezes when the mad house door is sprung? These small respites are a simple gift, yet what the gentle old breeder can afford.

We make the road by seven-ten and cruise to Bertahl where the morning traffic slows, he considered, *finish at the market by eleven, then to the park to see the swans.*

He filled a few pails from the pump and threw more corn into the roost.

Through the woods he could make the cottage and saw that Frederick had just lit the kitchen lamp to start his day.

A strong breeze blew against the hutch door with a slam; his eyes shot from the dark tree line upward, where a single cloud sat looming on the

132

crisp ascending air; a searing white cloud cut and kneaded to an enigmatic shape, edged tightly by an icy blue remoteness that he failed to ever realize before; the sky had never looked to him more pregnant with intelligence.

He walked back toward the truck, feeling for his keys; it was critical he remembered, to clean the cab of any foreign hardware and stray coffee cups, to set the window crank just right; pausing an instant to smile at just how great a difference such a minor slip could make; could set the strange young lady off her keel, but each small effort paid back twice the price of Helen's joy; no perfect happiness compares outside her laughing eyes.

He drove the truck around to the back of the garage to the clearing where the hutches stood and began loading the bed with the cages. He would stop inside the cottage once more for a cup of coffee and say goodbye to Frederick before swinging by Sharon's cabin to pick up Helen.

XXXIII

"Thank you Kenneth," he said, handing the towel to the butler's waiting glove.

It was Wednesday. Lord Penworth had no scheduled business at the Court that day, saving his late afternoon for the first of two reserved appointments; the grave matter for his family's privacy was now on secret trial and the Prince, by Giov's shrewd reckoning, would not rebuff the charges; his Charlotte's image in a photograph had tripped a very treacherous wire.

"I've seen to it that some extra ham from last night's table has been packed inside the basket, with your cherished creamed herring and a pot of English mustard, sir."

Penworth smiled at these words, putting the finish on his comb, adjusted the clips on his suspenders.

"How's Charlotte, would you mind? She's always rushing, always late you know. Her age I suppose."

Kenneth turned around from the laundry hamper and informed him that a very excited young Charlotte waited downstairs at the ready; was on the phone just now with Gloria, who had graciously forgiven her and accepted the invitation to join their pleasant picnic in the park.

"Which jacket would you prefer this morning?" he asked.

Penworth still struggling with the mention of Gloria's unexpected company dismissed the half-digested question; politely giving leave to his *most-efficient* valet by offering to retrieve the jacket for himself.

"I'll catch up with you in a few minutes; I've something to prepare before we leave. Ask Charlotte to advise Gloria to be ready for the car by quarter-past eleven. Please."

Kenneth placed the hamper by the chamber door for the house staff; turned to Lord Penworth,

"As you wish, Sir. Will that be all?"

The Duke turning his collar down, reconsidered, asking Kenneth to look in on Alistair, still asleep for all he knew, and extend for him every privilege of a Penworth.

"Oh, and Kenneth, please inform him that we've gone to picnic down at Silberfluss, most likely near the carousel. Thank you. That will do."

"Yes sir."

It was a matter of habit that Giov could not pass the office door without inspecting some small thing or other on his desk. An open advance upon a Prince is a slight at best; his four-thirty with Eugene required exacting preparation for which he groomed in a fever; devouring the charts and figures in his brown valise; working all of yesterday whilst oblivious, the shadow from a poplar tree outside his window crawled from end to end across the hardwood floor.

There was no Hobbes here in the townhouse with his silver tray; no eggshell snifters poured with cognac for a friendly holiday. Touchwick was all business. Kenneth was not Hobbes.

He pulled the folders from their sleep and laid them in an order on his desk. He flipped the cover on the grey one and examined page seven once again, shook his head and switched the placement of the gray one for the black and piled the reports again. He dropped the empty valise toward the edge of his desk, pulled the drapes and left the office, locking the door behind him.

"Charlotte!" he shouted, "What say we go and picnic?" and skipped down the staircase to hug his precious girl.

XXXIIII

Queen Francis returned from her morning exercise in the garden with a thin mat rolled loosely under her arm, discussing with her yogi the unusual brilliance and clarity of the sky; about how much of the fabulous energy one draws from such a spectacle is strictly barometric, how much is isometric and the needless distinctions people employ to separate the unity of the true Life-force which binds it whole.

"And yet that solitary cloud," remarked the Queen, "how it sits up there on its blue throne; one senses that it draws the sky behind it like a train; that one proceeds, the other abides.

"I'm helpless not to feel as though my private thoughts were resonated somewhere inside that brilliant mist. It looks very much like a conductor at his podium, wouldn't you say? See, he even waves a white baton."

The Yogi hugged the Queen and jumped into her Aston-Martin, speeding down the drive quite recklessly. "How will I ever attain such Chi?" Fanny mused, waving her off.

In the window a very stern looking Gloria stared back down upon her mother, waiting impatiently for her examination to be finished before the Penworths arrived.

Prince Eugene's chauffeur was out front of the Palace, wholly absorbed, caressing the fenders of his limousine with a soft shammy cloth, waiting for the brief visit to be ended and the drive back across town toward St. Pontificate to begin; the Securities office from there and back to *Fleiss*.

It could not have occurred to the simple driver that there was anything more to be gained from living; his was a principle wherein a rich life was attained through a solid character and that a solid character could be had for nothing less than a sincere effort toward personal excellence at one's vocation. Choose a vocation young, he believed, and strive to be the top name in the register above all whoever worked the task before. He was a fine chauffeur and retired home each evening to his wife and child a very satisfied man.

The Queen walked back toward the great house passing the obsequious driver with no evidence of having noticed him, standing straight and stiff with his shammy, head bowed. The cloud was shaped now like a baker's hat, she decided, realizing how hungry the exercise made her.

"Princess Gloria is in the salon, Your Highness; she awaits her inspection."

Her Majesty's personal assistant had a clear, direct voice which revealed no weakness, such as some who suffer humor or emotion; hers was an efficient house, her schedule pedantic.

How the Queen could unwittingly turn her screws.

Gloria ran from the window toward the entrance of the comfortable salon where her mother, Queen Francis Dubois, had just entered; withholding every indication of the exacerbation now at war for control of her reason.

"Mother, I see the Penworth car at the gate. Please don't hold me too much longer," she pleaded.

The Queen was no more moved to rush by these words, handing the rolled mat to another waiting pair of hands; dropping into an over-sized recliner stretched with satin, dyed in harmonizing stripes of pale Wedgewood and Prussian blue. She kicked her sneakers to the floor.

"I should think that's no way for a fine young lady to address her mother, the *Queen* no less!" chastised the dour aide.

"Nor any way for a *servant* to speak to the Princess," she shot back. "Mother, *please!*"

"Yes Gloria, turn around; let me look at you."

"It's an outfit Uncle Eugene bought for me in Vienna last week. I think it's wonderful, don't you agree it's wonderful Mommy?" Gloria spun around again and again before her mother, "It fits perfectly!"

"Stop that spinning Gloria! You make me dizzy. Where are you going dressed like that? And where did Eugene get that *garish* ensemble, did you say?"

"To a picnic with Charlotte and the Duke at Silberfluss Park; and he said he bought it in a fine shop in Vienna, Mommy. Look again, *please*. All the young people wear such things Momma; I shouldn't expect you to understand!"

The Butler appeared in the doorway and cleared his throat with such delicate excellence as one could only demand from years of meticulous refinement. "Lord Penworth and the young Lady Charlotte have arrived for Princess Gloria, Your Majesty."

"Wait five minutes and show them in," replied the regal Yogini, looking quickly to the clock beside her.

"I should expect them to dress that way in Vienna. For the record, Gloria, I haven't the faintest concern for what the children are wearing in the slums and ghettos of the world. You are nobility and you will dress like nobility. Madam, take Gloria to her chamber and see that she returns wearing something less distasteful."

"My pleasure, Your Highness," she replied marching Gloria out of the salon.

The Queen's chance for a moment's repose was once again interrupted, this time by Uncle Eugene, as ever smart and as polished as his limousine out front.

"My dearest Sister-in-law!" he entered, arms outstretched.

"Oh, it's *you*. You really needn't bother."

"No trouble at all! I was just on my way out; thought I'd look in on my favorite niece, that's all."

"One favor I ask, Eugene, and then you are more than free to go."

"Anything for you, Your Highness."

The Queen could be quite droll when the situation called for it.

"Next time you invade Vienna, please leave your plunders in Austria."

The Butler returned with Lord Penworth and Charlotte; the Prince froze instinctively, all color drained from his face.

"Your Majesty," the Duke bowed toward the satin-upholstered recliner. Charlotte performed a most splendid curtsey.

"Penworth," the Prince snapped.

"Your *Prince-ness*," smiled the Duke. Turning back to our regal Yogini, Giov asked for Gloria.

"Gloria will be down any moment. She is suffering a wardrobe exchange at the moment; seems a mother can't suspend her diligence these days."

At which point Gloria entered the room in an outfit chosen by the Queen's aide; entirely appropriate for a pre-war debutante preparing to observe a polo match.

Gloria took one look at Charlotte, dressed like any other young girl from the streets of Vienna. Uncle Eugene looked very amused.

"Shall we go then?" remarked the Duke, "I'll have her back, exhausted, by three o'clock, your Highness."

Gloria could not take her burning stare off Charlotte; how wonderful she looked. A deep black cloud of ink ran from her brain, coating every chamber wall inside her spiteful heart; such rage as tricks the voice into an utter, abject silence.

"You look absolutely chic, my dear!" shot the Prince to Charlotte as the trio exited the salon.

Charlotte stopped in the doorway and turned round, replying, "Thank you so much, Your Lordship."

XXXV

"You've got to move your truck, Mr. Gregory; someone needs your space," called the kid from in front of the old blue truck. "He's waiting."

It was clear through the front window of the shop that a large truck was blocking the passage of traffic trying to make their way in the opposite direction. God, how Gregory hated the city!
"He can wait," replied the old man, "truck stays where it is 'til I finish here."

The proprietor smiled at his unflappable supplier and continued to calculate the bill.

"That's thirty-five at seventeen, then . . ."

"Or forty at fourteen and eighty-seven; is it I come all this way to take two-per on the cheek, Tom?"

Gregory studied his multiplication tables with apparent and equivalent alacrity.

"Couldn't you just move it up some, Mr. G.?" pleaded the boy among the growing chorus of trumpeting car horns. There's a space just up front and he can roll right in. Everyone could move on."

Gregory looked out at the cab to see that Helen was getting agitated by the horns.

"I'll keep the girl where I can see her!" he shouted back above the din, "Now if you'll stop the foolishness, Tom; *oh* what's the *bother!* Give me seventeen for thirty-five, then! Take five on my account. I can't wait here and argue with you anymore!"

Tom, seeing his old friend of twenty some-odd years finally lose his composure, simply laughed and handed him cash for forty at seventeen,

"Here you go; now move that piece of junk away from my shop and have them stop making all that noise. Till next Wednesday, then."

Gregory shook his head and made out the door to his truck. Tom followed him to the front window, studying the young woman, now flailing about in the cab of Gregory's truck.

"My God! She looks as she might hurt herself," he thought. He watched his old friend open the passenger side door and calm the woman; holding her in his arms and pressing his face against hers, his hand holding the back of her head. Tom caught himself getting soft and quickly made the sidewalk to begin directing the truck into its space.

Gregory climbed behind the wheel and made for Silberfluss Park.

XXXVI

It couldn't have been a more splendid morning for a day by the river; Silberfluss Park was near empty this morning save a few members from the free-run dog society, talking amongst themselves while their pets frolicked within some invisible yet well-regarded boundary.

Lord Penworth led the two girls past the dogs onto a separate, favorite meadow nearer the carousel, far more remote and set closer to the river bank opposite the narrow drive which ran parallel to the Silberfluss most of the length of the Park.

Some swans were busy preening on the pebbled shore line, paying little notice to the others, gracefully paddling, or as it might seem, posing for snapshots by the tourists who would then speak of their great numbers back at home.

Lord Penworth chose two spots at odds with young Gloria's preference, compromising on a third which was isolated from the main view by a half-round berm topped with lemonwood hedges and here spread the large red and green blanket on which he dropped the basket, poured a glass of chianti and lay down to read. The two girls eagerly broke into the pastries, splitting a cannoli and washing it down with cola.

"Gloria and I will go and see the swans now. Is that alright?" asked Charlotte, anxious to catch up with her friend who had already taken it upon herself to make for the river. Penworth was somewhat surprised and called out to Gloria who seemed to pay him little mind.

"Yes, of course dear. Go keep an eye on that one, would you?"

Charlotte ran off and Giov lay back down, head cradled in his woven fingers, watching a bright, single cloud cross through an opening of treetops above him; how crisp the deep blue sky seemed this morning; how noiselessly the cloud slipped through its window, pulled from the grass into the air and yet pressed down from the very edge of space.

How would he stay airborne against the Prince tonight?

The evidence crushed down upon him from specific forces high above, he knew; yet something always present, something trusting, also seemed to pull him from the ground floor of disaster up into the ethers of society; a trusted place inside the halls of privilege where he bound himself to the less favorable principles of moral governance; his was the chance, come once in a generation, to force the Council's authority into the Nation's bleakest neighborhoods, while endeavoring to break no eggs about his own house in the cause.

The cloud had drifted through the trees now, cut by the fluttering green coins into its million parts against the brilliant blue.

"What's meant to be is what will be," he thought, "lest I change my way. And that is not to be."

He rolled to his side and read his book; his thoughts now lighter than a cloud, then fell to sleep.

XXXVII

The Princess grabbed Lord Penworth by the arm and shook; "You must wake up!" she cried, "Its Charlotte, by the carousel; bleeding from the head! Wake up!" she screamed, blouse soaked in crimson.

The Duke raced toward the carousel; woke in a fright he stumbled over the berm, crashed through the lemonwood and ran toward two figures by the carousel; one kneeled, the other stood.

On the ground the broken body of a young girl lay, blood formed a circle round her crown into the grass; a bearded man bent above her, speaking softly as her eyes rolled back inside her head;

"Now don't you leave us darling Charlotte, don't you go. Old Gregory has a hutch of hens; you love those hens, this much I know."

The Duke held his tiny Charlotte in his arms; old Gregory standing to the side by now as a park constable came running toward them from the carousel.

"It disturbs me very much to tell what I've seen here today," Gregory told the officer while detained on a nearby bench, "very much indeed. That one so young could raise her hand unto another; and with that stone? What is wrong with this city is what's become wrong with the world."

He broke into tears.

"Where's my Helen!?" he cried, suddenly remembering and shooting to his feet, "Helen!" he shouted.

Helen had by this time, wandered off to the river bank where the swans gathered.

The constable pushed Gregory back down onto the bench.

"Who's Helen?" asked the constable, panning the area with squinted eyes.

A long black limousine pulled up just then from which emerged two well-dressed men and escorted the Princess discreetly from the scene.

141

The old blue truck, now purged of hens, was rolling up the steep incline of a deep green flatbed with the curious image of two mythical lions from an ancient time of Regal majesty painted on the cab door.

The limousine sped down the drive and out from sight.

The gurney was loaded into an ambulance while Lord Penworth, dazed by the terrible events, was led into the back of another black car. Gregory was nowhere to be seen.

The grass was combed, the blanket and the basket cleared; the sun shone like magic through another crystal clear autumn sky onto a sleeping carousel; just another quiet day in Silberfluss Park.

A pair of cygnets left their preening for a swim; the gander first, the second followed him.

End of Part Two

Part Three

I

Once upon a time there was a great old Mountain wanting sorely for a name, but met as yet no traveler come to lend it such, and so sent a river from its crest of melting snow down through the bustling robes of spruce and balsam onto the distant flower covered plain below as artful invitation for whoever might discover such a tonic for their thirst.

But these were lonely times and while the other mountain folk with names like Dom and Weiss and Rosa each had hosted mighty battles in their folds, there were as yet no lips within the winding river's reach; no archers in its festooned fields, nor cavalry among the forlorn mountain's chestnut hills;

and so the sun did rise above and set behind a nameless peak for lo, these many, many thousand years.

One translation tells it as a brave retreat; an army from some distant place divided from its goal; whilst courageously withdrawing through an unmapped pass by chance discovered the unspoiled tracts of brightly colored fields and sumptuous woods cut through by a swelling silvered stream.

These were meadows, streams and woods not scribbled on their map; a wreath of gilded hills and hollows rolling like a carpet wove from articles of tender baby's breath and sassafras, hemmed by towering walnuts, oak and apple branches heavy slung with tempting fruit;

An army here dropped down onto its wearied knee, three hundred thirsting helmets filled to quench the battered day; and so beside these crystal waters paused the bold campaign in paradise.

The General, much convinced he breached the parlor entrance of his Lord, bent up his head unto the sky for prayer, greatly shocked to sight the old peak standing there, above the foothills in its snowy cowl, a great white granite stallion waited for his yoke; the General gasped and stabbed his standard in the ground and they did celebrate a fortnight in the garden they had found.

The stones came next, cut from the quarry's face; some for a great cathedral in the sodden east, up from the musty cellars rose the great *Pontificate*; the others stacked onto a castle for the new King and his

143

legions, vaguely west arose the grand portcullis gate, these both along the graceful banks and swan filled waters baptized thus: the *Silberfluss*.

The woven fields of sassafras and baby breath, the vaporous gold, the speckled red and shaded blues divided next, into some handsome shapes by men with axes, horse drawn ploughs; field stones upturned and stacked in checkered walls bisecting his from theirs and ours from yours;

the curious math imported from the ancient scripts, survived from ancient realms and ancient wars; that one may look down with venal absolution on the beggars face outside the gate; defending access to the surplus bounty of what one rakes in; this the menace of their Western race;

and thus a cloud was stalled high in the air, that choked the sunlight from a hopeful corner on old Pater's face.

For yet inside the deep green darkness whereby the vanquished fields were hedged, survived the authors of another version of a tale just told; of how the pleasant flowers and the orchards of the fields had come to be, and of the venerated mountain staring down into the lea.

For Pater hid some children there, inside the covering fir and spruce; in smoky camps among the fox and mink, migrating with the seasons up and down the icy river's bank; seldom settled long at any single place; for there was no honor owning what defending might disgrace.

Peering unseen from the cliffs and trees the children watched the axes and the horse drawn ploughs; saw the walls and fences, a castle and the great cathedral rise; in sorrow as all liberty and access to their hallowed fields expired;

And pushed into vexation an assault upon the quarry came and went, a futile gesture raised against the conquering sacrament.

But one does not provoke a healthy hive and still expect to track and feed his livelihood in peace; and so the reckless campaign on the quarry changed the world for good, and thus six hundred years would pass with no peace in the neighborhood.

They named them conjurors and savages, philistines and gypsies in their countless yarns and history books; vandals running scrimmage in the unmapped woods; the purloined heifers, the ransacked fields; who drag unwary children from their cabins and their chores for no more trespass than their golden hair and flawless looks; the tenterhooks of wars;

"We are a select people, come in all Christ's innocence to settle in selected land; we, the doleful victims of a culpable and jealous race," and raised a marching army with great cavalries and taut-strung bows, who turned the rustic fields and hills into a multi-blazoned hazard.

Broke-hearted Pater with his newly Christened name looked down in sorrow, apprehending at long last his cousin Rosa's woe.

The campaign drew on simple words to rally such a fight, and thus it was decided that "no good gypsy but is dead" more than the rest sufficed; and they poked their foils and bright fires deep into the murky shaded woods, yet with eight hundred horses, tireless forges, endless kegs of ale, all conspired to the odious phrase, but for the cunning poor-armed rascals in the caves, the General strove to grow his Liege's neighborhood.

And for six hundred years all hope in truce seemed tangled in astuteness whose supplies were in the dearth, the casualty of toxins from an underworld discharged when those first stones were turned out from the green and peaceful earth;

and through the generations tales of anguish told before ten thousand fires, avowed across a million supper plates, both sides concur, no single name more loved or loathed than of the Generals line who call themselves Penworth.

II

A pair of heavy wooden doors crashed open to the entrance of the hospital as seven paramedics steered the gurney to a pale green room, hung in drab curtains, packed with trays and winking instruments; shone like crystals crossed in icy chrome and silvered lights; a tight white sheet stretched across the surface of poor and battered Charlotte's sad new bed. In the hall, a small crowd marshaled where her father leaned against a Uniform for cold support.

Images of swans across the surface of an ink-black pond, exchanged for laughter over breakfast toast and marmalade; the cherished smile wreathed in golden curls all caked in blood; exhausted clock hands by the nurse's station standing still;

A rush of disconnected images inside his crushed, bewildered head.

"You all right, Your Grace?" asked the uniform, "take a seat here."

Lord Penworth failed to answer; did not hear.

"Where is Gloria?" he managed, weakly, "where's the Princess?" He slid down onto the bench.

The Chief Inspector had arrived to the Hospital and studied the Duke from some distance while listening to a second man recite from a palm-held pad; Penworth managed somehow to lift his daze up from his trembling hands to briefly meet the Inspector's imprecise expression.

"The Princess is safe. She's back at the Palace. Can I get you something to drink?"

Again, the Duke seemed not to hear.

"I've got to make a telephone call. I've got to phone someone."

And so saying stood abruptly, making to the lobby where a bank of empty payphones stood along the wall.

"Stay with him."

"Yes Inspector," replied the uniform.

III

Morning in the pleasant cottage, yanked like an old rug from under the good Pastor's malingering feet, witnessed a moderately agitated Frederick dodge two cats and one pair of Gregory's bedroom slippers, snatch the nearest jacket to the kitchen door and fly from the cottage into the old Volvo, waiting obediently in the shaded drive to take him first to the white Chapel under the hemlocks, where a small collection of burlap bags, over-stuffed with donated clothes, blankets and food waited to be driven to the secreted camp in the forest where Grigoras lived with his family and fellow villagers.

The newly ordained Priest was typically late, typically distracted and typically oblivious to any allusion that other people thought these things about him; moving through life typically undisturbed by concepts like punctuality or focus, leaving all custodial attention toward life's minutia to those incapable of appreciating the Lord's finger in every day experience; and so a quiet morning of Schumann and Grieg, of cobwebs and bacon and laundry and the fresh pine air gave sudden way to the

146

stabbing realization of the implication behind the alignment of all those little arms and hands on all those wonderful clock faces on the sitting room walls.

Frederick's anxiety, one might appreciate, was not so much provoked by an imposing expectation for punctuality on the receiving end of his labors, for the recent monthly visits by Father Frederick with donations from his well-meaning congregation had caught the small gypsy village off guard, eliciting a reaction mixed in equal parts gratitude and a certain, measureable degree of resentment at the perceived infringement upon tribal dignity. They had, you see, an acute suspicion of almost every expression of colonial beneficence; attributing the motivating sentiment to some ritual verification of an anointed, albeit compulsive philanthropy; happier it is to live amongst the poor that they might provide for them, yet never inconspicuously so; and in thus, the bitter dynamic of one who receives a gift with little or nothing to exchange.

No, in fact the Minister's urgency rose from the need to be back home from the delivery with time enough to begin what has been a house ritual for over fifteen years, the Wednesday night supper; and tonight was to be a broiled leg of lamb, something special for Gregory after a long hard day in Touchwick.

The jacket he grabbed was one of Gregory's thick knit flannels, not really a jacket at all, but served the purpose of dulling the edge of his clerical appearance enough to dispel his vague intuition that the reference provoked an antagonism that his less-than-vague intuition had just recently begun to decipher.
And it smelled of Gregory.

He arrived within the hour, the Volvo chasing squirrels and crushing fallen branches on the last, wooded leg of the journey; the blue smell of a smoky camp growing stronger as he approached the brush screen and through, to eventually park on a level patch of space a short distance from the spot where such terrible memories are still evoked. It was cold here and activity was sparse.

Grigoras left his trailer, turning to relay one last brusque instruction to his wife inside, and climbed the short ladder to the ground.

"Poppy!" he called, arms stretched wide as he walked across the open space to meet Frederick. The two men embraced and turned back to the Volvo where they took the bags of clothes and food to a table under a heavy canvas tarp set for socializing under protection from the elements. The day was beautiful but the signs were telling Grigoras of inclement conditions waiting to strike within the next day or so.

His trademark pipe hung where one might suppose, and the two spoke uninterrupted for about half an hour, white smoke squeaking through both corners of the round man's whisker-girdled lips.

"This bag of blankets, a nice touch, Father; the clothes? . . . Maybe not so much."

Frederick smiled quizzically, "All right Mr. Grigoras, let me have it. What's wrong?"

It was obvious by his face that Frederick was immediately struck by the profundity of his trespass.

"Oh dear. I sincerely meant . . ." and was interrupted here by the large man's hand which rose to indicate that the topic produced an acute degree of awkwardness for both parties.

"How can Masha, who needs these clothes for her three little cubs, dress them in poor-box when Loka calls her *beggar*? These things, they are deep here; to go naked is sometimes better?" he laughed and shook his head. "*Maybe so* . . . I don't pretend is right; I *know* you! I know you as good soul. How do I explain such foolishness?"

"Pride," replied the priest. "These things have a way of working out. Anyway, enjoy the blankets."

He smiled and nodded to Grigoras, "Now, would you please take me to see Besnik? I brought him another book and then I've got to get back."

IIII

It was a mistake for Kenneth to believe that Alistair was still asleep upstairs, (*the Professor, among many other accomplishments, had written several well regarded essays on the Circadian reflexes of both fauna and flora in the Northern Andes , using himself, a classic insomniac, in one particular study as the subject*), for at the very moment when the front door chimes rang, the Professor was still inside the locked office, where he had trespassed not minutes after hearing the two Penworths leave for the Palace, engrossed in private papers that he found still lying unguarded on the Duke's work table.

148

Hearing his name sung in the hallway just outside the sun-filled room, Alistair coolly replaced the papers to their proper order, stacked the folders as he found them, neatly along the table's edge, satisfied that once again his instincts, but for some minor corollary revelations, were soundly supported by the practical record, and waited with his good ear to the door for the sound of footsteps to fade down the hall.

Kenneth had his hands full at the door as Alistair descended into the front hallway toward the voices which betrayed a tone less familiar than one might expect from so early a call. He slid a palm across his thinning silver mane, above the ear as was his habit, to reassure the placement of his comb, then crossed the carpet to meet Kenneth at the door.

"Thank you, Kenneth; I'll relieve you to more pressing duties."

Poor Kenneth took no unreasonable offence at the Professor's curt interference; and as recourse to his brash dismissal, the good Butler's countenance, unable to unfrown itself, full and likewise counter-dismissed his esteemed *Principal*.

The Professor moved easily to his next business at the door where two well-presented chaps stood abreast out on the portico, fully expecting to be welcomed inside. The garrulous half was not so much imposing as he was tall and polished in a blue-gray window plaid sport jacket and a pair of smartly cuffed black wool slacks; he had a long neck and proportionately tiny ears topped with a small brimmed black fedora.

His companion wore a light suit and glasses with a fashionably sculpted moustache barely visible beneath a crooked nose, napping just above a thin gray lip.

The Professor, to their immediate misfortune, lacked in social etiquette what he in equivalent proportion vindicated with academic brilliance, continuing his inquiry comfortably separated from the odd pair by the intricately fitted door jamb.

"Might we at least come in, sir?"

Alistair ignored the audacious solicitation by turning his attention to the tall man's less eloquent associate, replying, "How can I be of assistance?"

"I'm Special Investigator Jules Ombreux and this is my partner, Private Investigator Marc Damian," the tall one persisted, presenting his card.

"I'm afraid, sir, the purpose of our intrusion is of a most disturbing nature; perhaps best served within the confines of a more discreet milieu; somewhere providing greater intimacy."

"You want to come in; is that what you're saying?"

Kenneth, situated within ear-shot of the front door, skillfully positioned himself between the two parties and resumed his proper role and duties as head butler, inviting the two inspectors into the foyer and stopping, in so far as the Professor's silent, yet admonishing insistence made it fully understood, just short of offering to remove their hats or jackets.

"What's this all about then?" snapped the upstaged academic, "You're inside now; what "disturbing" news? Who sent you two?"

A terrible foreboding gripped the old man's flesh; the figures from Lord Penworth's confidential *Allocation Proposal* still fresh and swimming in his mind.

"And whom do we have the pleasure of addressing?" continued the vocal one.

"I'm the Lord's uncle. Who sent you?"

"Well then, I'm afraid I have some terrible news for you sir. You're grand-niece has suffered a critical contusion earlier this morning. I dare say that her injuries appear, at this moment, life threatening."

Stung by the callous presentation of the events, Alistair placed a hand out to the wall, a ready aid to steady his balance against the weakness now shot through both his knees. Kenneth placed an arm around the Professor's waist and walked him inside to a rather large wooden chair with heavily carved armrests in the likeness of two figures from an ancient time of heraldic majesty; offering the sort of semi-comfort one might tolerate for the brief interval required to remove a pair of muddy galoshes; harsh luxury and little more.

The two men, assuming full advantage of the repercussion from the dreadful news, followed the Butler and the old Scholar further into the house without invitation, having yet to learn that the stunned Professor is more likely at the height of his intelligence, making a formidable and eccentrically cagey adversary.

"A glass of water, if you please, Kenneth," spitefully neglecting to extend any similar offer to his *guests*.

"Where have they taken her?"

"She's at Our Lady of Uncontestable Mercy."

The quiet man had by this time wandered from the doorway toward the staircase, offering himself as wide a view of the house as he could drink.

"It's our hope continued the larger man, "that we might have a look around for the sake of the investigation."

"I see," replied Alistair, his eye drew a bead on the gentleman in the light suit, "so there's an investigation?"

Kenneth returned with a glass of water and word of a phone call for the Professor, "You can take it in the hallway, sir."

"Excuse me gentlemen, I'll be back to escort you out briefly. Until such time, I wouldn't at all mind if your friend over there could restrict himself, with you, back to the area of the vestibule pending evidence of a legitimate warrant to search this home. Kenneth will remain here in the meantime to entertain you with tales from his boarding school days."

Inspector Damian shot a contemptible eye to Jules, who simply grinned at Kenneth.

"So, you're a public school lad, are you?"

The Professor lifted the phone.

"Oh god, Alistair . . . it's Charlotte, my baby!" said the scarcely decipherable voice over the phone.

"Yes, my boy. I'm just aware of it, now. Two inspectors are here with the news. How are you?"

"Alistair, I need to figure this out. Nothing makes any sense. There was a man who saw *everything*! I recognized him immediately. *I know his name*; I'm just having trouble remembering . . . I need to find him. He saw what happened, *Damn it*! . . . *He* saw everything! And now the police are here, pursuing the most offensive line of reason," he paused.

"Can't talk now; have company. Listen to me, son, listen *carefully* and say nothing more," the professor whispered. "Your valise upstairs will be repacked with the folders you left out on the desk. It will be secure and traveling with me. Keep your wits about you. You must meet me in Mayfair. Can we trust Hobbes? Simply answer 'yes' or 'no'."

"I don't know anything anymore, Alistair. I need to see Charlotte. They won't let me in to see Charlotte."

"Yes or No Giov; it's urgent and I've *got* to know." He remained as cool as the situation demanded.

"*Yes* then, of course. Please come down to Our Lady as soon as possible, Alistair. I need you right now."

"Pull yourself together and meet me back in Mayfair. I'll bring Charlotte. I will explain what I know when I see you. *Get out of there*! I repeat, you must leave that place immediately if you hope to ever see Charlotte again.

And *trust* no one! . . . Mayfair in three days, got that? Good bye."

The phone was silent before Alistair heard the iconic click from the other end.

Now, back to formally unwelcome his two unwelcome guests.

V

The cottage had a remarkable way of redirecting the long orange rays of autumn's dusk through the dense and lightly dusted configuration of angled shadows, tossed haphazard by each article of sentiment nailed or balanced, set, hung or leaned inside the cluttered space. No jar, no jacket, book or chair; no clock or swaying pendulum existed independent from the greater tapestry of rust stained beams and shaded tendrils now curled, now cut, then echoed past the brooding windows; stabbed through by a haunting nostalgia from deep inside the most impenetrable depths of an autumn twilight's melancholy.

The clock struck four, and in this singular and pleasant cottage way out on the edge of the purpled forest, any declaration of the hour commenced a full five-minute celebration wherein every spiked wheel and rail suppressed by pawls and cogs and springs discharged; and so a hundred hammers fell onto a hundred bells and bellows piped like gay nuthatches and the crimson cardinals; doors flew out and cuckoos rushed and then snapped shut again; a wooden girl in a painted dress spun circles with her lederhosen *knabe*; a hunter raised his rifle at a dancing bear and always missed, and through it all the knock and click of every clock continued to prepare for the next hour's fête.

Frederick looked up from the open rack where he was basting a fresh leg of lamb, the special meal he saved each week for Gregory's return from the city, hoping to see the headlights down the road approaching home after dropping Helen off into the anxious arms of her waiting mother. It was getting very dark by now and more than time to fire up a couple lamps about the house to chase the thirsty gloaming.

The phone rang and Frederick closed the oven, wiped his hands on a small towel and crossed the kitchen to answer it.

"No Sharon, he hasn't come back yet. I'm sure they went to the park and just got caught in some traffic."

That's right; Gregory mentioned they would go to feed the swans. You know how much she loves her birds! . . . I expect them fairly soon. I'm making supper and it's almost there. I'll *kill* him if it spoils! . . . That's right. Call me when he reaches your house, will you? Thanks. Goodbye now."

Frederick walked into the sitting room and leaned over the andirons to begin a small fire, wondering why his hands quivered the way they did. He stopped and looked over his shoulder to the amazing collection of time pieces humming away on the far wall. It was already ten minutes past four.

VI

The rectory in late afternoon was best understood as little more than a series of comfortably furnished rooms surrounding an enchanted kitchen, which under the finicky stewardship of Miss Crumbe, filled the house with such fragrance as to discourage one from ever exhaling. Dinner would be another hour and already the Archbishop, reduced by this time to the mere servant of his appetite, could scarcely focus on the matters before him on the desk; the North transept renovation, still closed to the public amidst protracted architectural and financial complications; the curious rise in worship attendance against a drop in tithe revenues and perhaps most galling, the arrival of the guest-Bishop from Antwerp in less than two weeks.

153

"This ought to be a circus! . . a small glass of Chianti might serve to quell the pain," he thought to himself, and so convinced, rose from his chair to slowly navigate the intricate geometry of the broad Persian carpet, over to the burl wood cabinet across the room where he filled out his prescription.

Looking to the clock, Bishop Grieble lowered his wireframes to the end of his long, narrow nose and massaged a thumb and finger deep into the sockets of his exhausted eyes. *"Will the Lord's work never end?"*
Breathing deep once more, he raised the glass to his lips and took a swig; half closed eyelids and exhaling, then began the familiar journey back to his desk when the piercing ring of the telephone shattered what little respite he had just then worked so hard to manage.

"Let it ring; I'm done for today."

But on another phone somewhere else in Touchwick, a body was persistent and the Bishop's bell continued to sound for longer than his rather formidable will to withstand, and so swung him into the chair and pulled his paunch up to the desk.

"Hello?"

His Eminence kicked against the floor, rolling his chair back from the desk and opened a thin drawer looking for a small appointment book which held the times and dates of special functions not recorded in his official calendar.

"Your Highness," he replied with no subtle derision, "Yes. I've been apprised; very unpleasant. No media as yet. Very prudent."

Still rifling through the contents of the drawer, Bishop Grieble produced an old prayer card from the service he performed so many years ago for the Duke of Dortpen, Lord Silas Penworth, Giov's father; a rather odd keepsake to be found floating loosely, he thought to himself.

"No, no Eugene. I'm unprepared to discuss this. I'm quite sure that I don't *want* or *need* to know. Listen to me Eugene, I suggest you finish containment of the situation before dividing the spoils; give it a few days and see how the cards play out."

He held the prayer card distractedly, waving it before his face like a painted fan. "No! That's exactly what I warn you against doing. Please listen to me, this can't escalate! So far, we've got a solid enough basis to discredit the man; he's finished."

The prayer card fell from Grieble's fingers like a feather from a molting goose; a click indicating contact with the floor.

"What man?" he slammed the drawer closed, no longer interested in the appointment book, "the media never mentioned a witness, and a *woman?*"

He swallowed the remaining contents of the glass and placed his open hand against the underside of his chin, slowly massaging his throat, continuing to listen as the Prince explained the situation further. A wave of relief washed across his capillary'd cheek.

"And the woman is a *girl?* . . You mean, she's an *idiot?* Oh!, this is priceless. I will say, Eugene, you've certainly stepped in it this time. What about the other witness, the poultry vendor?"

His fingers dropped from his throat and now danced across the keyboard of his cassock buttons, up and down from spirited into dark agitation as the Prince led on; this was not an easy phone call for the nervous man of God to navigate.

"Oh Your Highness, no. I must ask you not to involve the church, and that especially means its Archbishop. No, I think I've heard too much already . . . no. but you're positive you've contained the story of the *imaginary* witness . . . the chicken man? Perhaps it would behoove us to discuss the whole matter later this evening."

He lifted the glass to drink not remembering that he drained it a moment earlier.

"What other thing?" he asked, unsuccessfully attempting to end the call before he found himself somehow implicated in the twisted labyrinth of Eugene's rather reckless campaign.

"The *Allocation Proposal?*! Eugene!" He rose from his chair and asked the Prince to excuse him for a brief moment while he hurried to the burl wood cabinet and brought the whole bottle of Chianti back to his desk. Looking down at the phone, he poured himself a full glass, raised his eyes to the ceiling fan and crossed himself.

"Yes, I'm back. Now, whatever possessed you to trust him to accept the terms? Eugene, that was a grave lapse in judgment. Some people are just ignorant and simply can't be suborned by the mere assurance of success. This is not good; *not good at all*. You must destroy his copy. We must get that proposal back! It could ruin everything! *And with Vandermeyer coming to speak, no less!* Do you understand!?"

Some troubles are even too grave to wash with Chianti. Archbishop Grieble had a sudden and most disagreeable sensation in his belly upon surveying the austere desk top; every page and paper neatly stacked, the edges arranged perfectly parallel to the desk's ornately engraved perimeter; the handsome green glass lamp shade glowing warmly over the leather jacketed cup of pens and pencils, set to touching the blotter's edge at a point of tangent corresponding precisely with the corner repeat of the gilded Greek key which traced its rectangular margin; and set upon the central intersection of the whole affair, a half empty bottle of Chianti rising from its basket like a hungry young bird straining from the nest; a plump glass filled two-thirds beside it. *Ah, were it only hemlock!*

"Two men? Well, did they recover it?" he reached for the glass, "No? Now why would a servant stop two Inspectors? That makes no sense at all," and took a swallow, "Professor Constantine? *Alistair* Constantine? Yes, I've heard of him. What's his business there?

"I see. Well, does he know anything about the *Allocation Proposal*? . . . Good enough. But we should be more sure. I think you owe him a visit; a consolation call, what do you think?"

A soft knock came at the office door, "Are you ready for supper, Your Eminence?" came the frail voice.

"Listen Eugene, I've got to go now. Meet with me tomorrow, then? Splendid. Breakfast; sounds wonderful. See you then. Goodnight."

He dropped the phone in its cradle, reached into his pocket and produced a monogrammed silk handkerchief and mopped his brow. "Yes, my dear Miss Crumb," he shouted, "Supper sounds wonderful."

VII

Chief Inspector Ramseier had a young daughter of his own back in *Luzern* where she lived with her mother and step father for the past three years. His was one of those exceptional split-ups, unspoiled by the residual toxins served up so often in litigious cocktails by legal parasites in oxblood wing tips. She, to her credit, stipulated no punitive settlement,

156

stated his sound judgment and even disposition toward her and their marriage for the record, emphasizing his exceptional qualities as a father.

He related his fondness for his wife, his love for his daughter and even a considerable admiration for his ex's future husband; all captured for posterity inside the stenographers little box with the peculiar keyboard.
It even became, over the brief course of the proceedings, a matter of professional vexation for the solicitors that the divorce proceeded so efficiently; no one quite sure in the end what actually constituted a sound marriage. Inspector Ramseier was a member of the Royal Touchwick Police force and his marriage simply failed to adjust to this capricious circumstance.

He was familiar, as were most, with the Penworth name, and like most, had a fairly specific opinion of the Duke which until this moment had never been challenged into words. He liked the idea of a swashbuckling legislator from a distinguished line of dignified, if not-so-recently swashbuckling legislators, but reserved all conditions of final judgment until his first opportunity to interview the man.

And yet, most incongruent to the inspector's impeccably honed paternal sensibilities, was the claim that a father so evidently attentive and doting could have committed the grievous act for which the Princess has accused him. Penworth was an official suspect of record as of two p.m., in accordance with the Royal Secret Service Department, among the first responders at the scene, and it was the Inspector's responsibility to perform the inquiry within the guidelines so directed; yet something was especially irregular as regards all intuition.

It was with such empathy, coupled with a time honored and conditioned sense of respect for the Nobility that Penworth was thereby accorded an invisible leash; permitted a reasonable degree of freedom to walk about the old hospital halls without suspecting he was under continuous surveillance.

"Where is Lord Penworth now?" he asked the Constable on current assignment, "I'd like another word with him."

The officer unfolded his arms and motioned to the adjacent doorway with his head. "I think he's nodded off; he's been quiet in there for about fifteen minutes."

"Wake him. I want to ask a few more questions."

The constable came back out of the room and made a sign to Ramseier that the Duke was prepared for more questions.

"How's Charlotte?" he asked straightway.

"To be honest, I'd rather you spoke with her attending. Right now, I'd say this case might regrettably escalate from assault."

"*Oh dear God!*" Penworth thrust his face into his palms and sobbed, "and you think I did this?"

"Is *that* what you're concerned about?" fired the Inspector.

"This is a nightmare . . . *a nightmare*. I tell you I was asleep, I was napping when Gloria woke me in hysterics. Please let me see my daughter, I beg you Inspector. *Do you have a daughter?* . . . Please let me in to kiss her."

"First tell me something about this *man*, you know, the mysterious old man you keep going on about."

"But I swear to you! . . . The old man was there; I'd seen him somewhere before..! . . ."

Ramseier stared into the wet, swollen red eyes of his suspect, unable to convince himself the Duke was not entirely deranged.

"It leaves you in quite a hole you know; You see, I'm simply trying to understand why a young girl would invent such a terrible account; it's just fantastic . . . where did your witness disappear to? Why hasn't he come forward? . . and then again, without some corroboration on your behalf, some solid evidence, it puts your word at odds with the daughter of His Royal Highness. Not looking good for you, no; *not one bit.*"

"No more fantastic than the idea that I could have ever raised a hand to my beautiful Charlotte," and buried his face again into the sweep of his open hands, sobbing.

The Inspector rose and instructed the Duke to stand and follow him to the young girl's bed, fully aware of the emotional powder-keg which awaited the grieving man.

VIII

Kenneth rolled the heavy garage door open, making a note to have the squealing wheels greased sometime over the weekend; giving the Professor's old green Citroen a brief once-over, the Butler made his way to open the driver's side door.

He smiled at the screwdriver in the glove box, exactly where the strange old man said it would be, slid it into the cylinder on the steering column, *where once upon a time a key did fit*, turned the handle, pumped the gas and grinned when the engine coughed its way back to life. The old car then rolled back into the white pebbled driveway where Kenneth drove it around to the carport; Alistair waited on the stoop in driving gloves, the Duke's valise clenched firmly in his right hand.

It was a short business to dismiss the pair of irksome agents earlier, as he was quite anxious to catch up with his two dearest friends at the hospital. Kenneth relayed the look of tender strength toward the eccentric gentleman, taking his hand in his own, saying "My regards, if you would be so kind."

The green car drove through the tunneled arch and out to *Dumont Avenue* where it covered the short drive to Our Lady of Uncontestable Mercy in a time that one would need to suspend all credibility not to wager against. There, to his great fortune, was an open parking spot on the street across from the Touchwick Post Office, half a block south of the hospital. He carefully placed the screwdriver on the front seat and closed the door, then walked toward Our Lady of Uncontestable Mercy.

"It's Fortune's move now," he reasoned.

IX

"No Sharon, I'm still not convinced that something's wrong. No, I'm *not* suggesting this is normal. Please, listen to me. It's seven o'clock, I know. But you also know Gregory; he's *very* capable and above everything else, he would never allow *anything* to happen to Helen. I expect a phone call at any moment."

Frederick was lying through his teeth. The leg of lamb was two hours out of the oven and Sharon's anxiety served only to exacerbate the sense of dread his feeble optimism failed to answer.

"I've been listening to the traffic reports and they seem to emphasize tonight's congestion; I'm sure that the two of them are far more agitated then the two of us at the moment. Please Sharon, try to relax. I'm sure that Gregory would have called if something were wrong."

X

Everyone has to visit the lavatory now and again, and now was Constable Olivieri's turn. Alistair's instruction's, though seldom sounded from the depths of *obvious intuition*, had nonetheless merited a remarkable reputation of progressing more often toward a beneficial resolution. It was time to leave the hospital and trust the Professor's direction that he would be reunited with his precious, broken Charlotte, back home in Mayfair. *Home*, where everything would come whole and clean again.

There was no time to waste. His first obstacle, a pair of double doors locked to entry for traffic from his direction, cleared when a young respiratory therapist exiting from a nearby elevator improved his prospects by way of a brief, extempore exchange; keying the door and permitting access for them both.

Penworth made a left at the freshman therapist's first right and disappeared into an unlocked changing room where he reappeared in scrubs, head cap and a face mask of surgical green cloth. Discovering a pair of aviator frame eyeglasses, Giov slid them on his face and finished the disguise, however complicating his efforts by virtue of the severe prescription of the lens, a detail managed by hanging them off the tip of his nose and looking over.

The constable, having drained his bladder, returned to find the room missing one Duke. Fearing first for his pension, the rookie officer, in a controlled panic, discreetly began a search of the ward.

The Duke had simply taken a short stroll to calm his nerves; perhaps he's in with Charlotte right now.

That's where he'll find him, he was quite sure.

It was getting later on and Olivieri was, to his faintest relief, the only officer on duty; the Chief Inspector having left the floor to complete several phone calls over three quarters of an hour earlier. A middle-aged RN at the nurses' station was halfway through her account of the Duke's movements when Olivieri turned to nod toward a surgeon walking past toward the stairwell exit. Turning back to the nurse, he impressed

160

himself by positing questions regarding the witness' perception of the subject's possible state of mind at the time of his elopement.

In the lobby, Alistair was already identified and cornered by the Chief Inspector who found great relief and success in landing such an interview.

"I'm headed back up to ICU right now, if you'd care to be escorted."

"If it's no bother," the Professor artificially replied.

"Come, the elevators are right this way."

As coincidence would have it, a surgeon with a pair of heavily prescripted eyeglasses had just emerged from the stairwell, proceeding briskly toward the lobby exit which was situated only seventy feet from Alistair and the Inspector.

Professor Constantine, recognizing something familiar about the gait of the approaching medic, paused to ask, in an exaggerated volume,

"Excuse me Chief Inspector, but I've parked my car directly across from the Post Office on *Verlaine*, I hope I shan't be ticketed."

"I don't see a problem, Constantine. Bring the ticket down to HQ if I'm wrong, I'll see it fixed."

The surgeon placed his finger along the right side of his nose, nodded to the Professor and resumed his march toward the lobby exit. The professor, passing the doctor, followed Inspector Ramseier to the elevators and up to the drama which awaited them both on the fourth floor.

XI

No proper gentleman's library can conceivably forego the installation of an ornately cradled globe; the Prince's reading room was no exception and the Commissioner, marveling at its eccentric scale, surrendered to his more prosaic impulses and pressed a finger from his right hand onto the Saudi peninsula, giving the great ball a delicate spin. His left hand was, of course, occupied with a cheroot, lending the beguiled lawman a provocative lift with each pull.

"More single malt?" asked Eugene, freshening his own drink at the bar across the great room. Commissioner Dumitru turned his head from the globe toward the Prince, catching his smallest reflection, far away in the face of the large mirror hung behind the rows and rows of bottles lined against the wall.

This one diminutive image; this inverted figure of a tiny man inside a sumptuous space, caught the Commissioner thoroughly unprepared, for outside the surreal atmosphere of the superlative opulence presently smothering the shrewd careerist, Dumitru had always fancied himself a sophisticate, a bit of a raconteur and lady's man. But inside this room, a separate and enthralling dynamic was at work; here was, for this little man, the next logical step up.

"Fresh ice," he answered, strolling across the room to the bar where the Prince acted as publican for the term. The Prince had dismissed his butler, leaving the two men alone to talk, an indication understood by the Commissioner to simply reiterate the singular capacity of his services; undone through disclosure of any kind.

The scotch was delicious, he thought to himself, the cigar flattering, but the secret to realization was in the ice; for it was the ice alone that steered such a treacherous discussion; he was most clever sober, and the mirror, he decided, was quite unreasonable to his exceptional shrewdness.

Walking over to the envelope lying on the small conference table, Dumitru retrieved his glass and joked, "Do you suppose I should count it?"

"Why of course," replied the Prince, "in such private matters as these, I'm left to a singular drudgery that under any other circumstance I'd naturally delegate. I was forced to prepare it myself; and I'm afraid that money, Dumitru, simply *bores* me to distraction. You'll find the instructions in the envelope simple enough to follow. . . . Your glass?"

Dumitru met Eugene at the bar and motioning toward the conference table began, "I only ask because the package startled me by its size. Two and two apparently fits in a much cozier space than I would have guessed, Your Highness."

Eugene smiled and dropped fresh balls of ice from the silver tongs into the Commissioner's glass.

He half expected this.

"Well, I must admit; it seems rather premature; negotiating a raise, first day on the job and all. I commend your enthusiasm Dumitru; no man is prosperous devoid an out-sized appetite. But I must respectfully decline. We have an arrangement. I have your word and that envelope on the table clearly expresses mine. Now stop being unreasonable and come, let's go onto the veranda for some air."

"Your Lordship, must I remind you that many things have progressed markedly since our initial discussion of the terms? I've already needed to recruit a small yet talented team from the within ranks; appreciative and loyal officers, anxious and able, to assist the Crown out of a sense of duty *and* . . . an appropriate degree of compensation."

Filling the glass, Eugene's smile dissolved into a totality of exception which he directed toward the Commissioner, his arm outstretched with a fresh scotch; Dumitru took his drink.

"How many and what is *appropriate compensation?*"

"Four. And as I mentioned, all can be arranged for a mere two and two."

It certainly wasn't the money. ₤2.2m amongst the five of them to contain the situation meant he could still retire into his damp sarcophagus a more prosperous man than he would ever be without the trouble or the expense; this was simply an extemporized resolve to seize upon an adversary's misfortune; a rudimentary commercial decision. No, it was far more a matter of *order*.

He abandoned the bar to retrieve the *Jean Jarreau* he left in the ashtray on his personal desk, silently considering the unpleasant development. Here was yet another example of the escalating erosion of propriety between the classes; a tendency which offended him deeply. Such insolence! Who dares play the Prince?

Re-clipping his cheroot, Eugene drew a flame against the tip and puffed a great cloud into the room, saying, "I'll see it to seventeen; but I caution you, no more confederates into play without first consulting me. And may I also offer this piece of advice?" he turned around, now staring Dumitru down, "You, Commissioner, are the little plover which cleans the crocodile's teeth and nothing more. Cross me with such impertinence again and see how quick the blue-blooded lizard snaps his jaw. Now, some air?"

Commissioner Dumitru looked at his reflection once more, emboldened by the metaphoric progress in the scale of its impression; his elbow on the bar and boot on the rail, he was five times the size he seemed a short moment ago; he took a large swallow and followed the Prince out onto the veranda.

The night was chilly with cold air rolling down from the black mountain cliffs; the veranda awash in blue moonlight. The two men stood near invisible under an artificial grove of potted palms, soon to be taken into the warm botanical gallery for the winter; our two covert entrepreneurs' betrayed by the occasional bright red glow from the ends of their cigars.

"So," he began, "who are these confidantes of yours, Bogdan?" His voice was trained, very smooth; his mind, laced with bitter herbs.

Dumitru thought about the strange circumstances which led him to be sharing a fine smoke and single malt with the brother of the King of Hoffenstein; what his wife would think of him, could he only tell her.

"Marceau coordinates the dispatch staff; instructions are that all media and witness calls are triaged to screen for their relative bearing toward the security of the investigation. Level one calls are managed by Marceau himself. Jakob Fein is instructed to anticipate the family of the two occupants of the work vehicle; the witness' spouse and the young lady; at this time we're unsure if she lives at the same address and are moving as if she did. His instructions are quite clear: stall the husband until the witnesses are safely rendered across the Portuguese border where your staff will receive him."

"Husband? I thought the witness was an old gent; raises chickens, no?"

"Right. Witness is a *homosexual*. Married to a priest named Frederick Pye; Brennan-Pye that is; Frederick Brennan-Pye."

Eugene sipped from his glass. "Does this present any unique complications?"

"That's where I had to bring in Thomas Keynes; seems the *husband's* something of a local hero! Archbishop just collared him."

"*Grieble?*"

"I suppose."

"Oh dear *God*!" thoroughly disgusted, Eugene tossed his cigar into a puddle of rain water collected in the base of the Palm tree, rustling gently in the crisp night air.

"You have a handle on this mess?" he snapped.

"Will I earn your confidence, do you mean? Don't you worry, Your Highness. Anyone who can testify will be deferred for whatever time it takes to insure that no one believes them when it's finally their turn to talk; which brings me to my first observation, if you please, my Lord."

"Yes?"

"Well, as it happens, the girl appears to have the potential to severely complicate an otherwise neat little package. Her disabilities render her *incommunicado* and as such, an impossible witness."

"Yes, I've learned as much; from men paid *far less*, I'll remind you."

"Touché, Your Highness," he replied, "I simply hoped perhaps I could arrange to throw the press some chum while vilifying the other witness in one sweeping gesture of Police efficiency."

The Prince finally allowed the faintest breath of relief wash across the whole tense canvas of his likeness. "See to the matter," and took a sip.

"We're extremely fortunate," the policeman continued, "that Lord Penworth chose such an isolated region of the park for his nap. The department is also prepared to present the weapon at a press conference for tomorrow morning. This should prove the *coup de théâtre*. You see, I have a confession to make," he knocked the ash from his cigar, "I don't particularly care for this Marquis any more than you do; and there's no reason to report on events that never happened, now is there?"

"That's all well and good Dumitru, but I need you to handle *der Kücken-händler* personally. Where is he now?"

"What *Kücken-händler*, Your Highness?"

The Prince, concealing his profound agitation, asked the Butler to show the Commissioner out and paced his study trying to piece the new information into the greater picture. Things were apparently under control for the present; the timetables have simply changed, that's all.

There was now much, much more to discuss with His Eminence than previously considered. Tomorrow was going to be *some* breakfast.

Bogdan sat in the back of the cab, admiring the fabulous lights of the Pont Dubois; how beautiful Touchwick was at night. Here he was, an important, well respected man in the very jewel of civilization; having just finished a private conversation over fine cigars and single malted scotch with the Prince of Hoffenstein. He settled back into his seat, a self-contented smile crossed his face; his eyes closed as he imagined how the money would change his life.

XII

Giov sped down *Dumont* hoping to retrieve some clothes and the pistol; his mind now freed somewhat to begin reorganizing the days grotesque events along a timeline at particular odds with the presentation against him all afternoon by Inspector Ramseier. The Citroen was a five speed, engineered before the advent of synchro-mesh gearing, presenting the city driver with a terribly unnerving growl-shift from time to time; Giov was spared none of the grinding.

There was a tall, well-dressed man on the sidewalk in front of the townhouse, he wore a blue-gray jacket and a black hat; a cigarette pinched in his fingers. The Duke decided to pass the townhouse and circle the block. Who was this man? Was it really so strange, in a city of a couple hundred thousand people, for someone to pause in front of his townhouse to have a smoke?

He seemed far less capable of distinguishing legitimate suspicions from the false illusions born of tangled nerves. He could see a squad car parked in the archway tunnel as he passed the house. There was no block to circle he concluded, heading for the *Pont Dubois* and his home in Mayfair.

I now trust you with all that I have, Alistair.

XIII

It was just after two o'clock on the morning of October the twenty seventh, when the Archbishop was roused from his sleep by the telephone. He had been losing his battle of wills with that damn bell all day and night; he cursed, resigning himself to unfold an arm from within the warm confines of his comforter and feel, spider-like, for the incessant receiver. Placing it against his ear, the half-woke Minister of Virtue, thus began his inquiry, "Yes? Who in bloody hell is this? Can't you see what time it is!?"

"Your Eminence. You are speaking with the Prince of Hoffenstein. I have some news that won't wait for breakfast."

Grieble rolled the covers from his chest and swung his thin legs over the side of the mattress and sat upright. "What is it Eugene?"

"It's the girl. The charges against Lord Penworth have just been raised to murder. There's a manhunt combing the entire city for him as we speak. He's eloped on foot from *Our Lady*; we've got his house under close watch. He can't escape."

"*Heaven help us*," whispered the Archbishop of St. Pontificate.

XIIII

The Office of the Söfenzin Royal Police Headquarters was crowded by the only two desks needed to administer the services of the entire on-call duty roster at any given time. The five rifles in the gun case remained behind a warded lock whose latch was turned but four times a month outside game season for the single purpose of a weekly regimen of oiling and cleaning.

During the autumn and winter hunting months however, it was unlikely to find one or two not missing from behind the glass, wandering somewhere in the foot hills of Mt. Pater, where the stock pile of the Department's humble cache of ammunition was provided the disbursement required from overflowing the munitions chest. The steady arrival of a modest supply of replacement rounds was arranged by the Chief of Police, Officer August Richter, another recently reinstated celebrant at St. Humility under the Hemlocks; eager enough to patronize Jacob Mueller's General Store in town, whose family coincidently celebrates the same late service each week in an adjacent pew.

Every officer, by their own volition, also owned a personal handgun which town ordinance forbids from being carried while on-duty, with the singular exception of Chief Richter, a quiet but capable man who used the license to parade a pearl handled .44 magnum in a shiny black, custom-made holster tooled, on the occasion of his having made Chief of Police nine years ago, by a very grateful Romani craftsman for a singular act of compassion which also helped to neutralize most tensions between the two bordering communities for the past decade.

Outside the small Police Station was a white painted bench set on a tiny porch under the eave, where Frederick and Sharon sat together under the bright porch light, waiting for any news to be dispatched from Touchwick which could help explain the terrible circumstances which brought *the Gay Priest* and *the Girl's Mother*, as the two were regarded by the town, together at Police Headquarters at two o'clock in the morning.

The door opened and the Desk Sergeant emerged to inquire if more coffee would be welcomed.

"Oh, and it's a bit premature yet, but Inspector Keynes from Touchwick has just informed me of some good news regarding the discovery of a girl who fits your Helen's description, Sharon."

A shock of elation wrought with horror chilled the hopes of both sad figures on the bench; for in that single phrase was a tantalizing promise framed in the bleak omission of any explanation for the strange circumstance that she might be found with no mention of Gregory.

Sharon wept.

Frederick gripped her hand, sitting upright, stared into the blank darkness of the early morning air, struggling to keep Sharon from having to see his own tears build to overflow down across his face.

"I'll put these coffees down here for the both of you." He placed two small cups on the porch railing. "Why don't you just consider going home to get some rest? There's nothing I can tell you here that I can't tell you just as well over the phone. Please, do us a favor; you'll get the flu sitting out here all night like this. I'll send the squad car immediately when something turns up."

Sharon collapsed into Frederick, a gesture he understood to suggest that it was his correct but painful decision to initiate the journey home.

And just like this, the jubilant hood of Death descended to bud inside these two defenseless forms.

XV

Alistair waited in the back seat of the car, while Kenneth made his way round to the driver's seat and then followed the long white hearse out to Mayfair, young Charlotte's true home. Here she will be placed amid her ancestors in the family plot where she rightfully belongs.

Present among the long train of state cars and private limousines making the journey out to Hoffenstein's rustic perimeter were Their Royal Highness' and an extremely morose Princess Gloria, Prince Eugene and Lady Belladonna, Lord Waxman and of course, His Eminence, Archbishop Grieble, who agreed to assist the Service, scheduled to be led by Father Frederick Brennan-Pye, the Hero Priest and neighbor.

A line of seventy vehicles made the three hour drive without stopping, as the motorcade was ushered in every case through the intersections and highway entrance ramps by coordinated traffic patrolman waving white gloves and blowing into silver whistles. Through each small town and village, streets were lined by mourners waving the heliotrope and puce flag of Hoffenstein in honor of the tragic life and death of one so young.

It is an uncompromising condition of the human character that an event so desperately solemn does, for its brief duration, eclipse all thoughts of correlated intrigue; freezes the clock from its stalwart curiosity to linger in the moment; no thoughts of the case, no mention of murder or the absence of the poor girl's father to desecrate this somber passion play; *but that the gaze of fathers on their daughters did with dumbstruck tongues and weak translations lay.*

The sun burnt through another crisp blue sky onto the tiny hole where a sorry nation prepared to lay one of its children; drifting clouds dotted the ground in slipping sleeves of shade.

Felis, hours dry from his shower, looked from a top floor window through the thinly parted drapes far out upon the crowd assembled round the slightest hole he ever carved; *first pit I ever dug to lay a diamond in.* Sadness seemed as loyal to the young man as a stray-dog.

Closing the curtains, he went down the back stairs, made his way through the house and out the kitchen door to reach a path beyond the line of sight from way out where the party assembled for the memorial. The police had situated themselves *en masse* to apprehend the Duke should he be brazen enough to make the day. There was no reason to suspect, within the confines of their limited reserves, they should allocate manpower to areas of the property with no view.

Stealing to the back of the garage, Felis entered through an old door, until recently congested with antique artifacts of husbandry and cultivation, cleared yesterday in preparation for the suspicious undertakings of the young fugitive and his new mentor, the faithful

169

Hobbes, already waiting efficiently beside the deep green Land Rover which split from the motorcade upon arriving.

Hobbes peeled his driving gloves from his fingers and unlocked the rear door of the truck, motioning to Felis that it was time to slide the beautiful Maplewood casket out from the back and place it in the waiting space beneath the loft which they concealed again with ancient artifacts of husbandry and cultivation.

XVI

Bishop Grieble read the service before a mountain of stuffed toy animals and flowers; exhibiting every molecule of discomfort a body should expect from one so dependent on exacting preparation and substantial forewarning; for Father Frederick, having begun his third day with no significant, tangible progress in the mystery surrounding the cruel and terrible disappearance of his beloved Gregory; the unusual discovery and reunion of an extremely agitated Helen with her mother; being too despondent, regrettably declined the offer to perform.

The little white lacquered box was lowered into the earth; Bishop Grieble swung the smoking thurible and made the sign, signaling the lines to form and pass Alistair, the closest living *relative* available to receive the guests who then proceeded back to their cars after tossing the tributary pinch of soil down into the hole. Gloria, as it turns, took ill and was being tended the duration of the service in the Royal limousine.

There was no Press to dip their pens in such sad ink; no shutters snapping beyond the patrolled property gates about half a mile away.

Alistair had uninhibited occasion during the ordeal to match glances with King Maximillian, whose present complexity of emotions confused him but for the singular sentiment which rose with clarity above the fray; that he intended to talk privately with the distinguished Professor before the Royal limousine left Mayfair again for Touchwick.

XVII

The vast fields below him curved within a bright white bowl, now
reflected through a wreath of dangled chestnut leaves;
Giov, grief struck stood inside its crown; lost among her thick branches,
looking through the space between the sky and she far off; the fields and
trees; the tiny, fresh dug hole and he. And to feeling anything was by this
time no more capable of him than should the bright blue sky reach down,
if called, from the farthest stratosphere, and stroke his face.

There was no longer any more to the entire story than this; and here against his moistened fingertip, a small white lacquered box pushed ever far and far and far away . . . to disappear.

"This image I perceive at every pause in vague astonishment, behind these eyes pressed into my blood soaked hands, caught unawares and speechless inside a jar;" he mourned, "the cursed day light bouncing here to there, mad as a fly against a pane of glass; the unremitting silence in my aching skull; unaware if what I crave remains just outside of reach because my ear is closed or my tongue too thick; to learn you cried and I turned drunk and anxious in my sleep.

"This bright, clear, cheerless day in the country, just standing there, menacing in its silence; its deep perspective; its dead silence.
The cows and goats way out on the grass, mere holes in cow shapes and goat shapes; and Poppa, up here hidden in a shade tree all confused and spangled like a gypsy tambourine; whipped by the sunlight and this cruel autumn breeze;

"How much color, my love, is already gone away by your side by now? The reds I see are orange brown; the yellows and all the splendid yellow seeds and yellow bangel-ettes the other children sit down on clouds in the long soft grass upon?

Where would you hide these? . . . and why and where upon?
You know you needn't go so far away to prove my love for you."

The kind Duke overcome; convulsed a tear that drew a bead from his chin to the bed of moss way down.

"Look there!

"my young girl cries just now for help to put her shoes on the proper feet;
and not a single sound from there but the light on her small beautiful feet.

"Oh, dear babe! let a time before I ever mentioned you, before they ever spoke your name, let it carry you softly, oh dearest God! Carry her to *you!* Mary, for safe keeping; my dear, *broken* little girl, my babe; across the field, far across the white grass;

"See now! . . . my eye plays tricks, for she is there without her tiny shoes again;

"and Poppa, silly Poppa; hiding in his yellow chestnut tree; who loves you, my *most Precious*, evermore, with all of life's grotesque, heart broke fragility."

Eventually climbing down, Giov went back to wait, deep into the wood.

XVIII

Bob was a patient man who never regretted the situation he and Sharon shared, raising a young girl like Helen; happy working at the automotive shop, dispensing gas when he wasn't changing someone's oil or plugging a hole in some pitiful tire. He was *not*, as the good folk from the church socials used to carp, "a very ambitious provider".
No wonder the girl turned to be such an animal.

The cabin was not quite a cottage, needing windows on at least two more walls, I suppose, to be considered such; and despite the rather rustic material from which it was constructed, was exactly what Sharon considered cozy. They only needed one bed after all, (Helen hasn't slept alone but one night since the day she was born), hid behind a curtain which described the nether reaches of the kitchen and the main room where she placed two chairs below the window and a porcelain lamp with a paper shade by which she passed the quiet hours listening to the radio and watching Helen read her upside down picture books. Helen simply took over Bob's chair when she got older; he's been gone a long time by now and would want her to sit there.

It was the third night after Helen was found and returned home that Sharon, now temporarily housebound by her daughter's freshly minted, obsessive agitation at any suggestion to going out of doors, sat mending the buttons on another one of the young lady's sweaters while listening to *Mystery at Seven*, a radio program which recently replaced one of her favorites and for which she had not yet formed an opinion.

Sharon watched as Helen rubbed her thumb back and forth across the page, when the radio program switched to another scheduled commercial break, explaining how Lesaffre has been distributing the finest yeast products for over one hundred and fifty years; how Botot natural toothpaste promises to whiten her smile and Michelin provides added years of safe, pleasurable motoring with superior steel belted tire technology.

172

The station then checked the time and briefly reviewed the four top news headlines, including the arrival of Bishop Vandermeyer next week and some mention of a truck being towed from the Silberfluss, north of Touchwick, that evening while divers were busy searching for survivors.

" . . . and now back to your scheduled program, *Mystery at Seven . .*"
Sharon hugged her baby, eyes filled to spilling, and dialed Frederick on the telephone.

She tried three times; receiving no answer, surprised Helen with another embrace, kissing her eyes.

XIX

The ancient face of the beautiful silver river would tell Chief Inspector Ramseier absolutely nothing of what he desperately wanted to know about the cold wet world which raced on beneath the rippling strobe-red surface, out from which the tow-winch almost finished pulling the old blue truck.

Water blasted from the cab through the door seams, no longer packed by the rubber stripping long since cracked and rotted away while dozens of emergency personnel, some dog handlers, combed the shores and grassy margins of the bridge and roads around the scene.

The Police Commissioner's car pulled up just now on the shoulder of the road above the banks where the operation was currently under way. Both front doors opened and two gentlemen stood out from the car. One was highly decorated and wore the Commissioner's cap; the other officer returned to the rear door and opened it for a frail man wearing the cassock of a priest. The three men began their descent down the slippery banks of the Silberfluss.

"Matches the report of that missing delivery truck . . .some old . . . *I don't know*, What in hell would you call them? Chicken Men, I suppose?. . . Well any way, it's definitely his vehicle."

Commissioner Dumitru turned to where Ramseier was pointing, "No body yet?"

"*Poulterer*," whispered the Priest.

XX

"It does me a profound honor to accommodate you, Your Highness." He stiffened his frame, locked heels and gave a quick, respectful bow of the head, "Please allow me to see to your drink. . . *Hobbes*?"

"Oh relax Professor! On such occasion; simply remember me as Max, the spoiled prince who once filled the conservatory with a thick brown smoke on a vandalous lark. I'll not tell."

Prince Eugene and Queen Francis both winced at this. Lady Belladonna, ever facile, contrived a sudden though ostensibly intense fascination with landscape painting; became much too absorbed to acknowledge the jibe.

"So, that *was* you? *Terrible*, Max. . . .*very terrible*. Could have died happy never knowing. You destroyed my *Cuphea carthagenensis,* you know. Never tried replacing it; *too rare*. A first rate scandal!"

The Professor could not hide the sincerity of his disappointment in the amused King's confession.

Prince Eugene, as it happened, was far too suspicious to relax. This Professor Constantine was the true *unbestimmt* in his design. With every other aspect falling neatly into place, the Professor represented a unique conundrum; more of a threat by what *wasn't* known of him than what has been recently gathered about him. Either way, his familiarity with the Duke was enough to include him as a subject of immense interest with regards to recovering the *Allocation Proposal* before his brother sniffed it out.

Among the many regrets and irritations in the ambitious Prince's life, the recent ability of Lord Grimstone to leverage his confidence in the *Proposal* against the better instincts of his own aspirations was first and foremost salacious. He would, in due time, see the Councilor answer for his egregious advice, but first he must secure that copy of the report, safely back in his possession; all else will wait.

"Well Professor, I must relate the consequence of my own failed judgment; having incorrectly gambled on the cathartic power of confession. I do sincerely apologize. There is of greater substance however, the matter of the young child passing over; *tsk tsk*, such an unspeakable tragedy. May I, at this heartrending time assure you, dear old, friend, that the entire resource of the crown stands behind you in your grief; which I assume, in the eccentric manner given you as an academic includes making sense of the insensible."

Eugene, at this, coughed himself into a fit, which timed perfectly with the arrival of Hobbes and a small tray of refreshments.

"Perhaps Your Highness would care to sit down," offered the benevolent Butler to the terse rebuke of the Prince, whose ghastly behavior served to wrench Lady Belladonna out finally from the rendered Dedham countryside and back into the conversation, suggesting, "Shouldn't we be as concerned about poor Gloria, outside waiting all the while in her sorry state? There's really not much more we can do about her friend now, is there?"

Alistair's head snapped to stare into the eyes of she whose lips had just executed such egregious sentiments. He placed his trembling glass down toward the side table where Hobbes reflexively slid a perfectly timed coaster.

"There is a good deal of sense in this" he replied. "Our nation's youth must suffer our due diligence or spoil in the brine." - the Lady far too self-distracted for the gibe to sting.

"Alistair," the Monarch spoke, "I'm sure you'd like to have some time; we've a decent drive besides."

He took Alistair's hand inside his and bade off; his entourage behind.

Hobbes returned to the library after showing His Majesty to his limousine, atypically unburdened by a tray of fresh drinks. The Professor was slumped into a chair before the fire, his lips moving to form the silent speech he was reviewing with himself. Hobbes quietly made his way to the windows where he began drawing the drapes against the late afternoon sun.

"It's a puzzle, Hobbes."

The good Domestic, having completed the full round of windows, made his way to the fireplace, adding more fuel and stirring old coals. It would be a considerable oversight to ignore his gnawing uncertainty as regards his own future. Jobs in his line of work, though available, seldom ignore the surreptitious intangibles; the superstitious forces always trying to gain access into other people's homes; one tragedy expends the family and moves to feast upon another. These are the habits and traditions of country life; no purse however large or small has yet divulged a secret sense against it. Hobbes was little more than bad meat now, a sobering consequence to many faithful years of service.

"Yes sir," he spoke as from a foreign place, "a devilish puzzle."

The Professor reached out for his glass, spoiled now by the melted ice; Hobbes in reflex once again acted on cue, made his way down to the galley for a fresh tray of drinks.

Oh, such sadness in the canton today; the world of shadows has for once outpaced all joy inside of Mayfair.

Alistair stared into the fire, lost completely to his thoughts; unfolding his right hand which he just now used to bid farewell to a King; where sat a regal calling card, prepared to further weave the day, already overwhelmed in spells of evil and despair, this one small light of hope; a calling card on whose white face there was embossed the Imperial cipher: a rack of colored billiard balls.

XXI

The small wagon stood barely visible on the path outside the garage; the moonless night was stabbed by a seasoned chill, forming thin ribbons of vapor to rise from the mount's wide nostrils. The solemn walk to the second hole commissioned in a single day was far enough to keep the most discreet surveillance at bay; the small parade, a cook, a hand, a butler, a fugitive and a professor; a solemn pageant on a star filled night; a maple box rolled indigo on the horse drawn wagon in the light-starved night; a little girl rolled to her secret final bed to rest.

In a tiny clearing through a country mile under hemlock boughs, the horse stopped obedient near a fresh dug hole. Out from a dense patch of oldest brush, the figure of a Duke showed himself like ink against a backdrop just inside the twilight zone; this figure who bent over the maple box and pried its lid. There was never so much sorrow gathered in one single place; a kind and broken man of honor dripped his tears onto the pale white child's blank and lifeless face. He bent into the casket, stole one final kiss.

The hole was closed, Alistair and Hobbes, with an arm draped 'round each their stubborn necks, walked the Duke of the Dortpen through the shadows back to his bed for one last night; dividing watch amongst them until morning light, when out through the tunnel, dug for safe exodus from assaulting savages and gypsies some four hundred years hence; out through the tunnel, Lord Penworth would initiate the next installment of his everlasting flight.

XXII

"You need permanent asylum my son!" declared the Professor in the dim lit galley where they lay their tired friend down, "and this thing cannot wait!"

Hobbes nodded once again in total agreement, "We can hide you until we arrange some final passage."

"Passage? There is no passage! I need to fully clear myself," his eyes now four days wet and swollen red by grief and constant worry.

"This nightmare is a dream from which I must awake or be consumed. There is no hiding here. The Prince will sooner raze this house and salt the fields. Help me find an old man who represents all true witness to the crime I did not do; who has for reasons I can't comprehend avoided every chance to clear my name!"

Alistair's face suddenly awoke; like when a single thought amalgamates a dozen baffling and arbitrary cues.

"By God! I think I begin to appreciate! *Giov*, listen to me very close and carefully. You say you've seen this face before; the man who knelt over Charlotte on the ground?"

"I'm certain of it! If I could only recall . . . it's becoming more and more like a dream, each day that passes."

"Was the man alone?" the Professor continued, "Was there a young lady of a strange, dissociate temper, perhaps?"

"No, he was definitely alone, Alistair. He knelt over Charlotte, trying to tell me something. Do you suppose he did it? Did he murder my baby?" Giov shouted, "Oh my God! I'm so *responsible*! I'll kill him with my naked hands, I will!"

Hobbes joined Alistair restraining Penworth. "Calm yourself son, *calm yourself*; things are beginning now to fit together somehow, though I can't yet see the whole picture. Are you sure you remember the face?" Hobbes released his tight hold of the Duke, apologizing.

"I'm certain as I'm innocent."

"Then let me try this; did he have anything to do with chickens?"

And thus the entire sketch of stray coincidence took its fledgling form from here; Giov purged his memory of first meeting the man named Gregory down the road through Söfenzin, alongside the brilliant Professor's recollection of a situation which has played with modest interest on the inside pages of the local press; his only clue the tragic concurrence of place and time.

Such correlations are never quite so obliquely noted in the academic's mind as same such things tend to be among the throng.

"There is a point at which these two ostensibly separate activities share a common horror, if you would forgive my speech; and this point is where the witness that you tell about has left behind a next of kin equal in his sense of loss and desperation as your own.

"Your *witness* Giov, I deduce, is that same Poulterer, who entertained young Charlotte on the road that day in the company of a young woman with a similar habit; whose disappearance must have been connected to our recent travesty; who leaves his husband, Father Frederick mad with grief; who could not make, for suffering's sake, dear Charlotte's special service today."

All was progressing far too rapidly for Hobbes, one minute nervously wiping the kitchen counter, the next preparing a kettle for tea, the next dropping ice in a highball for a stiff Tom Collins to the distraught Duke's taste.

"It was the connection between the disabled young lady's happenstance to have been together with your witness that same morning on a delivery of forty birds from Söfenzin all the way into Touchwick, when she became separated from him only to be found and returned the next day, while his delivery truck was pulled from the Silberfluss only last evening."

". . . as I mentioned, this Gregory wasn't the neglectful sort," muttered Giov.

"And so I gathered. *How* and *when*, then, did these two become divided? This is all beginning to indicate an atmosphere most sinister and essentially dangerous the closer we come to the actual facts."

Hobbes turned back to the counter and prepared a second Tom Collins, this one for himself, then asked, "All well and good Professor, but you seem to overlook one little thing," he took a swallow.

"And that is?" inquired the academic.

"Well, *and I'm no scholar as you know*, but you keep removing access and motive, eliminating suspects; then who but *nobody* did the deed?"

This talk would prove too much for anyone to bear, just having laid such precious cargo in the ground; Giov sat head down, arms wrapped tight around his waist. Alistair gestured to the well intentioned butler that perhaps they stop or take the conversation off beyond the grieving father's ear, when Penworth startled both by raising his head imploring, "Yes Hobbes, go on!" Alistair nodded to Hobbes.

"Well I haven't much more to contribute I'm afraid than this: Somewhere someone sleeps these nights with memory enough to drive a General mad; and great efforts, it would seem to me, have been employed to sanitize the trail."

The Professor nodded grimly.
"Precisely, my dear friends. The woods are now chockfull with hazard."

"In light of your startling interpretation," the Duke spoke up, "or more accurately, your revelation of the facts, I can only accept my next responsibility as a private visit to Father Frederick and advise him of the most plausible truth. His whole world might well be trapped forever in a vicious lie; I at least owe him the attempt. Oh, Alistair, when may I find time or place enough to grieve?"

Lord Penworth walked briefly from the house into the night to think.

XXIII

It was an unfortunate consequence of the effectiveness of the Tom Collins that Hobbes did indeed forget his obligation, woke on his watch by the loud, sunrise pounding on the front door of the house where Chief of Police August Richter announced himself. The force was small but reinforcements from the National Guardsman made the dispatch an impressive total of nine constables and agents, already positioned strategically around the home and immediate grounds. Escape for the Marquis, whose presence was most assuredly the conjecture of some anonymous scoundrel of influence, seemed nigh impossible.

Hobbes handled the front door with a progressively proficient alacrity, while to his enormous credit, the Professor provided every aid to the successful spiriting of the troubled Duke through the tunnel and off into the high fields; far off into the dense wood; far from the police and the ancestral home he left behind; now a tiny spired silhouette in grey against the wide expanse of dawn's first light; far from any knowledge if or when they should ever reunite; the farthest of far.

"Perhaps you'd like to come around to the barn and answer a few questions," suggested the good Sheriff, leading Hobbes around the great house, along the driveway leading back about the greenhouse and down a short ways to the first stable past the car garage.

There were four uniforms milling outside the stable; the grim expression of the first copied directly onto the face of the second, continuing without variation to the last. An attitude of protocol reinvested itself among the clutch on first sighting of the Chief with the pearl handled revolver. "Martin still inside?" the Chief asked a young female officer.

"Sargent Martin's in there still" she responded, circling around the others to open the door for Richter and the Domestic.

The pervasive sound of police prattle and the surreal events of the past few days had taken their toll on old Hobbes; for so many years devoid any influence or reference to or from the department of law enforcement had left him entirely incapable of processing the intense concentration of police activity monitoring his every move over the past week; he simply couldn't remember ever bothering to call upon their services in the past.

How in God's name have they trapped Lord Penworth like a rat inside his own compound? . . and why was it so *Goddamned* necessary to bring poor Hobbes directly to such a scene of unqualified humiliation; *such abusive disrespect indeed!*

"What is the purpose of this exercise?" he demanded of Richter, stopping in his pace.

Chief Richter turned around and looked the Butler up, suspiciously annoyed, "I don't particularly care to be dragged out from my home before a proper sunrise or a cup of coffee, Mr. Hobbes." He put his right hand on his hip, letting it rest on the carved pearl handle of his signature. "But I go where the dereliction is; where the trouble just seems to sit and beg for me to be. And *Trouble* Mr. Hobbes, doesn't wear a bloody watch, and I certainly can't apologize to you enough for that."

180

He grabbed the handle of the door and pulled it open, turning back to Hobbes, "Now if you'll simply come and identify the body, we can all make it home before noon."

Hobbes slowly grabbed the knob of the door, stung by notice of a "*body*" and followed the Sergeant into the dark stable, lit brightly across the roof and rafters by a host of portable spot lamps at the far end of the murky stable row, past a series of head high partitions; the sound of more babbling from the waiting team of officers. There's been far too much tragedy these last few days, he thought, unprepared to suffer any more.

The last stall partition finally gave way to the well-lit, open space of the barn, where another group of four uniforms now milled within a ring of hay bales neatly stacked, way high up, stacked to reach the loft; neat bales stacked like Jacob's ladder to the highest loft from where a rope slung down just long enough to free the poor black African; his chest-high boots left to finally swing free, in peace for all eternity.

There's been too much description by this time of sorrow; I rest this piece, saying only that his kind new friend, poor Hobbes, the faithful mentor to the young man in Christ, suffered nothing less than an un-mendable grief.

XXIIII

The tunnel exit employed to full advantage the estate's exceptional disposition toward each landlord's most surreptitious endeavors, depositing its inhabitants far across the compound to a discreet but unremarkable opening in a craggy fold of Pater's limestone robe.
A track of twisted crab-apple, drizzled in honey suckle, populated the summit twelve feet above a small meadow dense in sassafras, briar and scrub cedar, stretching a short sprint from the edge of a green and unnamed wood, providing continuous cover for most of the four mile hike to the threshold of the dark Dortpen forest proper.

Begun by Lord Gerald Neuhaus Penworth in the late seventeenth century, completed by his son Albrecht Neuhaus some sixty five years later, the tunnel served to provide that certain remedy from restiveness required of a man so frequently engaged in ambulated matters of State and battle; so infrequently at home.

Bands of vandals from far up the Silberfluss would come, you see, out from the black wood to chase across the barren fields in a day when little more stood in the whole region than the one great house on the hill. The wives and children left at home by the wayfaring Dukes were a persistent distraction which no domestic force, regardless of number or loyalty could effectively neutralize. And for this reason Lord Gerald initially commissioned the great tunnel.

Lord Penworth slipped out from the passage, turning back in the day-break gloam to grab the back pack from Alistair who was himself just climbing from the hole. The sky was purple and red; two silhouettes, no less part of the entire hushed surrounding splendor, silently exchanged farewells; the elder took the bereaved with a hand onto his should saying, "Hold."

Giov slung the pack, "Too much to fix, Alistair; too little time. There will be dogs soon enough my friend," and turned to leave.

"I *will* show you this, however," the Professor pressed.

He produced a small white card from his vest pocket, embossed thereon a rack of multi-colored billiard balls. "How do I use this?" he asked.

The Duke turned to his mentor and replied, "With every caution. The mirrors have ears in Touchwick, I'm afraid; and Max can be quite a devil himself sometimes."

"I will uncover your innocence."

"I like you much better chasing at weather balloons around the Antarctic; until then," and Giov made his way into the woods.

XXV

It was a busy Sunday outside the magnificent Cathedral where another crisp Sabbath morning intensified the harsh engraved depressions cut by centuries of rain and ice across the complex array of dimpled curves and deep, thick creases on her ancient face and ribs; scores of Touchwickians milling about on her wide stairs. The circus had come to town.

Today's sermon was to be given by the visiting Bishop Vandermeyer from Antwerp, an older, thin framed activist who had once again made headlines for his recent explosive interview in *WHEN*, the enormously popular weekly magazine, regarding his call for widespread outrage to the recent trend in world economics away from social programs for the poor, the dismantling of the middle class and toward riskier investments in longer term adventures for essentially private interests.

Touchwick's recent prolonged rate of high unemployment and looming recession provided the perfect backdrop for such an event; while still evolving, the scandal of the most progressive Member of Council, Lord Penworth, simply amplified the public's acute sense of powerlessness and despair.

Even Archbishop Grieble was unable to mollify his congregation's demand for the reformist Bishop's appearance behind the lectern.

Vandermeyer's arrival on Wednesday appeared in every respect to have been coordinated with an eye to outwitting all unwanted attention from pesky antagonists, anarchists or the Press; he drove himself across the *Pont Dubious* in a dull red, late fifties Volkswagen with a leaking tan colored convertible top, split-seamed seats and two hub caps; a vehicle which certainly turned no heads.

The dash was the cracked and brittle consequence of time under direct sunlight, which permitted him to excavate a small hole just left of the steering wheel, large enough to protect such profane valuables as loose change for tolls or an emergency guitar pick.

The car also blew an oily screen of faint blue smoke, stunning the occupants in all vehicles caught most unfortunately to the rear, in a throat coating, lung filling film of improperly digested fuel exhaust, which he swore one day to have fixed, provided the disposable credit miraculously manages, in metaphorical fashion, to waft his way. Grieble's impatience for the visit to become another forgotten aberration of the past cannot be over-emphasized.

A spectacle of vibrant anticipation could be observed outside the great carved doors this Sunday morning, where the whole of Touchwick's irascible periphery, it would appear, funneled inside to satisfy the grave and unique purposes that combine, divide and isolate us each and all as brothers and sisters of some ill-defined and tessellated whole.

Dark limousines pressed with an obliquely veiled contempt through the eclectic throngs of celebrants and the curious; media cameras bobbing through it all like the ridiculous papier-mâché masks on any Fat Tuesday on Bourbon Street. A few dozen placards nailed to hand-held sticks with messages that ranged from *Spread the Wealth* and *Jobs not Dole* on one side of the police cordons, answered on the opposite by boards reading *Say NO to Socialism* and *Vandermeyer Go Home.*

Vendors of fruit, hot cakes and coffee were out-selling Monday morning by the trains.

Here, before his God, the old minister from Antwerp climbed to the pulpit and took his place at the rear of a parade of venerated orators come through history before him; trying to impart some small insight, some toe-hold toward understanding a system so large, so unethical, so inconsistent and so old as to dwarf both definition and solution;

but in the act, attempt, at the very least, to continue exciting through an eloquent sermon those very passions desperately amiss in the voiceless, powerless mob mixed in among the few power-brokers still brave enough to take communion in the great Cathedral of St. Pontificate this wonderful autumn morning; to reaffirm the classic *inalienable right* and expose the mechanisms of uninhibited voracity and self-coroneted righteousness and by so doing, strategize the *Great Push* back to the fundamentals of Christian equity.

"*That* some will most *assuredly* overreach *His* greatest commandment, *warp* the boundaries, tip the scales of our most sacred contract, our *humanity*, toward a singular, highly focused dysfunction is all the *Science* you or I will ever need to over-fill the most impassioned *Prophesy*!

"For everyone here, you wealthy, you poor and you who simply struggle day to day; living in your own *quiet desperation*; you who walk this earth, *every one of you* know full well what is right from wrong; and I will further propose that even the most wicked among us work their sincerest efforts with every flourish of the saint; who simply scorch the earth lest he or she are touched in flame by it; yet leave His message safe protected in a vault, as even Judas kissed the Savior, one hand across his black heart.

"Which begs what Good doth *any* that proceeds without some reasoned compromise, some self-interest? We all make our concessions; we all make deals," he paced the dais, ever searching for the Lord's face, somewhere mixed among the sea of crowded, shiny expressions in the great room.

"For what is *Fact* anyhow but a piano bench? . . . and *Truth*? . . . Truth my friends, but the *quality* of light which passes through the window of the room in which you found it. Who here knows it different?"

The congregation stirred.

"But does this make it right? And don't, my dear friend, don't bother looking to the great books for any clue to what undoes the appetites of this world; you will not find it in any of them! . . . in these books you'll only find the best conjectures of our greatest minds perhaps, but not *one* single, final answer to the cure for the greed that consumes our sincerest intentions!" pushing his thick frames back up the slope of his nose and pressing an open fist onto the pages scattered across the stand.

A flash went off somewhere within the endless ranks of pews where ushers quickly swarmed, providing brief distraction from the podium as the shutter-bug was reproached.

"What goes here?" begged the good Bishop, "Leave that woman be! No harm certainly in remembering such a day, I wager," to no avail.

"Perhaps then, if you act quickly enough, constable, this morning will have never happened!" he quipped to the mildly amused assembly.

"It's easy enough these days it seems, to point at the stain on my neighbor's tie; unmindful of the small scrap of spinach lazing on my own tooth; my own compromise of faith; no good friends, what is wrong here, what is charged against Pharaoh, cannot be righteously appraised without first calibrating the scale; which conveniently recalls us to our own, *unconfessed*, complicity."

The Bishop continued on for three quarters of an hour during which time the number of well-presented in the audience were eventually reduced to a small handful as their thinner-skinned colleagues rose and haughtily navigated the long, carpeted aisles to exit the great doors at the rear of the nave. His thesis progressed, as was his well revised manner, from complicity through duplicity unto harsh toxicity; elaborating on the misappropriation of *Advantage* by those *Skilled Brokers* who synthetically inflate its value through a manipulated scarcity of means; wherein the sacred tool becomes a most dreaded weapon.

The appalled Archbishop of Touchwick sat dutifully civil on his throne opposite the lectern, periodically referencing his wrist watch in a private wager that the effectiveness of his guest's diatribe could be measured simply relative to its duration; stealing an occasional glance over the audience to privately assess the general mood of the room, wherein sat expressionless, the thickest skin in Hoffenstein, Prince Eugene Dubious.

XXVI

The exiting procession stretched from the glorious sanctuary up front, way back to the farthest rear corner of the great chapel where the baptismal font stood in a bright alcove under a walnut covering; holding the emblematic place in line where Hoffenstein's incubating prospect may one day wake to rise beneath the sacred splash of Chrism, taking up the ploughshare onto the great new battlefield of conscience just now illuminated by his Eminence, the good Bishop of Antwerp.

The tired old cleric, anxious to sit and rest back at the rectory, would not permit his fatigue to interfere with the congregation's need to ratify their private epiphanies with the press of flesh onto the *Beacon's* paw. Closure was his own elixir, discovered through insight, delivered like snake oil; the cunning man of God understood the resonance of intimacy and staked his popularity against all measures ineffectively pursued against it.

Archbishop Grieble, stood to his right, reading the articulate expressions of the fresh inspired celebrants as they passed; it wasn't all that much to smile, take a hand inside his ring encrusted own and breathe a word, but more than he could marshal, as the unanimous consensus was to associate his Eminence with the good works and message of the *Rebel* from the north.

Prince Eugene met his desperate glance from the rear of the nave, where the last mingling parishioners, mostly elder regulars, stretched the occasion's conclusion into a painfully drawn, obdurate business.

"Excuse me for a moment, please," he explained to Vandermeyer, pontificating before the small ring of acolytes standing about the alter rail.

From the construction scaffolds of the North transept ambled the figure of a priest, his manner slow and pensive, his intention not altogether uncommon, but whose access was indeed modestly particular. Walking close beside him, a woman dressed in classic knee-length skirt and matching lapelled jacket, white gloves and short cap with a modest veil; his wife.

The Priest had come to meet Bishop Vandermeyer in the absence of the multitude, having come from the country earlier that morning with his wife to hear for himself the man who had been accused of upsetting a continent. Vandermeyer, still anxious to retire, found one last reserve of focus and engaged the Priest, computing the depth of his philosophy by the anticipated length of time it would take for Grieble to conclude his private discussion and relieve him back up front by the alter.

"And I'm no more reluctant to admit, as I first expected, that in fact your position begins to make the better sense; on the contrary, I'm actually dismayed at how vigorous my thinking had initially been set against it," the Priest confessed, "I beg your indulgence." His wife squeezed his hand, a private indication that he needn't debase himself further.

"Oh please. What good would it do any of us to all borrow from the same opinion on all matters?"

"I've brought my message to the pulpit these many years and throughout that time have enjoyed watching many good people look with a parental pride at their own sense of empowerment; experiencing the thrill of emancipation and credit it to my words, but for which I served only as the courier for a package they themselves had sent for. And yet, having said that, I've turned as many back unto their vile schemes with renewed vigor. The score remains rather even I'm afraid; that's the thing we like to call *human nature*, but is in reality all *nature* and nothing like the cipher in the chromosomes the good Lord set aside exclusively for us as his shining example. We all see, Father, into such issues that to which we were predisposed but are nonetheless reluctant to engage."

"Ah!, Your Eminence! I was just preparing to retire back at your wonderful home when this young man approached me with his lovely wife. Excuse me, your name again Father?"

"Crispe. Nice to see you again, father" interrupted Grieble.

"Your Holiness," Father Crispe bowed to kiss his ring. "This is Monika, my wife."

"Mrs. Crispe, a pleasure."

"Wonderful to meet your acquaintance, Monika," added Vandermeyer.

She smiled, nodding her head.

"Why don't you come back to the rectory in about an hour for some refreshments and discussion before you head back to the Söfenzin? I'm curious how things are managing for us out there in the Dortpen," offered the Archbishop in another characteristic moment of premeditated benevolence.

"We'd be delighted."

XXVII

The path to the hutches wound around the old garage as it always had, up the narrow sweeping incline, around a rotting canvas tarp tied years ago, protecting a skid of spare concrete bags, now the rock hard home to slick beetles and centipedes, much too cumbersome to move;

a curious bundle of moldering rake and shovel handles nuzzled headless inside the moist crook of a colorless window sill set grey and wrinkled in the moss and lichen covered wall; thick pine and hemlock branches swept just above his head, leaving streaks of blackened sap stains shrouded by the various climbing vines, as Frederick made his way, stumbling in Gregory's black rubber boots, to feed the hens.

The routine was off and the poor birds knew as much, scattered now as plentiful outside the fence as in, pulling at worms from their holes and beetles from the punk; chicks were dead or dying; the eggshells thin. Frederick walked from the garage where he replaced the shovel, having buried another clutch, anxious to replace the memories up behind the barn with another phone call to Chief Winkler; by now, his only thread to Gregory.

He kicked off the boots and left them to dry in the mud room, washed his filthy hands in the kitchen sink and followed the pattern of thick shadows into the sitting room where an empty fireplace gaped beneath a cluttered mantle where amongst the clocks and candles was a gold framed photo of two men in suits sharing a slice of chocolate cake.

It was Sunday; time to wind the clocks.

XXVIII

The young priest pulled his car around the *Frère Jacques* traffic circle off Gillette Street onto Boulevard Viceroy where all indications of the morning's eccentric assembly surrounding the Cathedral were vanished, replaced now by the more conventional, slow and easy pace of a chilly autumn Sunday on Inner Touchwick's sleepy east side. A long, tree shaded stone wall began from its corner tower at the intersection of Dubois and Viceroy, extending three full blocks before the wide stone driveway cut through a pair of tall iron gates, swung perpetually open in wide welcome, and on into the churchyard.

To reach the rectory, Father Crispe sped around the fifteen foot bronze statue of St. Pontificate, captured with his left hand upon the forehead of an errant, kneeling gypsy having thrown aside his bag of pagan amulets, holding both hands tightly to *The Holy Bible* offered in the great man's right. This path cut directly to the Archbishop's residence, avoiding the cathedral entirely.

Miss Crumbe had pulled out all the stops today; the few select guests invited for a pleasant afternoon with the Belgian Muckrake would first discover for themselves, before the front door chanced to close behind, before surrendering their hats and jackets to the row of copper hooks, the fabled truth behind such claims of other worldly stirrings in the nose; the kitchen swelled with such exquisite fragrance as to beg the abstract nature of perfection and the pious provenance of her skills, bewitching as they were.

A set of four silver trays presented quartered tomato-basil sandwiches, oyster mushrooms stuffed with locatelli-drizzled herring in flaked puff pastry shells and glazed caviar canapés, all served with a youthful Beaujolais beside a delicate leak and raspberry soup filled inside small individual raisin-rye bread bowls for starters; a twenty pound goose, plucked fresh and bled on Friday, remained primarily responsible for the balance of whatever olfactory intoxication pervaded the charming atmosphere of the cozy salon.

There was a small living room Steinway in the corner of the space which no one played.

Leaning on one elbow, Prince Eugene placed his tiny plate and tiny fork down on the top of the celibate piano, mopping his neatly trimmed moustache with a napkin and continued.

"Whereas it seems to make perfect sense, that without the *derring-do* of the well-heeled, well educated, entrepreneurial set, there'd be no Hoffenstein; the greater the risk, the greater the gain. Now, why a chap shouldn't be compensated accordingly, I've no idea. Nothing blasphemous in proportionate compensation *yet*, is there Your Eminence?"

He gave his Beaujolais a small victory swirl before relishing a taste.

All attention had been given over to the tired old priest who really had no interest in the conversation; for what purpose should he volley such trifling philosophy? This was a picnic, nothing more and *Conscience*, the birdie popped back and forth atop the net; and he was truly tired; this Prince seemed rather self-satisfied to him, fresh charged and persuasive enough, provided the listener is only half informed and even less than half invested. Who in this comfortable gathering could openly admit to the existence of such a problem in the first place?
Ah! . . . to be back, cat napping in his old apartment in Antwerp.

"*Proportionate compensation*? . . . There's a spin!" the dissident Bishop muttered, hesitantly aware nonetheless, of his histrionic reputation.

"Let me inquire, Your Highness, as to when it became proportionate for our *derring-do-entrepreneurs* to leverage these same advantages in the service of iniquitous influence in the Parliaments; and while exercising this privilege, insure that the Entitled preserve most of their earnings, effectively destabilizing this same *risk* you just now mentioned? Wouldn't it be as fair to simply reduce the compensation proportionately?"

It was weak, he knew, but enough to sense the temper of the room; he placed great hope that it would tire the subject and inspire a distraction. The Prince however, looked un-amused.

"I see how you've collected your reputation for bold insolence, Your Grace, or may I substitute *frankness* in the interest of civility, seeing as there are ladies in the room." He lifted his glass and began slowly away from the piano, dramatically forming his response while silently strutting his *Prince-ness* before the guests.

"You might be correct if the world were as corrupt as you imagine it to be. Your premise however, holds insofar as it can be postulated that our governments, and by correlation our laws, are inherently unfair across the gamut; you state this as if it were some known fact. Need I remind you that I represent the House of Dubois? That I am also a principal member of the ruling council? Do you suggest that you bring a greater knowledge of the business of State to the podium than do I? There are only two implications in this and the first is that I am not as sharp as you, for having seen the corruption and done nothing about it would place me in your snare; and I am a far more clever adversary than you credit me. The second is undeniably a black mark on my character."

Bishop Grieble knocked his plate of canapés to the floor breaking the tension which had gripped the room. Eugene was caught again, the cunning Bishop's hook set firm into the fleshy ego of the Prince; but would he say too much? Had he indeed already said too much? Grieble needed to get Eugene out of the room to conference.

"You mistake an old man, who has given his passion over to a Higher Power, of having intentionally offended you. Good Gracious, no! . . . I can't see much point in that, Your Highness. I'm merely trying my best to respond in a spirit of sincere consideration of *all* the consequences; we're all pleasant here, no? As I am your humble guest, and servant through God, allow me to translate my meaning more agreeably."

Grieble stood from his chair while Miss Crumbe swept the mess from the side table and floor, also fielding compliments from the guests for her sorcery; every attempt to gain Eugene's attention was eclipsed by Vandermeyer's deftness with the rod and reel; *a true devil at work here! . . . but then again, Eugene is always best undone by Eugene.*

"Let us say only that, in a strictly pragmatic sense, it is not always a trespass before God that one hones one's advantages; our welfare programs and orphanages are beholden to the excess of such talents, I confess."

Father Crispe sat riveted to his place on the short sofa, his wife appearing quite restless beside him. An odd thought had come to his mind; a memory from his visit to the Archbishop some weeks ago.

"But when the average working man is brought to financial ruin through his best and noblest efforts; dare I suggest, set towards it by a dapper-suited swindler's promise of achieving the unlikely; be it a lack of financial savvy or simply a naïve, vestigial faith in our most *stable* institutions; and by this I refer of course to that which we all have most injuriously suffered as our mutual Financial Establishment's recent collapse from fiscal solvency, resulted directly, I will further add, from unsavory infringements of principle;

"and then compound this setback by the collateral rise in unemployment, sky high utility bills, rising food prices or an untimely transmission belt on the slip; where are the similar efforts in your council chambers to provide us with a safety net proportionate to a lifetime of labor? Is there a chair for this family at our Round Tables? Our average working stiff is certainly not invested in a second vacation home or a ridiculously expensive handbag for his wife is he? Yet he gets up every morning and works the day, never knowing if or when his mortgage will be foreclosed or his son or daughter will need hospitalization; he is probably unsure if or when he will ever be financially sound enough to retire. I ask you, is this what you describe as *proportionate compensation?*"

Grieble spoke up, "Ahem . . I need a moment, if you would all be so kind, um, Eugene. Please may I have a brief word with you? We'll be but a minute."

Bishop Vandermeyer turned his tired eyes first to Grieble and then to the Prince.

"I'm sure it can hold for a time, Your Eminence. We're just about through here," snapped the Prince.

"It's rather urgent."

Prince Eugene was the star of the room and *no one* would spoil that for him.

When did it become common practice for just anyone to tell the Prince of Hoffenstein where to go, what to say, what to do? Damned insolence!

"You're a very clever speaker, Bishop, but you can't solve the problem by pretending that poor financial comprehension is a consequence to be ransomed by those of us who pay our bills; who studied mathematics in school while the rabble played at skittles; who focused our opportunities and trained to steer the great forces of the country's factories and trading floors. We are the ones who prepared against the predatory fangs of nature herself; who build the dreams that the *complicit,* as you like call them, inhabit and pollute. We've simply taken our place because we are fit and determined; no litany of excuses can erase this fact; let the lazy mob and the lame subsist; I've enough trouble trying to figure out which handbag is in vogue this season, don't cry to me about some ne'er-do-well's slipping transmission."

A chill descended over the room, a stillness broken by a most unexpected voice, "I think I've heard just about enough! Please Linus, let's go home."

Monika shocked her husband, who found himself paralyzed by incompatible loyalties; the pause was all His Highness needed to turn his rapier tongue toward the little sofa.

"Leaving so soon, Mrs. Crispe? I do hope it was nothing I said," at his cynical best.

"Please Linus."

The young priest stood, numbed by the fact the occasion turned suddenly so sour; that sides were drawn; that his side was so clearly opposite the side of those he always admired.

"I'm terribly sorry if I caused you to feel unwelcome, my dear. That's the trouble with mixing politics and pleasantries. Please do forgive me and lets not let these little problems spoil our fine afternoon," pursued the Prince.

"*Little Problems*?" Monika snapped, "You stand there and speak dismissively about the people who trust your institutions to look out for us, the way you trust that we'll always be there to buy your junk, drive your trucks and breathe your foul air. We're the ones who pay more of our salaries in taxes; building the bridges and the roads to move your rotten nonsense about. *You were born to it!* How could you possibly understand the first thing about struggling for *anything*? You and your despicable surcharge fees and private Swiss bank accounts! You move our jobs to Portugal, you rape the Congo, Angola, Indonesia; you get us into wars and who carries your rifle? These little *ne'er-do-wells*, that's who! Bishop Vandermeyer, please keep speaking so at least *someone* can answer back to these privileged . . ."

The words caught in her throat. Linus stood and took her arm to leave; a very proud man. The Prince stood motionless, realizing that Monika was actually a very attractive woman. A faint smile turned the far right corner of his lip.

Archbishop Grieble escorted them out of the salon and to the row of coats.

"I'm terribly sorry to both of you, please reconsider," he began, aware that any attempt was pointless.

"It's time we started back, Your Grace. We have quite a long drive," Crispe replied "and do apologize to Bishop Vandermeyer for us please; I found him fascinating and wish I had said goodbye."

"Of course I will, son, of course." He followed them out to the driveway. He held the door for Monika while Father Crispe circled the car to the driver's side.

"A word, Father," Grieble started around to meet Linus; he was not prepared to speak loud enough for anyone to overhear.

"Yes, Your Grace?"

"It's about Father Frederick. Have you been over yet to see him? Terrible what's become of his *friend*, don't you think? Any news?"

Father Crispe saw for the first time that Grieble's eyes don't always track together; that his left eye was a bit yellow and lazy. Funny, he thought. *How did I not notice this before?*

Father Crispe then did something that would prove to change the whole course of his career and character. He simply replied with a faint smile, out of all context with the dead stare of his eyes, pulled the car door past the Archbishop, and drove off.

XXIX

He had gone over the *Proposal* a dozen times, modestly aware that his sumptuous intelligence did not necessarily predispose him to artfully detect the more subtle properties of whichever financial pretexts were embedded throughout the great heap of tedious digits and references twisted in obscure legalese; an area far better suited to his talented protégé, whom he hadn't heard from in a matter of weeks.

Much had progressed, much had stalled. The press had finally picked up the story of the fugitive Member of Council; the accusations that he fled to avoid prosecution for the murder of his own daughter were now embellished by the curious claim from some *unnamed sources* that allege his crime corresponds with the disappearance of a considerable sum of cash and gold which is queerly assumed to have both provoked and underwritten the affair; speculations and theories were about as numerous as the articles which posited them; no two stories from any variety of publications need ever echo the other, for both continued on, fresh with unique facts and analysis of the inexhaustible diet of officious fabrications supplied by the Prince's rumor mill.

News of the whereabouts of the Poulterer had come to a dead end; the story had simply lost the public's interest, replaced, for example, by bulletins of growing civil unrest to the north and east of the small fiefdom; a modest demonstration on the steps of the Touchwick Stock Exchange having made the front cover of the *Chronicle* this past week in fact.

Alistair pored over the pages for hours each morning until his mind could no longer sustain the elevated focus he so studiously cultivated over his lifetime of academic endeavor; a rewarding attribute when exercised on practical applications of scientific hypotheticals but torturous in the present context of a surreptitious and torturously mundane specimen of fiscal virtuosity.

The pages seemed after a time to sincerely enjoy his growing addiction to rejection; squandering his talents on sordid statistics and an integral calculus; a temperament more gratified devouring research money toward the employment of a differential calculus and quantum theory in some god forsaken, inhospitable geography somewhere north or south of forty degrees latitude. Life in Europe, in Hoffenstein, in the Dortpen, in Mayfair, at Burlwood; this *civilized* excuse for subordinating mathematics to such pedestrian mischief filled him with an incubating resentment toward his race that only the predicament of his beloved pupil could entreat him to ignore and persevere beyond.

The pages were hiding something.

Hobbes knocked at the door and entered with a decanter of coffee on a tray of quickbread and jam before Alistair could reply; the latter barely raised his head from the desk.

"Ready for a respite?" he inquired.

The professor stopped his pencil, grabbed the page of frenzied scribble in his fist and tossed it in a ball beside the small pile of similar casualties near the waste basket. "It's trying to destroy me Hobbes."

"What's that Alistair?"

The old man rose from the desk; the thrill of imminent victory accelerated against the stubborn brake of his topical illiteracy. *Something has to give; these men are not that intelligent!*

"This terrible puzzle; I've struggled with the figures in all three separate papers, all seem innocuous; that is until page seven in the top report. It references a body or an account for which, incidentally, I have little knowledge or regard, but that it reappears in a number of graphs and

195

tables in the other two sections of the opus with absolutely no supporting reference of any arithmetic consequence. It seems a ghost of significant influence; my pencil would appear to pass right through it, time after time, like a mist."

"That is a mystery, Professor. Please, take a break. Let me pour you some coffee."

"That would be kind, Hobbes. Please, sit; distract me for a spell."

Hobbes mustered a faint smile and placed the tray on the low coffee table between the settee and the wing-back chair; memories of sharing cognac with the Duke last winter added to the burden of his more recent losses. A looming melancholy had since descended upon the house; humor was the great rock of Sisyphus and evenings since have found them all the more exhausted from the curse.

"Please try some bread, put something in your stomach; the mind will follow."

Alistair chuckled, "Never could tolerate that quickbread! Maybe the bi-carb . . . I'm not sure."

"Then allow me, good sir, to present you with," and he lifted the small pot of delicious blackberry jam, held between two long, slender fingers and the thumb of his left hand, deftly removing the lid with a second pair of prodigious digits from his right, "homemade blackberry preserves from the enchanted kitchen of Miss Doris, matron of the galley over at Fishwell Park, our distinguished neighbors, nearest to the west."

"Where we recovered the two hounds last week sometime?" ignoring any mention of its proximity to the tunnel exit.

"Precisely. Miss Doris and I have known each other for many years, going back to her first interview with the Charmings; met her at the train station and again at the butcher only days apart. People tend to place a great deal of credence in such coincidence; *me* for example," he smiled briefly.

Hobbes was quick to replace the lid in his fingers with a short spreading knife which he used to spackle a generous portion of the jam across the warm biscuit. "There, now try that. Sometimes all you need is a little help from a sweet old neighbor . . . simply intoxicating, tell me I'm wrong!"

Alistair smiled at his new friend, admiring the tenacity with which he concealed his stabbing moroseness; took the biscuit and popped half of it into his mouth. There was no denying a sense of pleasant surprise; a phenomenon like nothing he could have possibly forecast.

Not only did the blackberry neutralize the unpleasant effects of the harsh dough ingredients, but served to modify the remaining elements of the long avoided treat into a sublime harmony of epicurean delicacy; a transcendental moiré of the sweet and bitter halves of every kitchen's essential mischief; the cumulative effect was nothing less than astounding.

"Remarkable," and he devoured the remaining half; closed his eyes and let the crumbs simply fall from his lips down to his vest. Hobbes was preparing a cup of coffee with sugar and cream.

"If I might offer a small piece of friendly advice, Mr. Constantine."

Alistair opened his eyes to a saucer and cup, extended from the figure of Hobbes, seated opposite the table and in possession just now of the most terrestrial eyes he'd ever seen; pools of crystal blue ponds sunk down within the private folds of time worn hills, features on the face of one who'd seen and heard and lived unshielded in the thick of life, through all its seasons. There was much inside this look for which there were not yet words; yet in his hallmark humility, the proprietor of this exalted backdrop proposed to speak; and speak he did.

"Yes Hobbes. By all means, talk freely. There is no ceremony between us."

"Well, *and I'm no scholar as you know*, but it would seem very plain to me that you are trying to describe blackberry preserves by examining the naked biscuit."

"I'm on about a biscuit?"

"In a manner of speaking, sir, I'd say you're quite right in saying you're *'on about a biscuit'*," repeated the butler.

Alistair screwed his eyes and took a sip, suspiciously eyeing half a dozen buns still warm and cushioned in the napkin nested in the broad wove basket on the tray. He nodded that the good man carry on.

"You see, it becomes quite plain to me when seeing you discuss your similar distaste of biscuits and statistics and how Miss Doris' splendid preserves seemed to miraculously change things between you and quickbread; that maybe sir, you're trying too hard to reconstruct a recipe for blackberry preserves from the merest scrap of some second-hand reference to it on a slice of dry quickbread; I believe you referred to it just now as a *mist*. It can't be done that way; you'll just drive yourself into a hole. What you are seeking, Alistair, appears to be the missing *key*, without which you are at an exceedingly stubborn disadvantage. "

Alistair stood and went to the window.

"Hobbes, let's you and I stretch our legs and take in some of this fine countryside before I inevitably take my leave of it. What say we go and pay a call on old Miss Doris?"

Hobbes smiled and stood preparing to clear the small table.

"No, no, please. Let that tray sit there a while. I believe I owe it my sanity. My hat!"

XXX

The morning rain tapped against the window; somewhat discouraging in light of the forecast for sunshine rumored yesterday among the school's custodial staff where she worked her odd schedule scrubbing the halls and stairwells for a meager stipend and additional respite for her darling *Lovely*.

The shade was still drawn; it was six-thirty in the morning and Helen had already started Sharon's stressful day an hour and a half earlier, caught ineffectively trying to manage the smooth plated brass chain which secured the front door from her aimless yet unremitting elopement; an onerously compelling feature of her peculiar affliction.
Perhaps the rain will stop.

It was Saturday and Sharon was struggling to bathe a fully developed child, getting them both ready to leave the house in an hour; *rather a cat in the sink for fleas!*

The church was a half mile away and she was expected to have the housework finished in time for the Ladies Auxiliary lunch meeting at twelve, requiring her to be there no later than eight to begin.

The congregation had by now long forgiven itself for the seven year hiatus in observance, reinstating committees, resolving into familiar social cliques segregated by the usual, unsurprising economic circumstances while autonomously providing for the appearance and maintenance of the splendid little shrine under the hemlocks.

Frederick's personal situation had become once again the renewed topic of contention which seemed only to revitalize a timeless dichotomy of principled benevolence pulsing just beneath the fabric of unity promulgated by the faith which coerced them whole; as each of the hundred continued nonetheless to ornament their Savior in a hundred separate, multi-colored robes.

Some expressed a devotion to the order through an ostentatious harmony throughout the hymns; others just conspicuously loaded the collection plate, while still others, working behind the scene, maintained the electric, water and oil contracts, a chore which, during excessively trying periods over the many years, nearly brought Frederick himself to an absolute confrontation with his own higher power.

The return to normalcy was, rather simply, a call to the retirement of that noble earnestness stringently employed during the time of the *great upheaval,* the temporary banishment of Sunday observance in the *good* name of Leviticus; it being now a time to reinstate the symbiotic complacency all initially prayed might reward the effort of creating a self-maintaining system worth launching in the first place; and with this finely tuned organization back in good stead, old Vandermeyer's principle of *duplicity* had prodigally returned to roost.

Sharon understood none of this as she chased Helen from the refrigerator only after the last half of the milk bottle went splashing to the kitchen floor, thoroughly soaking the startled young lady's clean outfit. Dodging her mother, Helen sped to the chained front door where her continued shriek for breakfast over-filled the small cabin; milk stained footprints tracked across the littered sitting room carpet.

Her tired hands trembled as she wrung the towel of spoiled milk into the sink, wondering how to fix some substitute breakfast without it. Helen ran back by her mother, stood in the puddle of milk, attempting to pull Sharon's hand back over to the refrigerator, pecking at her arm with a multitude of the sweetest kisses, pleading for breakfast. Sharon looked at her pants and blouse, wondering what clean clothes she had left in the basket to replace the wet shirt and pants now clinging to her *Lovely's* thin body.

The clock told of another half hour gone.

Sharon grabbed Helen into her arms attempting to break the spiraling anxiety, pressed her face into the wild bale of hair, smelling the fresh scent of the shampoo, kissing her tears off the soft golden ringlets. The girl broke from the embrace, held her mother's arm extended toward the refrigerator, urgently signing the words *father* and *cookie*.

It was time to prepare for the rain and Sharon could never get a hat of any sort onto Helen's head. It was of the utmost consequence that a reasonable grip be maintained on the young lady's hand until they had at least passed the fourth mailbox toward the corner where they would lose sight of the cottage and the road was far less traveled; as the obliging umbrella in her opposite hand left nothing free for her purse, it became essential to arrange everything in its proper order before unfastening the soft plated brass chain above the door.

It was now seven forty-five, they were going to make the church about ten minutes late but this was nothing unusual. Reaching down to grab the umbrella handle, Sharon's purse slid down the sleeve of her rain coat and over her wrist; Helen remained calm by the door.

Panning the house one last time before pulling the front door open, as was her habit, Sharon caught a glimpse of something under the couch, something shiny. Her heart beat in panic.

Throwing the umbrella to the floor, she ran to the couch and dropped to her knees;

"What have you done!" she wailed stretching the tin can into the air, looking on its emptiness with crazed bewilderment; "For the love of God, Helen, what have you done!?"

It was eight o'clock and two figures made their way through the gentle morning rain toward the little church where one would spend the next three agonizing hours cleaning to cover her frightful loss; the other would sit in her pew, singing with an old wooden spoon and look upon the colored rays of light through the great window, silently floating behind the alter.

XXXI

A deep blue van pulled up to the Söfenzin Royal Police Headquarters on the rainy Saturday morning around ten o'clock; painted emblems on the cab doors alluding to its active service in *His Majesty's Interior Security Command*, with further implications that the two gentlemen observed leaving the vehicle, in impeccable uniform, were officers sent all the way from Touchwick.

Chief of Police Richter had opened the little station an hour earlier in preparation for the scheduled arrival, aware the unpleasant spirit of such appointments is customarily mollified with a preemptive cup of fresh coffee, pastries and promptness.

The two men were seated across from Richter's tiny metal desk, each with a paper cup of black coffee rested in their opposite fists on opposite knees; perfectly mirrored bookends with the conspicuous absence of anything remotely narrative between them; Chief Richter broke the faintest smile.

"No. I can't say as I've noticed either of these two fellows around the village. Of course, I haven't asked around either." He lifted the top photo, further scrutinizing the face for future reference.

"Is that a hole in his right lobe?"

The officer to Richter's right, Colonel Krutch, indicated as much; "Yes. That's Victor Grübek; sometimes wears a silver hoop in there." Krutch was the senior officer, in charge of the search and recovery of the fugitive, Lord Penworth; a mission elevated to *ISC* intervention after three months of inadequate results by the regional authorities.

"The other one is Dominic Pedroni" he continued, "Victor was a merited officer from *Immigration* before an early, forced retirement freed him to pursue his more innate, belligerent tendencies. Dominic, as far as we have been able to piece together, was a climbing guide and survivalist in Lombardy before turning his talents toward freelance fugitive recovery seven or eight years ago. Both men are honorably discharged veterans with active overseas service in the orient.

"It is important to remember that neither of these men have broken the law and there are no outstanding warrants for their arrest. That having been said, however, it is the concern of *ISC* that these two men are intercepted before they interfere with the Penworth case."

He drank from his cup, neatly replacing it to his knee in an exaggerated effort to present himself as the zenith of discipline; an individual of superlative breeding.

"Chief Richter, we've come here to intercept these two freelance lawmen in the hopes of apprehending the Duke in a condition suitable enough for trial."

"And these two don't share your concerns?" The Chief rose from his chair, walked to the north window, gazing on old Pater; absorbing the vast forest at its base, stretched endlessly into the swallowing mist of rain. What could possibly remain of life for the once proud father; the distinguished heir of the Penworth name; whatever could possess a man to hide among the shadows in such infinite wilderness?

"And just how do you want my officers to *intercept* these two? We write parking vouchers; we help the senile find their way home; maybe Lars in a drunk will beat on Jenna again. No one in this district has leveled a gun at anyone more dangerous than a brown bear in the past twenty years."

The visiting officer then stood from his seat to meet Chief Richter's objections without the disadvantage of posture.

"We have reason to believe these two are not concerned about a trial or even motivated, for that matter, by the ransom money."

He finished his coffee and placed the cup on the desk adjacent them.

"I do not expect you or your officers to try to make the pair feel unwelcome; I simply instruct that you relay any information regarding their arrival in Söfenzin to me with unmitigated urgency. The newspapers, Chief Richter, are disseminating dubious reports, gossip really, regarding an unsubstantiated embezzlement, a fortune which by now has remarkably grown to dwarf the official ransom and which is also claimed to have been hidden somewhere here, in the Dortpen country; strictly conjecture . . . but then enough to inspire the cunning of these two characters of interest."

"I see," and walked the two officers out to the van, "We love the Penworths here in Söfenzin, Colonel. I'll keep a sharp eye; you can be sure."

XXXII

The weather made parking outside the small chapel especially difficult, as fewer worshippers seemed willing to hazard an unreasonable stretch in the rain, preferring to wage the good battle for car space along the tiny street or the modest muddy lot adjacent the barn; all in the good service of joining the community in mass.

Frau Campbell and her three daughters arrived earlier to arrange the Hymnals and Prayer books in the pocketed shelves secured to the backs of the pews, changed needing candles, laid the alter cloth and replaced the chalice and ciborium.

Herr Campbell and the handsome young Dieter Jacobs positioned themselves on either side of the chapel doors, both of them glistening, freshly bathed and drizzled in a budget aftershave; dispensing programs to the arriving celebrants.

Johannes Sloan sat upstairs in the balcony behind the organ with the Ladies Auxiliary Choir milling there-abouts, fussing through last minute program details heavily spiced with sundry gossip.

A visitor had arrived this morning, garnering modest attention by way of his clerical dress and beautiful escort. Herr Campbell dutifully offered to make room for the couple up toward the front; a more difficult task these days, but a wholly opportune resource for a visiting rector with such a mind as to impose upon the local hospitality. Linus Crispe had no intention of unseating anyone, rather preferring a more discreet pew in the back row where an odd young lady sat restless beside her mother.

The organ let loose with the keynote of *My Jesus as thou Wilt*, the Ladies Auxiliary Chorus filling the hall with mellifluous evidence of their time dedicated to rehearsal; six acolytes bearing staffs, bibles and candles escorted Father Frederick in file up the aisle toward the altar, where each followed their prescribed paths to various spots on various benches for the duration of the service. Father Frederick naturally took his place in front of the altar.

The hymn subsided.

"You all look wonderful this morning. I'm so glad to learn the rain was not enough to keep you home."

A murmur of amusement echoed the good man's introduction as he used the next ten minutes to outline the week's lesson and make first mention of the fund raiser scheduled for the end of the month to help one of the more desperate of their congregation make ends meet during an especially troubling time.

Sitting in the last row made it more difficult for heads and eyes to turn on Sharon, while Helen's song continued to fill the empty space during pauses in Father Frederick's honeyed preamble.

"Which brings me to a subject we all assume to know a great deal of, except the way in which it works; a notion which directs three quarters of our deeds, independent of our reason and for which we are more readily prepared to chastise its eccentricity in others while blindly forgiving it in ourselves; I want to speak with you this morning about the special relationship between *Loss* and *Need*."

The good Priest placed his left hand into his right and stepped from the lectern, away from his notes, looking at the floor while struggling with his trembling voice.

"It is commonplace to complain to anyone who'll listen that we've lost something we used; something we've grown attached to, maybe something or some*one* we claim to have loved and respected; something we would say, in all honesty, we *need*. I guess it can also be anecdotal to remark that it seems the more we need something the more likely we'll find it missing."

A brief, low titter arose from the pews.

"But can we honestly lose something we're then able to prove we never really needed? Is it really worth this enormous, epic preoccupation; this combing of heaven and earth to uncover every last trifle that we can actually describe as being inevitably essential?. How great would it finally be if we discovered that we actually needed nothing at all! Is this even possible?

"Well if so, we'd never have to feel the pain of losing; the wretched emptiness of *Loss,* would we? We could be free from wanting; when all we should really need or want is knowledge of the truth in His Word; and you can never lose Him, can you?

"Yes; that would be convenient.

"But that's not how this gift works, is it? Life. It's just not that simple. He, in His unknowable wisdom gave us more than a stomach and a pair of eyes; He gave us a hunger and a vision! He pushes us to explore, to ask, to fashion, to build; to expand ourselves. To Love.

"We did not invent the *Miracle*; we merely found it lying there, by the river, in the forest, inside a flower, up in the stars at night, in the sand. And so we gave it a name; we took it home and built a shelf for it. We filled the shelf and built another; filled that one and built seven more shelves.

"We then raised a barn to hold more and looked out our back kitchen window one day to realize, in our obsession, we built a second barn! "But we didn't stop there, did we? . . . no! We worked weekends and over-time hours just to have the very last one from our neighbor who then forgot his own wife and family that he could scour the shelves and barns the whole world over for the perfect replacement for the last one he sold for the money it cost him to build another shelf."

The chapel was silent; each looking on the priest; a man they hold as having recently lost the most.

Father Frederick paced the altar slowly, deep in thought; silently returned to the pulpit.

"Why would He then tempt us with His blessed Miracle, which worked at too hard trying to achieve, is in the end, only corrupted? I will also ask you to consider, at what point does *Loss* become just *enough* to be sacred? . . . or too *much* to be sympathized; and when does *Need* overrun a true love of life, if given these two beautiful eyes to see and these wrinkled ears to hear, the miracle of sight and sound becomes less credible than the discipline to turn them away from seeing all there is and hearing everything?

"Where is the balance dear God, between being and doing?"

He lowered the glasses from his face to ritually wipe the lenses; looked again at his ring.

"Well, one answer might be that it's simply wrong to discipline yourself from hearing and seeing all there is in the world. That turning from Life is turning from the Truth; and turning from Truth is a great sin in itself!" He looked over the congregation; at the confused, the rapt, the tolerant and saw finally, there in the farthest row, the pastor from Mayfair. He continued,

"I might look at a beautiful sunrise, but I don't say to myself, 'Frederick! I simply must get me one of those!'

"All the overtime in the world isn't going to help me to ever own one of Life's most sublime and majestic events. Think how handy it would've been to simply pull out a nice sunrise this morning for instance."
The congregation purred.

"Look now to your side; I seriously ask each one of you to think of the person you love more than anything else on this Earth; Are they here with you this morning? . . . Remember when you met; how you met. Think of the years you've spent just trying to get by; taking all the variety of junk life's thrown at you, knowing that this person; these people have always been there, struggling with you; or are waiting for you to come back home. Now think about the truth in knowing you can never lose them; because they are like the sunrise;

. . I never owned you to begin with . . ."

His voice dropped off; unheard by anyone beyond the front two or three rows and confounding even to those up front who heard.

Pulling himself together, the intrepid minister concluded,

"Do not live hiding from His miracle; and that means turning a blind eye or a deaf ear to life; but instead fight the pain of Loss by sharing every day the love of these things you see and hear in life; share them with someone near to you; but do so never *needing* to do so. There's nothing *sacred* was not sleeping when a need for it was formed. Learn to rid yourself of Loss by simply borrowing from life . . . and share these things never claiming them; learn to recognize the cages as you build them; the snares you set by imprisoning the very things you love and admire the most.

"And let the mystery of His reasoning simply be another curious gift to be experienced, not dissected; without needing to understand why He gives and takes the way He does or when He does.

"Accept the perplexity of our personal relationships; accept your humble place inside His great beam of light, shed criss-cross along the ground before us; this simply cannot be explained away like distances or time; by ingeniously spinning some fingers on a clock or sending airplanes into empty space.

206

He just simply *does*; and we're all blessed quite enough to play our small parts in the whole exalted confusion of it all. *That* is His way."

A high, vaguely perceptible C *major* drifted from Herr Sloane's keyboard over the balcony rail, swirling down into the watery atmosphere of the town folk below.

"If you would all turn now to your Hymnals," the cue to a preamble of *Immortal, Invisible, God only Wise,* permitting time for the good flock to comb their blue books for the page.

The remainder of the service was a study in contrasts ranging from those few simply offended by their bewilderment to those who received genuine comfort from the sermon's first, inadvertent peek behind the stoic posture of the troubled Priest; a love letter to the voyeuristic among the congregation, written from the deepest crevice of his undressed wounds.

The doors opened to a breaking sun, the morning's rain in evidence across the ground in diminishing puddles. A street once lined with cars now bare.

"Father Frederick, this is Monika."

"Father," she smiled, taking the Priest's hand, "pleased to finally meet you."

"Well, I must admit to feeling a bit awkward, Linus; I was totally taken by surprise, seeing you in the back there. If you're taking communion in Söfenzin, who's doling out wafers in Mayfair?" he chuckled.

"Oh, I've got that covered, I hope. Grieble's been sending some of the students out to St. Andrews to scare them, I suppose. Today's service was entrusted to the trembling hands of a young scholar from Bünsch; a real talent for the sermon, I believe."

"Well, if you'll bear with me while I change out of these vestments, we'll continue your interrogation back at the cottage."

Monika stood waiting with her husband on the steps outside the chapel; Linus flicked his butt into a puddle, "He's every right to distrust me."

Father Frederick climbed into the back of the car. "Not far, just make a left down here, by that old greenhouse."

"Your service was inspired, Father," Linus watched the old priest in the rearview, "I've heard about your considerable gift, but I must admit, I wanted to hear you first hand; I can tell you it was profoundly moving."

"I feel much the same way, Father. You made me feel somehow comforted despite the pain you describe."

"Oh, don't you two get too invested in a plateful of meaningless words," Father Frederick unrolled his window for some air, "This town's been anxious to hear me give something up since his disappearance; *that poor girl's terrible death . . .* ; simply can't stand not knowing if their venomous natter will be born out. I pretended a confession and they acted out a little sympathy. Now I can be left to myself, for a time at least."

The car pulled up to the hedges now carelessly tended, hanging over into the narrow lane, pinching the driveway to a scarcely navigable entrance; Linus pressed the accelerator as the small car sped up to the small cottage and followed the driveway around to the back where the ground was more level.

Standing from the car, both of his guests panned the bucolic property; a great smile broke across Monika's face as she remarked on the splendor.

"Thank you; you're very kind."

They followed Frederick in through the mud room into the kitchen, both reasonably shocked at the sorry state of things. The whole of it was an indescribable mess; filthy plates and piled clothes; a sink over-flowed with pans and flower pots. Newspaper lay dissolved on the floor where food for cats was spooned into crusted bowls. The curtains hung from cobwebbed rings. Muddy boot tracks led the way into the sitting room, drowned in the music of its hundred clocks.

"Please forgive the place; I've been quite . . ."
"We're fine, thank you," offered Linus, moving toward the couch.

"I'll put a kettle on; please have a seat inside."

Monika led the way from the kitchen, followed the mud track into the living room, marveling at the great collection of pendulum clocks, cuckoo clocks, spring driven clocks; every model of hung, standing or sitting clock, plucking and bowing its small part in the symphony which filled the room.

Yet odd as the sheer number of clocks may have at first seemed to the young couple, finding their seats upon the sofa, odder still, much weirder, that the ticking boxes on the walls and shelves; the great Grandfather clock against the wall; the mantle clocks, each one with its hands plucked clean; stood or hung or sat freshly wound with nothing but a naked, numbered face.

"Now, Father Crispe he entered the room with a kettle in one hand and three tea cups on the finger of the other, "You have news from old Grieble, have you? What have I done this time?"

"I'm afraid I've come to spoil your sanctimonious bitterness, Father," Monika shot her husband a look of cautioned horror; silently pleading for him to be kind, "I've news of circumstantial relevance which I nonetheless feel obliged from a sense of moral clarity to share with you. You're a good man whom I'd consider it an honor to count as a friend; there's little I wouldn't sacrifice for a friend."

Frederick softened his guard. "Sugar, Monika?"

She shook her head, looked kindly into the glazed eyes of the old Priest, "It's just that I fear Bishop Grieble is somehow complicit in your situation."

XXXIII

A weather had blown into the Dortpen; stubborn cold and showers filling the lakes and the gutters, softening the hillsides; biting raw into the hand and face too long exposed; a thick wet cloud sent from old Pater down into the valley where his children wander, over-slept, confused in absence of the morning's break.

A mist to turn the poor man's broken heart to mud; and with it come the web works of disease, the thin black fingers of a truth so centered, makes a lie of everything too proud to bend unto its vast enormity; that all the multicolored world will roll someday into some simple spot of black, and here forever in a vault, all dreams and loves will sleep; that all trouble and all secrets have outlived their usefulness.

Three Gypsies and their five hounds hiked an overnight in such a cutting mist; when gathering some wood for coffee and a kindling for the bones, the youngest called out from some labyrinth of brush and stone where he discovered fair protection for a spell.

·Three men and five dogs sat with coffee 'round a fire in the old cave's mouth, looking out as would-be noblemen from some fine and high-on precipice, out on the blighted day; ate and drank and soothed the knife-edge from their stiffened frames, off toward distant memories from some warmer refuge far away. A hound they knew as Kasper from his nosing in the cavern's throat made off a sorry howl; was how they found the wet and dying Duke.

Two men dragged the sick man through the forest on a stick, the third, picked to run the long way back and to the camp where Grigoras grabbed a set of keys and met them at the figured time and place along a roadside pass; inside the day had a wheezing skeleton piled thick beneath thin blankets in an ancient Gypsy mystic's bed.

The elders smoked five pouches of tobacco; spilled half a dozen fifths of vodka 'round the fire that cruel night.

XXXIIII

The sheer door side-panels served the past half century as an inconspicuous blind from which to spy on callers approaching the great townhouse; his soft white glove need merely part the curtain from the frame, half a pinch and behold, the whole of *Silberfluss* across the way observed.

Davis at his post prepared now for the pearl white limousine which moored beside the curb out front of the address; watched as Grieble's colored slipper breached the car door and touched the walk; aided by the chauffeur quickly circling to stand and brush his cassock, tap his zucchetto, retrieve his readied briefcase; *on with the show.*

"Yes, dreadful morning, Davis, *dreadful!*" complained the dour cleric, contemptuous of leaving the comfort of his rectory, resentful of the crosstown drive and ever spiteful of the tony *Fleiss* district and the prosperous heathen who nest within; surrendering his top coat and muffler to the doting aide, inquiring,
"Is His Highness prepared for battle this morning, Davis? I trust you've fed him well; he's going to need it today, by God he will," and was led up to the familiar library of the Prince of Hoffenstein.

A very anxious, subordinated Grimstone nearly jumped from his place at the large table; startled from his immersed reexamination of a neatly ordered pile of financial charts and tabulations, (infamously familiar to the small but opportunistic fraternity presently assembled) by the knock on the door where Davis stood with the Bishop by his side.

"The Archbishop Grie . . ." he began to announce, when the old cleric pushed past, entering the quiet Library with a style concocted to emphasize his status as co-principal of the conspiracy.

"Your Eminence," smiled Grimstone.

"Elmer," greeted Eugene, "Please take a seat so we can begin; there's quite a bit to cover this morning so I suggest we place a lunch order for one o'clock now so's not to be interrupted later. Davis, please?"

"As you request, my Lord. Will you be having your usual aperitif?"

"No, I'm afraid; coffee and iced water all around for today; thank you Davis, that will be all."

Davis exited the library, closing the heavy door behind him.

The Bishop took his seat, opposite the Prince, at the east end of the conference table, Grimstone between them to the north; a duplicate stack of neatly prepared folders before each of them.

"No aperitif? For God's sake Eugene, you must be grim!" Grieble rebuked, taking the red folder from the top and thumbing through, stopping to admire some of the strange, superficial symmetries displayed as colored graphics of some alien economic aesthetic.

"Rather," he replied. "I've asked for the revised *Pontificate* numbers, Elmer; as you'll notice in the blue report, all the numbers are coded to November. It is December the eleventh, your Eminence; I hope you've brought new figures with you."

The tone of the meeting, thus set, insured the one o'clock platter of shaved pastrami on pumpernickel-rye, side of sauerkraut, English mustard and black, pitted olives went back to the kitchen relatively untouched. The thick door hung on a double set of frowning hinges like a cenotaph, adequately serving to confine the vigorous clarification of an ever widening division as regards the spoils of the enterprise, vastly lucrative as it was, within the gloomy conference room; *and all the consequence of a baffling little key.*

Grimstone throughout, faithful to his Prince though cravenly cautious for his soul, dutifully interpreted the figures and reiterated the complex mechanism of his *Dynamic Trust Consortium,* a technically adroit financial breakthrough of his own inspired fecundity, wherein a specified sum is spun upon a carousel of wide ranging investments like corpuscles through the veins and capillaries of a sleeping griffon, each uniquely programmed to a self-determined pace through erratically timed gates, yet all beholden to one simple key; the conductor on the podium, without which the spine of the entire compendium dissolves; the art as meaningless as hieroglyphs without the carved Rosette tablet.

A wonderful advancement in the criminal stratosphere of high finance, no doubt, yet for the malevolent confederates conspired behind the stacks of septic calculations, nothing more compelling than to place the great *Cathedral of St. Pontificate* along the tracks, where like the heart of sleeping Hoffenstein all blood will in its own time pass and exit clean; tax free and clear; a dance so perplexing that none without the key could ever guess a single coin had left the track.

"You suggest we change the *cipher* at this time?" Grimstone, emboldened by the brash enormity of the proposition, deserted his subordination for a relatively audacious strike at the Prince.

"That would be supposing I could knot the laces on a rushing *striker's* shoe! Whatever for?"

Grieble, well out of his technical depth, sat motionless with the appreciation that something dreadful was afoot, watching for more indications of the severity of Eugene's paranoia.

"It may well be the single enterprise which rescues the entire project from detection."

Eugene's thoughts, earlier sharp and crisp, now dripped softly from beneath his thin moustache; his eyes fixed through the thin drapes across to the silver river and its supple flakes of liquid winter sun.

"Detection? What do you mean *detection?*"

Grieble caught wise; interjected, "But you have assured me that everything bought has been paid for; services subscribed have been

212

rendered! Relax dear fellow! I've read the papers, listened to the news. You've done quite well thus far, am I not correct?"

Grimstone closed the folder on the table before him. "Would it be so impertinent as to inquire into the nature of the business whose collateral influence upon this meeting appears to both mystify and threaten my interests?"

Bishop Grieble continued, "You have the *Allocation Proposal* back from that doddering academic by now, haven't you?"

Grimstone shot a glance to Eugene.

"The *Proposal*?" and chuckled to himself, drawing the attention from either end of the table; "The *Proposal*? You're worried about Penworth? That *Meddlesome-Spur's* hiding in the hills somewhere if he's not already dead! He's got more important worries on his mind these days, I should guess; moreover, my work remains unfathomable without the key."

Prince Eugene looked across to Grieble, "No. I haven't managed to retrieve it."

He drew a lighter from his vest and rose from his seat to glide over where a cherry wood humidor beckoned.

"There's that delicate line before alarming the unsuspecting; I'm loathe to draw attention to a meaningless pile of financial detritus; worthless pages wanting of encryption . . . and yet."

"Yes! . . . *and yet* indeed!" snapped the good Bishop. Lord Grimstone shook his head in puzzlement; Grieble continued, "That Alistair Constantine still has the *Proposal* will forever be our sincerest hazard. He's a first rate mind and those, gentlemen, come marinated ever more in instinct than in logic; his reputation provides evidence enough to suggest that nothing of such *innocuous* value can survive undetected within reasonable proximity to his compelling curiosity. Penworth will try to contact him, if he hasn't already done so. We must turn our resources toward seeing that nothing comes of this possibility."

Eugene rolled the cigar in his wet mouth, drew deep and exhaled. "I've never been able to enjoy one of these without," he paused and walked the library floor across to the bar, took three snifters and poured a splash of *Di Sorono* into the belly of each, ". . . one of these."

XXXV
Leaving the Church would do no good.

Frederick drove back to the cottage from his unscheduled stop after Jacob Mueller's General Store to have a talk with Chief Richter who expressed no interest in opening a case against the Archbishop of Touchwick on the grounds of no evidence and a petty motive. It was obvious to *him* that Frederick's accusations were based on an indelicately paranoid suspicion of homophobia within the Church; the Good Bishop was merely the figurehead of a developing conspiracy percolating in the grieving vicar's mind.

It was increasingly apparent, at least to Frederick, that the past months had witnessed in him the rebirth and fruition of a shadow character in whose muted existence all his former strength seemed more and more absorbed, leaving less and less of *Frederick* available or recognized by those who grew to know and friend him over the past twenty-odd years.

Gregory had been the key he reasoned, to opening all access for his passions to the world beyond his private fiction; without whom he now suffered an acute, reflexive decent, returned unto his darkest depths. *How odd that in his disappearance I could lose more Frederick than should Gregory have come home to me in death.* His foundering faith alone sustained against the fierce attraction of a total implosion; the key was out there, the hearth must hold a burning log at any time should he come home.

A pair of brown leather gloves gripped the cracked red plastic steering wheel of the old Volvo; the odd old town sliding across the windshield like a movie he had seen ten thousand times; whose ending always caught him by complete surprise; his breath floating from his lips in gossamer laces, drawn out the slightly cracked window.

He always admired the evolution of the hedges, rising as rambling scrub brush from the roadside woods into an open patch where they assembled a formation less irregular, denser; the spaces between them ill-defined until the row became a solid wall, broken only by the gap carved by the driveway entrance, where to Frederick's surprise, a white van sat idling, the exhaust curling like effigies up into the gray sky.

"I need you help again Father; he's very sick. Doesn't know even who he is."

214

"I'll follow in the Volvo; we mustn't waste any time."

XXXVI

She was eighty-eight years old and wore an amulet; a fashioned piece of conch strung around her fluted neck, drawn in folds from weather, gravity and simple age; her long black island hair now white and grey beneath a head-scarf tightly wound; excessive piercings did their patient work, dragging her lobes down to a muted jaw; who came upon the caravan those three score years ago; a young girl lost from any ties, singular in her silence.

That she was a mystic suited the lot; who read into her oddness all such matters of portentous note, as a mirror might show favor on the desperate vanity. She worked in cards and palms with eyes telltale enough for sixty years to compensate her dumbstruck voice, revealing meaning otherwise confused from there.

The Duke still besieged by fever'd dreams and chills, shivered beneath the pile of quilts arranged on the kind old woman's bed; who though eighty plus and rheumatoid took him in upon herself, watched over the poor man like a nurse; slept on the floor beside him overnight, cooked his gruel, brewed his tea and read his cards inside the dark lit trailer where the two were hid. A harsh light from the open door cut through this murky scene as Grigoras introduced Frederick to the gypsy dame, smugly panning head to toe; dismissed him for his collar.

"He's good Mama! He come to help Mama," the good man tried to no avail, "Father, this eez Madam Piko; she like you very much!"

"Yes," he replied dryly, "so I can detect." And moved over to the bed where the delirious patient lay.

The months of harsh weather and rudimentary survival skills had left the fugitive white haired, white bearded and broken; not a face for either man to straightway recognize; though in his formidable privacy of thought, Frederick dared a most fantastic estimate; the mere suggestion filling him with a passion to invest himself, that somewhere for his trouble he might find the antidote to his suffering.

"Fetch me some water, he must swallow these" he instructed holding a pair of tiny yellow tablets, "Please, the lamp."

Frederick stood beside the man for some time; rehearsing text, changing cold rags from his fevered brow, attempting to unravel the cryptic mutterings into some vague coherency. The hours passed, when Grigoras finally returned to the trailer hoping to relieve the tired priest.

"It gets late. Not much sun left for you. Madam Piko watch him for you tonight. Tomorrow we take him to the city, no? To hospital?" Frederick panicked at the suggestion, replied, "No!" startling Grigoras, "absolutely not. Grigoras, I need this man's presence in the camp to remain our private knowledge. I must trust you to protect him."

"You mean *hide* him . . . here in the camp?"

"That is exactly what I mean. I'll return tomorrow with some stronger medicine; perhaps a doctor. Please Grigoras, you must trust me as a man of God; as a friend. Promise me that you will keep him safe."

Grigoras stared Frederick in the eye. "You are my brother; my brother *Frederick! . . . as if I ever wanted such a thing! . . .*" and laughed. "You ask for nothing my friend. Your truth eez truth enough. We don't like so much talk to people from the towns anyhow. Tomorrow you explain some better, no?"

"Tomorrow I will know much more, Grigoras. We talk tomorrow."

Piko pushed past the two men in the tiny trailer, opening the door where she wrung another cloth from Giov's head; his fever had broken. A sound came from the patient, so like a breath as to have almost escaped notice but for the pause, "*Alistair,*" he came again.

Frederick replaced his gloves on the table, going to the bedside, leaned over the Duke, "Yes my friend; what is it?"

Penworth gripped Frederick's hand; a cold grip onto the Priest, ". . . *call on Alistair, Padre; red billiard; tell him.*"

Frederick placed his left hand on the sick man's head, convinced the words were mere inventions of the grippe and little more.

"Three swans scheming on the banks outside the temple; the brother, clerk and faithless host . . . red billiard ball is key"

"Please hand me that water." Grigoras passed the glass to the Priest who spilled the smallest drip into the man's white lips. "Now take it easy; lie

216

back and don't speak."

"*. . . go on, pet the hen's Lotti;. . .like in the book . . . . tell Alistair. . .*"

"Piko, another cold rag please."

And with these words, a stunned Frederick fastened his safety belt and made back to the village where he began a frantic search for this *Alistair.*

XXXVII

A braided leather bracelet was the only intermission in the fluid totem of his life, rendered in a technicolor semaphore of ink stained dates, iconic references to Jesus, guns and mother, running from the deltoid down his arm, extending to his four thin fingers and a ring abiding thumb; stretched from under the food stained covers, out to the clock on the bottle littered nightstand. The thick vinyl curtain allowed for nothing but a razor beam of daylight to breach across the utter blackness of the room. It was impossible for Dominic to read the time; his hand swept a half filled bottle off the table onto the floor.

"What time is it?" he mumbled, face still buried into the damp mattress, "You there?"

Victor was an early riser, in fact already on his way back to the motel room from talking with Sheriff Richter, who withheld any sense of gratitude for the bounty hunter's sudden presence in the region or the service which compelled his visit in the first place; stopped just short of legal excess by not confiscating his Ruger.347 right there at the station.

Gregarious Dominic on the other hand, insisted the pub in town depended on his benefaction, getting back to the room about half an hour before sunrise; a good three hours after Victor had already turned in.

They were an odd pair.

It was ten past noon, still gray and drizzling but bright enough to lend a painful antidote to the slovenly, grotto atmosphere infected upon the motel room when Victor returned to open the door.

Dominic turned his back to the light, desperate to milk the next few minutes of rest before his partner enforced his own, all too familiar ritual revelry.

"Get up."

A caramel colored Camry drove off the gravel lot of the Mt. Pater Motel, hustling out of Söfenzin before Chief Constable Audie Richter rallied the moxie to engage the objectionable pair with additional, more persuasive tactics. They needed supplies for a long trek into the wild Dortpen where the key to their fortune hid among the vast cloak of primal wilderness, out beyond the last stone wall of Hoffenstein.

Hid among the trees, the pair convinced their work was a mere undertaking; simply waggle every branch on Pater's spine until the Duke fell from some propitious bough, down into their hands.

"There's a small village, eight, ten miles up Doggerel Path," said Victor, studying a road map, "I'm pretty sure we can get food and ammo there."

"What about some breakfast? . . . and we need gas."

Victor looked away from the map to the fuel gauge; "We have enough to get to Mayfair. We won't need any more than that."

XXXVIII

The relationship between the Romani and the population collectively sworn to defend and sustain the Royal Coat of Arms has always been a tenuous specimen of symbiotic dependency; the wandering people having only recently begun trading the sovereignty of extensive self-reliance for the less autonomous conveniences gained through a recent and circumspect participation in the more dynamic markets hard at work beyond the borders of the great Dortpen forest.

Affairs of the Hoffench rarely breach the foothills into the higher, more densely forested elevations, as a festering distain among the diaspora has effectively castrated any and all significance from the activities of their arch adversaries; likewise, the death of a gypsy has never made the obituary notices in town.

Monthly travel into Mayfair or Söfenzin for flour, butter, salt and a variety of other staples is a very stoic, detached business; the town folk, suspicious of the Romani, still want their money;
the Gypsy behaves with every caution of the afore-mentioned Nile Plover; ever welcome to clean the reptile's teeth, plain reckless to loiter.

The tax collector gave up rooting out the nomads centuries earlier when it became patently evident the custodial drudgery and peril entailed far outpaced any practical dividend; the Gypsies consequently reap no civic benefit from the Dubois Government, whose official survey nonetheless includes the entire forest where these disregarded people manage a paltry existence, maintaining meanwhile an uncommonly rich and distinctly independent culture.

The trifling raised from periodic descents into the neighboring valleys is then typically pooled; earned in most part by cyclical visits from the mythical hills and hollows of the dark Dortpen, down onto the slumbering valleys where otherwise quiet domestic evenings are, without announcement, shocked from a quiescent exuberance by the pandemonium of colorful wagons, trailers and livestock; nights of music, magic and trained animals, both domesticated and wild; acrobatics, dancing and perhaps, most compelling, a private reading from Madam Piko, soothsayer and healer, whose extraordinary reach into the vast and teeming *beyond* has established a reputation for unsurpassed precision and bewildering utility; whose reputation for oddness extends beyond the coarse amazement of the town folk, becoming years ago an inseparable element of the tight-knit Gypsy folk-lore itself.

Wary of strangers, especially mistrustful of the white colonials, this tribe, which has by no means crossed arbitrarily into our story, discovered the strange young girl wandering lost, unaided many years ago; Grigoras' own father was likely no more than ten years old at the time; took her in from the jaws of death by certain exposure and neglect; subsequently discovering on her person a stamped ticket-half for ocean passage from the Philippines to Portugal; train stubs from Lisbon to Saragossa; Saragossa to Toulouse and Toulouse to Touchwick; a letter of introduction, signed by Mr. Hortense Bidwell, folded among these documents to be presented to the conductor at each station, giving further aide and guidance to the young girl, hopelessly overwhelmed by the eccentric pace and habits of her new home; thoroughly confused, subsequently lost, mysteriously vanished for many, many years.

A doctor in Mayfair, now decades deceased, was full prepared by this same Hortense to expect the arrival of the remarkable subject, this young deaf mute with an alarming exuberance; beautiful black eyes seething to engage, with a tendency toward channeling the cosmic cipher, crisscrossing the barriers of human intellect; a plane where all events and creatures own equal share in the perfection of simply being part of something infinitely more complex, absent vindication; no longer bifurcated across imaginary logarithms of monotonous efficacy.

All these marvelous things inside her exiled mind detected by the compassionate Domestic on holiday; all observed in one simple act inside a humble window frame; two silhouettes: a young girl and her little blue and yellow barbet.

XXXIX

"And in the basket?" he continued, worming a finger under a corner fold in the sheltering towel, relishing, despite the gloomy ambiance recently descended on the grand old house, his unwavering capacity to tease the old cook, by this time worn to her last nerve, crying "*You* Mr. Hobbes, withdraw that finger or *suffer* it!" to which he complied, albeit only on finding the dozen or so eggs concealed therein.

She lead the way through the back door to the kitchen; he followed like an obedient pup, rambling on nonstop regarding all manner of local gossip and domestic intrigue; she placed the basket on the wood block counter-top, spun to face the mischievous butler; removed her coat and muffler promising to have a frosted spatula for him to sample later that afternoon.

"So! The desirable young Miss Barrett takes a merry pity on this anonymous Thursday, does she now? And I'm to benefit thereby! . . . well all's right by me my dear; and may the best egg lift the cake!" he laughed, helping to stow the groceries from their sacks onto the higher shelves where Miss Barrett used to employ a step-stool in her more nimble days.

". . . and Gretchen from *Morgan's* told me that Miss Doris has switched back from corn starch in her gravies; pinching the budget I suppose, things being as tight over there as they are here nowadays."

He rabbited on, disconcerted by the woman's irregular reticence on the matters of her foil next door; a topic customarily known to get the proud woman's goat, exposing a paramilitary talent for culinary punditry rivaling her singular gifts within the epicurean workshop she knew only as home for the past thirty some-odd remarkable years.

Looking down from his place among the loftier cabinet shelves, old Hobbes was mournful-struck by the distressing roundness of his dear friend's bearing; her thin back square between the counter over which she hunched and the sympathetic butler's weary gaze. Something viral was afoot and worse, *immune* to his most potent wit, dispensed to salve the inscrutable poisons fermenting in the sad woman's heart; a sclerosis on the soul when worries stubbornly elude the best intended interventions, the only clear prognosis of the circumstances played out here before him right now.

"What's that on the table by your hand, Mom?" holding for balance onto the cabinet door as he unclimbed the stool and crossed the few tiles to the counter where he laid an arm across Miss Barrett's boney shoulders.

"Ah, there now, Mom; looks like you went and got the mail early for me again this morning; suppose I owe you a token now, eh? . . ."

She moved a hand to rest atop the stack of envelopes; made not a sound; but for the slight arc of her wrist she remained wholly still, her head a vice in whose stern grip stared steel blue eyes, fixed and unblinking on the neat pile of cards and stamps, bound together by a thin elastic band.

"See here now mom! How'm I ever going to taste that spoon with you all done in like so? . . look lively my dear Miss Barrett! Let me have a look will you? Mr. Professor's upstairs at this very moment to triage the whole pile at my asking. I'll just take those if you wouldn't mind . . ." and swept the stack from under her light touch, spying the top address, typewritten   for one *Professor Alistair Constantine, PhD*, from the prestigious *Society for Global Geophysics , Christchurch, New Zealand*. *So the old bird's frightened much as me.*

"You been reading other people's mail, you *felon!*" as she struggled pointlessly to snatch the pile away from Hobbes.

"Thinking about tampering with the *His Majesty's Post*, are you? *They'll take a limb for that, you know!*" he laughed; it was so easy he couldn't resist; *and* it was effective; Miss Barrett came alive.

Snapped like a mesmerized subject from a bright, pendulating coin, the old cook cried "Give them to me! Give me back those letters! They belong to no one; they must be burned!"

"You just calm down Mom!" as he danced two steps ahead of the pitiful woman, who snatched a long wide knife, began waving it in spastic arcs about the kitchen.

"Calm down Mom! Calm yourself at once!" he tried to no avail; the old cook fatigued, dropping the knife, fell into a chair at the small counter under the double hung window outside which the view of the distant forest rose above the roof of the barn, just down the short, hedge lined path leading from the back door. She buried her face into her apron and wept.

Hobbes placed the knife onto the counter without taking his eyes from Miss Barrett, walked over to her chair and softly massaged her shoulders;

"It's been a long, long season, I know Mom," and picked up the bound parcel, "But you haven't forgotten wrong from right, have you? People like us . . ." he stopped short; briefly stunned by the spectacle forever framed by the window; a sense that it was suddenly transformed; a finer view today than all the casual years gone by.

"He'll leave us Robert; he'll go where they call him."

"And if he's to go, it's his right to do so, you foolish woman. We'll never stop him. He's meant to do important things; we can't just sit here and think of ourselves."

"What will become of us? Kicked to the road, that's us! . . . And me, an old woman, I've nothing without *Burlwood*!" She broke into a fit of tears.

"And that's precisely where you're wrong, Mom" he snapped, "Do you think for one minute that Mr. Robert Leslie Hobbes would ever leave *Burlwood* without a fight?! Our fortunes, you forget, are bound; I would no sooner abandon you than would I the Duke himself! We are an integral part of this great legacy, mom; the Duke will come to reclaim his place; sure as the Professor will move on.

"A house like this, it's become a living being; someone has to care for her, that's you and me, Mom! A King knows about such things; trust me."

He held the stack; slid the elastic band aside to read the whole address once more; his thin gaze focused to that faintest image which only those invested in the palest faith, who'd gamble everything against all odds could see.

"I'll have a talk with Mr. Alistair Constantine right now," and marched off to the front of the house, leaving Miss Barrett alone to compose herself and begin work on his marvelous cake.

There came a knock on the front door.

XL

Alistair was taking tea to open his atrophied sinuses in a futile attempt to shake a paranoid forecast of impending influenza, so the glimmering chrome of the approaching vehicle aroused only the slightest flame of hospitable curiosity.

As he was only half dressed and ill prepared to suffer any trifling interruption from his latest scholastic immersion (this morning's obsession being the nature and defeat of the influenza microbe), it came to his considerable relief that Hobbes had just entered the foyer from the library entrance with a bundle of mail in his hand which he silently dispatched to the old academic, fluidly sailing as befit his post, synchronizing his reception at the front door with the Professor's disappearance behind the same Library door on his way to the kitchen for more tea.

"May I help you?"

Here, the kindhearted butler was pleasantly surprised to find waiting on the opposite side of the knock, a weathered old priest with his hat held firmly in his hands before him; *evidence of genteel customs, quite rare nowadays*; a gesture served instinctively to parse any number of vestigial formalities and abridge the awkward ritual of establishing some base line for cordial exchange.

"Good day sir. My name is Frederick Brennan-Pye."

XLI

The Professor paced around the study like a puma in a cage, having neither taken the time to finish dressing nor the consideration to inquire as to whether the minister already had breakfast. Hobbes, endowed with impeccable instincts, had already accounted for the eccentric's complete lack of social decorum, knocked and entered the room, *as had become his exceedingly casual style*, holding a tray of muffins, a decanter of coffee with three cups and accoutrements.

"So he's taken ill, has he? Is he in any other sort of danger?"
Hobbes placed the tray onto the low table set between the sofa and the two wing-backed chairs opposite.

223

"I assure you Professor; the Duke's situation is tentative at best. His only allies are a peculiar old clairvoyant who seems to have taken a sincere shine to him and a middle aged man who I proudly consider a relatively recent, yet dear friend; a Romani of reasonable influence whose absolute trust I accept implicitly but whose capacity to suppress the situation shall inevitably out-maneuver him."

Hobbes poured a cup for both the Professor and the Priest before filling the third cup for himself. "So, Hobbes." The Professor took a most sardonic tone, "I'm delighted you've chosen to join us! Please have a seat and make yourself at home."

Frederick was quite taken by the remark; instinctively placed his cup and saucer down onto the coffee table and switch-crossed his legs.

"I'm heavily invested Alistair, as you well know;" Hobbes rejoined, vaguely piqued, yet full measured and respectful, "only takes a fourth level education to read the envelopes I've been delivering. Now unless my presence here poses some impediment toward a solution to my Master's dreadful circumstances, I'll continue to proffer my humble assistance."

Thoroughly satisfied, Alistair grinned and turned back to Frederick.

"It's insufferable to stand here powerless while my boy lies bedbound in the den of wolves; his very name a certain death sentence! We must take measures to liberate the Duke; this much, aside from every consequence, is paramount."

"His convalescence, however, dictates he remain where he is; too ill to move," the minister rejoined.

"I will return with medicine tomorrow, hoping he will soon gain strength enough to speak more clearly; his ramblings I fear more than his unlikely detection."

Hobbes screwed his eyes, remarking "Good Lord! . . . Surely his Grace's portrait should already have provoked suspicion, no?"

Alistair turned sharply to the Priest, measuring his response.

"News from the valley seldom rises higher than the foothills; the Gypsies, for their part, seldom wander closer than an eagle's view of Mayfair's outer wall; little news but what they absorb from a brief visit to the General Store is ever considered up there; they're fine enough with their own troubles.

"As for his appearance, I hesitate to alarm you further, yet I must admit, the months have taken their toll, gentlemen. Were it not for his incoherent mutterings, I could *never* have placed the face with the man, so transformed he was."

Hobbes placed his trembling cup into its saucer, leaned over to place them on the table; his eyes were red, tired and red. He looked over to the window where the Professor stood; a surprisingly small silhouette against the great bright plane of glass, looking out onto the rolling miles of bucolic Dortpen, ever rising to its snowy peak where Pater mutely stares back down into the same great window on three small men before a crackling fire.

Alistair suddenly turned to Frederick.

"You mention these *muttering* and *ramblings*; were they even marginally intelligible?"

At this the Minister's face lit up. "Why of course! This is what brings me here today, for the love of God! I've been so caught up with other details; I clear forgot my initial reason for seeking you out!"
Alistair rolled his eyes, "Yes, yes Father! What is it you want to tell us?"

Hobbes sat transfixed, his eyes intent on the minister's lips, his breathing stopped.

"He pleaded for me relay a message; quite broken, as to be cryptic, but the exact words were thus:

> *Three swans scheming on the banks outside the temple;*
> *the brother, clerk and faithless host.*

To which he added a reference to the game of billiards."

The Professor looked a blend of intrigue and puzzlement as he coaxed the collared courier to continue.

"More precisely, he said: *red billiard ball is key* . . ."

Hobbes had by this time searched the Duke's writing desk for a pen and paper on which he recorded these enigmatic words. *What in God's name could this possibly mean?!!*

Frederick continued with his best account of his encounter with the Duke; remembering at long last to adapt into the separate yet related tale of Father Linus Crispe and his encounter with the *Brother* and the *Pompous Host.*

Alistair beamed; threw off the house robe and exclaimed, "That's it, Hobbes!" so loudly as to make the nervous Butler jump from the desk about a foot.

"That's *what*, sir?"

"Miss Doris' *jam*, Hobbes! . . . I believe our Duke is not quite as illogical as you suspect, Father! Did he have anything more to say?"

Frederick, now pleasantly bewildered, added "He then made reference to *Lotti*, who I've come to know through a tragic coincidence as the young girl, Lord Penworth's daughter Charlotte, who stopped Gregory, my husband, to examine his truck loaded with hens one day by the side of the road. Gregory told me the whole story over dinner, later that same evening. He thought it absolutely enchanting. *And now the two of them-*"

It was pointless to engage the Priest any further.

Alistair flew from the room to finish dressing, taking no time to excuse himself or show Frederick to the door.

That was fine enough for Hobbes.

XLII

It is typical for the otherwise migratory band to choose a practical place well before the first snow bends the cedars with its icy emphasis; a base camp wherein to brace against the hoary months 'til spring returns and wakes that epic restiveness; that *wanderlust* so often called upon, yet whose tedious embellishments less than half explain the full character of the clan.

Resurrected in early December this year, for example, are the manifestations of a dormant skill and attention toward intransience; ropes

226

replaced by timbers, canvas by tin sheets and sod, stone ringed fire pits by brick laid stoves, wine with whiskey; all subtleties, *save the latter*, most impractical in June.

Grigoras pulled from his pipe to confirm, with irrevocable proof, the bothersome fact that it was time to relight the bowl with kindling from the roaring fireplace situated at the far side of the communal lodge, where at the moment, a gathering of adults mingled in the late evening firelight, beneath the flickering shadows of hung dried meats, small cages, traps and other artifacts; gathered tonight to discuss the arrival of the hermit now recuperating in the old psychic's trailer.

Conspicuous was the absence of Madame Piko.

"So, you would leave him to die, cold and alone in a cave." Grigoras paused to draw the long flame deep into his bowl, puffed half a dozen times against the stem, filling the vent above the door with a column of thick blue smoke.

Cosmo answered for Alina, "Some have families here who want to know first where the old man comes from; who, *let's be honest*, I hear he speaks like a *Colonial*. Tell me about some of these things, *then* I worry about details like *cold* and *alone*."

Grigoras paced the hut, ducking to pass beneath the small cage where an old squirrel curled inside the slightest blanket of a tail, drunk in squirrel dreams;

"Then I find out!" he replied, pushing Kafka's nose out from his pocket where, the brazen hound had ascertained, on rich occasions hid small scraps of cured jerk-beef.

"How small a problem! Alina, Cosmo; all of you, Poppy comes tomorrow with some medicine. Just look at the picture here: an old man with a white head and silver beard shivers in an old woman's bed. *You think he wants to mess with these?*"

A great smile broke beneath the kind man's thick black beard as he patted his formidable biceps in a lark.

"Besides, Poppy will take him back if he belongs to the *Colonials*, I promise all of you; otherwise, men like him, they go back to hiding on their own. We shouldn't bother learning how to treat strangers in the way of *Colonials*, should we?"

Yoseri, a generation older than Grigoras and skillful *Rom baro* since a time before Grigoras shared the blood bread with Roxanna, tamped his pipe and sighed; all that was required to lure the room's undivided attention and began his cross examination.

"Cosmo, you have no children . . . when did you become such advocate for family?" he grinned, "not that I don't like unmarried boy who likes family, just asking is all."

"*Alina* has family," he shot back. "I speak for a woman here who has no man to speak for her!"

The group then traded riotous cackles for jeers, drowning the explosive indignation of Alina toward the hubris of Cosmo's shocking oath of youthful gallantry; guinea hens woke from their makeshift roosts and ran diagonal patterns throughout the cluttered space, in between the legs and feet beneath the long table on whose back the hand warmed scotch bottles freely traded sweltering whiskey for chilled night air; tobacco pouches, unzipped lying there.

The old Baro, dressed in multicolored rags, tucked his well-worn fiddle tight into his chin and drew the long, frayed bow across the strings, *the key G#*; all heads turned and voices dropped until the serenade concluded yet another chance for each to muse into the vapors of an antique past; a history which bound them all into a single phrase, artfully described once more upon the bridge and guts of the old man's precious instrument.

All but Cosmo; in a youthful scorn, ashamed stormed from the lodge into the cold; into the night.

"He'll practice many years to grow a beard," Yoseri sighed and packed his pipe.

Flakes of snow were falling through the trees.

XLIII

Back to Burlwood from a long hike in the fresh morning snow, Professor Constantine stomped his boots in the coat room behind the galley, hastening the knotted laces, then removed them; storming the kitchen where Miss Barrett bent into the oven to remove a tray of quick bread;

228

her wide rump providing a berm over which the anxious academic spied the indefatigable Hobbes, napkin tied efficiently about his throat, finishing a cup of boiled brown eggs, side of sausage and coffee; the *Touchwick Chronicle* in a rail-car fold held deftly in his long fingers.

"If you would be kind enough to send a tray upstairs to Master Penworth's study, Miss Barrett; loaded with warm bread and a pot of Miss Doris' most pleasant preserves; fresh coffee, sugar, cream and leave them at the door. I've no wish to be disturbed this afternoon. Hobbes, you will be enthusiastically astonished at my progress thus far! . . . *Nothing like a morning walk to clear the mind!*"

Dropping his paper, Hobbes respectfully stood from the table and nodded, replying, "A very pleasant morning to you, Professor. I'll see to your breakfast *exactly* as you prescribed."

Miss Barrett spun around, having almost dropped the tray at Alistair's explosive introduction; still entirely unfamiliar, after all those many docile years, with his degree of unrefined élan; she looked to Robert, as was her way, for any clue to what her best response should be; *silent focus on the task at hand*, his usual prescription.

She continued filling the napkin lined basket with the hot biscuits, *stung by the reference to Miss Doris' handiwork*, avoiding the radioactive core of his gaze by staring everywhere but.

"As you require, Professor."

The hours passed, transfiguring the short morning shadows into longer strokes and wider fields of bluest blue across the smooth white meadows and hillocks outside the upstairs library windows, where Hobbes passed the many hours absorbed into his latest mystery novel.

It was four o'clock and not a sound had breached the study since the nine o'clock event wherein all mayhem was invoked, moving the large rolling blackboard from the play room downstairs up into the study; the mad scramble for a fresh pack of chalk no less droll than the great Beethoven's celebrated rage over a lost penny.

Finally, at six-thirty that afternoon, as was a tribute to the *Great Intellect's* focus, intuition and inimitable tenaciousness, the door opened and the manic old man crossed its saddle into the hallway where he called out into the great empty space of the old house, "Hobbes, come quickly! *We've done it!*"

XLIIII

Hobbes was himself absorbed by the scene outside the library window, where the headlights of a black sedan were groping their way up the snow plowed drive, quickly approaching the house; his heart, for the briefest moment, stopped its beat; behind it, the lights of a second, identical black sedan.

"*Hobbes! We've done it!*" came the cry, as the practical Domestic quickly sprang into action.

Charging from his cozy indentation in the library's most agreeable reading chair, Hobbes reached the Professor with an urgency so dire, so sincere, as to gain the reason with a directness mere words are not equipped to provide.

"Inspectors are here. Whatever you've found is most likely what they've come to take from you. Think quickly Professor and act quicker still!"

For the first time in this whole tale, I must admit, I've never had the cause to write about Alistair Constantine caught so thoroughly off his guard; and yet here he was, unable to switch from a day of ponderous analytical labor to the proactive hyper-animation required of the situation; his greatest asset, Hobbes.

"You will use the time descending the staircase to collect your usual cynical humor; greet our guests with all the vinegar and honey of which you are masterfully capable. Most important, *delay*! Give me time upstairs to do my work! *GO!*"

There came a knock.

XLV

"What brings two of Touchwick's finest so far from the city?" the Professor asked, having employed the staircase to maximum advantage; "Two cars?, my, my . . . How may I help you this time, Special Investigator . . . *Jules*, isn't it? . . . with Private Detective Damian. Please come in, the cold is blowing into the house."

The two Lawmen entered the foyer, marveling openly at the massive chandelier suspended from an impossibly high ceiling, left to dangle its bottom finial some fifteen feet from the floor, above the tessellated likeness of two figures from an ancient time of heraldic majesty, set into the tile by anonymous craftsmen centuries ago.

"Professor Constantine. It is my officious happenstance to inconvenience you at yet another of Mr. Penworth's . . . *unpresumptuous* abodes," replied Ombreux. "Thank you for not holding us outside on such a cold evening."

His memory of the previous interview at the *Dumont* townhouse was fresh; a harbinger of his attitude toward the unbecoming coup tonight; the Old Gent was a cagey study alright, but Special Investigator Jules Ombreux had come in force this time, all antes hedged behind the authorized scribble on the warrant folded in his right breast pocket. *No need to strike capriciously; still plenty of time to exact a reprisal.*

"Is it your habit, Professor, to always avail yourself at the door? It seems a number of things tonight are exceedingly familiar with peculiarity."

Detective Damian, ever sparing with conversation, appeared less agitated, peeling his tight black gloves down from his wrists and clasping them with his left fist, held inside the right hand behind his back; more than delighted, giving the full stage to his more affable accessory.

"Having you wait," Alistair replied "until Hobbes was finished in the commode *was* my first thought; *very intuitive of you Inspector*; but the night being cold as it is. . . Now what business brings you all the way out to Mayfair?"

The hour was late, the night poor comfort to the traveler; Ombreux here conceded to his impatience far more quickly than he had rehearsed those many bitter nights.

"I've come to look around the house for evidence relating to the disappearance of the fugitive, Charles David Geoffrey Penworth, or *Giov* as he's commonly known, formally of this address. Recent developments have revealed enough circumstantial activity for a warrant to search the premises for tangible support specific to certain, related allegations."

He produced the warrant to dramatic effect. "I've brought additional manpower, but desire, as one gentleman to another, a willingness to cooperate, for which I'm prepared to avoid the need to populate this beautiful home with a half dozen heavy handed mercenaries looking for a pebble in a quarry."

Alistair learned much from his busy blackboard calisthenics that afternoon. The warrant, he estimated, was worth several hundred million francs to anyone with influence enough to fortify it with a fabricated essence of legitimacy; someone with enough power to fill its maw with teeth. With so much at stake, he reasoned, money was motive enough to trade a life to avoid scandal; his life for a scrap of paper.

"Well, if you have a warrant, I suppose you're going to come in," he recited, and waved his arm to summon them away from the entrance hall, drawing them deeper into the house.

"May I impose, *as one gentleman to another*, to examine the warrant that you so *officiously* exercise?" he stalled.

Images of a desk covered in a sea of numerical sketches, notated reports and diagrams with names, account numbers and perhaps most damning, hard implications of ecumenical intrigue. And then there was the blackboard. *Hardly time enough for all the air to clear of chalk dust.*

He was finished; it was over.

"Be my guest," and handed Alistair the tri-folded papers. "But you're going to have to study them *in motus* my friend; while we search. Detective Damian and I would be no sooner pleased than were we in transit with our evidence, back across the Pont Dubois."

"This *evidence*; can you describe it? Perhaps I can be of help. Seeing you two off and across the Pont Dubois would be a genuine pleasure, I can assure you."

Jules simply turned his back to the scholar and continued on toward the salon.

Damian began his investigation at the very entrance of the house, lifting paintings away from the wall, spilling cabinets, curios and side table drawers; he even pulled letters from opened envelopes; all this industriously completed on the way to the great staircase, the trail to where Inspector Ombreux suspected the real treasure lay.

The genuine irony of the whole situation struck a chord deep within the Professor, half skimming the warrant while otherwise musing how the Penworths fought for twenty-two generations in the name of the crown; who for three quarters of a century endeavored on construction of a tunnel to escape the savages once reviled for vandalizing the peace and properties of the same territory now pilfered by minion of the Crown's own corrupt appendage. This time, the irony brought no upward curl to his lips.

"Excuse me Inspectors;" his voice pitched high with excitement, "Stop what you're doing there, Detective!" He had discovered something in the warrant.

Ombreux rolled his eyes, repeating the Professor's call for Damian to stop turning the hallway inside out.

"Yes, Alistair; it was only a matter of time. I had every confidence in your ability to read," a monotonous sarcasm in his voice.

"But the warrant clearly restricts your jurisdiction to the Duke's study upstairs. You've absolutely no authority to finger anything else in this house!"

The old academic, now shaking, wondered with fresh agitation what might have delayed the faithful Butler for so long. He had grown over the time, somehow dependent upon the humble man for genuine moral encouragement.

"The secret to many an important distinction, Professor, lies not so much in its elaboration, but instead in the absence of any detail. For instance, *and I'll spare you the tedium of poring over the rest of the warrant*, you'll concede that neither does it dictate a limit to the number or quality of agents I instruct to execute the search. I consider this entire house a crime scene!"

"The warrant apparently begs to differ!"

"You play hard ball with me, Alistair, and see how I earned my reputation for a vicious volley. How would you write this scene?"

"We've nothing to hide, Inspector. But as I'm currently ill-compensated for my many years of effort toward the advancement of a better understanding of our world through science; a place you would arbitrarily choose to safeguard; I ask again, as one gentleman to another, for your investigation to be as brief and unobtrusive as only a professional of your tenure and bearing can capably provide. The Butler has received no allowance since the loss of His Grace's daughter and Detective Damian over there has already confirmed the poor domestic's itinerary for the next several days."

"And speaking of your Butler; does he suffer from dysentery? I'm inclined to surmise, but for the weather, your Domestic has taken leave for want of wages."

Enter Hobbes, on cue, with his signature tray of coffee and a plate of Miss Barrett's holiday cookies.

"Compliments of the kitchen, gentlemen."

Inspector Ombreux approached the Detective to request that he dismiss the second car outside; "We've got this well under control; no need keeping the boys waiting indefinitely in this cold."

Exitus Detective Damian; ascensus scalae.

XLVI

The doors were all stripped of their many coats of white paint about the time Lord Penworth returned from Angola; restoring each to its original wood flesh, then hand finished in a natural chestnut varnish, the Study entry sat just past midway of the long hall; breathing, it appeared, in anticipation of the condemned academic and his magistrate.

There, opposite the paneled surface of the sealed study door, behind its indiscernibly respiring face, the shrewd Inspector could foresee the hideous crime scene, strung in all the charismatic disarray he eagerly envisioned; preserving one last drop of innocence; some small sting of encounter the shock of true discovery has not yet ceased to proffer. *Inspector Jules Ombreux* would be commended for this night, he was assured.

"It's locked, Professor. Would you be so kind?"

Alistair fumbled with his ring of keys, investing any small tablet of time at his disposal upon the series of unlikely occurrences which drew him here; dropped the whole set onto the carpet.

"For a house with nothing to hide, you act quite unnatural, Alistair."

The Professor stooped to retrieve the set, stood again, redirecting, "I've spent the better half of my time living in a tent somewhere north or south of the Polar circles, Inspector; keys are a very cumbersome exchange for the comfort of a warm bath."

Jules broke the smallest laugh, "You are a character indeed. Perhaps some other time; some other circumstance, we'd share a bitter over laughs."

Alistair responded with a dour face, "I should think not," and unlocked the door.

"Step back from the door if you please," and the law man slowly swung the heavy panel to a darkened room. He tripped the wall switch, lighting a number of soft glowing sconces throughout the magnificent room. Alistair braced himself upon entering behind the Inspector.

The desk lay in perfect order. The blackboard wiped clean of intrigue and reworked with figures from the household budget. The air was free of chalk, the smell of cinnamon permeated throughout.

Inspector Ombreux's slumped like a Dali clock upon his collar.

Wordlessly he drifted through the room; floated like the last surviving victim through the scorched alleys of Pompeii, stunned by the devastating mass of evidence that was not waiting for him there.
He went over to the desk.

"I suppose it's pointless to request you unlock these drawers, but for the sake of diligence, please humor a tired old Inspector, would you?"

Alistair, for his own sake, was equally stunned, if not more so. *I had left this room in total ruin.*

"Yes . . .," he stumbled, "but of course."

Then regaining himself added, "But only to satisfy the warrant! I've absolutely no idea what could possibly interest you or any one back in Touchwick with the Duke's private study. He certainly isn't suspected of plotting the assault on his daughter from this room."

Further emboldened by the good Domestic's meticulous attention to detail, he continued, "And if it's clues to his suspected whereabouts, wouldn't the warrant have included a broader range of targets; his bedroom or the garage for instance? What business have you anyhow, rifling through the desk of a notable member of Parliament? There's something very untoward to this whole business and I've just the mind to accept my invitation with the good Duke's old friend and colleague at the Palace!"

Now perhaps, was time to stop. A chill seeped into the Professor's agitated bones; *had I said too much?*

A knock interrupted the two men before Inspector Jules could respond.

"Detective Marc Damian, sir," he was announced.

"Very well Hobbes. I suppose you *had* to," Alistair replied, and the Detective joined the Inspector in a two hour long, thorough turnover of the poor Duke's old study.

Constantine and Hobbes meanwhile, struggled to provide mutual comfort to the other's jagged nerves just down the hall, in the library, during the ordeal.

"They're calling for a slight dusting tomorrow. Is the plough still fixed to your truck?"

"Yes sir. I don't usually remove it until middle March."

"Quite right to do so," noted the preoccupied scholastic.

The Professor joined Hobbes at nine o'clock, sending the two policemen on their way back to Touchwick; the good Butler waited at the sumptuous door while Alistair accompanied his *guests* outside; walking them to their cold and waiting automobile.

"You won't reach Bertahl until half past eleven; in this weather, maybe later. I'd invite you to stay for the night, but the house *really* is a mess, you know. How unsatisfied you must feel, having made your grand play only to leave with a more compelling case for his innocence."

The Inspector smiled. He genuinely grew to like Alistair, almost wishing they could collaborate one day; *our two extraordinary brains at work on the same side of a warrant!*

"You make a very good point, Professor. When we return, *and you can expect us soon enough*, I'll be sure to give myself more time. The Duke's innocence is another matter entirely. Good night to you, sir."
"Yes indeed. Godspeed gentlemen!" and turned back toward the house against the muffled sound of a large sedan driving quietly away, down the long snow coated drive.

Hobbes waited dutifully in the doorway for his good friend, who stopped for a brief moment in the lot to admire the nighttime portrait of the grand Burlwood estate; its magnificent neo-Gothic stone work, its fabulous glowing windows, its numerous spires and countless chimneys stabbed into the belly of a crisp, star filled winter sky.

It was a breathtaking sight to be sure, his caressing eyes circling back now, across the copper work and buttresses, toward the great doors where Hobbes waited with his characteristic patience beneath the well-lit study window, *recent scene of intrigue most fantastic*, one floor directly above the ivy covered vestibule, where a small satchel hung suspended by a leather strap; an odd sight, he smiled; *as if someone were attempting to hide something.*

XLVII

The snow made it impossible for Frederick to convince the old Volvo to drive him any further than a few miles out of Söfenzin, where he sat helpless once more; stopped along the road with his head and hands against the steering wheel, praying for guidance.

With a vial full of tablets in his jacket and a very ill man stranded somewhere, far out there, it was a most desperate effort to resist the overwhelming impression of perplexing entrapment, beguiling his battled reason ever closer to the darkest side of providence; a place within the mind where all events are rationalized biographically; nothing risen or befallen by coincidence, but rather further confirmation of an undetected force *again* at work against him.

He raised his eyes up from the wheel and looked out on the clear bright valley; such a perfect morning. *Gregory will be just heading off to the city in his old blue truck, filled with cages filled with hens.*

A hawk far off, chased in cork-screw patterns by a stubborn pair of senseless crows, drew his eye ever farther from his place; to where the distant tree line edged the meadow; pushed lazily away by napping gusts of expanding, frigid space.

Never in his many years had such loneliness taken hold; an emptiness unfilled by good deeds, by prayer. *There was a God*, he well believed; the evidence out there, spread wide across the landscape; but on which side of all this wondrous faith was he?

Seized by an impulse to confront the long ignored appraisal of his own self-worth, Father Frederick pulled the gloves off from his hands; the windshield now laced in a thin film of his breath; reached behind his neck to pull the scarf out from his coat. *It's not too late to stop.*

He unbuttoned the clerical ring about his neck, pulled it away from his throat and placed it on the seat beside him; never pausing from his strict consideration of the hawk in bold retreat.

A sudden thrill of blasphemy had overcome the creeping gloom now deeply dyed and threatening to his soul.

XLVIII

The old green automobile had sat as it did for the entire duration since the Professor's arrival, started and superficially maintained on few occasions by Felis, *and never since*; whose mechanical curiosity far exceeded his technical proficiency; motivated to start the motor more by a romantic compulsion than by any sincere obligation to its legitimate upkeep.

So the car sat motionless inside the garage for half a year.

It was for this reason that Hobbes found himself struggling at the last hour with a very ice packed, very stubborn garage bay door, as Alistair had suddenly announced he would present his findings to the one authority he could marginally trust; an ear located hours away in the fabulous and bustling town across the Silberfluss.

The odds were barely even on his success, but less against him than should he bide another day at Burlwood, waiting for some vapor of alternative to blow his way. Ombreux would certainly return with greater influence; the house turned inside out.

Better to make his introduction to the enigmatic King, than gamble that his further hesitation would insure a worthier thing.

"I should go with you, sir. You know this."

His breath condensed in the cold, thin air. The Professor circled the car, rested his briefcase on the back seat then turned to Hobbes.

"Who'll stay with Miss Barrett? No, my friend, the Inspector will return at any time; I'm gambling that he's already been admonished for his uninspiring performance! Master Penworth would require one of us to speak up for this old shack, and *you* know this much as well. Goodbye Robert. Wish me success."

"Then be well, Professor Constantine. And accept one final apology for erasing the blackboard."

Alistair hugged the old Butler goodbye, "Don't be ridiculous! My mind, for better or worse is made one half from sponge, the other half a solution of silver nitrate and potassium iodide. Nothing lost by your inspired action but our innocence preserved. Now speak of it no more. I'm off to the Palace." He subconsciously felt inside his jacket pocket for the small white card given him one somber day by a king.

The old green Citroen puttered down the driveway out of sight.

XLVIIII

The access afforded to the bearer of such an unsuspecting voucher astounded the Professor, as he passed through half a dozen gates and doorways with every ease of a member of the Dubois family itself; observing how, at each sentry post, the stern countenance of authority yielded to a more relaxed flexibility of bewildered compliance at the underestimation of the old threadbare figure with the even older valise.

His hours in the library waiting were well spent, devouring *obsolete* articles of meteorological import, *soon enough upstaged* by graphs and numbers gathered by *his* more sensitive instruments, hard at work in God forsaken regions throughout the southern hemisphere.

Approximately four hours had passed before a Page entered the library to announce His Majesty's brief audience was now availed.

"Please follow me." And the Professor followed.

Through the back stage labyrinth of ancient halls and staircases; dim lit galleries and, in one amusing instance, through a secret passage disguised into a wainscot wall, the silent vassal led on.

The Palace, though formidable an edifice against the city backdrop, assumes the scale of twice the size within; most fascinating!

Their journey ended at a door; instructions were then repeated by the dutiful Page for Alistair to continue through to the hallway's end; there he would be left to decide whether to continue to starboard or port.

On both ends of the short passage were identical doors, equidistant from the primary hallway's intersection.

Each door led into another small chamber, ten foot square, wholly unfurnished and thoroughly uninviting, with a second door on the opposite side, reached only by releasing the first door, operated on a set of weights which dropped to close it automatically; locked to prevent reentry.

This second door led either to a short hall where a stairwell to the billiard room upstairs waited with a stick, a table, chalk and a King; the other to a garden where a sentry stood to lead the confounded guest to his car, a cab or the first bicycle heading off the Palace grounds.

The choice was, in every respect, that very wager, so awkwardly amusing to His Majesty; a gamble of his own that pedaling indignantly away was not also the solution to his Fiefdom's privation. . . . *Ah, but isn't this the very spice of life?*

"I'd very much enjoy circumventing this nonsensical distraction and be directed to the Billiard Room in the more familiar manner of my previous appointments, *thank you very much.*"

"As his Majesty instructs. Good luck to you, sir," bowed his head and disappeared back into the darkness from which they came.

"Max! This is ludicrous!" echoed Alistair's voice in the empty hall. "Juvenile!" and began down the passage.

L

"As if *Luck* had a finger on *any* scale!" he spat. "Four bloody hours wasted in *your* squalid little library to be humiliated like this! *Maximillian!*"

He reached the end of the diminutive corridor, where his *luck* was contrived to suffer a trial. By this point he had already considered simply reconfiguring the Palace maze inside his remarkable brain, by which practice he would naturally arrive back at his current location, this time with an exact reference to the hallway's compass orientation; from there it was a small effort to establish the relative proximity of both the billiard room and the garden. He had every intention, every confidence, of outwitting the little upstart . . . *that is* . . . with one *awkward* exception;

There was a very narrow spiral stair, reached just beyond the secret portal in the wainscot; on the wall beside the top step, a framed lithograph of New Zealand, courtesy of *A. Hoen & Co., 1844*; a print he admired as much for its detailed depiction of the southern Otago district, *where he was presently in collaboration with the Society for Global Geophysics,* as for its showcasing of the printmaker's skill.

The difficulty presented by this unique article, was not in the trigonometry of his compass orientation departing onto the downstairs hallway with respect to the leading top step; (for the count of the steps was twenty two, at roughly fourteen and one half degrees per step with a four inch leading edge, making his decent ending at an orientation three hundred and eighteen degrees clockwise from his initial, embarking coordinates). Entering the top from a Northern perspective, facing south, for example, descending clockwise three hundred and eighteen degrees would leave him on the bottom landing facing South-South-East, and so his solution could begin from knowledge of this; no, the trigonometry was sufficient enough.

And herein lay the good Professor's dilemma: the surreptitious doorway, by his impeccable recollection, was fabricated into a North-South oriented wainscot wall, entered from west toward east; *this much was not subject to reconsideration.*

But at this point the trail becomes confused.

His guide, sharing no interest in the framed likeness of New Zealand, had continued forth at his rather brisk pace, descending halfway down the staircase before admonishing Alistair to keep closer quarters, leaving the preoccupied Scholastic to rush the spiral passageway from points unobserved, urgent not to be left behind.

It was a complete blank in his memory; from which direction did he start the stairs? A wave of distracted flames rekindled for the contemptible acts and privilege of the adolescent King;
. . . memories of a glasshouse filled with toxic gas;

a boy whose conjuring intelligence proved ill-provided, through a ritualistic enablement, for any natural consequence regarding such a puckish repertoire.

He looked left and saw a sleeping door; a handle which demanded at the very least a brief examination; the professor took his time to engage just so; the polished handle tossed an arbitrary ray of sconce light back into his tired eye; here he could discern no clue.

The door just opposite, aside from its reflexive correlation to the one just now observed, bore nothing more or less to satisfy the keen Professor's eye or mind; a perfect set; a perfect riddle; a gambler's perfect dilemma.

The valise switched now to the opposite hand allowed his left fingers free to rummage through the loose change in his trouser pocket; feeling for the largest coin; *a toss would end all consternation in a turn; responsibility thus transposed*; but the stubborn man of science simply wiped instead a handkerchief across his running nose. He proceeded to the right with every sense of decorum.

LI

The sun was hanging very low upon the horizon, almost dusk. Alistair stood in the company of officers in winter dress; smiling as the old Professor placed his valise onto the ground and clasped his hands behind his neck, legs spread in a posture of ultimate subordination, there among the skeletal rose hedges and topiary planted seven feet above the snow covered Royal cesspool.

It had been a tough week; a tough year for the old man. He was a gentleman of another world; one of scholarship and inquisitive isolation; the customs of such present culture were progressively alienating; more foreign and forgettable to him than the indigenous habits of the scant populations happily survived beneath the commercial radars, south of the Antarctic circle.

He simply desired to leave.

"You'll come with me, sir." An officer of the guard instructed Alistair to retrieve his leather bag and follow him back into the Palace.

Within moments, Alistair recognized the familiar door, behind which were a stick, a table, chalk and a King. The officer displayed every protocol expected of his rank, knocking without the slightest tell to announce the arrival of a guest whose unprecedented significance also excluded any call for a valet, a cabby, or a bicycle.

The door opened and Alistair Constantine, PhD entered, absent any previous presumptions of reprimand or vague familiarity; the sense was that he had entered into the realm of an exceedingly complex and formidable character; Max, as he was, had gone *forever*.

In as much, Maximillian had full fulfilled his least subtle intention: *no regal awe toward any common man;* this *finally* included Professor Alistair Constantine, PhD.

"Your Highness," and nodded his head.

"Professor," the host exclaimed, "So kind of you to pay your respects. Please, drop the formalities and take your coat off. I trust you had no trouble finding the place?" A short burst of laughter.

"None, your Highness, none whatsoever." Alistair was immediately overcome with Master Penworth's own words, *With every caution. The mirrors have ears in Touchwick, I'm afraid; and Max can be quite a devil himself sometimes . . .*

Here was the lion's den now, for sure; his valise in its inimitable order. The moment's next wager was entirely his to call: *the brother's hand upon a treasonous hilt; evidence sufficient to excise a Bishop; the exoneration of a good man, unjustly aggrieved; and most traitorous of all, a murder inquiry turned upon a father's only real connection to the world;* thoughts now turned from ending well to simply . . . *ending.*

Alistair looked about the room, its quaint familiarity; the times he chalked his cue; raised his glass to Max's father; the precious reunion with the Duke just last summer; his head rushed with strange timidity. Maximillian for the first time in his knowledge stood before him as a King.

"Four hours in my library, waiting . . . A busy man like you must have something extraordinary in your briefcase, Professor. Pray tell, what could it be?" Maximillian took a drink, bent and shot the cue ball at the seven which dropped with a snap off the far side bumper into the corner pocket, where his glass of brandy balanced on the molding just above.

"If you're attempting to unnerve me with your goading, your Highness, you've quite succeeded; but I'll tell my tale regardless as the truth and fate of one we both regard hangs in the balance."

Maximillian bent to sink the eight, which missed and bounced to roll and land behind the nine.

"Oh . . . bad form!" and stood his cue onto the floor.

"You feel tight? I don't like *tight*. Tight just cost me the eight." He turned his back to the table, adding *"Relax* Professor; I'm wanting this to be a sort of *fact finding* discussion, not a debate."

He sauntered over to the bar where he refilled his glass, asking Alistair what he wished, "See, we're alone here. It's how I like this room. Let a King pour you a favor."

"Scotch. Single malt over one cube. I've an allergy to ice."

"So I've heard Alistair," smiling in that indescribable *King-like* manner. "Now what are you protecting in your little school bag?"

The tableside telephone restricted interruptions to the merest set of vetted candidates; usual suspects being immediate family or agitated Heads of State. In the course of this evening however, instructions following the last of three forwarded attempts were that no further interruptions of *any* kind would be tolerated upon threat of severe reprimand.

The felt was soon overrun with sheets of paper; some offset in small groups, some lain side by side; pages filled with tabulations, charts and graphs; to the left of all this work lay the fresh plucked folders, having given of themselves to make a case against the villainy now engaged upon the tiny kingdom. The time was late; the King enthralled.

"But these amount to little more than serious accusations, Alistair; and don't get me wrong, I do believe your instincts are correct; your heart is in the right place. There's just too much here to digest!"

The King paced the length of the gaming table, hands clasped behind him. It was clear that he sincerely wanted to pursue the matter right through to litigation, but doubted whether the Professor had yet made a fool-proof case.

"You say the scheme, when put in motion shares the elegance of a fine chronometer . . . *Alistair*, all I see are wheels and levers, cranks and pendulums. Where are the axels on which these gears hang and spin, on which the pallets rock? Where is the spring? Without these things our case is air! The money enters from the left and disappears on the right; this much I understand. Make me see how in these stacks of hideous charts and calculations one can make a fortune disappear."

Max was as earnest to learn as the Professor was hesitant to solve the riddle for him; for throughout the long evening he had withheld the key to the puzzle's grip on His Majesty's imagination, knowing full well the sudden clarity toward avarice would consequently shine its light onto a collateral, much more sinister affair.

Lord Penworth's innocence would thus be mightily inferred; the elaborate frame now with its motive caught inside a jar; which leaves a very awkward hole inside a tale of murder that a restless nation had not yet put to bed.

"There's something more Professor, isn't there?" Max studied the old man with a developing trepidation; as if by some dark secret the Great Scholar's own clock had stopped its wheel; locked inside a calculus of finite facts against an infinity of separate truths; *to save a life will cost a life*, is but an axiom; poor Alistair, a man of heart, unable to outfox the truth in this.

Max brought his hand down softly onto the Professors shoulder, "Alistair, I would not be you right now for all the headaches of a King; to share the news you bear, must be a frightful thing. Let me proceed and by so doing, help to find your voice; I'm more informed than you suspect, but play you ignorant by choice."

The old man turned his eyes slowly onto the King; *time to wind the clock.*

Hunching back over the documents spread helter-skelter across the great playing field, Alistair began collecting the separate piles and laying them into three distinct groups, each group divided three times by virtue of calendar association. Max stood transfixed; still confused but utterly transfixed.

"You were always quite astute; *though unnecessarily disruptive*, so I will now present the same set of data through a finer lens, courtesy of your beloved friend and confidante, *Giov Penworth, Duke of the Dortpen*; who I might add, deserves credit for being the first individual to have successfully deciphered the scheme."

The King's face lit up, "Well, Alistair, you certainly know your way around an audience. I'm perfectly paralyzed with anticipation, *lead on!*"

The Professor led the King through the mechanisms of the elaborate laundering scheme, wherein an ever changing third of all payments made to the vast holdings of the *Atlantic Trust Alliance* were transferred to one of the three rotating investment groups, represented by documents lying there on the billiard table. All these shares are then atomized into smaller and smaller packages which then dissolve into accounts represented by the other two separate piles of pages, anyone of which rotating account is aligned with the holding of the previous institution, exchanged like valance electrons, all designed to pass eventually, in accordance with a regulated, calendar-operated pendulum, through the comparably vast accounts of the Great Cathedral of St. Pontificate, from where it rejoins the primary *Atlantic Alliance* arsenal through a reversal of the same mechanism; yet somehow lighter than money that should have been (albeit illicitly) exempted from tax responsibilities.

"The missing tax money is then coded within these pages as the mysterious unnamed account, initially on page seven of the blue report, and then again in a number of graphs and tables throughout the opus. You see, Your Highness, the axle to your crown-gear is the number *three*; the key by which each formless part and substrate of the whole elaborate scheme takes shape; *but does not finish there!* For three is also the number of confederates, whose names I beg you to disclose; save me the infernal disgrace."

The King was astounded by the pages on his bench; wordlessly digesting details of the scheme he knew intuitively to exist, but like a virus, impossibly dreadful to behold under the lens.

"I'll say the names Professor, for they each occur on a separate charge I have sleuthed with the customary incompetence afforded a Regent."
He took a long swallow from his glass and went to the bar to refill it. "My brother's greed is greater than his talent for it, but somehow I know he leads the tryst. So there, I've named one already, Alistair. How do you like me so far?"

Alistair sat on the sofa before the fire and swirled the remaining small cubes in his empty glass. "A fine start, Max."

"The next one is almost too easy; yet the greasy one of the bunch. I'll not drag the Church into the Press; but have a talk with Grieble myself. He's simply a bad boy who should place his aptitude for corruption to better use; perhaps grafting for the State?" he laughed.

Alistair simply grinned; bitter bones of irony shook like dice inside his gnawing head.

"And the third?"

His Majesty turned to look out of the window, onto the night-lit city, bustling below.

"The third, Alistair? The third is the architect." He paused to sip once more, "Are you familiar with the tale of the king and the architect Professor?"

"Which tale, your Highness? I know several."

"In my tale, the architect, for his inimitable skill, is blinded by a King who holds a length of iron heated in a roaring fire."

LII

"I'm to see that no one disturbs His Majesty until he further instructs me otherwise. I'm sorry your Highness."

It is said that Hoffenstein boys are fed on meat and grains; that grow more likely into well-built men. The guard outside the Billiard room was valid proof of this.

"Your insolence will be rewarded, mark you."

And the Prince stormed from the hallway outside the billiard room, back to his limousine, waiting just outside the Palace doors.

LIII

Alistair attempted to collect his papers from the table and sort them back into his valise.

"And just how far do you expect to go with all that evidence, Professor?" The sound of rifled pages stopped; he dropped his palms flat onto the table, stared straight down into the sea of numbers.

"I'm through with this place! I've had enough of this Max . . . *you people*! . . ," half astonished that he recognized inside the quavering sound his own sequestered thoughts.

The smirk evaporated from the King's face.

"You play cruel games with other people's lives; you cheat and steal and threaten those who might unwittingly hinder access to your ridiculous obsessions! How many more lives over this, your Highness? How many more *children*? I'm a scientist; that's all I know. You can have this world of noise and nonsense; I aim to seek a better place; *less civilized,* where people still look after one another! . . . Leave me and those I *love* be! . . . *is all I beg of you Max.*"

Perhaps it was true, that even a King might hold a certain allowance of awe for the common man. He let the crackling fire answer for the tired academic's outburst; for Alistair had just now cut a hole into the fabric of decorum; through which all pomp and circumstance marched lockstep into the hearth and out the stacks, high upon the Palace roof, there to fall like rain upon the tired city.

The old man shook with cold; Max removed the rocks glass from his hand, carried it to the bottle still standing on the bar top, dropped two fresh cubes of ice and topped them with a single malt; handed it to the scholar and placed another log upon the coals.

"You've something else on your mind Alistair. Pray, relieve yourself to me."

The old man took a belt and looked onto Maximillian Dubious III.

"You mention a King, evoked for punishing an architect whose crime was little more than his talent; how sorely you will despise my own gift for seeing into madness, there finding truth."

"You speak of the charges drawn against Penworth for Charlotte's tragic fate? It would all seem rather too convenient, I see. Your fascinating demonstration this evening certainly outlined a very strong case for certain, well placed individuals to protect their interests against a viable threat. How he ever came upon such evidence is still quite a mystery to me . . . and yet, there it lies," motioning to the billiard table.

He poked the log to snug it deeper in among the coals.

"But upon my recollection of the facts presented in the Police report, there were only a small handful of suspects; none but the Duke and the mysterious Poulterer, now vanished, are of any practical interest, no?"

Alistair drew upon a rush of courage, speaking so, "Takes more temper than strength to strike such a blow, your Highness."

Maximillian stopped staring into his glass, raised his head. "I also recall being informed of a mad girl at the scene. How did she ever make out? *The whole story such a pity.*"

Alistair, defeated, spoke no more. He did his work; tried to save the Duke; there was no further audience or cause to plead; *alas, the mirrors here have ears of stone, young Duke.* He wanted very much now to retire for the evening; back on his cot in his tent on a desolate island far, far across the southern seas.

"I'm certain you'll appreciate this."

Max handed the Professor a packet of folded documents and envelopes. Clearly scribed across the top envelope in the stack was the address to the prestigious *Society for Global Geophysics, Christchurch, New Zealand.*

The old Professor dropped his eyes; slowly shook his head.

"We Nobility all have our own society of infiltrators, derelicts and spies, Alistair. Eugene is simply more ostentatious with his toys than me. I've already arranged for your passage tomorrow morning.

"There's simply no way to insure your safety in Hoffenstein anymore. Rest here at Silberfluss tonight. A train leaves for Genoa tomorrow; you'll be on her, travelling under the name *A. Capella.* Once in Genoa, your journey will ultimately reacquaint you with colleagues in Christchurch. Go and make your *science.* I, for one, shall miss you very much.

"Oh, and a final toast to your health, dear Professor." He raised his glass, "it would do you well to remember *two* things; Your instincts led you to a garden where you presumed to find the back staircase to a billiard room; you're not infallible old man; Second and most dreadfully important: *you'd do very well to steer clear of a lion and his cub."*

LIIII

It had been a month since Frederick placed his collar on the seat, where it sat the entire drive back to the little white church beneath the hemlocks; once arrived he knelt before the altar, prayed until his legs grew numb, filled with glory that the collar, tried again, still fit.

Ensuing storms prevented access to the camp; the snow piled high in drifts throughout the hills and valley; nothing left to do but pray for the good Duke's health and soul; *a secret he would take with him to Gregory.*

He circled back from the garage, where he finished loading the wheelbarrow with wood for the fire. It was the kind of bright winter morning where the faceted iced crystals slung their beams of sun like long, slender brochettes through the eye, shot deep into the soft, astonished flesh of the brain; the cold wind whistled through the pine trees; but for the phantoms drawn out, rising from his clouded breath, the good priest was alone.

Helen had not visited since that fateful time; a merciful turn being as the hutches were by now as empty as Gregory's side of the bed. Sharon watched over the young lady these months with such a bond that folks in town remarked how two so close cannot but meet along some mean; although the gossip of a mother nearer now to mad than a daughter driven sane was inevitably spread.

An unexpected visitor had just rounded the hedges and parked at the bottom of the drive. It was Father Crispe, climbing out of the car; alone today; pushing the door with force enough to plow spare room into the high drifts which made a narrow corridor up the incline and round to the back of the cottage. He waved at Frederick, still far up beyond the house, about half way to the barn. Father Frederick placing the barrow in the snow, waved back, delighted to share the beautiful morning with someone, especially glad that he went grocery shopping yesterday.

The change caught Linus by complete and pleasant surprise; the kitchen was spotless, the floor waxed to a shine, the rugs beaten, fresh and bright, the curtains washed and cob webs dusted. Frederick placed the kettle on the stove; cut a Danish in its box, transferred it to a chipped blue plate.

"Let's go inside and talk," and led the way.

Seated, Linus began, "You look wonderful Frederick! I'm very much relieved to see you off this way."

Frederick turned from the fire, placed the poker in its stand, repeated, "*see you off?*" His eyes remained on the younger priest while he crossed the parlor to join him on the far end of the sofa.

"You going somewhere?"

Linus grew emotional upon these words; their scant vibrations acting as a finger might upon a trigger or a switch; his eyes swelled up in a mist.

"Yes, Father. It would seem that the *good* Bishop Grieble believes my work here in Mayfair is either well enough complete, or that my soul needs the added experience afforded by my new appointment in South Touchwick."

Stunned, Frederick stood to circle the coffee table; very slowly, "I *see*. Never came around, did he?"

"It's not so bad at that, I suppose. The neighborhood is vital, *most dynamic*; the congregation, good, hardworking *felons*," he joked. "It's come as quite a shock to Monika, though, having just made so many new friends here. But we're young!"

"Excuse me," and went into the kitchen to pour the coffee.

Father Crispe surveyed the unusual room, now transformed into a right comfortable space again; the tables polished, the curtains thrown wide to the bright glare from outside; yet something was peculiar, something different about the room for which neither dust cloth nor broom could answer; something extant in its very want; missing perhaps.

He returned with two cups of coffee on a tray with sugar and cream.

"Would it help for me to speak with him?" the old priest faintly offered.

Linus smiled. "You've been a good friend, Frederick. Somehow I can't see your influence with Grieble serving to help in any way but another appointment, perhaps *Africa* next!"

They both laughed at this, had Danish and coffee; talked for about an hour when Father Crispe rose to leave.

"When?"

"My appointment is to begin in the spring, early March. Perhaps we'll get together again sometime before then, yes?"

"Splendid! I'll give you a ring."

Sitting in his car at the bottom of the driveway, Father Crispe placed both hands on the wheel, lost in thought about moving from the odd old Priest, who progressed from pious regard as a menace to a friend inside the small space of a year;

he looked at the beautiful cottage; considered the deep sense of loss and suffering his new friend endured with such strength, such grace.

And there it struck; the *parlor*! . . . It was indeed changed. The trembling walls once harried by platoons of switching pendulums; long flittering shadows, tracking back and forth across in sweeping arcs; the deep, hushed throat of palpitating waves, spilling and swallowing against some sleeping beach; the sliding pallets, steady crown escapements, all now still; all now asleep; the sitting room, in its obscure serenity, now all the more unnerving.

LV

He leaned about as far back as he could, reluctant to dismount and walk the steep trail separately; his boots were thick, but once a frost got inside it was an ordeal to warm his feet again; yet horse and rider paired was a four-fold risk.

The spill timed perfect with the epiphany of his indecision, now standing from the fall and subsequent landing into a soft bank some twenty feet down into a hollow where he quickly appraised the situation for broken bones and missing gear.

Kinter was fine, gracefully up righted, conspicuously delighted to be free of the extra weight and obediently waiting for new instruction; large black eyes looking down on her stumbling partner, brushing snow from every crevice of his torso while absurdly calling for the sensible beast to come and help. She stood her ground.

He was a day's ride from the camp, making the round to check his traps; empty full ones, set fresh ones and reposition others; a token pile of rough shaped pelts tied with jangling traps across Kinter's rump; an awkward moment passed and two dark figures carried on, cutting a fresh path through the mountain snow; a jagged trail stretched from trap to trap; a mountain gypsy and his mare.

It was getting late; Cosmo looked up from his bloody work, a shoulder and some ribs still tender; *two hours to dark*; time to find a place to spend another freezing night. Panning the valley, he watched the shadow of one looming hill mask the base of its neighbor, whose top half glowed like garnet in the winter's last afternoon light; sparse diamonds rippling on the surface of the stream far, far below.

A column of thin blue smoke rose up from a blinded gulch against the trees from somewhere not too far, then black against the upper orange of the tired, purpling sky; the valley everywhere reverberating with the evidence of spirits.

One fire always sheds more warmth than two; this he remembered from his father, who believed it always better use of a gloaming hour, reaching for a stranger, sharing some kill, than settling in alone.

Kinter followed Cosmo down through the darkening hill side, through the deep snow, cutting sideways and back against the strong forces pulling at his boot straps from the crevasse far below. A ring of light glowed by now against a crown of branches curled high above the intriguing fire; the camp was now a simple hike; his heart raced, not certain of the vein of hospitality which awaited, yet fairly certain in these woods, in this snow, a friendly tribute to the belly and the spit will unlikely fail.

He tied his roan mare to a young birch sapling; snuck up to the small clearing under the sailing sparks to gauge the circumstances; the snow aiding his vocational stealth. Through a space the camp was now visible; a shelter, some sacks strung down from high branches and a fire. Where were the residents?

There is nothing with which to confuse the distinct sound of a pistol's hammer, drawn back and ready to fire; and this was precisely the deliberation young Cosmo labored under when such a noise came up from behind.

LVI

Kinter stood nervously tethered in the darkness for over half an hour before Cosmo returned to bring him back to the campsite. Two rabbits were prepared on stakes to roast, two men in soldier uniforms grateful for the feast. The storms, it was learned over whiskey and pipes, had trapped these two from all familiar compass points; set out one month ago to trail a fugitive with dreams of wealth and buried fortune; caught now not so much struggling to live but to survive, for which they were the better trained.

They knew the battlefields, they knew the towns and cities of the world; they knew the taverns and the women all; but in their vast experience the thing they knew the least was everything they needed to absorb now to survive; the Dortpen forest was the pitiless master, Cosmo their reluctant savior.

"Name's *Penworth*, he's a Duke; refined nobleman." He spit out a piece of grizzle and laughed.

"*Refined nobleman*, that's a laugh! . . . But this one's a swashbuckler sort; lived for a time in the jungles of Africa. He's out here somewhere all right; we'll catch up with him."

The fire's heat was trained into a half cup shelter formed of woven saplings crossed by supple switches cloaked in thick fronds of evergreen and mud; the bright glow affording Cosmo a grotesquely frank description of the trail worn pair.

To his left, a mangled black beard shook as the tattooed goblin spoke; a wiry nest to sundry oils, spit and food particulates which bounced into, among and out again with every syncopated syllable his rambling jaw could mete. An enlisted soldier's top coat hung, open to the fire, from his shoulders like a second skin; a row of large metal buttons hung their mute insignias from timeworn threads, the shabby swansong of some pleasantly antique and twisted memories.

Inside the dark folds of this coat, a leather belt secured an ivory handled knife which he took no great pains to hide.

Cosmo tore some meat off the hind quarters of the smaller hare, trying to assess the quiet one. He seemed more refined; he looked to have shaved within the past two or three days.

"Murdered his own little girl; cracked her head with a paver; in the presence of no one less than the Princess herself! This is the cold blooded sort we're tracking, *I tell you right.*"

The uniforms, suggesting efforts in the service of the Crown, were from a previous war; evidence of a long, nostalgic intermission preceding the previous month so woefully accounted for by the bearded one. The quiet soldier now spoke, "You know these hills. Seen anyone out here over the past five months?"

He produced a folded photograph of the Duke, taken shortly after his return from Luremo over ten years ago; fifteen pounds heavier with long black hair, clean shaven and dressed in the traditional cut and collar of Parliament.

The old hermit back in Madame Piko's trailer was a stretch; besides, this was a matter to be labored by Colonials upon Colonials; he had no respect or allegiance to *any* Crown; these men were not, nor would they *ever* so much serve as friends.

"My work make it helpful to enjoy being alone; sometime I share food with stranger; he share a fire, tobacco maybe. In five months? I see no Duke.

"Penworth not a name I share tobacco with, besides. Tomorrow I leave you two traps. Maybe I see you in spring? You not travel far in this before then, trust me."

They went to sleep.

Cosmo slipped away from the tent under a star filled sky, leaving the two soldiers deep in sleep; untied Kinter then stole silently away from the camp. He never felt comfortable with Colonials, these two especially; something about the uniforms and the violent atmosphere referred upon the whole purpose for their being. *This tiny camp o'er-filled with wretched spirits!*

He led the old mare through the waist high drifts for about ten minutes, through the waning darkness, as far and fast as he could; musing on the distress of the soldiers when discovering how skilled and silent a seasoned gypsy can be; he smiled at this.

"Wasn't gonna steal your horse."

Victor stepped out in front of Kinter from a dense holly patch to Cosmo's right; he'd been waiting there for some time.

"Expected you might leave us like this he smirked; "No breakfast?"

"I'm the busy man, leave early, let you sleep. No trouble, good?"

His hands were unsteady.

"I look asleep to you?" Victor replied. "No, I guess I don't. Just didn't want you going off without mentioning something I don't want *him* to hear, is all."

Cosmo looked directly at the uniform, a bronze and silver pin just discernible; the sun about ready to crest the hills; said not a word.

"There's a reward in it for you. Just give us the *Colonial* if you see him; it's worth a very fine reward, son. More than you'd ever suspect."

Cosmo hated the two soldiers, yet tribal legend holds the Penworth name most despicable of all.

"I should see him, I take your money, all right," the gypsy smiled, pulled on Kinter's tether and led away to finish the long trek to empty his traps.

Victor knew that following the gypsy was a waste of time; drew his pistol and held it to the small silhouette of the young trapper, now almost disappeared far off into the deep forest snow.

Bang! he scoffed; putting the gun away in his long wool jacket; turning then to trudge his way back to his comrade, start the morning's fire and have some coffee.

We're so close, I can smell him.

LVII

He came around, the ticking sound against the front window enough to lead his delicate notice out from a soup of dreams; out into the stark brightness of the room. He rolled onto his side, pushing the thick pile of blankets onto the floor, pulling the sweat stained gown back down below his waist; an instinctive effort to preserve some measure of dignity should the old woman suddenly return to learn his strength had finally improved enough to right himself.

Such strange configurations of memories and visions, fused inside this fevered head; a broth of restless lies and facts a fortnight simmering in that sweated bed.

He panicked, rushed to stand, discovering in the act a vigorous fragility which knelt inside him like a faithful hound; a point within the collapsing spiral of confusion where his aimless arms and leaden legs, his weary eyes withdrew; a delirious nap which called him home to rest another thousand years; there was no hurry where there was no name;

and I most nameless of them all.

His head then fell in weakness through the air; forever falling through the whistling air; a song bird tapping on the window with a stick. He was sound asleep when she returned.

256

Madame Piko pulled the blankets back to cover her new friend, looking down on his curled body. She lit a flame on the stove and touched it to a pipe; walked over to the couch and sat her tiny frame into an embroidered cushion, studying the small parcel found strung around the sick man's neck the night he was delivered.

It caught her eye that fateful day; soaked by cold rain through and through; and so it hung to dry among her feathers and collected amulets inside the small room where she stacked her tarot, patient under candle light; a small space described by fairest lace and long strung beads; where the curious and desperate might come to dodge a brief moment from the noisy world, have their future traced into the air by the exceptional ancient mystic.

She pulled an old fur mantle across her ice cold legs and held the pouch by its thin leather thong to spin inside a beam of sunlight cut across the trailer through the window where the feeder hung outside. A small leather pouch she'd seen a thousand years before, with tight embroidered threads stitched into its flesh. She took a small pull from the pipe, a faint smile cut into her harshly wrinkled face.

She was far too old to cultivate the smallest tear.

LVIII

"I suppose there's something wrong with your cue?" teased the older brother, "perhaps you'll try that shot again using mine?"

Prince Eugene smiled at Maximillian, disposing all misgivings of his eagerness to upstage the fool; watching him circle the table like a pick-pocket on a rush hour train; an unfair break and two consecutive lucky sinks had begun their work to undermine his pretentious familiarity with the game; yet opportunity, he reasoned, had not altogether deserted him.

"You see the four? . . ." took his shot, "and there little brother as the small violet ball rolled into the leather net below the side pocket, ". . . is the only *true* object of the game."

Eugene smiled. "You didn't invite me over tonight for dinner and billiards, Your Highness, come clean, what's this theater all about? It stands to reason you play a better stick than me; the many hours spent in this room! . . . if governance were nine ball, Hoffenstein would have a navy on the Silberfluss for Christ's sake!"

Max chalked up and placed the small blue cube onto a handsome round inlaid side table dominated by a gilded lamp; the warm glow waking lazy bands of colored light, struggling through the chiseled prisms lined along a whiskey glass two fingers filled; he raised the drink in a mock toast toward the Prince and smiled.

"You're quite right about that, dear Brother; *Damn those infernal swans!*"

The orange ball shot off the rail across the felt into the corner pouch. Eugene worked his Cuban with an eye on the table, "You've dismissed Gerald early, I've noticed."

"Green ball, opposite corner," and sunk.

"Nice shot . . . ."

He drew from his cigar and retired the pool stick against the nearest chair.

"Seven, side pocket, off the rail." Maximillian circled the table now, more like a tiger; dropping the brown ball quicker than the green one before it; Eugene left with little else to do than tease his weed, scrutinized the marked change drawn upon his brother's face like some stalled cloud, here to block all light.

"Eight," and motioned to the opposite side pocket with his cue; gone.

"I'd like to switch to some *Grand Marnier*, care to join me?" Eugene asked, moving toward the bar.

"I received a most fascinating visit the other morning," offered King Dubious, breaking his brief period of silence, "an extremely interesting man. But, really I suppose, I can't say that I wasn't expecting him."

Eugene uncapped the bottle, looked directly at his brother and poured himself a glass. "Care for one? Offer still stands."

"No, please!" replied the King, "I'll save one for a night cap, thank you. The evening is still *so* young."

Eugene poured himself a generous snifter; deciding which direction to approach his brother's patient assault; far too confident to assume the King held cards enough to shake his impenetrable hand.

"We've an important vote in chambers tomorrow, Max; I should hope you'll put more effort into finding a proper rest than extending your campaign against whiskey bottles. I postulate the efficiency of your attacks upon my current proposition inversely proportionate to your alcohol consumption. I'm more anxious to defeat you in a fair debate."

Max threw back the remaining Scotch and held his glass out for his brother to attend; it was time.

"Then need I *postulate* upon the whereabouts of a certain *missing* poultry merchant from Söfenzin?"

Eugene crossed back to the game table, a glass in either hand, smiling. "So! . . . my big brother's decided to become a detective? How rich. From your hypnotizing performance just now, I'd encourage you to tour the gaming halls instead. You're a regular *Renaissance man*, is what you are!"

"And the number three; mean anything to you?"

The words stopped Eugene cold with a sudden appreciation for the snare. "Hear me now your Highness," coolly reaching down to place his cigar into the silver tray, "what was done was nothing more than required to protect the throne. I assume the capable Professor Constantine just couldn't resist bragging to you how he broke the code? How droll. I should have arrested him weeks ago," he smirked.

Max placed his glass onto the green felt, positioned directly between the cue ball and the striped yellow nine ball.

"Oh, Eugene; perhaps you care too much. You've made a poor man disappear; put Lord Penworth out with the cat. Perhaps it will all become more sobering for you once you discover what happened to poor Grimstone at about seven o'clock this evening. I wish so much you could have been there!" he laughed, "And *all* to protect my good name and the integrity of the throne."

"To protect my *niece!*"

A storm passed across the King's face; arrested there behind a pair of dreadfully frosted eyes.

"There is urgent business for you in Angola, dear brother. You and Lady Belladonna have one week to decide how you will manage your affairs here. I will settle all difficulties you've managed between the State and Azevedo. The Trinity is dissolved."

Eugene stood before his brother as an image in ash; placing his full drink onto the side table, stunned with disbelief.

"Think about Gloria!"

"Nine ball, corner pocket."

The white ball left the stick, caressed with just that subtle kiss of English only skill and practice can avouch; avoiding by a feather's breadth the scotch set on its arched path; struck the yellow ball which sailed into the corner hole; game over.

King Maximillian Dubious III raised his cue to slide the beads along the rack above the table; *"Race."*

LVIX

The week of sun gave way to sudden winds and warmer showers, the melting snow forming deep iced puddles; mud filled lawns and gutters, waking rheumatoid connections all around the Dortpen. Sharon had taken Helen with her to St. Humility that morning to sweep, scrub and polish, as was her routine. Helen, for her part, being somewhat older now, found certain basic comprehension of the situation, amusing herself in a pew with magazines and other various objects from home with which she passed the tedious hours, enrapt.

Father Frederick had no business at the church that morning.

It was two o'clock that afternoon when Sharon finally closed the beautiful red door of the chapel behind her to begin the sloppy walk home; Helen being incapable of managing an umbrella of her own, stood reluctantly under Sharon's, bolting repeatedly from its cover, into the icy rain; an impulse born of agitation at the first gesture of confinement in any form; the icy afternoon proving wholly insufficient against the tired widow's impulse to perspire.

Rounding the last corner to the cabin, dreadfully anxious to be home and sipping hot soup in dry clothes before the radio, Helen broke once more from her mother's hold, recognizing the cabin and racing for it.
What are those vehicles out front? Sharon mused, surprised at having only then observed a police ambulance and a squad car.

Helen, far beyond her mother's reach, was promptly apprehended by two medics in rain gear, while the shouts of her mother drowned inside the sudden thunderous downpour. Chief Richter at this point stepped from behind the van to intercept Sharon, swinging like a wildcat in the futile recovery of her only baby girl.

"Take it easy, Miss Sharon!" he tried, his loudest voice a whisper against the harsh weather. "I have a warrant for Helen's detention for the accidental homicide of Lady Charlotte Penworth."

The rain crashed down onto the echoing van; Sharon lost her footing, slipped into the mud, where she slithered and scrambled to stand. She had cut her lip and the blood now mixed with the rain and mud, washed off her chin in a savage mingling with bewildered tears.

"What are you doing to my baby?! August? Please! . . I beg you, *please give Helen back to me!*"

She struck Chief Richter on his cheek, trying to tear past him to reach the medics loading Helen into the back of the vehicle.

An officer subdued Sharon into handcuffs where she eventually traded hysteria for bewildered exhaustion in the rear seat of the Chief's patrol car.

Rain beat hard against the thick steamed windows; Sharon watched the nebulous white shape and flashing red strobes of an ambulance back out of her driveway to disappear; her whole wretched life inside it.

LX

Frederick rushed up the small stoop, one hand keeping his hat from flying off into the wind and rain, crossed the porch to find the tiny police station already overcrowded with regular staff and medical technicians; Sharon was being held elsewhere while the few reporters sent to pick up the *dead* story squeezed Chief Richter.

Conscript guardsman Odin Denis stepped out of the headquarters onto the porch for some fresh air; the cold wind a relief against his sweated face and neck; *another hour in that oven would be my fucking death,* he muttered before recognizing Frederick as the Hero Priest.

"Forgive me Father. It's just so *Goddamn* hot in there!" the words outpacing his awkward series of regrets and apologies.

"It's all right!" Frederick finally appealed, "I'm looking for Sharon; Helen's mother. Where can I find her? I've been told a most terrible account and I'm convinced there's been some very terrible mistake. Please, tell me where I can find Sharon, will you?"

The embarrassed soldier looked to the Priest, "Oh no, Father, not this time. There's been no mistake here. This information comes directly from the Royal Forensic Labs in Touchwick; most well equipped and modern facility in all Hoffenstein. Blood work confirms the crazy girl swung the rock; prints are all over it; a full report with color photographs was issued late yesterday. Don't you see what this means?"

Frederick grabbed the railing, stood weightless on the porch at these words; stunned by a force which seemed to simply lift him out from his shoes; finally perceiving that one, single concept perpetually hid behind every soul-reaching principle, *the pure ethical plasma*; circling high above the puppeted reality of the frenzied station house and unified toward some shifting spot inside a clear white tunnel of maddening wind and convulsive rain, stressing great cracks along the inside seams of his own diminishing faith. *No God could sit so still and watch this much drift past.*

He suddenly gripped the rail in every effort to avoid fainting.

"You all right, Father Fred? Listen to me. It means the Duke didn't do it after all! How's that for you? God! Life's pretty funny sometimes, don't you agree?"

He recovered from his brief dizzy spell with a faint salty numbness in his mouth; the officer's remarks echoing with an acute pathos; a dull spike pounded deep into his sweating head.

"As a matter of fact, I couldn't agree less! That young lady's about as capable of murder as am I! Where's Sharon?"

His voice rose at this, apparently loud enough to attract notice from a few individuals inside. Chief Richter looked over to the window, saw Frederick and excused himself, abruptly ending the Press release.

The station house door opened and August stepped out into the cold refreshing air, fully aware that the Priest would serve him harder than the Press inside.

"Father," he nodded, reaching into his shirt pocket for a cigarette.

Denis, would you mind?"

The Guard looked at Father Frederick with faint suspicion, returning inside only out of obligation to the Chief. The wind slammed the door closed; the two men stared into the rain, avoiding eye contact; it was, without question, the Chief's cordial responsibility to break the silence.

"Where is she, Richter?"

August took a drag, breathed the smoke into a gust which only pushed it back into Frederick's face.

"Sorry, Father. I should quit these things, I suppose," clipping the head and throwing it over the porch rail.

Frederick stood unresponsive, staring at the silent street lamp across the small lot, diligently aiming light out into the storm.

"What do you expect me to do Father? I'm *law enforcement*. Hell, you know how hard I pressed to find her! I just serve warrants; the courts sift the evidence. She'll get her day."

Father Frederick looked directly into Richter's eyes, "Her day? . . . *that's a laugh*. You believe she could do this, Chief Richter?" August reflexively reached for his shirt pocket; caught himself and shook his head,
"I not only believe she *could*, Father, I'll go further and confirm the case closed."

Father Frederick took a cigarette from the Chief, asking, "Please take me to see Sharon."

End of Part Three

Part Four

I

I kept my pact with the Professor, squandering my youthful allowance, enjoying a gay life in the murky shadow of far-off taverns; haunting the race tracks, galleries and casinos; wagering against all sensible odds; breaking vows, surviving broken vows; all whilst making my art and discovering the art alive all around me; saving for my future only those same two coins, hung now from doleful scraps of ribbon, like medals, from my heart.

For I am indeed a rake reformed; I was a Duke, a retired libertine and played it fair; I fell in love with all my soul, not once but twice; and for this extravagance recite the Beggar's Prayer.

Much had recently ensued to bait the idle Press these past twelve months in Hoffenstein; so much upset, so many scrubbing brushes splashing in as many swampy pails;

a vast ignoble industry, the *Fourth estate*, dissecting scandals on its printed page, hazarding the disinterment of a truth, but in due course, the treatment always mortgaged to capricious kiosk sales;

The sordid type-keys busied tapping onto blindly spinning rolls; headlines hawking episodes and horoscopes of the shameful or forsaken souls; no mention of eradicated courtiers, no whisper of the empty jails;

Thus the time of many dishes broken from a priceless set; so many shards and fragments to be matched and glued; where now an anxious nation looks toward its little King to steer; Maximillian Clemency Dubois III, who shades instead a felted table with his chalk and wandering balls of colored ivory, delicately cued.

And I who lay here dreaming in my little gypsy bed; who hear the banshee in the wind; who fears to wake into my loss of everything; has shaped his new home in this old discarded head.

II

There came a knock on the trailer door; Madame Piko having left before the second daybreak, (when the sunlight crests the shoulders of the east-most hills) in search of edelweiss, most precious for midwinter conjuring; leaving me distracted from my work to rise and see to it.

I was at the moment busy with an auger at my belt, sitting half clothed in my long johns on the lace draped couch, cutting a fresh hole to describe a much diminished waist.

The sound of an outraged engine chorusing with pungent tires, whistling in a muddied track outside near-off, announced some fresh restiveness for which I labored earnest on my strap to cheerfully investigate; only recently come round from weeks of fever to a drowsy camp, delighted for the synchronized vivacity of us both.

Behind the door, perspiring Grigoras.

"Good day!" which served preface enough for him to tender up his harried cause; that even in such weakened state, my service in the cockpit of the mired van might break the odds so stubbornly fixed against the crew now shouldered to upset it. More than anxious to oblige, I proved the talisman; the wager won and every muddied beard stretched wide in spontaneous cheer to praise it, but for one, who under Grigoras' keen watch, preferred to wander off alone and brush his mare.

"Never mind him," filling his pipe, "He'll come around. How you feel? Madame Piko says you're eating."

The band of muddy shoulders having broken toward their separate interests left me to the first true interview with Grigoras since my rescue; whose instinctive trust in mankind thirsted for substantiation; a comfort which he solemnly longed to find in abundant supply from me.

"Madame Piko has been very kind, as have you all. Your hospitality has provided extra pages to a story that I've yet to write, but toward which my overwhelming debt exceeds the slimmest chance to clear it."

The large man with the black beard laughed at this, more confident in his intuition, "I look at a wet, white haired old man with long white whiskers pushed up into his chattering face. I say to Madame, *he won't eat much!*" He laughed some more. "And pockets which have not held coin since *Hector* was a pup!"

He had a remarkable talent to amuse himself; a prodigious advantage for a merry soul and one which seemed, with each grin, to shave years from his age. He was sincerely likable.

I looked around at the muddy camp through a vague film of smoke and ash; everywhere the melted ice transforming any permanence to a twinkling, transitory sight; the snow receding from the tin roofed huts, the painted trailers in a settled ring through which the hens and dogs cut separate crisscross paths; the tethered goats, the children rushing through their chores; anxious, I supposed, to play.

He looked at me; the heavily employed pipe lost inside a massive paw now rested on his knee, the smile having given over center stage to a sober face, and asked quite deliberately, "You a Colonial like Cosmo thinks?"

I recalled the peaceable cocoon of my fevered hiatus, incapable of remembering much before I woke in the old woman's bed; each attempt to piece my fractured story into a coherent narrative aborted by a regiment of telepathic infantry engaged to screw its course. In truth, at this point I could not answer yes or no, and told him so.

"You're honest; so odds very slim you're Colonial. You look pale old man. Maybe too much excitement this morning. Sit and breathe fresh air. I get some friends and take van through the snow to the road. We need supplies from Söfenzin, maybe find the Priest. You rest up some more, get your strength."

With that he was off.

I sat in the warm sun for another half hour before I spotted her tiny figure against the distant snow field of a hillside to the south; at the rate she was hiking, it would be another hour before she made it back to her trailer with a handful of fresh picked edelweiss.

III

It was a night I will forever remember as the anniversary of my second Communion; resurrected to an antiquated world of fellowship and good will; the warbling violins, brisk dances, the open fire throwing riotous shadows across the walls and roof inside the common hall; foaming mugs and bottles flying off the tips of table-kicking boots; the haunting songs, laughter; the drunken, sentimental proclamations.

I have no memory of having shared in such heartfelt happiness outside a cause less subtle than a winter's thaw; my own recuperation serving most conspicuous to most, a simple metaphor for spring.

My strength by now had been restored, relative to this present, *over-ripened,* much reduced form; in due time even fashioning a tiny

266

residence for myself several yards off the main ring of trailers, that I might relieve the cramped hospitality of my gracious *infermière*, while providing for my separate need to privacy.

I subsequently joined Madame Piko on her frequent, silent walks; learned very much about the herbs, flowers and plentiful mushrooms spread abundant amid old Pater's own fertile lawns; hiking solo, at her behest, on more numerous occasions as her age progressed and health piecemeal declined.

Tonight she sat among the revelry on a make-shift throne beside the fire; regarded as a treasure in their midst; content to be among, to rest and watch, her children.

A fat yellow moon began the evening from a spot within the trees, behind the massive compost pit opposite the formal entrance to the camp; sits smaller, platinum, now straight above Madame Piko's trailer situated midway; an indication of the lateness of the hour, a harbinger for members of the polarized extremes of life's parochial punch clock; the young ones struggling vainly against heavy eye lids and conspicuous yawns; the elders simply nodding off, more than anxious to retire.

I saw enough in Madam's eyes to take her arm; offer our contrite farewells, escorting her to the trailer where she spent the past sixty-odd years of her amazing life; I marveled at her tiny frame. She motioned for me to come inside; crossed the room to her tarot behind the long curtain of strung beads and sat, sliding the soothsaying deck off the old chenille table cover, cards spilled helter-skelter on the floor. I must admit, I felt a little uneasy as she motioned for me to sit across from her. She looked tired; very tired.

Tired of her silent world, yet not out of love with it; simply tired of sustaining it. She pulled her paddles for the last time in; wishing now to simply float the river she had loved so much in life; let the languid landscape slide; the water lift her head.

I never felt such melancholy beauty in all my life as in the stillness of her weary eyes just then.

She reached out to me with a leather pouch; embroidered threads much in the likeness of a dragon and a boar; held it from a thin leather twine, where it spun before me like a diamond pendant on a silvered chain. The image struck me wonderful yet harsh with pain, for I knew somewhere very deep inside that I could not follow her, such was my fear; and yet such love as I had hid but could not conjure here.

I knew this bag; reached out for it, she let it go; the faintest memories like spices in a consommé began to turn in clock-like rings, spinning off the sorcery of her edgeless spoon, the mesmerizing passion of her mystic reckonings.

I thought of a shipwreck, of a man named Bidwell and an idle King; and still my mind swam helpless down, unable to define the context of a hope so filled with memories clothed; so ominous and threatening.

I owned that purse, this much I know.

I spoke now to her, knowing that she could not hear; confident that my meanings and intentions were unambiguous, abundantly clear.

"Where did I lose this? What does it mean? Does it answer who I am?"

She rose and shuffled to a trunk which lay hid beneath a thick pile of quilts and blankets, also tossed haphazard to the floor; raised the lid and moved some old pieces of her past, expressly saved to reminisce; withdrew a small square of the most astounding fabric I have ever seen, a young girls skirt, though having in my buried past the strongest impression of having once before encountered the weave.

A jacket presented as a wedding gift by my trusted friend and aide, Hortense Bidwell, to Mary, my departed wife, the mother of my lovely little girl.

I collapsed beneath the daunting weight of countless dormant memories; sobbing like an orphaned child.

"My name is Charles Penworth; I am the Duke of Dortpen, falsely indicted for the murder of my angel, Charlotte! . . . my heart and fortune, by this means, interred."

The white haired stranger collapsed onto the couch, face buried into his hands; *the soup now ready to be served.*

A wind blew hard against the flame tipped candles closest to the open window by the front of the trailer. Madam Piko placed her thin hand on Lord Penworth's head, then crossed the room to close it.

She could not hear the footsteps below the window sneak in blackness through the thick mud outside.

IIII

It was a fitful sleep; daybreak a relief. There were still some eggs left when I visited the hutch, the late night revelry no doubt accounting for the aberrant tranquility of the camp; taking three I crossed the commons, making for Madam Piko's trailer to poach her favorite breakfast. I let myself inside after waiting through a full and courteous series of well-mannered raps against her door.

She looked peaceful, almost smiling as I pulled the blankets up to cover her. I decided to go immediately to tell Grigoras of the sad, inevitable news.

The bright sun continued where it left off the previous day; access to the streams, roads and forest, long since swallowed by the winter's ice, now piecemeal thawed away.

V

The interview with Sharon played like running water through his exhausted mind; as images inside the head of one whose tired legs dangle from a bridge in a hard earned rest; watching clouds reflect in moiré configurations; skate across the rippling creek face below; to just sit and watch the water come and go, *was never really there*, to come and go again, pressed down into the river bed against the stagnant, mildewed air.

They broke her this time; it was clear to Frederick she was nothing but mere collateral overhead, the cost of doing business; as one might slay a lamb for Easter feast.

He could think of no chapter, verse, no hymn or prayer to find the woman in those lifeless eyes who once lived there; and with Sharon gone goes everything she ever touched; a cabin leans that was a loving home; a little white church beneath a sweeping hemlock tree, became a pair of dull red doors beneath a rusted bell and nothing more.

Helen never understood, could never say goodbye.

A chapter in the legal books was closed to show the anxious kingdom that some healing had begun; condemned her to a gilded cage, to swing upon a diamond perch and sing her curious lament inside a surreptitious tower window carved on high; a gamble that the busy world would soon enough forget; erase the memory of all incident; a new act, fresh to incubate onto a disinfected stage; ten thousand years in isolation for a charge she could not comprehend; for the hand she never raised.

The Priest went round the cottage to his old Volvo and drove it to a place on the rural road about ten kilometers outside of the town limits, a few kilometers from the forest edge where he pulled off to the shoulder. The vast meadow spread before him like a brown and yellow blanket of wild rye and bramble; the woods far off maintained their crisp edge against the field; all the stubborn snow had gone. A hawk far off was chased in cork-screw patterns by a stubborn pair of senseless crows.

He stepped out of the car and circled around to the trunk where he found a small red can of gasoline which he poured into the front side window on the seat where his clerical collar sat alone, bent wide and helpless.
He walked for miles then, never looking back to see the jet black column stretching into yawning space, to where the crows chase hawks and little children point when asked where Jesus lives; and walked and walked until his tired legs hung dangled off a wooden bridge.

VI

Preparations for the festive burial consumed the mournful days before the feast; a hole into old Pater's ribs was dug and coins thrown in; Madam Piko dressed in verdant luxury, her tarot placed with reverence by her side, was lowered while old Yoseri sawed onto his cat-gut strings; much whiskey drunk, some poured into the open ground, that she might find familiar celebration in the great abroad.

Two days had passed without an end in sight, the dancers taking shifts; the noisy pig sty emptied of its swine, for no greater love had any but the village for their Dame; and such was the joyful habit of the camp, until the soldiers came.

I knew at once, with young Cosmo at the lead, *who missed the Mystic's burial while otherwise loathsomely engaged,* that my time among my new found family had come abruptly to an end. Grigoras marched up to the front and greeted the two strange Colonials as one might welcome guests into a family's home; the soldiers bearing pistols pushed their way past him into the throng where I surrendered hoping to avoid all further disgrace of Madam Piko's dignity.

"He's not the hermit that you think he is, but a fugitive I overheard, who spoke of a treasure buried in the ground! . . . *My fortune, by this means, interred . . .* His *very* words!" the trapper barked.

270

Grigoras spat in Cosmo's face.

I was led off in irons through a baffled crowd;

"He's no Colonial, nor could ever be!" Grigoras cried out loud.

My time among the good Romani people, *Pater's children*, had come to an end; my time among the Hoffench had begun again.

VII

"Look here Mom; it's a post from Touchwick. How curious!" Hobbes held the pale blue envelope against the dazzling sunlight, attempting, it could be surmised, to surrender in silhouette any hypothetically revealed contents disguised within.

Miss Barrett turned her head up from the oven where she had just fed the insatiable fire box below, seeing Hobbes busy with his unauthorized examination of the mail, remarked, "Well, Mr. Hobbes! *They'll take a limb for that, you know!"*

Hobbes turned sharply toward his accuser, simply smiled and confessed, "Not if the subject of the investigation bears the same address as the *accused."*

The old cook cocked one eye at her friend, suspicious of his proclivity toward mischief and unfolded her rheumatoid frame from the furnace, closing the heavy steel gate.

"You mean to say you got a post from Touchwick, there in your glove… addressed to *you?"*

"Not just Touchwick, Miss Barrett. This letter bears the return address of no less a residence than *Palais Silberfluss!"* Concluding his fruitless inspection, the cagey domestic then added, "As for your assumption that this letter is addressed to me, I enthusiastically inform you that you are only *half* correct."

He danced over to the drawer where Miss Barrett kept the house silver; (the dull flatware given to prosaic utility and not that which is customarily dispensed on the great House's more ceremonious occasions), found a bone handled butter knife and slit the crease, freeing the folded document within.

"What are you going on about Mr. Hobbes? How am I only *half correct?* Give me a look, now. Let me see the great mystery," and ambled over toward the bright window where her old friend stood, unfolding the letter. He handed Miss Barrett the empty envelop to inspect.

Mr. R. Hobbes and Miss R. Barrett
Burlwood Estate, Mayfair
Dortpen County, Hoffenstein

The return address:

Professor Alistair Constantine, PhD
Palais Silberfluss, c/o His Majesty, M.C. Dubois III
Touchwick, Hoffenstein

"It's addressed as well to me, Mr. *R. Hobbes!*" she remarked, her reading glasses on the table clear across the galley; "I'd naturally want to hear what he has to say, if you would. *A letter to the pair of us . . .* from *Palais Silberfluss? . . .* how remarkable. Wait until Doris gets wind of it!"

Hobbes was intent upon the missive, unresponsive to the old woman's carrying on. His face dissolved to a solemn, reflective smile; a tender countenance; the singular expression of a pleasure drawn from losing something wonderful in a bid against an inclination far superior; he smiled at his old friend, suggesting she take the page across the kitchen to her glasses on the table; to read the letter for herself as he was suddenly disinterested in speaking.

She took the paper from his listless hand, shaking with distress; all thoughts of Doris having suddenly turned in against her. Slowly crossing the familiar space, Miss Barrett pulled a chair from under the table and sat herself, tugging the spectacles onto her marvelous nose and began to read.

Dear Mr. Hobbes and Miss Barrett,

By the time this letter arrives, I more than suspect that I shall be standing at a pier in Genoa, Italy observing my trunks and various crates of interest being loaded into the cargo hold of the Vegeto, in whose austere hospitality I shall endeavor to cross any number of oceans toward my eventual destination; a port, which for the moment, must remain a confidence I have agreed to share with no one but my recent and most unexpected benefactor.

It is with the deepest regret that the specific urgency of my departure precluded any wish I had to pay my deepest regards and sincerest respects in a manner more befitting a farewell between comrades of our mutual, profound experience; but in accordance to sobering advice, I elected to defuse, through my impulsive conduct, any further, potential adventures (including any future visits from Warrant-bearing Inspectors) as regards its interference with the tranquility I have always wished to return upon Burlwood.

Let it be herewith comprehended that in light of Lord Penworth's absolution of any charges related to the tragedy regarding young Charlotte; the estate of Burlwood shall remain in a condition of perpetual readiness upon the hope, against all present unlikeliness, of his most anticipated return; a charge for which a pension toward your mutual, indefinite services has been arranged forthwith and for a duration not a single day less than a period described exclusively within the specific, albeit wholly unsolicited, terms of your own prescribed resignation. Best of luck and health to you both; you've certainly earned as much.

Sincerely,
the Professor

P.S.: Please extend my valediction and eternal gratitude to the lovely Miss Doris next door and convey also my undying affection for her confections.

Miss Barrett looked up from the letter and dropped the glasses from her nose; her eyes now moist with a similar sentimental desire for the distinguished academic; the same who frightened her so profoundly, to suddenly round the corner and announce another set of impossible, arbitrary parameters for the morning's breakfast performance. It was then she noticed Hobbes completing the last toss of a muffler around his neck, strutting toward the back door of the kitchen.

She looked at the stove, now warm and ready to begin frying up a flat of bacon, which she knew her old friend enjoyed as much as his brandy; shouting, "And where do you think you're going?"

To which he snapped, "To relay the Professor's sentiments immediately to Miss Doris!"

And popped out the door.

VIII

Of all the inopportune times for the miserable old van to be stubborn, now seemed especially loathsome; it was a matter of the utmost urgency that it turn over and take him into town without additional delay.

Grigoras began to suspect he had flooded the carburetor, thankful that the battery at least was fairly new. He dropped the accelerator pedal to the floor and held it a moment, lifted the motor cover and removed the air filter. To his great relief the strong smell of gasoline filled the cab, reassuring him that he would be on the road to Söfenzin in a minute or so.

What could *possibly* have possessed the young man to betray an old, defenseless friend like that? The image of his honorable surrender, sparing every further blemish to the sanctity of the occasion; *I've known Cosmo when he was born; I remember his father . . . maybe this explains enough.*

He held the pedal halfway down and turned the key.

Half an hour from the woods on a small road cut through the wide stretch of Dortpen lea, still gray and brown from Winter's latency; the vast rolling softness always captivating in its uninhibited service of sheer horizontal nothingness, a feature most exquisite for its sheer abundance to the thirsty forest dwelling eye; Grigoras recovered from his mindful wandering by the peculiar sight approaching to his left about three hundred meters up ahead. It was a policeman circling a very distressed vehicle, the squad car appearing from its place behind the wreckage as he drew up alongside the scene.

"Chief," he offered through the open window. "Anyone hurt?"

"Grigoras," he replied, his hand subconsciously dropped to pat his holster. "How's Yoseri?"

Grigoras looked with expressed concern at the burned shell sitting most forensic by the side of the road, "Yoseri very well. Two more great-grandchildren! I tell him you ask." Then looking back at the car, he asked again, "Anybody hurt?"

"Funny thing; no sign of anyone. Plates were stripped. Figure it was probably abandoned; maybe some raccoons having fun. Just got here and haven't had time to run anything. What brings you down here?"

"Look like an old 240DL" Grigoras noticed, "Friend of mine has one, *so I know*."

"It sure *was*. An old *Swedish tractor*; I know a few people with these. See a lot of them running around. This one's burned up so bad I can barely make a trace of the color; just some grey left back under the trunk lid. "Going into town?"

The gypsy smiled at this; always prepared to explain himself to a law man. "It looks black to me," he joked. "I was going to see Father Frederick; but now I see you. Maybe *you* who I want to see better. Maybe you help me better."

Richter made a poor effort to hide his sense of annoyance. "Kinda got my hands full here, Grigoras. Why don't you go into town and make a report at the station. By the time you're done, I'll probably be back and we'll talk there. Good?"

He tugged on his beard, half expecting this. "It's about the soldiers you send to arrest my friend. He's good man and didn't kill *nobody*. I want to see him. I get Father Frederick to tell his story."

August Richter rested his elbows on the van door; his interest now piqued.

"What soldiers? I didn't send any soldiers." It had been months, but he full expected news of the two bounty hunters to inevitably surface; "*Who* did you say these soldiers arrested?"

"My friend! Old man, white hair, white beard, almost die out there! They take him yesterday, right in middle of Madam Piko's funeral! They disgrace us!"

Chief Richter asked Grigoras to follow him into town. He had heard nothing of Lord Penworth's arrest; a very important piece of news all right. It suddenly struck Chief Richter, "Hey, Grigoras; Father Frederick; he drives a grey Volvo, doesn't he?"

"That's my *friend;* I say before."

IX

The thaw meant more productive traps, which translated into fewer irregular, far more substantial meals; *for Victor and Dominic, that is.* There was no doubt though, they were by this time sick to death of the forest and exceedingly anxious to realize the lavish new lives my recovered fortune would allegedly afford them; the months of freezing through a mountain winter a most disparaging cross to bear for the privilege.

Theirs was a moderately disciplined, reasonably effective codependency; an odd disparity of knowledge, patience and refinement which instinctively mollified most of the routine antagonisms detrimental to a mutual focus as required to imagine, to plan, then execute a scheme as rich in speculation as this in which I find myself entangled.

I have my fortune hid; *this much is true*; they will not continue on, however, into lavish lives endowed by it.

Taking half a dozen whiskey bottles from the funeral, we headed east, through the lower hills back toward Mayfair, still some fifty kilometers away. Dominic assumed absolute dominion over my back, arms and legs; over stressed on merciless marches, up and down, through the rock-strewn gorges, bent beneath a hefty load designed to break my will, under fed and parched; kept but a snake's shadow from absolute exhaustion through exposure by infrequent invitations near the fire, occasional tastes of whiskey and a quasi-suitable blanket. The cold night winds of a waning frost still held a bite which knowledge of tomorrow's arduous schedule only served to further ridicule. Many days passed in this same fashion.

The other one, *Victor*, gave his comrade unrestricted license to his sadistic diversions; silent but for spare, concise intervention with intent to safeguard the precious map inside my head. He watched me; I watched him. He asked each night, with some food, if I would like to sleep closer to the fire; have some whiskey; go home.

I would unconditionally answer yes; turn away and pull my blanket tight around my shoulders.

I was miserable, but wouldn't let them see me break or fold; knowing that in generous pieces I was unfolding all the same; memories, leaking into now familiar creases, out from fever'd dreams; reminders of the many missed appointments with a vision whom I once upon a time engaged upon some mystifying business, left abrupt, unfinished a short while back.

A strange priest dressed in a gilded surplice waved two bent fingers toward an ink black pond; his eyes were hideously blonde; blind as grapes. A leather purse hung round his neck, emblazoned with two figures from the vast green world beneath the surface of a restive sea; he held this in his other hand each time he turned his marble face to me.

"There's not much point, our going on in circles for a fortune you won't share; the ransom for your corpse is still enough to make things right." Victor waited till the flames surrendered to the stimulating devils in the coals; a dim light barely stretching past the fire's skirt; Dominic an image barely traced inside the whiskey-slumbered shadows of his wrinkled heap; the dull cataleptic snoring but a tribute to the godhead of his vacuous philosophy.

"I'm not the murderer I am accused to be."

Victor picked a piece of charr from his teeth and spit into the coals.

"You just don't seem to understand Duke. I don't care; I really couldn't give a shit." He took a swallow from the canteen, held it out to me. "I'm not sitting in a fucking jury box here. A lot of crummy things happen to a lot of good people, all over the world. I've been everywhere, I know what I'm talking about; I've seen things decent, high-brow people like you don't even imagine one person could do to another. The things they make a little boy watch his mother do before they disembowel her. Fire, electricity, ropes, knives, horses; you name it, I seen it."

He took another swallow from the canteen.

"The *kind ones* use a pistol. Gets to be impossible to turn it off after a while; just makes all the pretty rules we follow here seem ignorant; *hell*, your worst punishments for the worst crimes here wouldn't make a victim out there in the real world stop and say anything but *thank you!* I'm just making sure that none of that shit happens to me; and you know how I'm gonna do that, Duke?"

I asked him for some tobacco, he rolled one up and put it to my lips. "I think so."

He laughed. "Money. A bit of money gets you into trouble. A *lot* of money solves everything. You were gonna be my ticket. Now, I'll just

277

settle for a ransom, a bath and some clean clothes; tired of looking at that sorry son of a bitch over there anyway."

As if on cue, Dominic let out a loud snore and rolled his foot into the coals. Victor stood up and kicked his boot before the heat woke him and his burnt foot slowed our march by complaining. Besides, he greatly enjoyed the quiet that proliferated in the absence of Dominic's banal, wakeful rambling.

"Want to hear something Duke?"

The priest now rowed a little boat across the ink black pond, the pale white sun against the oars; his head a cage detaining thoughts of vanity from exercise beyond; the golden surplice shining like the windows in a house of whores.

I had never heard Victor talk so much.

"Would it matter one bit if I said *no*?"

I looked at Victor, pathetically staring with sentimental self-pity into the hissing coals; his moist drunken eyes reflected a pin point of red-embered light back into the black space hovering between his thoughts and the cold reminder of a dismal camp in a dismal forest on an endless quest.

"I was gonna kill you anyway." He chuckled and put his hand to unscrew the canteen again; this time he stopped; looked fairly provoked, turned to me and said, "Maybe I'll just kill you now."

Tilted east, the white star splashing meaningless across two ivory colored balls; the trespassed sockets where two eyes once hid; a crooked smile now broke across the chiseled creases to pronounce a squall; across the face one thousand years of prayer had bigoted.

"I wish you would, Victor. You will anyway. I'd like to see that jackass over there carry some of this weight for a laugh. Your ransom might, however, require some evidence of our time together, don't you think? How does the idea of carrying my corpse another fifteen kilometers grab you?"

"I'll get some of the weight out of your pack. Maybe you live, *who knows*? Anyway, we'll be in Söfenzin sometime tomorrow. Can I ask you something, Duke?"

The clouds converged above the boat, and on a bet, the minister pulled across the knotted lines against a heavy, dripping net.

The Duke did not answer; lost in thought. Victor continued, not wholly invested in the Duke's half of the conversation.

"I want to know; I mean, at this point, nothing really matters, does it?" he finally noticed the Duke's vacant expression. "Lay your cards on the table, you live; fair enough?"

He pulled a fish out from the folds, the rain now pouring down; inside its mouth he found two coins, and on its head a ring-shaped Crown.

"Do you really have a fortune hid somewhere?"

Lord Penworth turned slowly to the soldier and in a hoarse whisper, just as slow, replied, *"I am perhaps the wealthiest soul you'll ever meet."*

X

A squad car drove past the open gates, heavily cloaked in vines of English ivy, *Hedera helix*; splashing through the rain puddles as it bridged the distance to the great house. Nothing and no one ever made it nearer to the entrance circle without Hobbes' attention likewise intercepting; and so readied him to greet the policeman and his bearded friend.

There came a knock.

XI

It was noon, the site was as he had described, with rows and rows of soft hemlocks standing like the crenelated columns in a great cathedral; large sweeping boughs of feathered emerald fronds, absorbing all stray sound not already quenched by the soft carpet of punk and orange needles covering the ground.

A small disturbed clearing in a large mossy area led Victor like a lodestone to a hand cut nail. The poor Duke, head bowed, stood trembling in shame amongst the crocuses which devotedly raised their springtime heads; the air uniquely still of rowdy jay bird calls; silent.

Dominic came up behind the Duke to push him toward the spot where Victor stood. The Soldier looked to Penworth, smiled. Dominic threw a shovel on the ground.

"Your fortune, buried here?" He shook his head, skeptically.

The Duke nodded.

"My treasure's buried at this site; hidden in the night some many months ago."

He fell to his knees and wept.

"I disgrace the very earth by what I do; *dearest Lord forgive me.*"

Dominic unlocked the cuffs, releasing the old man to dig. Lord Penworth stared at the shovel, incapable of bending to grab it.

The blind priest took the coins out from the fish's teeth; raised his face into the driving rain; then swallowing the coins himself, politely tossed the old fish back again.

"Get started." Victor sat with his back against a wide tree and smoked a pipe.

An hour passed, the exhausted shovel finally stabbed against a box; the Duke collapsed. Dominic, exceedingly impatient by this time, grabbed the Duke by his collar and dragged him from the hole, jumped in and reached up top for the spade to resume clearing the trunk.

He never saw the shovel that undid him, which in the end was very kind.

Victor jumped to his feet, and laughed, drew his pistol and declared, "Very nice, Your Grace, but such a mess."

He pushed the Duke into the hole to pass the broken body of his comrade out; with all his strength the old man lifted the decapitated soldier from the hole, and stole from him an ivory handled knife; Victor reached to grab and pull him from the top; cleared the hole for work to resume; never observing his Lordship's stealth.

Penworth knelt to his knees, pulling small handfuls of the spongy earth, delicately, meticulously off the box, still half concealed; still sleeping in the frozen ground. He caressed the curve-formed lid, scraped the carved relief, *an emblem in the likeness of two figures from an ancient time of heraldic majesty*; scraped it free of encrusting dirt, he kissed the box.

Forgive me Angel for all I've done ; for what I now must do.

"I'll take it from here."

Victor helped the Duke from the hole, secured his hands in shackles again, the thick chain hung to another at his feet. "You just wait up there; and stay away from the shovel," he laughed, throwing it to the ground with him inside the hole.

Victor worked another half hour, clearing the top of the box.

XII

"My fortune, by this means, interred" he repeated; "Yes, I believe I can be of assistance. Are you certain those are the exact words you remember him saying?" Hobbes looked to the large Gypsy with the black beard. "Those were his words."

Grigoras, despite the overwhelming excitement, was enormously distracted also by the opulence surrounding him; an element of the situation long ago dismissed by the *Good Domestic* as the inevitable circumstance of his craft and nothing more; aware and concerned nonetheless of its detrimental effect on the chief witness' focus.

"What do you make of it, Hobbes?" asked Richter, "I'm bothered by the amount of time that's passed with no word from these two thieves; there hasn't even been an attempt to collect on the ransom. These two are armed and extremely dangerous, *to the wrong person*, that is. It's not a stretch to figure they still don't know the ransom's been revoked. I'm thinking they're more interested in a treasure hunt; *God help us.*"

Hobbes briskly exited the house through the empty kitchen, his two guests close at heel. The police car was parked in the gravel drive which circled out back; he motioned for all three of them to get in and instructed the Chief to drive past the garage house and down the dirt road about a mile.

The poor old butler was deeply distressed upon his frightful deduction; having been present at the Duke's brief appearance to poor young Charlotte's clandestine, unofficial memorial; dreadful, painful memories, awoke from shallow graves; remembrances of Felis tinkering with the old green Citroen; Felis swinging from a knotted line; sledding on a winter's day; finishing with hot cocoa and brandy.

The grove of hemlocks stood another half kilometer from the dirt road; the rest would be crossed on foot. A gypsy, a butler and a cop, hiking on a narrow path across an austere field; three tiny paper silhouettes in black against the fading blue and yellow-orange evening sky; the sun pressed *down* against the treetops; not much light left in the day.

"We're very close," Hobbes remarked, noting the path was now defined by hemlocks on both sides. The battered person of an almost headless man lay on a bloodstained plot of ground a few meters from an open hole where Hobbes confessed the funeral of a young and beautiful young girl took place so many months ago. No other sign of life or death but this to greet them.

"That's Dominic Pedroni lying over there," Richter said, walking toward the lifeless evidence of his tattooed skin, bewildered Grigoras right beside.

Hobbes instead made a brisk, straight sprint to see the open grave, despondent over the indignity of the scene; inside the hole, Lord Penworth's broken, bleeding frame.

"The Duke!"

Richter and Grigoras left Dominic, ran over to help Hobbes at the grave. He was bound in chains, bleeding through his chest; Grigoras scrambled to one side and took an arm inside his massive paw to lift; Richter positioned opposite, then counted to coordinate the hoist, "*three, two, one . .*"

Lord Penworth let out an agonizing scream; Hobbes nearly fainted.

"Take the car back to the house and call the station for support. I need an ambulance."

"But what about . ."

"Go!" he shouted at the Butler, "we'll have no light in less than an hour. The Duke's in terrible shape. Grigoras and I will get Grübek out of the hole; Penworth can't be moved like this. Go!"

And Hobbes was off.

Victor lay face up holding a pistol inside the open casket of the poor young girl; a knife pushed deep into his ribs; there was no sound when they pulled on him.

And there inside the little hole, dug by a pious poor young African, lay the peaceful body of a young girl dressed in satin, stitched with edelweiss; a sight which brought the two stunned men to tears.

Two small hands held to a rosary, a bible at her side; a white veil of dotted scrim across a sunken face, and two coins laid upon her two blind eyes.

Here in a distant peace beyond all comprehending grace, one man's only treasure and his tragedy revealed, two coins placed by *Poppa* on his young girl's sleeping face.

Grigoras closed the little box, both he and Richter said a heartfelt prayer; two strangers left to throw their separate fists of dirt into the hole; and finally seal the whole affair.

The End

Epilogue

Many years had come and gone since Lord Penworth had returned to Burlwood, the *Chronicle* observed; his voice long missing from a distressed and indigent Parliament; vague and vulgar speculations all of what remained to stoke the slumbering ashes of a once sweltering Society Page. Faithful Hobbes, but for Giov, more alone now since the passing of his dear friend *Mom*, far more needing of assistance than his distinguished charge, *and most sincerely hard pressed to confess it.*

And so, acknowledging the years to operate toward everything alike, was no surprise to learn that even *east* of Touchwick, people suffered just the same. Time being dutifully impartial in its pedantic dismantling of our faculties; of its ever expansive meddling in our misbegotten dreams; and worst perhaps of all, the sad, reciprocal association of the pair;
the mind, so dense embroidered over time in fading thread, should in the end regard its sutures from the smallest pinhole in a brittle head.

As such, it is of no astonishment to learn that somewhere undisclosed, high up in a surreptitious tower window carved on high, an aging woman looks out from a gilded screen, who trills her wordless songs into the towns and fields below, solemn as a mourning dove.

Who still enjoys the colored lights wherever she might steal a look, who still enjoys her cooking spoons, her memory of country drives, some soda and her picture books.

Her life, accorded to her by the law, is one of perfect solitude; her only friends, a revolving shift of duty aides and nurses responsible only to a prescribed routine and towards her relative comfort, both of which derive individual success from perceived attainment of the other; almost cruel in its monotony.

And in such a fashion the years passed, every day the very same; every night, routine; when from the steady rain outside one April morning, unannounced, the visitor arrived.

She stepped out from a long white, shiny limousine all dressed in widow's black; she wore a wide brimmed hat of the highest fashion, her face well hid behind a veil. It was midday dinner, a tray of the subject's favorite meal was brought into her room, rolled silently across the tiled floors upon a trolley made from spotless stainless steel, over to a table where a chair was set to taste her meal; a second chair then slid alongside.

Helen sat before her plate, eyeing the visitor with infinite suspicion, no frame of reference for the meaning of the tears which fell from high boned cheeks behind the veil, shaded deep beneath the broad black brim.

"There was a time I thought she might not try her meal at all," recalled the only witness to the queer luncheon, "but then the stranger fed her gently from her plate and all seemed fine until...." The nurse's voice broke off.

"Until what?" her distracted husband asked, folding his *Chronicle* to look over at his wife who was now standing by the oven with a spoon in hand, utterly frozen; tangled in the revolting spell of her strange experience.

"Until," she continued, "it all became chillingly plain as she bent down to tie the stray lace of poor Helen's shoe."

Made in the USA
Middletown, DE
03 August 2015